THORN BIRDS
of
DETROIT

Before you begin reading the Thorn Birds of Detroit series, you may want to order a FREE eBook of an introductory novella setting the stage for entering the mafia underworld in Detroit.

Detroit was a fast-growing boom city in the 1960s. But unknown to most, under the surface corruptive forces including the Italian, Greek and Black mafias and many gangs were at work. The *Gloom and Doom* novella is a synopsis of the tough life in the inner city of Detroit in the years after the 1967 riots. It was a violent time. The new historical fiction series, *Thorn Birds of Detroit* begins in the late 1970s. Les Cochran weaves a tale of the underworld and the effort of citizens to fight back from a state of anguish and despair.

Get Your FREE eBook at:

http://lescochranblog.com/gloom-and-doom-2/

SAX CLUB

THORN BIRDS OF DETROIT CONFRONT MAFIA

BY

LES COCHRAN

Bookstand Publishing
www.bookstandpublishing.com

Published by
Bookstand Publishing
Morgan Hill, CA 95037
4410_6

ISBN 978-1-63498-322-8

Printed in the United States of America

ACKNOWLEDGEMENTS

A special thanks to my wife, Lin, who spent countless hours reading each word, giving me feedback and providing "constructive criticism." Thanks, too, for devoting hundreds of hours to reacting to the storyline, raising questions to clarify and amend, and editing each chapter one more time, even after we thought it was completed.

I appreciate, too, the precise work of my editor LinDee Rochelle, Penchant for Penning, whose attention to detail and questions complemented her tedious task of editing and critiquing. Thanks to her for inserting a little levity into the painstaking process.

At the end of this arduous process, Darlene Stockman applied her criminal justice background and proofing skills to finely hone the manuscript. Thanks again, to Lin, LinDee and Darlene for their meaningful assistance and support.

In writing this novel I became acquainted with two men who made a significant difference in assisting me to narrow the line between fact and fiction.

The interviews with Oscar Westerfield, Supervisory Special Agent of the FBI Detroit Division during the time of the story, infused the fiction with real information and insights. His keen eye in reading the final manuscript fine-tuned the technical aspects.

Scott M. Burnstein's two books — *Motor City Mafia* and *Detroit True Crime Chronicles* — were of immense value in providing the context for my fictionalized characters. His reading of the final manuscript added a powerful sense of reality to the novel.

A special thanks to Oscar and Scott; their insights and willingness to share brought the book alive. They are the finest professional colleagues an author could have.

In each of us there is something that cannot be denied. Maybe it's a desire to be the best we can be — the best mother, teacher or banker — it doesn't matter what it might be, striving to climb the highest pinnacle, solve a problem or live one more day.

In the human flock most are not thorn birds; they are people who go on their merry way, day-by-day, without giving serious thought to their actions, shadowing others or doing what their told. They are the followers, the rank and file — the workers — the essential ones who get the job done.

Like the thorn bird who sings its own song, some individuals strive to play the most beautiful music of all. They are the doers; the leaders — the people who make a difference. They are thorn birds. They work their hearts out without fear of failure, reprisal or dying. They're driven, sometimes blindly, to accomplish a goal; they're on a mission. And so it is with the thorn birds of Detroit — they're driven against all odds — to take back their city.

The "Thorn Birds of Detroit" series is about regular folks fighting back, trying to maintain their dignity. It portrays the efforts of men and women in the inner-city trying against all odds to take back their neighborhoods — blacks unwilling to be slaves to the mob bosses like their grandparents were to their white masters; local entrepreneurs wanting to build their own businesses rather than working for the mobsters; people in their community fighting for freedom against the drug-driven gangs; and a detective who's roots in the city compel him to push beyond the normal limits.

CHAPTER ONE

𝕯etroit 𝕱ree 𝕻ress
July 31, 1975

HOFFA MISSING — FOUL PLAY SUSPECTED

At approximately 3:00 p.m. yesterday, witnesses saw Jimmy Hoffa step into a maroon-colored Lincoln occupied by three other men, and leave the Machus Red Fox restaurant on the corner of Maple and Telegraph in Bloomfield Township. He has not been heard from since.

For eighteen years Hoffa has ruled the Teamsters Union; the largest and most dominant union in the world. In recent years, he has been hounded by rumors of corruption in his administration and there has been rampant conjecture about links to organized crime. It's been widely speculated that he has several powerful enemies who have plenty of reasons to want him out of the way.

THE DETROIT NEWS
March 2, 1976

MOB COLLECTOR LaBERRIE FOUND DEAD

Internal strife continues within the Detroit Mafia. This morning the body of Tommy LaBerrie was found on the floor of a local restaurant. Informants indicate

1

LaBerrie, a bagman for the mob was taken out by local mafia member, Ronald "Hollywood Ronnie" Morelli and Robert "Bobby the Animal" LaPuma, both well-known mob enforcers. This is the eighth gangland murder of the year.

𝕯etroit 𝕱ree 𝕻ress
October 9, 1976

DETROIT DRUG LORDS CONVICTED

The long awaited end of court appeals has happened. Yesterday the United States Court of Appeals, Sixth Circuit, sentenced Eddie Jackson to thirty years in federal prison and Courtney Brown to twenty-one years. The two of them had established a drug empire in a few short years, taking in nearly a million dollars a day and becoming the envy of the giants in New York City.

The drug czars blazed the trail, establishing procedures and policies, along with a mindset that will be used by drug kingpins for years to come.

THE OAKLAND PRESS
March 23, 1977

OAKLAND COUNTY CHILD KILLER STRIKES AGAIN

The body of Timothy King was found late last night, a week after he was reported missing. He lay in a ditch along Gill Road, about three hundred feet south of Eight Mile Road in Livonia. With his skateboard beside his body, his clothing had been washed and neatly pressed. He'd been suffocated and sexually assaulted.

Authorities believe there is a strong possibility that Timothy was the fourth in a string of cases by a serial killer.

***

Early in the morning, well before seven, detective Clark Phillips waited outside the office of William Hart, the newly appointed Detroit police chief. Speculating on the purpose of his first meeting with the chief, Clark wondered if he wanted to discuss one of his areas of special interest. *Hart had been a tough cop who worked his way up through the ranks. He boasts a strong record of undercover work in the gambling and prostitution houses. With the mayor's plan to aggressively integrate the force, maybe he wants to draw upon his experience in internal affairs.*

The door to Hart's office opened and an imposing, sharply dressed African-American man stepped out and extended his hand. "Clark, I appreciate you getting up before the crack of dawn. Can I pour you a cup of coffee?"

"A large cup," Clark said, half-jokingly as he shook the chief's hand. "It's a pleasure, sir."

The chief closed the door and strode toward the coffeepot. "Do you use anything?"

"No, black will be fine."

The chief laughed aloud. "The same way I like my women — hot and black."

Having heard of the chief's "fondness" for women, Clark said nothing; still, he was taken aback by the chief's brashness. *Maybe he's been around the mayor too long.* His thoughts referenced Mayor Coleman Young whose reputation for using off-color language was well known. He had regularly stated phrases like, "If a word is spoken on the street it's one that's widely understood. If the 'f' word or 'n' word offends you, don't listen. I'm talking to the people of Detroit."

The muscular man turned toward Clark, a mug of hot steaming coffee in each hand and placed one on a coaster in front of him. Walking around a large walnut desk, the chief set his mug on the departmental insignia and eased into a large, black leather executive, swivel rocker. He glanced at Clark. *Looks like a chip off the old block; a full head of sandy-brown hair, not a strand out of place. A starched light blue shirt, his sleeves rolled exactly one-half inch below each elbow. If it wasn't for his dad's gray streaks he'd be an exact clone.*

Hart adjusted his tie, rocked a couple of times and leaned back, his normally steel-cold eyes, mellow with compassion. A partial grin creased his jaw. "How's your dad doing?"

"He ... he's doing fine." Clark stumbled over his words. That was the last question he expected.

"How long has it been since he retired?"

"Five years and he hasn't changed a bit. Whenever I stop by he's ready to talk." Clark paused and corrected himself. "Usually it's more of a lecture."

"With a cigar in his hand, I bet?"

"Right." Clark nodded and grinned, recalling the many nights his dad had puffed on a Corona on the back porch.

The chief smiled warmly; his eyes drifted to the open window observing the oaks and maples rustling in their grandeur. *Lewis Phillips, the one man I always wanted backing me up. I didn't have to say a word. He was there before I made a move. Best damn cop Detroit ever had.*

The chief straightened his shoulders and looked sincerely at Clark. "I'm proud to say you're one of the few rising stars in the department; our top detective. I'm impressed by your record, particularly the number of times you've demonstrated an innate ability to see facts that weren't obvious to others and to uncover leads that weren't readily apparent ... impressive!"

"Thank you, sir. I've worked hard."

"It's more than hard work, Clark. You're just like your father."

He'd heard that many times before, but often struggled for the right words to reply. Clark glanced up at the two pictures, President Carter and Governor Milliken, behind the chief's desk, and looked him in the eye. "Like he always said, 'do your best every day and you'll never be disappointed at the end of the week.'"

"Sounds just like him," the chief ruminated. He shifted to the matter at hand. "There's a sign of recovery in the city. Crime rates dropped 19 percent last year. People are beginning to lose their wariness about venturing into the city." The chief leaned over the top of his desk and lowered his voice. "It's time we put the heat on the mobsters and gangs."

"No question, sir. The mob has a stranglehold on the city and gangs are running wild."

"That is why I called you in." His voice lowered to a whisper. "I'm forming a Special Crimes Task Force and putting you in charge."

Clark stared blankly, frozen in place; he didn't say a word.

"You're a little light on big case experience but we've all been there once. It's time for you to take the next step. I'm confident you can pull it off."

Overwhelmed by the thought of the task, Clark stammered, "W-well … thank you, sir."

Chief Hart eased back in his chair; his words sterner than before. "Next week the mayor and Huston Nash have scheduled a press conference. He will announce their family's effort to help the police track down the murder of his grandson. I'll use my time at the podium to announce the formation of the task force."

"I appreciate your vote of confidence." Clark's blue eyes sparkled. "I won't let you down."

"Somehow I knew you'd say that." The chief flashed a slight grin, rubbed his hands together, pulled his handkerchief from his suitcoat pocket and patted a glistening brow. "I'm heartbroken over the deaths of those young people in Oakland County. The 'Babysitter Murder' has everyone on edge. Four killings from February '76 through last month … fourteen months. We have to take action."

"Do you think the Nash murder is connected with them?"

"Hmm, I'm not sure … a Grosse Pointe kidnapping and the body being found on Belle Isle. That's a long way from Oakland County." The chief contorted his lips into a grimace. "The youngsters there ranged from ten to twelve. Nash's grandson was just four years old, but I'm bothered by the thorough attention given to all of the bodies; so fastidious."

"That bothers me too." Clark tossed his crop of Robert Redford hair. "It's a real possibility."

"Maybe so." The chief rose, walked around his desk and sat with his leg propped on the front edge. "Initially your team will focus on the Nash murder. That'll buy you some time."

Caught off guard Clark managed a slight, nervous grin that ended with a bewildered look. "Buy some time?"

The chief slurped the last of his coffee and bent closer to Clark. "I want to keep the task force's efforts as low key as possible for as long as possible. I'll try to give you a six- or eight-week running start before I announce the actual membership. That'll give your team an edge before the Mafia catches on."

"Makes sense." Clark leaned back in the chair and sighed, feeling a hint of comfort.

"Also, I'd suggest you meet with the county prosecutor as soon as you can. He's in our corner and is one of the few people you can trust. If you ever need straight talk, give him a call."

"Thanks. It's good to have a friend in that office."

The chief shot him a positive look. "It's a two-way street, Clark. He'll need your help to gather the necessary information."

"I'll need some top-notch officers to pull this off."

"You have them. Pick any six individuals in the department."

"Could I add my sidekick Earl Walker to the team?"

"The Pearl?"

"Yeah, do you know him?"

"Not really. When I was on the street everyone knew Earl, 'The Pearl.' One night I saw him pour forty-two points into his team's basket."

"Yes, I know." Clark's face lit up. "We were at Chadsey. Every time he crossed the midcourt line he called, 'Give me the ball. I'm hot!'"

"What ever happened to him?"

"He went to NC State and blew his knee out twice. They zipped it up but he was never the same; still walks with a limp."

"Sure, add him, now you have seven."

"Thanks." Clark gave him a thumbs up. "Do you have any suggestions?"

The chief pulled a slip of paper from his inside coat pocket and handed it to Clark. "Here are three names to get you started. Talk with them and your dad. It won't take long to come up with a few more for a short list."

Still struggling to comprehend the magnitude of the charge, Clark asked, "Any other suggestions?"

The chief stared at him for the longest time.

"Yes, I can't say it too often." He glanced at the door as if someone might be listening. "Your team must limit its contacts within the department. You'll never know who's connected — people are watching."

Breaking a partial grin, Clark nodded. "You won't believe how many times I heard that from my dad."

"Maybe you've heard it a hundred times, but I can assure you your team members have not gone through the same drill."

Clark felt another lecture coming on.

"You have to pound it into their heads. Tell them again and again not to talk openly to *anyone* outside the task force. Long-time colleagues may *not* be their best friends on this one. A slip of the tongue or the wrong word said may be all that it takes."

Clark raised his eyebrows, having never considered his partner — the guy who'd covered his ass so many times — being in bed with the other guys. Sensing there was more to come, he eyed the chief. "Is that it?"

The chief pondered the question for a moment. "That's the beginning." His tone was firmer than before. "Follow your instincts; dig, dig, and dig deeper ... explore every angle. Sooner or later you'll find something that'll lead you up the ladder — pursue it like a bull terrier — it may be our only chance."

Clark gave him an admiring glance. *This guy is no dummy. He's been round the block a time or two. I'm looking forward to working with him.*

Chief Hart hesitated, making sure he used the right words, his eyes honing in on Clark. "Hunt down the bastards rigorously; don't stop for any reason. Ignore the detractors and the threats; pursue them with your utmost vigor. We have to turn the corner before it is too late."

"Is that all?" he jested.

"Not quite." The chief grinned, enjoying the levity. "I hand-wrote a letter to the head of the Detroit FBI unit telling him that I am placing you on temporary loan to them, and from now on you'd be reporting to him."

A wrinkle crossed Clark's forehead. He cocked his head. "I-I don't understand."

The chief managed a small smile. "Nothing goes through this office. From today on you're the point man for all interaction with the feds. It's your investigation."

Clark jutted his jaw. "But ..."

"Keep your voice down." Chief Hart interrupted. "I'll say this one time only — our relationship is over. You don't report to me. I assume this place is bugged. I don't trust a soul here. If I say something in the morning it's on the street before the six o'clock news. As far as I'm concerned this meeting never occurred. Do you understand?" he asked softly.

Clark paused for a moment, looking at the floor, before he glanced up at him. "I'm ready to start," he said, his voice perfectly calm.

"Good." The chief handed him a slip of paper. "Here's the name and phone number for your FBI contact. Do whatever you deem appropriate. If you have any questions call Oscar."

***

TV trucks filled the street, making one lane barely passable, in front of a three-story white limestone estate. The building traversed half a block in one of Grosse Pointe's most exclusive areas. Pictured as an "icon of wealth" in films and on television, the affluent coastal area of Lake St. Clair northeast of Detroit was home to the Dodges, several members of the Ford family, Paul Harvey, Roger Penske, and countless other wealthy Americans.

Stationed at the elaborate gated driveway, two of Detroit's finest checked credentials of VIPs and members of the press. Five rows of chairs in a semicircle ringed the massive portico where the podium stood with the City of Detroit insignia displayed prominently in its wooden center. Six empty chairs waited on the left of the podium; two were positioned on the right.

Early arrivals milled the grounds admiring the hedges and flower beds, manicured to perfection as if ready for a movie production. The clock neared ten; the guests and media took their seats. Stepping through the front door, an older couple headed for the first two chairs immediately to the left of the podium. A younger couple followed, obviously in distress, wiping their eyes, and sat in chairs on the other side. Two younger women joined them in the chairs at the end.

A sleek black Lincoln SUV powered up to the gate long enough to let a flamboyant African-American man step confidently onto the sidewalk. Nattily dressed in a dark blue suit with a white pocket square, he strolled up the driveway and took his time ascending the stairs. As he reached the portico, the mayor nodded to the elderly man and took a chair to the right of the podium. Another flashy African-American man hustled closely behind and sat in the last chair.

At exactly ten o'clock the entire group stood. A military ensemble played "God Bless America," and everyone took their seats.

The elderly man stood and walked with stately determination toward the podium. He paused before speaking to garner the attention of all. Huston Nash, the grandfather of the murdered child, was one of the wealthiest in the area. He had transformed a small auto parts supplier for the Big Three into a major corporation, and was now recognized as a national investment guru and philanthropist.

Accustomed to controlling his emotions, Huston spoke slowly, deliberately. "On behalf of the Nash family, I want to thank all of you for being here today. Our family has suffered a grave loss. There is nothing worse than having the life of a young person snuffed out before it has barely begun. Over the past ten days our family has grieved over the loss of my grandson. We've prayed for resolution." He paused and wiped a tear from his cheek. "There is none," he said, choking up.

His son stepped to the old man's side and placed his arms around his shaking shoulders. The two men embraced for several moments. The old man turned abruptly and ripped the microphone from its holder. "No longer will we tolerate such violence in our community," he boomed. "We'll hunt down the dastardly cowards who committed this despicable crime. We will search the bowels of this city with the tenacity of a bulldog, not one rock or pebble will be left unturned. We will move in a steadfast manner with the determination of God Almighty," he closed with emotion. Huston's body trembled, leaving him barely able to stand.

Grabbing the microphone, his son stepped behind the podium. Standing tall, the suave, thirtyish man cleared his throat. "Today we're announcing a five-hundred-thousand-dollar reward to anyone providing information leading to the arrest and conviction of those responsible for the death of my son." He turned to his father, took his arm and helped Huston to his chair.

Mayor Coleman Young stepped forward, reeking with power, commanding the attention of all. Setting aside his colorful, black-power style, he spoke like an Episcopalian minister, as he had many times from the pulpit. Having worked with Huston on several major city projects, Mayor Young showed great sympathy and compassion for his friend, citing numerous contributions he and his wife had made to the city.

The mayor's tone elevated as he condemned the shameful crime that had been committed, carefully avoiding the use of curse-words for which he was well known. After rambling for nearly twenty minutes, he addressed the crowd with purpose, "As mayor of the great city of Detroit, I'm here today to pledge that every local, state and federal resource will be channeled toward finding the perpetrators of this unacceptable act. My office, the city council, and the chief of police will not rest until our goal has been achieved."

Following the sustained applause, he turned and nodded to Chief Hart. The square-shouldered man moved to the podium with confidence, acknowledged those present, and spoke firmly. "Nothing is more appalling in our society than the loss of a young child's life. Those who prey on the innocent deserve no mercy. I'm establishing a special task force to search out and prosecute those responsible for this crime and other similar acts. We will maintain a zero-crime tolerance and will not stop until those responsible are behind bars."

CHAPTER TWO

A slightly built, penny-ante bagman opened the door of a small neighborhood bar somewhere in Detroit's inner city. Stepping inside the nearly pitch-black room, the nervous man squinted and turned toward the dimly lit table hugging the far corner. Bumping into a chair, he stumbled over something on the floor and stopped in front of the two steps leading to the elevated corner booth.

"Take off your hat," a deep raspy voice growled.

He snatched his brown felt cap from his head and held it with both hands at his waist, anxiously twisting it. Beads of perspiration popped along his receding hairline.

"Are you Vinny Castintino?" Blackie, the top lieutenant for the Street Boss, asked. An open philanderer, he was in line to assume the third highest position in the Detroit Italian-American Mafia.

"Yes," Vinny mumbled.

"Speak up, Vinny," Blackie roared.

Vinny straightened his shoulders and looked up. "*Yes sir.*"

"That's better." Dressed in black with large, dark sunglasses adding to his menacing look, the tall, square-jawed man continued. "Sit down on the chair in front of you."

Vinny stepped up, stubbed his toe on the top tread and stumbled forward. Grabbing the back of the chair, he caught his balance and slid onto the seat.

A black-haired beauty to the right of Blackie bit her lip, holding back a laugh.

"Are you nervous, Vinny?" he asked, brushing back an errant strand of graying hair from his face. "Would you like a drink?"

"I'm fine."

Blackie turned to his favorite lackey. The second-generation American of Italian parentage had a crop of curly black hair that made him look taller than his five-foot-five inches. "Joey, he needs a drink."

"It's vodka, right?" Joey Naples asked.

Vinny nodded.

Blackie glanced across the table at his mistress of two years. "Vicky, would you get Vinny a double Smirnoff?"

The voluptuous woman with high, Cherokee cheekbones slid to the end of the booth, bent down and slipped on her heels, her round cheeks inviting Blackie. His eyes glued on her firm ass as she stood and slinked away.

Moments later, she reappeared, placed an Old Fashioned glass in front of Vinny and slid into the booth, cozying up to Blackie. He slipped his hand up her miniskirt and caressed her slender thighs.

Vinny stared at the glass for a long moment before taking a sip.

"Drink it all," Blackie directed.

Staring blankly at the wall, Vinny chugged it and sat the empty glass down.

"Do you know who I am?" Blackie asked casually, barely masking the underlying threat.

Speaking meekly Vinny gave him a slight nod, "Blackie Giardini."

"Speak up. I didn't hear that."

"Mr. Blackie Giardini," he said more forcefully.

"And do you know why you're here?"

Vinny bowed his head, afraid to look up. "Because I messed up."

"I want to hear about the event from you, Vinny. Tell me everything that happened."

The insecure pawn shuffled uncomfortably in his chair, moisture peppering his upper lip.

"Take your time." Blackie's voice rumbled firm, compelling.

"I was in my car watching the kid like I'd been doing for the past six weeks. He was running around, having fun, and played longer than usual. The old-lady nanny placed him on a swing, said something to the kid, gave him a push, and ran toward the restroom. The kid was fine until the swing began to slow down; he turned, realized she was gone, and started crying." Vinny pulled a handkerchief from his pants pocket and mopped his brow. "I jumped out of the car, ran over and gave him a little push. He stopped crying, but started hollering when he turned and saw a stranger. I put my hand over his mouth to make him stop, but he kicked and screamed."

Joey interrupted, "Did you touch him inappropriately?"

"No. I just had my arms around him. I was trying to make him be quiet when the ol' broad came out of the bathroom, shouting, 'Stop … Stop.' Next thing I know she's all over me. I wrestled her to the ground and slugged her. Guess I knocked her out … I didn't know what to do so I grabbed the kid and ran for my car. I covered his mouth with one hand, flipped open the trunk with the other, picked up an old blanket and wrapped it around him to make him stop crying."

"Did he stop?" Joey asked.

"Yes. I slammed the trunk shut and took off."

Blackie squinted at him, "Did anyone see you?"

Vinny shook his head, rapidly. "There wasn't anyone else around."

"Are you positive?"

"Yes. I cruised around the block to double-check. Nobody around, so I took off and drove around town for an hour or more, ending up on Belle Isle. It was almost dark. I parked, made sure I was alone, and opened the trunk. The blanket was wrapped around his head; when I pulled it loose he was blue. I guess he got tangled up in it. I was scared. I didn't mean to hurt him." Vinny paused as he strained to mask his shivering. "I … I wrapped him up real nice and laid him on a park bench."

"Is that it?" Blackie asked.

"Yes sir. No one saw me." He shifted uneasily in his chair.

"And you didn't touch the kid inappropriate-like?" Joey repeated.

"No, no. I'm telling you the truth."

"Vinny, you have a conviction for molesting a little boy. Look me in the eye. Did you touch the boy?" The old man leaned forward, peering at Vinny.

"No sir, it's like I said." Vinny wiped his face with his handkerchief again. "I panicked … I didn't do anything … so help me God."

Blackie stared; his steel-cold eyes sliced Vinny's skin.

Vinny reassured him. "Honest Mr. Giardini, I didn't do anything."

Blackie cracked a partial grin. "I believe you, Vinny."

The tension at the corner booth eased.

"But we can't take any chances. You need to take a trip to Miami until the heat dies down." Blackie tossed him a large white envelope. "There's ten grand and a phone number in here. Drive to Miami right away. When you arrive, call the number inside. The boys down there will give you directions to your apartment. Any questions?"

"No sir," Vinny said, obviously relieved. "I'll pack my bags right away."

"Good." Blackie pecked his mistress on the cheek. "Sweetie, will you show Vinny out?"

She slipped out of the booth, tugged on the miniskirt that barely covered her cheeks, and pranced toward the door. Vinny stood and followed her. Turning to Joey, Blackie asked. "Well, what do you think?"

The stocky, square-shouldered confidant shook his head. "He's a liability."

"How about you, sweetie?" he asked Vicky as she returned and slid sensuously next to him.

Knowing her response meant nothing, she gave him a sexy smile. "He'll cave when the cops turn up the heat."

Blackie's mouth turned down momentarily before a smile burst forth. "You're both right. We have to take care of him."

"Want me to do it, boss?" Joey asked.

Blackie shook his head. "We can't afford anything to happen around here."

"Why so?" his right-hand man asked.

"He's a convicted child molester. The cops will be looking for any connection they can find. If Vinny is found dead, it'll be obvious that we considered him a liability."

"Makes sense … they could run him down in Miami too," Joey said.

"Not necessarily." Blackie smirked. "The boys there are taking him out for lunch at an alligator farm."

"Yuck!" his mistress blurted then covered her mouth, knowing she wasn't supposed to say anything unless spoken to.

Joey stared at Blackie and marveled to himself. *Blackie always has a grasp of the situation. His insights are always on target. I've seen the same behavior countless times. He's a decent man with a knack for saying the right thing and doing what is proper. I wish I could do that.*

Joey was right. While Blackie demanded complete loyalty, he gave back the same level of respect to his subordinates, never raising his voice or embarrassing any of them. He treated his mistress with the same dignity, never cheating on her, and making passionate love as if she was the only woman he'd ever had.

***

Lewis Phillips edged onto his cushy wicker lounger, flipped off his house slippers, adjusted the wicker footstool two inches and leaned back. Clark smiled to himself, having seen the routine unfold countless times. Before his dad retired the predictable practice had occurred at least once a week, sometimes twice, with his dad's best friend, Leonard Ralston. Sitting on a rocker on the other side of the screened-in porch, his longtime buddy would do much the same, slip off his shoes, and sip on a Vernors.

Dad had that thoughtful look again, Clark mused. *Next would come the cheapo Corona. He'd unwrap the cigar as if it were a piece of fine jewelry, bite off the tip and moisten it. Before striking the match, he'd admire his prize and light it up. He'd take a drag and exhale with a look of ecstasy.*

Tonight was no different. Lewis took a deep draw on his cigar and blew out one, two, and a third smoke ring. Watching the rings dissipate into the warm summer air, his father pursed his lips for another drag.

Clark placed a pad and pencil on the side table and eased onto Ralston's chair. Instead of a Vernors, Clark sliced into his favorite raisin pie with a large scoop of vanilla ice cream. Taking a bite of pie, he waited for his fatherly mentor to lead the way.

It didn't take long.

"I like Chief Hart's approach to cut off all communication with his office. Downtown headquarters, 1300 Beaubien, leaks like a sieve." He took in a long drag and let it out slowly. "Rule number one:" He paused for effect. "Mum is the word. You can't be too careful; your team has to understand that. They can't say anything, not a word, to anyone outside of the room. If you say it once, remind them again, ten times, hammer the point home. You can't trust anyone."

Having heard the same thing from the chief, Clark shoved in the last bite of pie. His dad rambled on. Clark set his plate on the end table, picked up a pad and pencil. "Got it."

"I know son, but this is really important." He paused, took another long drag, and released a lazy smoke ring, twirling upward. "It's easy to let your guard down, particularly when talking to an old friend or someone close. One slip of the tongue could reveal a plan, a strategy, or worse yet, cost someone their life."

Clark paused, assessing the point. "Maybe I could come up with a short phrase or quote that might serve as a constant reminder."

"I like that." The old man flicked his cigar in the ashtray. "Better yet, have the team come up with something like that."

"Excellent. I'll make it an agenda item for our first meeting." His words stirred excitement. "I could put it on the bottom of every agenda."

"Perfect … that way it'll be a constant reminder."

"Got that one right," Clark joked. "What's next?"

Running his fingertips across the stubble on his jaw, his dad started speaking in all seriousness, ready to deliver the thoughts he'd had during the week. "Clark, this is the biggest assignment of your career. There'll be no room for a misstep or an error in judgment. There'll be no second chances. It'll be unlike any experience you've had; they think differently — take no prisoners."

Clark stiffened in his chair; he'd heard countless lectures, but never one that started with such a sharpness of tone.

"Son, this is for real. It's the big-time. It can be for all the marbles."

Moisture gathered on Clark's upper lip.

"I've shared my thoughts many times — none more important than these — call them the voice of experience."

Clark wiped his lip and made a note.

"Regardless of whom you pick, remember each member of the team will have know-how and experiences that exceed yours. Rule number two: Listen and learn before you lead."

Clark tilted his head, listening intently, and mumbled, "Tell me more."

"It's an old adage from a professor I once had. Never take anything for granted. Take in everything you hear. Think it through so you understand it, and then move forward."

His words connected the dots for Clark. "Makes sense. Don't make premature decisions."

"Right, and in particular when you're dealing with Mafia. They're smart as hell, plan and calculate far in advance; things may not be what they seem at first blush."

Clark nodded, trying to get a handle on the full meaning of the point. "How will I know?"

His dad smiled, knowing his son would be fine. "That's the point. You won't; that's why you must be very deliberate, positive of the steps you take."

Lewis took a couple of short, final drags and snuffed out his cigar.

"Rule number three: Delegate, delegate, delegate."

"Okay," Writing the words down, Clark said hesitantly. "I'm ready for this one."

"Let the team carry the ball. You don't have to know everything or do everything. You're the team leader. It's your responsibility to draw as much as you can from each of them. Take advantage of their expertise. Give them a chance to shine. You'll be surprised; they'll run further than you ever thought possible."

"I hadn't thought about it that way."

"Last point, rule four." Lewis thought for a moment.

Clark sighed, knowing the end was near.

"Give each member as much responsibility as you can. You'll be surprised by the leadership they'll provide. Remember, each one has achieved considerable success. That didn't happen by accident; they're all leaders."

Clark nodded, understanding why his dad had been so successful. "Anything else?"

"One more point." His dad stared at him for the longest time. "Sooner or later one of the mobsters will slip up. Be ready! It may be the only chance you'll have."

The door cracked open. Fran, Clark's mom, poked her head out. "*Police Woman* starts in five minutes. I know you don't want to miss Angie Dickinson."

"I'll be right there, sweetheart."

"Angie Dickinson … she's something else. How long has that show been on?"

"Five years. The last episodes are coming up." Lewis picked up his cigar butt. "Let's meet next week, same time. That'll give me a while to think about the people you might consider."

"Will do." Clark rose, picked up his dirty plate and headed for the door.

"Lewis!"

CHAPTER THREE

Clark Phillips opened the Sax Club door on the first Friday night of June, as he had every month over the past two years, and glanced inside. Brian May's solo in "We Will Rock You" reverberated onto the street. Shouts and cheers bellowed for the stripper.

Tall and slender at six-foot-two, Clark's one hundred and eighty-five pounds were evenly distributed, revealing the intensity of his daily workouts. He'd driven himself hard all of his life — for the record, an honor student in both high school and college — an overachiever, he would say.

Slapping the bouncer on the shoulder, he brushed back his thick sandy-brown hair, whispered something in the bruiser's ear and headed for his regular stool at the bar. Straddling the red vinyl, he slid into position just in time to gaze into the crotch of the African-American stripper above him. *Why does a pussy turn a guy on? You've seen one, you've seen them all. It doesn't matter if the broad is black or white, big or small; twats are all the same. Why is it special when one is gyrating over your head?*

He glanced between her legs at the mirror behind, showing off her ass. *Now that's something that makes a difference.* He looked up and watched her slide up and down on the shiny silver pole, as if she was sliding on top of him.

He had screwed her a couple of times before; somehow tonight, she seemed extra special. Her long, tan-streaked hair flowed over perfectly shaped breasts. If he didn't know better he would have sworn they weren't real. *She's the sexiest woman I've ever seen. God, she's hot!*

He fantasized about her dancing alone for him. "Nothing better than being in Caroline," he mumbled aloud, recalling the last time they'd been together — they'd had marathon sex in a room upstairs. Afterward she had lain with her head propped on a pillow doubled up against the headboard. The two talked into the early morning. *And God, she is smart. She knows something about everything; her intellect can match anyone's.* She told him of her mission in life, to finish her

19

undergraduate degree at Wayne State and obtain a law degree, so she could help poor young blacks who'd been raised by a relative, like her grandmother had raised her.

She glanced his way. Raising his long drooping eyelashes, he flashed his sexy blue eyes giving her a *come-on* look. She broke a faint smile and wiggled her butt a couple times, just for him.

The bartender set the usual in front of him; a Tanqueray on the rocks with three olives. "It's on the house."

"Thanks," Clark said, taking a sip, his thoughts glued on Caroline's rotating hips.

Continuing her routine into a second set, her body flayed wildly. He folded a ten-spot and slipped it under her ankle bracelet. Acknowledging his interest, she caressed her pussy, bent down to nearly head level and turned, rotating her ass in a grinding motion. He adjusted himself, his heart pounding. Anyone watching could tell she could take him anytime she wanted.

His eyes moved slowly up her shapely body and connected with hers. She stared back at him, seemingly waiting for him to break the spell.

It didn't take long. He broke the trance; the dimple in his right check deepened. He gave her a thumbs-up. Caroline's sexy, sensuous look confirmed the deal; without pause she unhooked her string-bikini top, leaned down and hung it over his ears … her grapefruits teasing his senses.

The guys around him hooted and hollered.

Clark stood, rubbed her top around his clean-shaven face, took a deep sniff and smiled, showing off his pleasure. He slipped off the vinyl stool and paraded around the bar, waving her top over his head like a drum major in a big-time marching band.

Applause and cheers broke out as he made his way from table to table.

Feeling his oats, Clark stopped in front of a table of younger females and gave them a couple twists of his hips. Applauding, they called for more. He chuckled and said, "That's all there is, ladies."

During the commotion, Renzo Ricciuti, one of Clark's college buddies had slid onto the stool next to his. Renzo worked hard to graduate from college — he knew he'd attain his goals — his strong work ethic would not be denied. He had honed life skills gained from the tutelage of his grandfather, who could repair or fix anything. Over the past fifteen years, Renzo's inner-city building and renovation business had grown ten-fold.

Puffing on a stogie, he adjusted his sunglasses, peering over the frames to watch his college friend, still strutting around the bar, the stripper's bikini top looped over his ears.

The two made eye contact. "Cool your jets," Renzo shouted.

Clark gave him a quick wave and marched smartly back, stopping a foot or two in front of him. He raised his hand and saluted. "Detective Phillips reporting for duty, sir."

Taking another drag, Renzo shook his head. "Goddamn, fifteen years and nothing has changed. You see a pussy and your brain shuts down and your pecker goes wild."

Clark adopted a thoughtful expression. "Nothing wrong with a little pussy now and then."

"Now and then?" Renzo decided not to pursue the topic they'd discussed many times. "Forget it. Anything new happening with Detroit's best police detective?"

"Not much." Clark wrinkled his nose. "Hey, I do have good news. There's not been a rape, robbery or murder in the last two days."

"Two days? You'll never make police chief that way."

"Chief ... who'd want to do that? Hart's new on the job and people are already on his case. First it's the city council and then it's the *Detroit Free Press*."

"Hey, he has it figured out. Did you hear what he told a reporter last week?"

"Hmm, not sure ... No, I don't think so."

Renzo's chest puffed, being one-up on Clark for a change. "Hart said, 'all you have to do to remain as police chief is to be loyal to the mayor. Do that and he'll be behind you all the way.' And, he went on to brag about Mayor Coleman Young."

"Sounds like he's figured it out," Clark acknowledged the comment and changed the subject. "How's your construction business doing?"

A glow highlighted Renzo's face. "Couldn't be better. I have five rehabs under contract and am looking to add two more renovations. The southwest side has turned the corner."

Clark shook his head. "Too bad I can't say that about the rest of the city."

"Yeah, half the places in the inner city are boarded up." Renzo took another puff on his cigar. "Want another drink?"

Clark glanced at his watch. "Why not? We have twenty minutes before the guys arrive."

Renzo motioned to the bartender. "A Jack Daniels here and the usual for our boy."

"You got it." The tall, slender barkeep turned toward the rear of the bar and shouted over his shoulder, "I have to turn the strobe lights on for the other two pole dancers."

No sooner had he flipped the switch than a stripper jumped up on each of the platforms located on either side of the bar. Renzo turned toward the well-endowed blonde to his left. His gaze followed her bouncing tits; a glance into the mirror behind her rewarded him with a reflection of her pivoting ass.

Clark zeroed back in on the other platform and Caroline's swiveling hips; he watched her profile in the mirror. *Christ, what a great body. I could sleep with her the rest of my life.* His eyes followed her from one mirror to another; he felt like he was watching her sensual body in 3-D. *Twist and shout. Go for it, baby.*

Turning toward Renzo, he said, "Hear anything about the four-year-old that was killed three weeks ago?"

"Nah … seems like the town is loaded with crazies," Renzo said, glancing across the bar. "Here comes, Carlos. Maybe he's heard something."

Waving to his old buddies, Carlos took a step toward them and disappeared into the mass of humanity. A clean-cut Mexican-American, Carlos Montes was the entrepreneurial guru of the group, having several highly successful used car locations throughout the inner city.

"Looks like we've lost him."

Clark chuckled. "Carlos may be five-foot-five but don't worry. He'll likely sell a car or two before he appears."

"Ha. You're right about that."

"Right about what?" Carlos asked, popping out of the crowd and squeezing in between Clark and Renzo.

"We were wondering if you sold any cars on your way over here."

"Don't laugh," he said. "I handed out four business cards on my way."

"I told you," Renzo said, nodding to Clark.

"What's this all about?" Carlos asked.

Clark laughed. "Nothing. We were joking about you selling cars."

"Laugh if you want. I signed a contract today to open my sixth dealership."

"Wow! Six." He looked surprised. "How'd you pull that off?"

"Unbelievable, huh?" Carlos gave them a prideful grin. "My wife and I talk about it all the time. It's beyond anything we ever imagined."

"I remember when you got your first dealership, but tell me again how you got started?"

"Funny you ask," he said, pride lighting his face. "It goes back to when I worked at the Cadillac plant during the summers."

"The plant on Scotten?" Clark asked.

"Right ... ten or twelve blocks north of Western High, where you went to school."

Clark stared in wonderment. "And that turned you into the biggest used car dealer in Detroit?"

"It wasn't just like that ... one of my buddies from the plant introduced me to a big-time Cadillac dealer in Dearborn. Next thing I know, I'm buying his used cars. I have another contract from a dealer in Bloomfield Hills, and two contracts from the biggest Ford and Chrysler dealers in town."

"That's hard to believe," Renzo interjected.

"You're telling me. It didn't take me long to learn that used cars sell like hotcakes in the inner city. Then Rosa Maria hit the jackpot. She came up with the lucky horseshoe logo idea, with 'BUY AMERICAN' wrapped around the outside of the neon sign and 'CARS' flashing in the middle."

"Yeah, you can see it for miles."

"We've been going like gangbusters ever since."

"You ought to have your success story published in the paper. People should know about it."

"Shh." Carlos placed a finger over his lips. "I don't want the word to get out."

"You're smarter than you look." Clark grinned and gave him a thumbs-up. "Ready to go upstairs?"

"Sure am," Renzo said. "It's about time I had some of that used car money."

***

The three friends gulped the rest of their drinks and made their way through the crowd to the narrow stairwell in the back. Treading up the stairs, they reached the dimly lit hallway. The three musketeers opened the first door on the left and stepped in.

Their longtime colleague and friend, Father Dominic "Dom" Repice, greeted them. He'd been the principal at Detroit Holy Redeemer High School when Renzo and Carlos were students there and was recently elevated to a leadership position in The Roman Catholic Archdiocese of Detroit. Still his jovial self, he'd added fifteen pounds, and gray hair now covered his head.

Having returned from college to their old neighborhood, the three met often for morning coffee. Carlos had become particularly close to the priest during the past five years when his wife, Rosa Maria, had been the president of the alumni association. A dynamo in her own right, she owns a popular Mexican restaurant near the intersection of Vernor Highway and Livernois Avenue.

"Beer and wine are on ice, appetizers on the table," the priest announced. "Help yourself. Ted and Alsye are on the way."

The three heads nodded. Clark and Carlos walked toward the food. Renzo grabbed a Bud Lite, took a slug and plopped down at the poker table. Picking up the deck of cards, he started shuffling like a Vegas dealer.

Ted Moomau walked in, gave the short priest a nod and bear-hugged Carlos and Clark. A four-year member of the group, Ted was originally from Seattle. By his own definition, a gypsy gigolo. As a matter of fact, he was far more free-spirited than the rest of the group; yet somehow he seemed to fit in perfectly with the local inner-city guys.

He glanced at Renzo sitting alone at the poker table. "How have you been, man?"

"Terrific," Renzo chirped. "Grab yourself a beer and sit your ass down. It's time to play some serious poker."

Ted nodded, picked up a Stroh's and pulled out a chair to Renzo's right.

"We have two players," Renzo shouted. "Anyone interested in playing poker?"

"Hold your horses," Carlos called, still chewing on a sub. "Alsye isn't here yet."

"He's always late," Renzo lamented. "Maybe we should start without him."

"Let's give him five more minutes," Father Dom suggested which carried the day. The five took their seats and talked about the Tigers' win last night over the Indians.

"They played like world champions," Carlos said, with a twinkle in his eye.

Clark shook his head. "Maybe, but the Indians will be hard to beat, come September."

"I agree," said Ted, tossing in his two cents.

Renzo ruffled the deck impatiently and announced, "First ace deals." Going around the table, he tossed a card in front of each player until an ace appeared in front of Carlos. Renzo tossed him the deck. "Dealer's choice."

Alsye walked in. "Deal me in," the late arrival with a broad Magic Johnson-smile said. The African-American newcomer to the city had joined the group three years earlier after he and his wife, Nicole, moved to the city from South Carolina. Since that time, he'd established a small chain of thriving convenience stores in the city's blighted area.

Alsye grabbed a beer and tossed a roll of twenties on the table.

For the next two hours each man took his turn calling his favorite game and boasting about his superior play. The group laughed and poked fun at each other. They took shots at each other's successes and teased about their losses. Talking about the good ol' days, they told raunchy jokes while the cards were dealt 'round the table.

Precisely at nine o'clock, Father Dom rose and waved his arms like he was about to give a blessing. "Break Time," he called.

Jumping up as if an alarm had sounded, Ted hit the head and Alsye followed closely behind. Carlos and Renzo refilled their bowls of nuts and each grabbed another beer, while Father Dom and Clark chatted in the corner.

Alsye returned and joined Renzo at the table. Looking around, he asked, "Has Sax Club always been like this?"

Renzo smiled. "Pretty much ... back in the Sixties it was one of the hottest strip clubs in the city. Sometime after that everything collapsed. The place fell on hard times and closed. It reopened over two years ago with the retro theme."

"How did the riots get started?"

Renzo raised an eyebrow. "That's a matter of debate."

A curious frown crossed Alsye's face. "Whataya mean?"

"I remember that day like it was yesterday — early in the morning of July 23, 1967 — the Detroit police raided a blind pig."

Alsye shot him a puzzled look. "A blind pig?"

"That's what Detroiter's call an unlicensed, after-hours bar. Someone screwed up. When the police arrived at the joint, instead of being empty, it was loaded with clientele."

Alsye threw his hand up. "Stop. I'm still back at someone screwed up."

"Sorry." Renzo tossed him a pleasant smile. "People in the inner city knew the Mafia regularly moved blind pigs from one precinct to another. Working in concert with the Mafia, the police would raid a property after the gambling paraphernalia and equipment had been vacated."

"I can't believe that many people were on the take."

"It's hard to imagine, but that's the way it was," Renzo picked up the deck of cards and shuffled them. "At four o'clock on that morning it happened — the place was packed. The police hit the wrong place."

Alsye's jaw dropped at the cops' error, and waited anxiously for the rest of the story.

"As the patrons were hauled away, a crowd gathered outside — there was shouting, shoving, name calling — the disturbance escalated into a street fight and within hours rioting spread throughout the city."

"Wow, that's amazing."

Father Dom joined the table. "The civil unrest rendered the city a huge battleground-wasteland from which it never fully recovered. I watched the whole thing on TV; it was kind of eerie. The news filmed a white car pulling up in front of Sax Fifth Avenue five times. Each time two guys would jump out, load the car with furs and take off. Twenty minutes later they were back for another load. Crazy!"

"Where were the police?" Renzo asked knowing the question was on Alsye's mind. "Some were pinned down by gunfire in precinct

stations. The rest were simply overwhelmed — too many hotspots."
Renzo shook his head. "The worst was yet to come."

"How so?"

"In the aftermath, the tax base was destroyed as over two
hundred thousand people moved to suburbia in the next three years."

"Why didn't the people rise up and take control?"

"Good question," the old priest said, "There are plenty of
theories on that, too." He leaned back and took a sip of beer. "My view
is pretty simple." He paused to let his point soak in. "Since the time
Ford produced the first automobile, decisions about everything came
from the top — the auto industry, powerful unions, big government.
And I'm sad to say, the Catholic Church — the average guy didn't
have a chance."

"There were other places like Detroit ... they came back."

"You're right ... but not Detroit." Father Dom gave him a
reflective glance. "For some reason it didn't happen. Some of it was
the lack of leadership in city government, but the biggie was a lack of
individual spirit. For so long every decision had come from the top. At
the time, people had lost their entrepreneurial spirit; their individual
pride and 'can-do spirit' were gone. Instead, they focused on placing
blame and looking for someone else to fix it."

"That's hard to understand," Alsye said with a grimace. "I've
been in town five years and have seven convenience stores, and I'm
focused on helping rebuild the surrounding communities."

Father Dom smiled warmly. "Unfortunately we didn't have a
cadre of thousands like you."

CHAPTER FOUR

Clark strolled into the kitchen a week later. "Mom, what smells so good?"

"Apple crisp. It'll be out of the oven in ten minutes."

"Great." He popped a smile. "Let me know when it cools. I'll put a scoop of ice cream on it."

"I'll take care of it." She pointed toward the back porch. "Dad is out back pruning the roses. He planted six Yellow Peace in one corner and six Mr. Lincolns in the other."

"When did he do that?"

"Early this spring. He's been doing something out there every day since. Have a seat in your favorite porch chair. He'll be done shortly." She turned toward the oven and looked over her shoulder. "You better be ready. He's been fussing about that task force of yours all week."

"Sounds like nothing has changed." Clark kissed his mother on the cheek and headed toward the sliding door to the porch.

Easing back into *the chair,* he thought about the times he'd sat there with his high school buddies, Carlos and Renzo. Once in a while they'd light the scented candles, turn the ceiling fan on high, and party. Renzo and Carlos took turns providing the marijuana. Clark never bought it; too dangerous for dad.

We weren't into the hard stuff or doing anything crazy, he mused. It was a stick for each of us and a few beers; that's all there was. The camaraderie was the best part. We talked about school, the Tigers, Lions, and fooling around with the girls in the local theater balcony — it was for bragging rights — whoever got laid the most and whichever one was the best. Renzo was always ahead on the leaderboard.

Clark chuckled to himself, recalling the one time the three of them played in the same basketball game. *At six-foot-two I was the smallest front-line player for Western High. Detroit Holy Redeemer, just down the street, had a bunch of runts. No one taller than me. It didn't matter with Renzo and Carlos playing for them. They were all over the court, picking up loose balls, making layups, and tossing in free throws. It wasn't until the last minute of the final game of our senior year, when I made a ridiculously lucky shot and we won by a point. To this day, they never let me forget that shot.*

His mom opened the door. "Want some ice tea while you're waiting?"

"Sounds good, but I'll …" He flashed her a big smile. "I'll wait for the apple crisp."

"Figured you'd say that." She closed the slider and disappeared.

Watching his dad's head bob up and down between the plants, Clark couldn't help but smile. He recalled the pride his dad had taken in every aspect of his life. *It started in grade school. He found something positive to say about every report card. I learned the ropes early. On the first Saturday of every month the two of us would walk down the streets of the precinct. He'd step into every store and shake hands with the shopkeeper, pat me on the top of the head and say "this is my boy." The owner would smile, reach into his pocket and pull out a quarter or point to the candy bar rack, "Pick out your favorite one." I was special.*

Clark glanced out the porch screen, his dad's head buried in the roses. He remembered the nights after his high school basketball and football games. *Whatever time I got home, it didn't matter, dad was sitting there in that old stuffed chair. It was always the same; we'd replay the game. He gave me advice, asked about a particular play, and praised me on my performance — there was always a compliment. I still remember the basketball league championship game when I hit the winning bucket. His voice echoed through the gym, loud and clear … "that's my boy." It was the same when I walked across the high school stage to receive my diploma … "that's my boy."*

Clark shook his head. *We had plenty of talks over the years; most of them seemed more like lectures, yet, I knew they were well intended. Matter of fact, more often than not, dad was right on target.*

The slider door opened and mom handed him a dish. "Here's your apple crisp, honey."

Clark reached up and cradled the bowl in his hand, its warmth telling his senses what was about to come. "Two scoops. Wow, that's great."

"What's great?" a shout came from the back wooden fence. "That you, Clark?"

"Yeah, take your time, pop. I'm having apple crisp."

"Apple crisp … I'll be right in."

His dad rose, brushed off his overalls and rushed inside, passing Clark without saying a word. Within minutes, Lewis had washed his hands and sat down in a chair with a dish of his own in hand.

"Nothing better than warm apple crisp and vanilla ice cream." He took a couple of bites and set his bowl on the table.

Knowing the time was near; Clark placed his empty dish on the end table and picked up his pad and pencil. He knew full well "Uncle Leonard's" name would be the first words out of his dad's mouth. *He wasn't really my uncle but he'd been at our house so much when I was a kid, I called him uncle. I guess it stuck.* "So who do you think I ought to pick?"

"Leonard Ralston has to be on the top of your list," Dad said predictably. "He's …"

"No need to say more," Clark interrupted. "He's on top of everyone's list. Who's next?"

"Will Robinson. If you pick none of my other suggestions, you have to pick him. He knows the streets, the Black Mafia and the neighborhood gangs — they're the worst!"

"The worst?" He was surprised. "Why do you say that?"

"They're kids, most of them are black, and have no rules, no morals … no scruples."

"Dad, they're all crooks … evil people."

"The Mafias have rules; it doesn't matter who they are — Arab, Black or Italian — they're part of an organization. They have someone in charge; they calculate, connive and plan. The gangs though, are spontaneous, freelance. You never know where they're headed. Whatever suits the head honcho's fancy is what they do."

Taking copious notes, Clark glimpsed up. "Okay … who's next?"

"Two individuals come to mind. The first one is Eddie Grissini. He lives and breathes the Mafia. He knows so much about the mob I sometimes think he's connected."

"Really … is he?" Clark thought for a moment; his interest peaked.

"No, that's just a figure of speech."

"Anyone else with his kind of experience?"

"Without question, no one comes close." Dad pressed his lips and nodded.

Knowing that look, Clark understood nothing more need be said. "Who's next?"

"Max Cumberland. He's the best precinct captain in the city. You need someone from that level to help with the logistics."

Clark edged forward in his chair. "Tell me more about him."

His dad laughed heartily. "He's street savvy and … a real character, too. Max will provide a little levity when things get tough. You never know what he might say."

Lewis emptied the last of his dish. "You can't beat your mom's apple crisp."

The sliding door opened and Clark's mother poked her head outside. "The two of you going to talk all night?"

"Nah, we're almost done," Clark responded. "If there's any apple crisp left you can wrap it up so I can take it home," he said with a grin.

She laughed. "I'm way ahead of you. There are two pieces in a container on the kitchen counter. I'm going to watch my favorite TV show," she said, sliding the door shut.

Lewis unwrapped a cigar, wet the end and fired it up. Watching the smoke rings drift toward the ceiling, Clark smiled to himself, waiting for his dad to continue.

He didn't wait long. Lewis rambled for the next half hour or so; Clark had heard all of the stories at least two or three times. Finally, his dad looked up at him with a grin. "How many times have you heard those?" he joked. Turning his attention to the matter at hand, "You need to add a couple of women to the team ... they'll offer a different perspective."

He took a couple of drags and blew a large smoke ring. Watching the smoke curl and twist, Clark leaned back and smiled to himself. *This time I'm ahead of him.*

Lewis took another drag and paused. "Have any thoughts?"

"Yes dad, there are two women everyone agrees are good for the team."

"Oh." His dad released another smoke ring. "Well, let's hear about them."

"Kimberly Weston is one."

His dad's eyes lit up. "The one with the big boobs?"

"Yeah, she really knows her stuff. She's been an undercover agent and has plenty of moxie."

"She's currently in child abuse and prostitution."

"Right."

"Good choice ... she was on my list too."

Clark smiled to himself. "The other one is Nancy Sterling from narcotics."

"Don't know her."

"She's been on board six years, has a master's from Michigan State, and can recite the details of every drug bust in the city's history."

"Excellent. You need someone with that kind of expertise. Drugs are the biggest problem you'll face in the years ahead."

Knowing his dad had more to say, he asked, "Have any more thoughts you'd like to share?"

Two smoke rings floated toward the ceiling fan.

"As a matter of fact I do."

Clark reopened his notebook. "Fire away."

"Some of this may be a repeat of the points the chief mentioned ... if so just make a note, they're worth hearing again."

Lewis took a couple of slow puffs.

"Your task force must develop a sense of oneness — unity, cohesion, solidarity — the members must feel a total reliance on one another. The confidence and trust they build as a team depends upon total confidentiality."

"Makes sense."

Shuffling in his chair, his dad raised a hand and pointed his finger at Clark. "I want to talk about the obvious."

Clark looked puzzled, wondering what this lecture would be about. "Oh ... okay."

"Criminals are not all the same." Lewis took his time in making the point. "Remind your team about the significant tendencies of the major groups you're dealing with — they're quite different."

"How so?"

"In the past the Italian-American Mafia was the only major threat. They're all related; almost impossible to penetrate. Lean on Eddie Grissini when it comes to them. He understands the culture and will give you insightful advice."

"That's a good reminder."

"The Greek Mafia controls Greektown, but beyond that they're not a problem. The Arab Mafia is a group you need to watch. They're shipping heroin directly in and their power is growing in leaps and bounds." Lewis took a deep breath. "In contrast, the African-American gangs are ruthless. As I said before, they're nuts; they act spontaneously, have no rules. Be extra careful of them."

"I know, dad, they're already the biggest problem in our neighborhoods."

"We're way behind the curve; that's the next battleground. Will Robinson will be most helpful here. He knows gangs better than anyone."

The slider opened. "Lewis, it's past your bedtime. Save the rest for another lecture."

"Just one more thing, Fran, and I'll be right in."

"One more," she blistered. "How many times have I heard that?"

"Just one," Lewis said softly, snuffing out his cigar and turning toward Clark. "You've picked people with outstanding track records. Take advantage of them. Seek out their input. The more opportunity you give them the more you'll get from them."

"Don't worry, dad. I heard the same message from the chief. I'll take advantage of them." Clark rose, opened the slider, turned back and whispered, "I have to run before I get you in trouble with mom."

Twisting the corner of his mouth into a wry grin, Lewis glanced inside. "I'm on my way, Fran."

***

It wasn't long before Clark was home again sitting on the back porch with his dad — this time he was the more serious one. While Chief Hart had not released the names of the task force members, the word was out.

As was customary, dad lit up an old stogie. "So what's the problem?"

"You wouldn't believe it, dad. There are reporters and people from the media all over the place, asking questions. What do you think I ought to do?"

"What's that have to do with you?"

"Me? Everything. I'm heading up the task force. They're clamoring for a comment from whoever is in charge."

"Has the chief announced your name?" Lewis asked pointedly.

"No, but …" Clark stopped, trying to decipher the words his father had said, afraid to ask one more time and risk embarrassment.

Smoke rings floated toward the fan, dead on the ceiling. Before Clark knew it, the top portion of the porch ceiling was filled with smoke. The old man puffed away.

Clark broke the silence. "Okay … okay, I give in." He threw his hands over his head. "What do I say?"

Lewis smiled, took in another deep drag and released a perfect, seamless ring.

His eyes lit up. "See that, Clark, it's flawless. Did you ever see a more picture-perfect smoke ring?"

"It's a grand prize winner." Clark said, not giving a damn about it. With a deep sigh he waited until his dad was ready.

The two sat in dead silence. Clark committed himself not to say the first word. It went on longer than he expected.

A loud chuckle broke the silence. "They know nothing, Clark."

Clark scowled, trying to sort things out one more time.

He gave it to him straight. "If you say nothing; they know nothing."

Clark gave him a bewildered, perplexing look. "So I just play the waiting game?"

"It is not your game. The media knows nothing. They're only digging and probing, *hoping* to find out something. The chief set a process in motion to buy you time. The longer you say nothing the more time you have. Got it?"

Clark's eyes beamed. "Got it. There's nothing to be said."

"Have any other questions?" the old man asked. Clark shook his head. Dad glanced at his watch. "Twenty minutes before Angie comes on. I have a couple of thoughts about the future … something for you to think about."

"Angie … it's Wednesday night."

"Reruns, but haven't missed one yet."

"Do I need something to write on?"

"Nah, you'll remember this," he said, exhaling a flat-tire shaped ring toward the fan. "It's about how you handle things down the road … when you *do* have something to say."

Clark slid closer to the edge of his chair. "Okay."

"The media will ask you all kinds of questions, most of them likely leading in a direction you don't want to go. Pay no attention to their questions. Say what you want to say; it's your agenda."

"But dad ... how do I do that? I'll look like a dingbat."

"First of all ... it takes some practice. We're taught to answer questions asked, so it's only natural for you to do so when you're at the podium. Watch Mayor Young. He has the process down pat."

"What does he do?"

"Tell them only what you want them to know, not what some young reporter has been told to ask. The only way you'll look like a dingbat is if you fall into their trap."

"You're positive?"

"Remember what I said before — listen and learn before you lead — stay the course and you'll be fine." Clark followed every word. His dad snuffed out the cigar, started to stand then plopped back down. "One more point."

Having anticipated "one more point," Clark hadn't moved.

"Never take an interview over the phone. Take the time to meet with the media. It'll puff them up, but in reality it's more important for you."

"Why?" his brow furrowed. "I don't understand."

"Being in the room with a person gives you a significant advantage. You can watch his eyes to see if he's listening. If it's a female ... did she hear? What is she thinking? Did she write down your main point? It's a game, take charge and play it your way."

One more time Clark shook his head in amazement. "Dad ... how did you learn all of this stuff?"

The old man leaned back in his glory moment, knowing his son was ready for the big-time. He hesitated for the longest time then grinned. "Listen and learn before you lead!"

Clark rose and embraced his dad with a loving hug. "I love you, man."

His dad nodded. "Good, it's time for me to watch Angie."

CHAPTER FIVE

Following a scorching July eighth, the guys arrived before the after-five crowd. Three younger strippers slid slowly up and down the shiny silver poles in their final routine; each strutting her stuff, hoping she'd be promoted to the lucrative night shift.

Renzo glimpsed up at the one above his head — her slender body and modest breasts slinked sensually to Abba's "Dancing Queen." He turned to Carlos. "How old do you think she is?"

Carlos raised a heavy dark eyebrow. "Shit, don't ask me. They all look like kids to me." He glanced over his shoulder and nodded to a rear booth. "If you really want to know, ask Clark. He has an eye for that kind of stuff."

Renzo's brown eyes followed his nod. "Not now, his hand is halfway up Caroline's thigh."

Carlos turned for his own peek. Clark caught his eye and gave him thumbs up with the other hand. Waving to the guys Caroline turned toward Clark. "You're lucky to have so many good friends. I wish I could say the same for myself."

Feeling he should say something, he stumbled on his words. "W-When you get your law degree and start practicing you'll have lots of friends."

"I can hardly wait. I'd do anything to nail that 'Babysitter Killer' up in Oakland County. What an asshole. I feel sorry for the parents. They must be heartbroken."

"I'm sure. It must be devastating to have your child snatched right out of a local parking lot."

"From what I've read, it has to be some kind of a sex pervert. There have been others and it's been going on for sixteen or seventeen months. Every parent in the county must be on pins and needles. Do you think they are connected to the Nash killing?"

Clark's mind responded slowly, shifting his thoughts from being with her all night; he barely heard the question. "Hmm … I'm not sure."

Caroline gave him an uncompromising look. "I hope the chief's new task force will get to the bottom of it."

"So do I," he said, wanting to tell her more; knowing he couldn't, he changed the subject. "How about dinner at Cliff Bell's two weeks from tonight?"

"That'd be perfect. I'll be finished with summer school." She glanced at her watch then looked at Clark. "It's time to go. I want to take a short nap before I get ready for tonight."

"Will you be getting off at the regular time?" He pulled his hand from her thigh and kissed her on the cheek.

"Yes ... around one. I'll be there with bells on." She giggled and blew him a kiss as she slid out of the booth. He winked at her and headed for the stool between Ted and Alsye. Having arrived a few minutes earlier, Renzo had already briefed them on Clark's roaming hand.

Ted watched Clark ease onto the red vinyl; he grinned, shaking his head.

"What's with you?" Clark asked.

Ted looked down at Clark's slacks. "I'm surprised you can walk."

"What's that mean?"

"I saw where your hand was. If that had been me, I would have had a king-size hard-on."

"Get out of here," said Clark, half joking and then adjusted himself.

Alsye downed his beer. "I'm starved. I'm going upstairs to get some munchies. You guys ready to go?"

Heads nodded down the row. Clark winked at the bartender. He rang up the tab and placed it in front of Clark. Each of the guys chipped in a five. Alsye slid off his stool and led the way.

***

Father Dom was at the door greeting them with a beer in his hand. The guys took turns lining up at the head then surrounded the table of hors d'oeuvres — leftovers from Renzo's Fourth of July party. Standing around bullshitting, Renzo was on a roll, funnier than ever, his witty banter better than any *Saturday Night Live* show.

The last to load his plate, Clark sat down at the poker table.

All heads turned toward him.

Ted led off a barrage of questions. "It sounds like the Nash family is really committed to finding the killer or killers, huh?"

Clark nodded a positive expression. "They have tremendous resolve. Huston Nash is going to pump thousands of dollars into the effort."

Carlos glanced up with a sympathetic look on his face, almost in tears. "I can't imagine what the family is going through."

"There's no way to explain it." Clark didn't move; his face expressionless. "It's tough on everyone."

"You know anything about the special task force?" Alsye asked.

"Not really," he fibbed.

"It's about time someone downtown did something. Drugs and violent crimes are absolutely out of control."

Carlos shook his head very slowly, looking at Clark. "You can say that again."

Alsye popped a second beer. "Did you see the report last week on the significant downturn in the number of police brutality complaints since Mayor Young eliminated the STRESS unit?"

"Yes, I saw that." Ted frowned with a puzzled look. "What does it stand for?"

"Stop the Robberies and Enjoy Safe Streets," Alsye responded. "There were over twenty-three hundred complaints in 1975 … less than half that this year."

Carlos cocked his head to the side. "Yeah, the police killed twenty-two residents and arrested hundreds for no reason at all. It sounded good at first, but now it's obvious they were unjustly targeting African-Americans."

"You can say that again." Alsye's infectious smile popped up. "I'm happy to see they've finally hired some African-American officers. When the mayor came into office there were less than 10 percent blacks on the force. He's done a good job."

Renzo pushed his plate aside. "I'm ready for some serious poker."

"Me too." Carlos rose, picked up the empty plates and set them on the side table.

"What do we have here … a Mary Poppins?" Ted joked.

Father Dom gave him a well-meaning smile. "You'll learn about that when you get married."

"Married? Not me … never."

"Don't ever say never." Renzo advised, then flipped the cards around the table. "Dealer's choice," he said, when the first ace landed in front of Alsye.

Ted glanced over at him. "In all our years together you never told us how your parents came up with the name Alsye."

Pearly white teeth sparkled in Alsye's grin. "After two sons my momma was hoping for a girl. She was committed to the name. I think Alsye means exalted or noble. Anyway, when the she became a he, I got the name anyway."

"Funny, how things happen. I guess all of us have a story to tell." Carlos took a breath and asked, "How's your liquor store business going?"

"Terrific. I'm thinking about opening my eighth convenience store."

"Eight … are you trying to corner the booze market in Detroit?"

"Corner the market? No way … I'm trying to keep my head above water."

Carlos wrinkled his brow. "With eight stores, how can that be?"

"Nicole and I talk about that all the time. By the time I pay our employees and cover my insurance and overhead costs, there isn't much left … seems like the Mafia takes most of that."

"How much do you have to pay them?" Father Dom asked.

"Three hundred and fifty dollars a month — fifty bucks a store."

There was a long pause. "How can you afford that?"

"That isn't the point, Father. I can't afford *not* to pay. If I don't I'll be in deep shit city."

"Has it gotten that bad?"

"Bad? It's worse than bad. It's the only way I can survive. They guarantee that my employees will not be harassed. They assure me there'll be no graffiti on my store walls, no broken windows, or gang fights out front. Basically my locations are some of the safest places in town."

"Sounds like you've developed a good relationship with the Mafia."

"Today, yes … tomorrow who knows? Every time you think you're doing well with them they raise the bounty or come up with something new. They're always one step ahead of what I plan to do."

Father Dom continued to probe. "How'd you develop an inside track with them?"

"Inside track?" Carlos shouted. "They're screwing him. He's paying them three hundred and fifty a month."

Alsye paused, collecting his thoughts. He spoke slowly, "Good question, Father. Most of the liquor and convenience stores in the inner city are run by foreigners. That doesn't sit well with the residents. And, the Mafia is not happy about it either. They're doubling down on them, forcing them to jack up their prices. That means life is coming up roses for me."

"Sounds like it." Renzo nodded and turned to Ted. "You thinking about expanding too?"

"Me ... hell no. I have all I can handle. Keeping five apartment buildings afloat is more than enough."

"Managing five complexes can't be easy. How do you handle the maintenance? Seems like you'd need a carpenter, electrician, and plumber on call twenty-four-seven."

"I do it all."

Renzo looked surprised. "You ... you're the maintenance man for five buildings?"

"I used to be a high school shop teacher, so I know a little bit about everything."

"Still ... five buildings. That's hard to believe."

"I make my rounds every day." Ted's Cheshire cat smile suggested more.

Renzo thought for a moment. "Your rounds?"

"Yeah, I try to be in each building at least twice a week. I enjoy mingling with the tenants."

"Mingling?" Carlos cast a perplexed look at him. "What's that mean?"

"Over half of the tenants are single women. Someone has to *service* them."

"Service them?" Father Dom cocked his head questioningly, a grin tugging at his lips. "Are you saying what I think?"

"It's not like I'm doing a bunch of prostitutes, Father. They are all decent, professional women. They're not the type you see hanging around bars. They lead normal lives and are comfortable at home. They appreciate the fact they are not hassled by the riff-raff."

Father Dom leaned back in his chair. "How many women do you *service* in a week?"

Ted took his time counting on his fingers. "Six or seven. Maybe eight sometimes."

"Christ, son, when do you sleep?"

Ted shrugged his shoulders. "Guess, I never thought about that."

Father Dom turned to Clark. "You've been unusually quiet tonight. What's on your mind?"

Clark's expression went flat. "Ah ... thinking about the Nash kid."

"What a tragedy," Carlos said.

"A tragedy ... it's a real indictment of our society," Renzo lamented. "Detroit is the pits."

"I feel so sorry for the parents," Father Dom said as he stood up. "Would you please bow your heads while I say a few words?"

The group did so and when he finished they looked up with somber eyes.

Carlos turned to Clark. "Are the details I've been reading in the newspaper accurate?"

"All of the accounts I've seen are correct. The nanny put the little boy in a swing, gave him a little push and ran into the restroom. When she came outside a minute or two later she saw a guy pushing the kid on the swing. The boy was screaming. She shouted, 'Stop ... Stop,' and ran over and jumped on the guy's back. He slugged her, knocking her cold and breaking her jaw. Four hours later, the fifth precinct got a call that a boy's body, wrapped in a blanket, had been found on a park bench on Belle Isle."

Ted tossed a questioning look toward Clark. "That doesn't make sense to me."

"Me neither," someone else agreed.

"That's why it's so troubling," Clark said. "The pieces don't fit a typical crime scene."

Father Dom slid his chair closer to the table with a look of interest. "Do you have a theory on this?"

"Not really ... the body of the grandson of one of the most prominent families in the city found dead — no threatening calls, no ransom note — something went haywire."

"Do you think this is connected to the murders in Oakland County?"

"Hmm ... I really can't say."

"I know." A frustrated Ted threw his hand over his head. "We've heard that before. You can't say anything about an ongoing investigation."

Carlos came to Clark's defense. "Lighten up."

With that their attention turned to poker. Right on schedule three hours later, Father Dom called "Break Time."

Alsye bolted for the head. "I can't hold it any longer."

Clark and Renzo loaded up at the food table again, and ten minutes later the gang was back at the table. Another three hours passed and Clark volunteered to clean up — nothing unusual. Everyone knew he'd been banging Caroline for the last two months. That was all he could talk about. And when Father Dom mentioned her name during a hand of poker, the twinkle in his eyes said it all.

The one o'clock bewitching hour came as usual, and within ten minutes the guys were gone. That is, everyone except Ted; he lingered to count his loot. He was always checking his loot — between pinching pennies and women's butts — he didn't have time for much else.

"How much did you rake in?" Clark asked.

Ted gave him a thumbs-up. "Fifty-seven bucks."

"Wow … that's damn good. You were on a real roll over the last hour or so."

"Yeah, I was down big-time before the break." Ted took his time and looked Clark in the eye. "You okay?"

"Yeah, I guess … I just can't stop thinking about the Nash kid."

"That's understandable." Ted said as he glanced up at Clark, then looked down as he dropped his winnings in a small velvet bag. "I can't imagine why someone would do something like that."

"Things are crazy at the office. The chief has the entire department working overtime. That's all I think about."

Ted's voice hesitated slightly. "You need a break?"

"Right. I'd be happy if someone would come in and say, 'I did it.' Fat chance of that happening."

"No, I'm talking about you getting out of the rat race and having some fun."

"Christ Ted, I'm working my ass off!" Clark didn't look up, kept sweeping the floor. "I don't have time to see a Tigers' game. I haven't looked at the standings in the past two weeks."

"I'm not talking about going to a ball game."

Clark looked at him with a suspicious eye. "Oh no … you're not roping me into one of your maintenance jobs. I couldn't fix a light switch if I had to."

"It's not that. I need a favor."

"Ha … I suppose you want me to hold a flashlight while you're unplugging a drain. The answer is no."

Ted slapped his hand on the table to get Clark's attention. "Will you listen for a minute?"

Clark looked up, set the broom aside and flopped on the chair next to him. "Okay, I'm all ears."

"There are two classy ladies in one of my buildings …"

"Oh no you don't," Clark interrupted. "You're not sucking me into something like that."

"You can't say that. You haven't even heard my proposal."

Clark wrinkled his nose. "I know you. I don't have to hear your proposal."

"Both of them are MDs at Wayne State. They're sharp as hell. One of their daddies has a yacht and she wants to take a cruise down the Detroit River some weekend in August."

"You gotta be shittin' me."

"No, I'm not."

Clark stared blankly for a moment. "Don't look at me."

"Come on, Clark, I can't go alone. I need another guy."

"No, I can't. Caroline and I are really hitting it off. I don't …"

"Caroline?" Ted cut him off. "I can't believe Clark Phillips just turned down a piece of ass on a yacht."

"That's not important to me, Ted. I told you Caroline and I are just fine."

"Fine. You don't have to get laid. Just go with me. I'll get laid. The two of you can stay topside and have a beer, unless you're opposed to that too."

Thinking it over before responding, Clark said "Okay, but you'll owe me big time after this one."

***

Clark finished cleaning the room spick-and-span, locked the door and walked slowly down the hallway. After passing the door to the club office, two doors remained on the left. The first one was reserved for the dancers; they used it to change outfits, freshen up or take a nap. The door on the end was available for the dancer with the longest seniority at the club. If she didn't want it for the night she could sell the key to a newcomer or pass it to the next girl in line — rarely did it go beyond that.

Clark pulled the key she'd given him from his pocket and unlocked the door. Without haste he stripped naked, took a quick shower, double lathering his hair to remove the traces of Renzo's cigar smoke, and dried off with an oversized towel. After blow drying his hair, he slipped on his Jockeys, grabbed a beer from the small fridge and propped himself against the headboard of the bed.

Within minutes the door cracked open. Caroline peeked in. "I was hoping you were ready," she said, locking the deadbolt and loosening the buttons on her skimpy attire. Slipping in part of a dance routine, she slinked toward the shower.

Clark's urges fired up.

After a hot shower, she returned in quick order, wearing a short red top that left nothing to his imagination.

Clark's smile spread ear to ear. Her sexy eyes zeroed on his bulging shorts. He felt the heat as his desires elevated.

Slipping onto the bed, she teased his nipples, before running her fingertips down his sides. A small smile creased his lips. He swallowed hard and slid down on the bed.

Perfect. She'd been thinking about seducing him with every move on the dance floor — her hormones on fire — now's not the time. *Take it slow and easy, watch him squirm.*

Clark didn't move; his desires beyond control.

She bent over and looped her fingers under his elastic band. Placing a hand on each side, she slowly eased his shorts down, freeing him. He seemed bigger than before. She leaned over, teased and sucked gently, her mouth engulfing him.

Clark's head fell back on the pillow, his heart racing, his body wanting to explode. *Jesus Christ, I can't hold off. Think about something else, count sheep! Goddamn, think about something ... anything.*

Caroline half-closed her eyes and with a smoldering look, backed off and gave him space.

Clark caught a quick breath; his body teetering on the verge of losing control.

She gazed into his glassy eyes knowing he was hers whenever she wanted him. And so, she took her time, clamping his hands one-by-one on the headboard spindles and slowly inching her fingers down his arms and around his face. Leaning down she lightly kissed his nose, cheeks and lips, searching for his tongue in a French kiss.

He pulled a hand from the spindle and reached to hug her. She grabbed his hand and shoved it back over his head. "I'm in charge tonight. Keep your hands on the spindles."

CHAPTER SIX

Sitting in a small booth near the front door of the Sax Club, Clark watched Caroline perform. Rarely sitting that far from her crotch, he stared in amazement. *She looks sexy from here, maybe even more so — her body moves so gracefully — a real turn-on. And she's smarter than hell.*

The front door opened.

A very attractive African-American woman stepped in and stood stoic. Squinting, she rubbed her eyes trying to adjust to the smoke-filled room. Slowly her eyes scanned the dimly lit bar. In front of her, she eyed the fifteen to twenty tables, half of them full of men — their eyes focused on the center pole — a highly sensual woman danced to Rod Stewart's "Hot Legs." Off to the right a younger pole dancer strutted her stuff; more for her own enjoyment than anyone else's. On the left another dancer worked her pole.

Drawn to the center pole, the woman's eyes shifted to the sexiest woman she'd ever seen — perfect proportions, great legs — moving in ways she'd never dreamed of.

The bouncer tapped her on the shoulder. "May I help you?"

Her eyes remained on the unfamiliar environment.

"Mama," the two hundred and fifty pounder said more forcefully.

"Ah … yes." She turned his way. "I'm supposed to meet Clark Phillips here."

The flat-top pointed Clark's way. "He's in the second booth, over there on the left."

She glanced that way and saw his waving hand.

"Thanks." She gave the gatekeeper a faint smile and turned toward Clark.

As she arrived in front of him, he slid out of the booth and extended his hand. "It's good to see you, Nicole."

She gave him a warm smile. "Thanks, I feel like I've known you forever."

He couldn't help staring at her beautiful face; her perfectly shaped nose. "Alsye has always talked about the most beautiful woman in the world, now I know why."

She lowered her eyes with slight embarrassment. "You're most kind ... I appreciate your willingness to visit with me."

"My privilege." Clark flipped a hand to the side. "If Alsye wants to talk, I'm here. If his charming wife wants to talk, I'm here. You name it, I'm here."

Nicole smiled, graciously. "You're exactly like he said you'd be, open and friendly, willing to listen and lend a helping hand."

"Hey, that's what friends are for." Clark's hand brushed his crop of hair. "Would you like to have a drink?"

She glanced at his glass full of ice and olives and wrinkled her nose. "Not anything like that. I'll have a Diet Coke with extra lime."

Clark motioned to the waitress. She unloaded an order at the adjacent booth and turned toward them, pulling out her pen and pad. Glancing first at Clark and then at the black woman, she gave him a quizzical look. "May I help you?" she said, hesitantly.

"Yes. She'll have a Diet Coke with two limes and I'll have another."

"Any snacks?"

Glancing at Nicole, Clark raised his eyebrow. "The chicken fingers are terrific."

"That'll be fine." She gazed around the bar. "Have you been coming here long?"

"It'll soon be three years. Back in the Sixties this was one of the hottest places in town. Unfortunately it fell on hard times and closed. A couple of my college buddies bought it and replicated everything to its original splendor; they even put a sign out front like the old one."

She sneered. "Sax Club ... does that have a particular meaning?"

"In a way. They're open for jazz from noon to midnight on Saturdays and Sundays and feature some of the most famous saxophone players. They've had Sonny Rollins, Wayne Shorter, and Joe Henderson. The rest of the week it's strippers and good ol' times."

"The weekends sound like fun. Alsye and I will have to come here sometime."

"You should." Clark glanced at Caroline and turned back to Nicole. "In the beginning 'sax' was as close as they could come to 'sex.'"

48

"That was my first impression." She giggled. "When Alsye mentioned you guys played poker upstairs at the Sax Club I had my doubts. He told much of the story you just related."

"Ha … there's a lot more activity up there," Clark's eyes rolled upwards, "than he probably told you."

Nicole winkled her nose. "What else goes on up there?"

Clark hesitated, not positive if he should describe *everything* that goes on, then decided to go for it. "The dancers have a room they can use if they want."

"Oh." She did a double take of him. "Have you been in it?"

Stirring the olives in his Tanqueray, Clark took his time before looking into her piercing stare. He pointed to Caroline. "See that dancer on the center pole?"

Nicole's face brightened. "How could I miss her?"

"That's my girlfriend," he said pridefully.

Nicole took a moment to admire the raving beauty. "She's stunning; legs like Tina Turner."

"Thanks. That's what everyone says."

Clark's eyes jumped back to Caroline. Nicole gave her a fleeting glance, looked back at Clark and grinned.

"Alsye said you're always striving for the best. Looks like you've outdone yourself."

"I'm a lucky man." His blue eyes darted to Caroline and back to Nicole. "I've always worked hard. Putting forth a little extra effort in the beginning helps things work out in the long run."

"You sound just like Alsye." She brushed her long black hair to the side. "I really appreciate your willingness to talk with me."

"Not a problem. We hang together."

She leaned across the table and spoke softly, making sure no one else could hear. "Alsye is really stressed." She hesitated before revealing, "His momma is dying." She pointed at her melon-sized abdomen. "And I'm seven months along … the Mafia just jacked up the ante … and J. J. is on a new, expensive medication. I don't know if he can handle much more."

Clark took in every word, unaware of the issues she had described. "That's a load; no wonder he's stressed out."

Nicole bit her lip, holding back tears.

Clark took a sip of gin to buy time, not certain where to go from here. "Want to tell me about his mother?"

Nicole paused a moment, collecting her thoughts, not sure how to describe the woman she admired more than anyone in the world. "Joyce Weatherspoon isn't his momma. She's his grandmother. Alsye's mother died when he was born. His grandmother raised Alsye and his two brothers. She didn't have a cent but treated the boys like they were saints."

"That's amazing."

"They lived in a small house outside of Spartanburg, South Carolina. That's where she was raised. They worked twenty-five acres on the old plantation where her grandparents had been slaves."

"Wow ... that's hard to imagine."

"Alsye never said much about all of that. He picked cotton with his two brothers as a kid; he never complained." She sniffled discreetly and wiped her nose with a tissue. "He's never said a bad word about anything or anyone in his life."

Clark paused to think of something to say. "How did the two of you meet?"

Nicole's face glowed; her voice perked up. "I was a freshman at the University of South Carolina-Spartanburg. He was the star running back on the football team. It was love at first sight. I knew he was the one when he bought me an ice cream cone after the first game." Her twinkling eyes slightly dimmed. "Did you know Alsye has been driving to Spartanburg every other week for the past two months?"

"Alone?" Clark gasped.

"Yes. He's been driving straight through ... twelve or thirteen hours."

Clark tossed her a look of despair. "That alone is enough to wear out a person."

"We had a long talk before he left this time. Joyce is ninety-two and failing. The doctor doesn't believe she'll make it through the week."

"Is there anything I can do?"

"No. Alsye told me not to worry ... he'd take care of it. I know it's tearing him apart, though."

Clark reached across the table and squeezed her hand. "You know I ..." He stopped, correcting himself. "The guys will do anything you want."

Nicole seemed preoccupied. "I appreciate that. I just wanted you to understand the issues he's dealing with."

Clark paused, searching for the next topic. "How's your pregnancy going?"

"Fine." She took a long sip of her Coke. "Alsye worries more about things when he's gone. He's concerned about me, J. J.'s medication that costs five hundred dollars a month, and a hundred and one complications at the stores. If it's not one thing it's another."

"Do you need money?" he asked cautiously. "The guys and I would…"

"No, no," she interrupted, waving her hands. "It's just that Alsye thinks about the worst possible circumstances. It goes back to his two older brothers. He watched the oldest one die because they couldn't afford the medicine. And, there's William. He's two years older than Alsye but he watches over him like a kid brother."

Clark took in a deep breath; his mind swirled with everything Nicole had told him. He changed the subject. "You mentioned the Mafia had upped the ante. How much have they increased it?"

Nicole wrinkled her nose. "That's Alsye's biggest worry. He never knows what they're going to do. He opened our eighth store so we could put a little away for J. J. and …" She tapped the top of her bulging stomach. "J. D."

"Yes, Alsye told us."

"A guy was by the other day and said they're considering a rate increase — inflation. That's BS. Alsye said they're talking like that because we're doing well." Nicole wiped a tear trickling down her cheek.

"How much is it going to be?"

"Four hundred and twenty dollars per month."

Clark gulped, "That's insane; that's over five thousand a year!"

Nicole sobbed, "There's no way we can handle another increase. Alsye cried all night. I tried to console him, but he insisted I go to sleep. He's always more concerned for me than himself."

"You're lucky to have a guy like that. There are plenty of guys whose first thought would be about themselves. Are you sure there isn't something I can do?"

Nicole's face was pinched with fear. "I'm really scared for Alsye."

"Scared … did something happen?"

"Not with the Mafia." She delicately blew her nose. "Alsye has packed his trunk full of Mason jars filled with moonshine on each of his last three trips from South Carolina."

"That's a big-time problem, Nicole. It's a federal offense to transport liquor across state lines without a license."

"I know ..." Nicole's face went blank. "If the Mafia finds out he's selling it out the back door he'll be in big trouble with them, too."

"Trouble with the Mafia and trouble with the law — that moonshine can kill someone."

She grinned, just a little. "The guy back home says it's been tested and is as safe as regular whisky. Twice as strong and half the price."

"That sounds good. He probably tested it on a horse," Clark quipped.

Nicole gave him a tight-lipped frown. "I'm just concerned for Alsye. Things are closing in on him."

"All of us would be pleased to help. I'd be glad to tell the guys if you want. I'm sure ..."

She cut him off. "I'd love that, but Alsye would die if the guys knew... maybe you could talk with him. He doesn't have anyone else."

Clark understood her perfectly. "I'll get together with him as soon as he returns."

She sighed with relief. "That'd be wonderful."

"Wonderful?" Caroline said, sliding in next to Clark. "Are we talking about my guy?"

Nicole gazed into her lovely dark eyes. "As a matter of fact, I am. You're really fortunate to have someone like Clark. He's so kind and understanding."

Clark hand-gestured a time out sign. "Could I interrupt for a moment," he said, taking time to introduce the two women.

Caroline flipped her long dark auburn hair back. "Clark tells me you have a special guy too."

"Yes, I guess we're the two luckiest women around."

"I wouldn't trade mine for anyone."

Clark leaned over and kissed Caroline on the cheek. "You wouldn't receive much for a trade-in anyway."

Caroline playfully punched his shoulder and laughed. "I was hoping for at least ten bucks."

Nicole slid off the bench seat and rose. "I'll let the two of you visit. I have to be on my way. Thanks again, Clark, for your willingness to help."

"My privilege."

Caroline watched her go out the door. "She seems like a wonderful person."

"You got that right." He grinned. "She's one strong lady."

Caroline snuggled closer. "Management is trying out a couple new girls tonight so I'll be off by eleven."

"Sounds like a deal to me." Clark's white teeth shined brightly.

She pulled the key from her pocket and laid it on the table. "How about Chinese tonight?"

"Great. I'll have the carryout ready when you walk in. Want anything in particular?"

"Hot and sour soup and ... something with cashews."

***

A week later, the maître d' at Cliff Bell's picked up two leather-bound menus and led the way to a dimly lit booth in the rear. Clark slid in on the same side as Caroline.

Looking at a piece of history, she admired the dark paneling and crafted woodwork. "I bet these walls have some tall tales to tell."

"I'm sure." Clark pointed to a line of photographs hanging on the wall. "From the 1930s to the '60s, this was the place to be."

"I like it this way — quiet and romantic." She placed her hand on his thigh and caressed.

He gave her an excited laugh. "I'll give you a half hour to stop."

"Forget it." Caroline smirked. "You wouldn't last ten minutes."

Knowing she was right, he opened the menu. "What are you having tonight?"

"Hmm, I'm not sure." The two talked over a couple of drinks as they continued to look at the menus. "I had the soy glazed Atlantic salmon last time," she recalled. "Maybe I'll have the braised lamb shank."

"I was thinking about that too. Red wine okay?"

"Perfect ... you pick."

Clark ordered a moderately priced bottle of red Bordeaux and the two settled on a Caesar salad and lamb shank. Over a long dinner, heavy with romance, their eyes did most of the talking. He ordered a second bottle of wine. Caroline snuggled closer. "How are your parents doing?"

"Interesting that you ask," he said, his face aglow. "I was thinking about them on the way over to your place." An unconscious grin appeared. "Dad is always giving me advice. And mom, she's always flitting around the kitchen and keeping dad in check. They're a great pair."

"What kind of advice does he give you?" she asked, inquisitively.

"How to deal with the mob and how careful you need to be when talking to others."

"He's right. You never know who's connected with whom." She eyed him with a coquettish grin. "Still think you can last a half hour?"

CHAPTER SEVEN

Ted drove across the Belle Isle Bridge, pulled into the parking lot of the Detroit Yacht Club, and turned to wink at Clark. "How's that fit your fancy?"

"Holy shit." Clark's eyes bulged. "I've seen this place from a distance but I didn't realize it was so big. The clubhouse is three stories high … it's almost a city block long."

"Wait 'til you see the inside of the clubhouse and the marina."

The two men got out of the car and walked briskly toward the complex, like two kids headed for a candy shop. Ted marveled at the landscaping. "Look over there, world-class tennis courts and an Olympic-size swimming pool."

"Yeah, and how about that?" Clark pointed the other direction. "Bocce ball, volleyball and racquetball courts. This place is unreal."

Opening the front door, the two strolled into the rambling clubhouse and came face to face with two grand walnut staircases — the lobby spilled in front of it, with opulent furnishings accented by a tasteful Mediterranean décor.

"Look at the restaurant; it's really elegant. We could eat here," Clark suggested, still looking for a way to avoid being in an uncomfortable situation with Laverne's friend.

"I have something better in mind," Ted said, slicking back his long black hair with his hand.

Clark ignored him, opened the door and stepped out on to the marina deck. "I'll bet there are two hundred and fifty boats here."

Ted pointed. "Check the size of that one over there. It has to be fifty feet."

"Yeah." Clark gawked and pointed. "Look there on the side, its brand name is Ocean Alexander."

"I heard they're the hottest thing afloat."

Seventy-five yards down the dock a tall attractive blonde waved. "Down here, Ted."

"Is that one yours?" Clark asked.

"Yeah, we've been together three or four times. She's something else."

Seeing a cute brunette step into the open, Ted said, "That's your date for the day."

"I told you this is not a date."

"Okay … Laverne says she's really bright and a lot of fun."

Ted picked up the pace; his thin frame bursting ahead. Clark took two double-time steps.

The leggy blonde ran toward Ted.

He turned toward Clark and said softly, "She's a former all-state volleyball player from New Jersey and has been on staff at Wayne State University Medical School for three years. She's into pediatrics in a big way."

Clark eyed her. *I can see why Ted thinks she's so hot — great body.*

Laverne threw her arms around Ted and pecked him on the cheek. "I'm so glad you could come." Stepping back, she looked Clark over. "You didn't say he was so good looking." She extended her hand. "Hi, I'm Laverne Belk."

Ted wrinkled his brow, making his sunken eyes look even darker. "I don't think he is."

"Good thing," the cute brunette said, grabbing Clark's hand. "I'm Sharon Wilson. C'mon, I'll show you around."

Practical and down to earth, the thirtyish woman was the definition of success. Growing up as a farm girl, Sharon had picked berries and tomatoes, drove the tractor, and did her share of the farm chores. Smart as well as attractive, the former high school homecoming queen was bubbly and vivacious, setting the pace for every activity she undertook.

"Sure." He followed her onto the thirty-five-foot yacht.

Laverne waved to the man at the helm. "Let's go, I'm starved. I haven't eaten all day."

The captain powered up; the engines roared and the yacht pulled slowly out of the marina. Ted and Clark watched as they passed by one grandiose yacht after another. "These things must cost a fortune," Ted said.

Laverne pointed to the largest one. "That's an Ocean Alexander. It costs a million dollars."

Ted's square jaw dropped. "Wow."

Laverne grabbed him by the hand and led him below. Sharon and Clark followed the two down the narrow stairs. Pointing out the features of her daddy's yacht, Laverne beamed while the newcomers gasped in amazement — walnut paneling and a French chandelier hanging over the dining room table — not a hotel in the county could out do the lavishness.

After the short tour, the four gathered upstairs again. Clark learned the back of the vessel was the aft. Sharon tried to teach him the difference between port and starboard, but every time he turned around he got it wrong.

"Looks like we'll have to go on another cruise, until you figure it out," she said, only half in jest.

Laverne snickered. "Sharon ... you can't teach an old dog new tricks."

"What do you mean by that?" Clark asked, feigning indignation. He rose and proudly pointed to the wrong side. "Once and for all, that's port."

The group howled and red-faced, Clark sunk onto a cushion.

The women placed two large platters of hors d'oeuvres on the table fastened to the floor between four captain swivel-chairs. Clark took drink orders and Ted fixed doubles — a tall Crown Royal on the rocks for Laverne, Patron Tequila with double lime for Sharon, Clark's usual Tanqueray with three olives, and a Dewar's Scotch for himself.

Clark sat the drinks on coasters and joined the group.

The four chatted about the Tigers' winning streak, the mess in Washington, D. C., Detroit's growing financial woes, and the topsy-turvy stock market. Clark cleaned his small plate for the second time, while Ted poured another round.

The pace slowed.

Leaning back, Clark gazed up at the undergirding of the Ambassador Bridge. "Did you ever wonder how they figured out how all of that bracing should be placed?"

"No, and I really don't care," Ted exclaimed. "As long as it stays up on my way to Canada."

Sharon looked perturbed. "That's a strange way to look at it. You can always use the tunnel."

"Speaking of Canada," Clark piped up. "Did you know this is the only place in the US where you can drive south and enter Canada?"

"Hey, you're a real brain," Ted jabbed.

"C'mon Ted … I'm from Michigan and *I* didn't know that," Sharon confessed.

"Where are you from?" Clark asked.

"St. Joseph, it's on Lake Michigan."

"Oh yeah … I know where it is. Did you boat much there?"

"Not like this. We lived on a farm and used to go fishing once in a while."

"On a farm?" Clark wrinkled his brow. "I've never been on a farm."

"I can't believe that."

"It's true. See those houses over there?" He stood and pointed to the Michigan shoreline. "That's Scotten Avenue where I attended Western High School. It's across from Clark Park."

"Did your parents name you after the park?" Ted hooted.

"That wasn't nice to say," Sharon said, defending Clark.

"Hell, for all I know he might have been conceived there …"

"Ted!" Laverne cut him off. "That's enough."

Clark came to his rescue. "No harm no foul. Ted and I are always poking fun at each other. Truth is my mother was a history teacher and knew all there was to know about the Louisiana Purchase. She used to tell me stories about the Lewis and Clark Expedition."

"Ha, fifty-fifty chance you'd been called Lewis," Ted poked.

"I suppose so, except then I would have been a junior."

"How sweet," Sharon said. "Lewis and Clark … that's a nice sounding father-son combination."

Ted scowled at her, downed the last of his drink and looked Laverne in the eye. "Ready to go down below?"

Caught off guard, she blinked. "Ted …"

He extended his hand. "C'mon, let's go so these two can get acquainted."

"You don't have to be so blunt about it."

"Sorry." He tiptoed toward her. "I just thought they might like to get acquainted."

"Weaseling out of it again, huh?" She giggled, grabbed his hand, and led him down the steps.

Watching them disappear, Sharon said, "They're becoming a thing. Laverne's been looking forward …" Sharon paused and covered her mouth.

"Looking forward to what?"

"Ah, nothing." Sharon's face flushed. "I guess I opened my mouth one time too often."

Clark urged her. "C'mon, tell me."

Hesitating, Sharon's face reddened. "Ted has a large one."

Dumbfounded, Clark stared mutely, not knowing how to react; he figured he best let this one go.

She grabbed his hand and squeezed his fingers. "Laverne and Ted are a good fit." She pursed her lips prettily. "Guess that was a double-entendre."

"So let's talk about Ted's … I've never had a conversation with a woman about another guy's pecker."

Sharon bit her lip. "I can't."

"C'mon, there's just the two of us."

She shyly glanced away, trying to come up with the right words. "Well, according to Laverne he's really hung; it's big and dark like a horse's …"

"A horse?" Clark cut her off, curious. "Why do you say that?"

"'Cause … Laverne says he hasn't been circumcised and has a huge erection."

Clark belly laughed. "What does Laverne have to say about that?"

"She calls it 'Midnight.'"

"Midnight?" Clark covered his mouth with his hand trying not to split a gut. "Does she say that in front of Ted?"

"All the time," Sharon admitted, her eyes wide open. "So do the women in the other buildings. He's doing a lot of them."

"Ted mentioned that at poker, but I never realized he was that open about it."

Sharon scrunched her shoulders. "Apparently all of the women know. I'm sure some don't even know his real name and just call him Midnight."

"Where did she ever come up with a name like that?"

"Laverne named it after Black Beauty, the horse."

Clark gave in and doubled up laughing. "I guess … I guess Ted will call me pony from now on."

Laughing like crazy, Sharon tugged on his shirt. "Okay, okay, we need to end it."

Clark straightened his shoulders and sobered up. "So how does a farm girl from St. Joe end up as a doctor in Detroit?"

"It was pretty straight forward. I went to Michigan State to become a veterinarian …"

Clark cut her off. "No wonder you know so much about horses."

She gave him a disgusting look. "I hope you're enjoying your jollies." She shook her head.

"Sorry." He paused, letting her know he really was. "So you went to Michigan State University."

She smiled broadly. "It didn't take long for me to decide I didn't want to be around farm animals the rest of my life so I transferred to MSU's med school."

"How'd you end up at Wayne State's medical school?"

"I finished my degree and decided to focus more on the research end of things, so I'm doing a residency here in forensic pathology."

"You're cutting up cadavers?"

"That's part of it — determining the cause of death is just a fragment of the job — there's some cutting-edge research going on out there that's going to change the entire way you collect evidence."

Clark's brow turned down; his shoulders stiffened with doubt. "What are you talking about?"

"Some of the biggest names in the world are doing research on hair follicles, saliva, blood samples and tissues to see if they can connect the dots."

"Connect the dots." Clark gave her a look of despair. "I'm still not with you."

"I don't understand it all either." She sighed. "But they're trying to connect hairs found on a person's comb they used at home, with hairs found at a crime scene."

"Wow." Clark's eyes bugged. "Wouldn't that be something?"

"I'll keep you posted," she said. "The field is growing by leaps and bounds."

"We'll have to talk more about that."

"Yes, I'd like to." She turned and ran her fingers around his lips. "Did anyone ever tell you that you have a super-cute smile?"

Clark's eyebrows rose. "Ah no … you're the first."

"Your mouth curls when you laugh. It's really cute."

Feeling uncomfortable, Clark changed the subject. "I'm having a Stroh's. You want one?"

"No, but you can get out the condiments. There's a plastic container of pickles and olives in the fridge. Bring them and anything else that looks good. I'll cut up the sub sandwiches."

"Got it," Clark said, delivering the goods and plopping down on a deck chair.

Sharon heaped a stack of sliced subs in front of him. "How'd you get into police work?"

"I didn't have much of a choice." He smiled pleasantly. "My dad worked the beat in the district where we lived and my uncle Frank labored in the Cadillac plant, about ten blocks north of there. I didn't have many other options — be a cop or work at that plant, or the Rouge."

"The Rouge?" Sharon tilted her head with curiosity.

"That's the Ford plant along the Rouge River; the biggest auto plant in the world. We just passed it. I'll point it out on the way back." He sucked down a slug of beer. "I worked in the Cadillac plant a couple of summers. It didn't take long for me to decide it was college for me."

"It happened just like that?"

"Well … I guess I knew all along that I was going to be a policeman."

"Why so?"

"I used to walk the precinct with my dad the first Saturday of every month. People loved him. I knew from that point on, I'd be a policeman."

"And becoming a detective?"

"I'm a little like you — have an inquiring mind — I'm always looking for a solution."

"Good for you." She sank her teeth into a sub. "Are you working on anything special now, if I may ask?"

"I'm assigned to the case about the killing of the Nash kid last month."

"Wasn't that awful?"

"I can't imagine why anyone would do such a thing." Wearing his feelings on his sleeve, Clark's face saddened.

"Have any theories about what may have happened?"

"We've looked at a couple of angles, but so far we're stymied … I can't say much more."

"Sure, I understand." Running her fingers through her lush brown hair, she twirled a few strands around her forefinger. "I'm always amazed at the different angles you guys come up with."

Clark gave her an inquisitive look. "I guess you know something about criminal investigations?"

"Nothing formal. My uncle Lloyd worked in the Berrien County court system. He'd visit on Sundays and we'd talk about the latest shooting or bank robbery in Chicago."

Not understanding, a crease shot over his brow.

"Sorry … our farm was across Lake Michigan from Chicago. We got all of our news from their TV stations."

"Interesting." He leaned back on the chair. "Sounds like you're a real crime aficionado."

"I wouldn't say that." She flipped her hair. "I enjoy being the devil's advocate."

"Alright." Clark glanced at her cute button nose. "Do you have a theory on the Nash murder?"

She backed away. "I'm sure you don't want to hear from me … I'm just a novice."

"No. Go ahead. Maybe it'll trigger a thought."

Pleased with his request, she grinned. "I have two theories."

"Two, wait a minute." He rose and headed for the fridge. "Want a beer? I'm having one." She shook her head. Clark grabbed a bottle and sat down across from her. "Let's hear your thoughts."

"One is that a child molester happened to be in the area and tried to snatch the kid. Something happened and he panicked. Not too likely, I'd say." She glanced along the shoreline collecting her words and looked back at him. "The second one seems more plausible — someone was watching him. Maybe they planned to kidnap him or were collecting information on the family. Either way, something went wrong. They likely had the kid under surveillance, maybe for insurance … who knows?"

"Insurance? How'd you come up with that?"

"It's my analytical brain, I guess." She pointed to her head. "It just seems logical. Huston Nash is one of the richest men around. Pictures of him and his family in the paper were almost too perfect. The old man looks straight. The wife is … kind of dowdy, a Betty Crocker type. That leaves their kids. An older daughter returned for the funeral from college somewhere out West and the younger one arrived home from an Eastern boarding school — not likely either of them was connected — that leaves the parents of the kid. The wife looks like Miss Priss. I don't think she's in the mix ..."

Clark cut her off. "So what's the point?"

Sharon wrinkled her nose. "The handsome dad is the only one left. Something about him doesn't fit." Sharon shrugged. "Oh well, maybe I should stick to my forensic research."

"Not so. You've raised an interesting point."

***

It was dusk when the four gathered again around the table. Clark and Sharon were sitting across the table from each other. Ted asked if anyone wanted a drink. Following a round of noes, he fixed himself a double scotch on the rocks and slid into one of the captain's chairs. Laverne flitted around the galley like a queen bee, pulling leftovers out of the fridge from every shelf.

Clark pointed to the shoreline. "There's the River Rouge plant I mentioned before," he said to Sharon.

She shaded her eyes. "It's huge; it looks like a city."

"In some ways it is. It's home to thousands of Ford workers."

Laverne placed a tray of liqueurs on the table, unwrapped a plate of cheese and chocolate mints, joined the group and gave Sharon a subtle wink. "There are only a few more weeks of good boating left. I'll be out of town next weekend. How about we plan a trip north in two weeks? We could stay overnight somewhere around Port Huron."

"I'm all in," Ted said quickly, as if he knew the proposal was coming.

Laverne glanced at Clark. "Ah ..." He hesitated, trying to think of a reason why he couldn't stay all night — thoughts of Caroline flashed. "I can't be gone Sunday. My mom is having a birthday party for my dad," he fibbed.

"Oh ... that's too bad," Laverne said. "How about the following weekend?"

"No ... I really can't. I'll have to take a raincheck."

Sharon looked at him compassionately. "How about Saturday? We could have a nice lunch and be back before dark."

"That'll work," Clark said.

Laverne agreed.

Ted nodded, knowing he was the odd man out and would have to find another way to get in bed with Laverne.

CHAPTER EIGHT

Sharon braced one hand on the yacht railing and extended the other to Clark. "Welcome aboard."

Laverne glanced at Ted then turned toward Clark. "It's great to see you, again."

"Thanks," he said, giving her one of his patented Cheshire cat smiles. He stepped onto the deck and pulled his left hand from behind him. "Chocolates for the ladies."

The women looked at each other in total amazement.

Sharon reached for the box. "Whitman's my favorite," she bubbled. "It's perfect. We can share them as a special treat during the trip."

"Sounds good to me," Ted said, peaking over Clark's shoulder as if to say "Why didn't I think of that?"

Laverne shouted to the captain. "I'm untying the lines."

The engines powered up and the sleek vessel pulled away from the dock, heading north for open waters. Ted hustled toward the galley. "Ready for drinks?"

"Let me help." Clark walked over to the small bar. "Same as last time, ladies?"

"That'll be fine," the two women agreed.

Sharon placed napkins, plates and silverware on the table. Laverne pulled a platter of hors d'oeuvres from the fridge that included a large arrangement of smoked oysters.

Clark eyed them with appreciation. "I love smoked oysters."

Ted winked at him. "Oysters and olives, can't do better than that."

"You don't need either one," Laverne quipped.

Sharon's eyes bounced with a twinkle from one to the other, knowing it was best to say nothing.

The guys delivered the drinks. Ted held his scotch high and toasted, "Here's to a great trip with two beautiful women."

"And two handsome guys," Sharon said.

"I'll drink to that," Laverne added.

The foursome clinked glasses, took sips, and gathered around the table aft. It wasn't long before the guys filled their plates and dug in.

Laverne studied Sharon's new, shorter hair style. "I really like the cut around the back."

Clark looked up. "I like her bangs." *There's something about bangs; they're a real turn-on. Shit, I'm not telling her that.*

"Thanks." Sharon fluffed her hair and gave him a soft smile.

Over the next hour the four chatted amiably, catching up on the local happenings and the latest in town. Ted placed his empty glass on the table. "Enough of the small talk." He turned pointedly toward his longtime friend. "Clark, do you think the 'Babysitter Killer' in Oakland County was involved in the Nash murder?"

Clark took a long sip, buying a reflective moment. He hated questions like that; yet, had grown accustomed to hearing them. He took his time, making sure he said nothing truly revealing. "Hmm, there's some common ground in the cases, but personally … I don't know."

Ted shot him a glare. "If it's not the Babysitter Killer … who did it?"

Clark took a deep breath and smiled. "That's the sixty-four-thousand-dollar question."

"Sounds like the same old thing from you."

Clark smirked, knowing he couldn't say more. "What did you expect?"

"Humph." Ted took a couple more appetizers and slid the platter in front of Clark.

Laverne reached in front of him. "I need those. I had an extraordinarily busy week." She scooped her plate full then slid it over to Sharon.

"What were you doing?" Sharon asked, as she placed a piece of salmon on two crackers and passed the tray back to Clark.

"It was one deadline after another … all week." Laverne giggled. "The rest of the time I was fighting off the doctors."

"Tough job," Clark mused.

Sharon turned to Clark. "Anything new in the police department?"

Laverne raised her hand, and asked pointedly, "Do we have to start on that again?"

"Sorry." Sharon bit her tongue and picked up a cracker. "We'll wait until the two of you are in bed," she said, curtly. "What do you want to talk about?"

"How about the stock market?" Laverne suggested.

"The stock market!" Ted exclaimed. "You don't know anything about the market."

"Well Ted, what would you suggest?"

"How about the Tigers? They're playing better."

"Sports!" Laverne ruffled. "Is that the only other topic you can talk about?"

"Well ..." Ted jumped up and tugged her hand. "If you don't want to talk we might as well ..."

Laverne shot him *the eye,* followed by a disgusted look. "And is *that* all there is on your mind?"

"It is when I'm with you."

"Oh, all of a sudden ..." She gave him a prissy look. "Aren't we lovey-dovey?"

Ted raised his eyebrows. "Why not?"

"Okay ... *Midnight.*" She rose and squeezed his hand. "You need to freshen my drink first."

He rushed to the bar, refilled their glasses and held them high. With a giggle, Laverne shook her head, grabbed her glass and led the way below.

Sharon raised her eyebrows.

Feeling uncomfortable, Clark looked away. He stood and turned toward the galley. "Can I freshen your tequila?"

She raised her glass. "Make it a double. I think we're going be here awhile."

That tone sounded like a come on. For the first time ever, Clark thought about not getting laid. He took his time adding ice and booze to their glasses and then placed them on the table.

Sitting down across from her, he asked, softly, "How have you been?"

She gazed into his eyes. "I've been thinking about you."

"Me? I hope they were good thoughts." *Shit, why did I say that?*

"They were ... very good." She sent a surprisingly sexy smile his way. "I still can't believe it ... our backgrounds are so different and yet, we have so much in common."

"I've had the same thoughts." Clark nodded in agreement. *Crap ... that was a dumb thing to say.* He quickly shifted the conversation, not wanting to go where he thought she was headed. "What was it like going to school in St. Joe?"

Surprised, she paused. "It really wasn't St. Joe. I went to Lakeshore High School in Stevensville. It's a small community just south of St. Joseph."

"Does that make a big difference?"

"There's a real difference. Most of the kids at St. Joe high school live in town. At Lakeshore most everyone lived on farms. I was involved in 4-H."

"4-H?" he questioned, sounding unsure.

She laughed. "You sound like a city slicker ... it's a non-profit youth program for rural kids administered by the USDA. They have all kinds of courses so you can learn about raising animals, growing crops, cooking and sewing; everything related to ranching and farming. They sponsor the county fair, too."

Clark's eyes rose to hers. "I've never been to a county fair either."

She gave him an unforgiving look. "You really have been deprived, haven't you?"

"I guess so," he gestured, throwing his hands in front of his face, as if indicating "What can I say."

She paused, seemingly to pick the right words. "Is there anything you can say about the Nash case?"

"Hmm, I'm still working on it," he joked and shook his head. "I really can't."

"I'll be interested to hear what you found out when the case is closed."

"You never know what will turn up. Sometimes it takes a month or so before the entire picture becomes apparent." He smiled, knowing he couldn't say any more.

"There it is again," she said, then ran her fingers around his lips. "Your mouth curls whenever you smile or say something funny."

He shrugged. "What can I say?"

"You don't have to say anything." She leaned over and kissed him firmly on the lips. "They kiss pretty well, too." She giggled.

Sensing she was headed in that direction again, Clark stood and extended his hand. "Come over here; there's something I want to show you."

Acting like she'd rather be making-out, she rose and followed him. Heading portside, he hoped she'd cool her jets. "Look at those mansions along the Grosse Pointe shoreline. I bet half of them don't look as nice from the street side."

Stepping next to him, she placed her arm around his waist and squeezed tight. *Crap, here she goes again. I have to find a way out of this.*

Sharon laid her head on his chest and snuggled.

He pointed. "Look at that one. It's unreal," his thoughts more on how to avoid a difficult situation than the mansions he was pointing to. *She's a very likeable person, but ... I can't betray Caroline. I've played around all of my life but Caroline is really special ... for the first time in my life, I'm feeling she's the one. I could spend the rest of my life with her. I love her.*

Sharon raised her head. "Isn't that something? How about that one over there?" Keeping her arm around his waist, she pointed with the other hand, "Three stories, a pool and a bocce court. Can you believe that?"

"It's unreal."

Clark headed for the galley. She walked toward the table and plopped down next to it, with a thud. He didn't turn around, assuming she was pouting about not being in a bed below. He paused for a long moment, giving her space and him time to develop a strategy if her hormones fired up again.

Turning around with a plate of munchies, he headed her way.

She gave him a disinterested glance over the top of a fashion magazine.

Unsure of her next actions, he stepped forward and surprised her with an Old Fashioned glass. "Tasty tequila for a beautiful lady."

Thankfully, that seemed to break the ice.

She laid the monthly aside and rewarded him with what he was learning was her standard shy, sexy smile. "Thank you very much," she said demurely. Sharon looked him square in the eye. "Are you seeing someone?"

Surprised by her forthright question, yet relieved, he sighed. "Yes, I have a special friend."

"How long have you been dating her?"

"I've known her for a couple of years; things became serious in the past few months."

"Good for you." She leaned back and looked at him with admiration. "You're quite a guy."

"Why do you say that?"

"Laverne said you were a really neat guy and that I should 'go for it.' I'm not that type, but when things seemed to go so well, I said to myself 'what the hell, why not?' Anyway, when I came on to you, you politely moved away. Lots of guys would have jumped at the opportunity, regardless if they were in a relationship or not. I respect you for that."

That was nice of her to say. He flushed and glanced slowly away. "Thanks ... I guess." He stumbled, knowing it was only the second time in his life he'd turned down an offer — both with her.

"You're really embarrassed, aren't you?"

His face reddened. "I'm kind of old school ..."

She cut him off. "I had you pegged totally different." She raised her glass and clinked his. "Here's to a really cool guy."

"And here's to a very attractive woman."

She blushed and turned away.

"So you're not as worldly as you try to be, are you?"

She smiled, seeming to unwind. "No, I'm just a little ol' farm girl from Stevensville."

He nodded with a big grin. "That little ol' farm girl is very nice. Don't ever change."

"Thanks. What you see is what you get. Whoops." She covered her mouth. "I didn't mean for it to come out that way."

He waved it off. "Not a problem."

Sharon leaned back and gave him a quizzical look. "When was the first time you did it?"

Surprised, Clark's eyes opened wide. "Why did you raise that question?"

"I don't know. It just came out."

Clark hemmed-and-hawed. "In junior high, I guess."

"Junior high, I can believe that." Sharon looked at him sideways, digging a little more. "*Where* did you do it?"

"In the balcony at the theatre. There were Saturday matinees."

"You did it every Saturday?"

70

Clark rolled his shoulders. "Ah … most of the time."

Moving uncomfortably, she almost fell off the chair in disbelief. He spoke up, "Okay smarty, when was the first time for you?"

She bit her lip. "College."

"College?" He laughed.

"Why are you laughing about that?" she said, sharply.

"I don't know. Why did you raise the issue anyway?"

"Because." She looked bewildered. "You're so different. I've never met anyone like you."

Clark raised his eyebrows. "I hope that's a good thing." *There I go again.*

"It's very good." She paused, realizing she shouldn't have said that. "I'm hungry again. Want to see what's left in the fridge?"

Clark jumped up. "I'm for that."

***

Clark and Earl stopped at the receptionist desk in the McNamara Federal Building on Michigan Avenue, downtown Detroit. While Clark signed in to see Oscar Westerfield, his contact for the Detroit FBI, Earl gazed at the expansive lobby of the new complex. *A long way from the old police station at 1300 Beaubien.* He glanced at the building directory. *Twenty-seven floors — other than an airplane I've never been that high.* Seeing everyone in suit and tie, he rolled down his shirt sleeves and buttoned his collar.

Clark pointed to the bank of elevators. "Twenty-sixth floor."

"God, he must be one of the biggies."

"I think he's the FBI's number two man." The two stepped inside. Clark hit number twenty-six and winked at Earl. "I told you this was the big time."

His African-American buddy pursed his lips and waiting in anticipation tried to lighten the situation. "Do you think they have Cokes up this high?"

The door opened before Clark could respond to the inane question.

Mr. Westerfield greeted them with a self-introduction. A slightly built career man, dressed like most of the rest in the building — dark suit, white shirt and somber broad tie — he led the two toward his office.

Stepping inside, Clark turned to Earl. "So what do you think?"

Earl looked around. "Nothing like 1300 Beaubien ... everything is brand new ... carpeting, chairs and desk. It even has drapes on the windows."

"It's a real upgrade for us too," Oscar noted. "We just moved here from West Fort last year. That was really the pits."

Earl looked Oscar in the eye. "I don't want to sound condescending but ... a big shot like you, I figured you'd have a corner office."

Oscar flashed a big grin. "Interesting you'd mention it. That was my wife's first comment. Fact is there are no corner offices. Check it out when you go outside. All four corners were recessed, eliminating corner offices in the building. The official word is that it strengthens the building. That's bullshit if you ask me. It's designed that way to eliminate the battle for the corner offices."

"Hah ... I bet you're right," Clark nodded and looked around at the plush surroundings. "Are the plants real or plastic?"

Oscar mused. "Plastic. This is the FBI, not the White House."

"Seems pretty fancy to me."

Oscar grinned, sat down at his conference table, and walked the two through FBI procedures. "Any questions?"

Clark and Earl were so overwhelmed they couldn't respond — only nodded.

"Good." Oscar stood and headed down the hallway to a medium-sized conference room — an eight-foot long walnut table commanded the center area surrounded by eight fabric-covered swivel rockers — three on each side, one on each end.

Earl's eyes popped out. "Looks like we'll have to rough it."

"I think this will do," Clark jested.

Oscar gave him a thumbs up. "Hey, I assume you'll be spending a lot of time in here. I've ordered a coffeepot for some of your longer sessions. When should I start reserving it for you?"

Clark sighed. "We're probably a week away. I don't think Chief Hart can hold off much longer. The media is on him hot and heavy."

"You better get used to that."

"I suppose ... Earl and I have been conducting individual one-on-one sessions with each of the team members — sometimes over lunch or coffee — whenever we can to make things look as normal as possible. We're about to the end of the line on that too."

"No problem. I'll reserve for every other week."

CHAPTER NINE

As customary, the wait staff arranged the table in a rear booth of a plain but serviceable neighborhood restaurant near the Macomb Mall in Roseville — a suburban area north of Detroit. Following the first Monday of the month routine, they draped a white tablecloth — hanging it equally on each side — added water goblets, wine glasses, and two black plates on each side. Today, a fifth plate was placed on the end.

A plump, dark-haired Italian-American waitress carefully folded five large white napkins into a common tent design, centering them on each of the plates. Filling five sauce dishes with olive oil and herbs, she located them precisely to the left of each plate. Next she placed a large basket loaded with fresh baked Italian bread in the center of the table, along with two bottles of Sicilian Castello Svevo — a ruby red intense wine with notes of licorice and spice.

Exactly at one-thirty in the afternoon, five well-dressed men wearing long-sleeved shirts filed into the Spaghetti Place, a popular ristorante with twenty-two pastas and twenty-four sauces. Jake Nicoletti, a local businessman and active philanthropist with an air of command, led the way. Known as a devoted father who set high standards for his children, he regularly spoke of their successes. His appearance begged comparison as a sophisticated businessman rather than a crime czar. In an earlier part of his life, he'd been tied to several gangland beatings and murders, and was the Boss of the Detroit Mafia.

He slid in on the left side of the booth and waited for the rest of his entourage to follow. His old friend, Anthony "Tony" Minelli, eased in next to him. Raised in a family with long-standing mob connections, Tony had worked his way up to Consigliere, the Boss's chief advisor. Over the years he had mastered the art of negotiation: "Never get angry; never make a threat. Reason with people, ignore insults and threats, and try to persuade."

Sliding in across from the Boss was Angelo Travaglini, the Underboss who functioned like a vice president for operations. A handsome man with black slicked-back hair — a playboy of the first order — he'd recently drawn the ire of Jake because of his womanizing and public display of vulgar behavior. Still, the two worked together effectively.

The Street Boss, Joe DiGregorio, the number three man in the organization eased in next to him. Last to be seated was Blackie Giardini, Joe's top assistant who was being groomed to become part of the triumvirate. Dressed in black and wearing large sunglasses, Blackie picked up a bottle of wine, filled each of the glasses half full and toasted the group's success.

The men broke pieces of bread, dabbed it in the oil, and entered into conversation about their favorite topic — their children and grandchildren — updating the others on the latest successes and accomplishments of their kids.

The waitress placed the special "chef's treat" of calamari in front of each one. The men ordered pasta specials for the day and nibbled on the specially prepared calamari.

Blackie refilled their glasses.

Taking a sip of wine, the Boss wasted no time in getting into the agenda. "Any thoughts about Chief Hart's special crimes task force?"

"It's a PR stunt," Underboss Angelo claimed. "It's an effort to appease the media. Hell, if they wanted they could round up two hundred child molesters in the blink of an eye."

"My sources tell me they've met three times," Blackie said. "Nothing has happened."

The Consigliere wrinkled his forehead then provided some sage advice. "Maybe it's a front for some other undercover activity."

"That's a possibility, but ..." The Street Boss set his wine glass down. "None of our contacts in the chain to Washington D. C. have heard anything."

Sitting with his hands folded under his chin, Jake listened.

Being a non-bona fide member, Blackie spoke guardedly. "I don't like the smell of this."

"We must know more about the task force," the Consigliere suggested with the slightest trace of an Italian accent. "Who are the members? What's their background? Who's in charge?"

"Makes sense," the Boss agreed.

DiGregorio turned to Blackie. "Get on it."

Blackie jotted a note in his black book and slipped it back in his shirt pocket.

The Boss rubbed his jaw in his reserved, calculating way. "Let's move to the Nash family. Anyone know where all of this is headed?"

"Nowhere," Angelo said, sliding closer to the table. "Huston will throw a bundle of money at it — fund some extra police efforts and hire a couple of private eyes — that'll be it." He curled his lip with a sense of distain. "Huston presents a great image; he has no backbone."

"You sure there's no way to connect anything to us?" the Boss questioned.

Blackie removed his sunglasses, twirled them once and placed them beside his plate. "I don't see how. Vinny is gone … there's not a trace of him."

"How about his child molestation conviction?" the Boss probed.

"There's nothing."

Jake frowned, still not positive. "What if they dig deeper into Nash's past, anything there?"

Looking more solemn than before, Angelo pursed his lips. "His record over the last ten years is impeccable. They'd have to go back into the Sixties when he headed the banks for us. Even then, the bank examiners gave him a clean bill of health — case closed."

"Hmm." The Boss rubbed his upper lip with the side of his forefinger. "How about the younger Nash?"

"Don't know much. I've heard he's a playboy, likes the women," DiGregorio added.

Jake shot a concerned look across the table. "Have Blackie do some digging on him. We can't afford not to know about him."

***

September poker started on a down note. Alsye was in South Carolina at his grandmother's funeral. Father Dom delivered a compelling prayer on behalf of the family. The guys talked about the work ethic Alsye had gained from her. Carlos suggested they make a donation to whatever group Alsye wanted. Everyone agreed and each one pledged a hundred dollars.

Renzo perked up the group. "The first hand is for Alsye, down and dirty, deuces are wild." Smiles emerged around the table for the first time.

Over the next three hours the group's spirits grew. Renzo was his typical comical self. Carlos made fun of his heritage, joking about Mexican stereotypes. Ted told several stories about gypsies. Even

Father Dom chimed in with a pun or two about the church. By break-time the group was back into the normal swing of things.

After filling a small bowl with munchies and grabbing a beer, Renzo flopped down on his chair and tossed the cards to Clark. "Anything new in your life?"

"Same ol' same ol', I guess."

"You guess?" Ted blurted. "Aren't you going to tell them about the woman on the yacht?"

All eyes turned to Clark; he looked as guilty as a teenager who'd come home after hours. "Geez Ted, there was nothing to it. Why did you mention that?"

Renzo raised his brow. "C'mon, let us hear about it."

Clark gave Ted a revolting look. "We went on two river cruises with a couple of classy ladies."

"Cruising on the Detroit River …" Father Dom confessed, "I've never done that."

"No big deal," Clark tried to shrug it off.

"No big deal," Ted shouted. "You said she was very nice."

Carlos looked at Clark. "Well?"

Clark fidgeted with his cards. "Okay, okay, she was nice."

"You better hope Caroline doesn't hear about this."

"God, we didn't do anything. We just talked."

"Sure. I know you," Carlos said. "Clark Phillips on a yacht with an attractive woman and he just talked … tell me another one."

"This is sounding better all the time," Renzo chimed in.

"Better?" Clark looked at Ted. "That's nothing compared to Mr. Midnight. He was down below banging the other one the entire trip."

Question marks filled the guy's eyes. They looked from one player to the other.

"There's a distortion in the way you think," Ted claimed.

"A distortion?" Clark threw his hands in the air. "You're the one with the big one."

"Big one … what's this all about?" Renzo asked. "Mr. Midnight?"

"It's nothing," Ted shuffled the cards.

Clark spread his hands a foot apart. "She said your dick was as big as a horse's. And they call you Midnight."

Father Dom raised a hand, trying to mediate. "Maybe some things are better left unsaid."

76

"I don't think so." Renzo turned to Ted. "Do you have something to say?"

Ted slicked back his hair. "So I have a big dong ... no big deal. Clark has a little pecker." Ted raised his thumb and index finger, separating them three inches.

"It's not *that* small," Clark shouted. "It's only little when it's compared with yours."

Ted tossed the cards down. "We're talking about the difference between a horse and a pony."

Renzo chuckled. "Ha, ha ... a pony ... that's funny."

Carlos belly laughed. "Wait 'til Rosa Maria hears about this."

"Truce." For the second time Father Dom raised his hands. "Enough. Let's move on."

Eyes shifted back and forth across the table, not knowing what was coming next. Renzo picked up the cards and stacked the deck in front of Ted. "Dealer's choice."

"Want a beer?" Ted said to Clark, ending the jabbing contest.

"Grab two, I'm buying."

The tone mellowed, and each player was happy to win a hand. It was poker in its best sense. Toward the end of the night, Father glanced around the table. "Anyone have some last minute thoughts?"

"Yeah, I do," Renzo proclaimed, unhappily. "One of the heavy-duty construction fences around one of my sites got ripped down. It's happened each of the last two weekends."

"Have any ideas who might have done it?" Clark asked in a serious tone.

"It's probably a local gang." Renzo threw his hands up in a frustrating manner. "Seems like kids don't have anything better to do."

Clark's eyes projected serious concern. "Did you contact the precinct chief?"

"Yes, he suggested I hire a night guard; said kids don't normally mess with things when someone is on site."

***

Opening the Sax Club door, Alsye was struck by the unusually high mix of blasting music and people shouting. He stepped back and glanced left and right. Catching a blur, he looked back to the left and saw Clark's waving hand, his lips mouthing, "Over here."

Alsye smiled then weaved his way through the maze of tables jammed in the center of the bar. Pulling up a chair next to Clark, he spoke loudly, "It's good to see yah, man."

"Same here." Clark leaned closer. "How did your trip go?"

"It was okay; it seemed like a really long trip home." Alsye tried to put on a good face. "Old memories kept coming up."

"I understand that … want a beer?" Alsye nodded.

Clark motioned to a cute young waitress with narrow hips and a small round ass. She hurried his way. "Two Stroh's?"

With a sexy smile she aimed at Clark, she asked, "Would you like anything else?" Her body language made it clear she wasn't talking about anything on the menu.

He eyed her. "Not now," he jested flirtatiously.

Alsye leaned across the table and looked at Clark in a curious way. "You banging her?"

"Nah, she's too young."

Alsye glowered, his face showing doubt. "I didn't know you discriminated on age."

Clark gave him a who-cares look. "I do. There are ones too young and others too old."

"Ha." Alsye spread his arms apart. "That leaves a huge range."

Clark seemed mollified. "One has to keep his options open."

The waitress returned with two bottles, placed them on the table and gave Clark a come-on look. He returned the overture with a wink then watched her wiggle her butt for his benefit.

Alsye scowled. "I thought she was too young."

"You never know." Clark glanced over his shoulder, taking another look. "Good thing about the young ones is they get older."

"And better too," Alsye agreed.

Clark took a slug and returned to Alsye's trip. "Did you accomplish everything you had to?"

Alsye gave him a feeble nod. "There wasn't much left to do. Momma outlived her friends … had been in the nursing home for the past year or so. I'd made all of the arrangements a couple years ago so all I had to do was sign a few papers."

"Still, it had to be tough."

"Tough … she was my mom, my grandmother; she gave me my life, showed me how to use a knife and fork, how to dress myself and how to … if it wasn't one thing it was another."

"You're fortunate to have had a person like that in your life."

Alsye's face glowed. "You can say that again."

"How was the overall trip?"

"It was okay as long as I was around other people. The funeral and all of that was tolerable. I faked it as long as others were around. As I said the trip home was the pits. I cried most of the way. Shit city if you ask me." He downed a slug of beer. "Other than her and Nicole, my older brother William is the only one I have." Alsye noticeably stiffened. "I don't know how William is going to deal with the loss. He used to stop by and see her every day."

"It must be special to have a brother like that."

Alsye's face filled with pride. "He has an analytical mind and can repair anything."

"What does he do?"

Alsye fidgeted uncomfortably. Clark wondered why.

"He's a laborer for a big contractor in Spartanburg," Alsye lamented. "I feel sorry for him."

Clark's brow furrowed. "Why so?"

Alsye didn't move; he stared back at Clark. "William is extremely talented; graduated from a tech school with an associate degree in construction technology."

Clark cocked his head to the side. "I don't want to pry but with that kind of a degree you'd think he'd be higher up."

Alsye gave him a grim look. "He's black and lives in South Carolina, need I say more?"

"I can't believe that's a problem nowadays."

"Huh … things haven't changed in a hundred and fifty years. The owner is a bigot, probably a Klan member if the truth be known." Alsye sniffled, his demeanor saddened. "I'm not sure if William can make it on his own."

"What's wrong?"

"He's insecure. We talked a long time before I left. He was ready to chuck the whole thing. I gave him a long pep-talk. He can't keep his life together without someone beside him offering encouragement."

Clark rubbed his forehead, trying to think of something to say that might be helpful. "Maybe you should mention his name to Renzo. Sounds like he'd be a good fit with him."

"Renzo. I hadn't thought of that. What a great idea. We have an extra room upstairs. I know Nicole wouldn't mind at all."

Alsye's mood changed; he pepped up and looked Clark in the eye. "Thanks for talking with Nicole. When she first mentioned the idea of me talking with you, I wasn't too keen on it. She kept saying, 'Alsye, you can't keep things bundled inside. You have to share your feelings. There's no better friend than Clark.'"

"That's what friends are for." Clark noticed Alsye's glassy eyes, thinking maybe he'd said enough. "Want another beer?"

"Yah, this one is on me."

"Fine with me." Clark gave Miss Hot Pants a cordial smile.

She was there in no time, looking like she was ready to spread her legs. "What can I do for you, Clark?" she said, her sweet voice sexier than ever.

"We'll have another round." He gave her a wink then watched her prance away. "I think she's getting older," Clark said, only half in jest.

Alsye ignored the remark and glanced at the featured pole. "Looks like it's Caroline's time."

Clark's eyes lit up. Taking a slow sip, he caught her eye and blew her a kiss. She pointed to her crotch and mouthed, "Later."

That's all it took to end the conversation. Clark's eyes glued on her body for one song, and then another and another. He stared, mesmerized.

Watching her step off the platform, Alsye asked, "When are the two of you getting engaged?"

"I'm ready, but it isn't in the cards right now. Caroline attends classes all day and works late most nights. As soon as she finishes her undergraduate degree, she's going to law school."

"That's terrific. I told Nicole she should finish her social work degree. She has less than a year to go."

"That'd be a great insurance policy."

"I told her the same thing."

Clark spoke deliberately. "Nicole told me the Mafia raised the fee."

"I worked that out."

Clark gave him a quizzical look. "How so?"

"When I told them about J. J.'s medical issues and our other financial problems they backed off a couple hundred bucks a month."

80

Clark gave him a dubious look. "That's a bunch of bull. The Mafia is not in the humanization business; they don't send out sympathy cards."

Alsye gulped, knowing he couldn't fool his inner-city friend. "I hired one of their women."

"One of their women?" Clark frowned. "A prostitute?"

"No, she isn't," Alsye said, with conviction.

"Where's she from?"

"A small town in Mexico."

"Is she legal? Does she have a green card?"

"It's in process."

"Process hell, she's working for the mob and you know it." Clark slowed, feeling he was pressing too hard. "Okay ... tell me the rest of the story."

Alsye seemed nervous. "They have a deal with one of their providers to send one of the girls home every year to show the progress she's making."

"Jesus Christ, Alsye, the Mafia doesn't give a shit about her; they're in it for the bucks."

"No Clark, this system is different. They recruit poor girls from small towns and help them out. She can send money home, rent a small apartment, and have a little spending money."

"I don't think so ... sounds like they are using her."

"No. They're sending her for Easter to see her parents."

"That's bullshit. She's a recruiter. You're part of the scam." Clark slammed his fist on the table. "It's the same as you working for the Mafia. I can't believe you fell for it."

"I didn't fall for anything." Alsye bit his lip. "I made a practical decision. I was short-handed and needed help. In addition, I'm saving two hundred bucks on my monthly tab."

"You're not helping her; she'll never escape the system. You're only helping them recruit more girls. Have you told Nicole?"

"God no, she'd kill me."

"See." Clark threw his hands in the air. "That proves it. If you didn't think it was wrong, you would have told her."

Alsye stared away, didn't say a word.

"How do you know you can trust the girl? She could be an informant ... who knows *what*?"

"I suppose." He shrugged. "I never thought about that."

Clark shook his head. "I suppose you brought a load of moonshine back with you too?"

Alsye looked up slowly. "I told Nicole not to say anything."

"Christ, she's worrying about you. You're dealing with fire."

Alsye fluffed the comment off, trying to hide his discomfort. "White lightning."

"That's not funny." Clark downed a slug. "How many fruit jars did you haul this trip?"

"Two hundred."

"Two hundred!" Clark exclaimed loudly, then covered his mouth. "You're driving a firebomb. You'd go up in smoke if you had an accident. Did you ever think of that?"

Alsye stared across the room with a blank look.

"What would happen to Nicole if the feds caught you? What if the Mafia found out?"

Alsye bristled. "No one's going to find out. I'm selling on the side to friends."

"You have to stop, Alsye, sooner or later someone will find out."

"I'll think about."

"*Think* about it? You have to do more than think about it. You have to stop."

Alsye paused. "Anything new happening with you?"

Clark bit his lip, knowing what Alsye was up to. *Maybe I've hammered him enough. I'll play his game and come back to it later.* "I'm still working on the Nash killing. So far, I haven't come up with anything. Nothing but dead ends."

"Keep digging." Alsye smiled broadly, showing his white teeth. "I have confidence in you; sooner or later you'll come up with a lead."

"I hope so. Most of the time it feels like I'm spinning my wheels."

"Spinning your wheels? Welcome to the club." He stood. "I have to go. Take care."

"Will do," Clark shouted across the bar as he gazed around the club. Spotting the hot little thing leaning on her elbow at the bar, he raised his empty bottle, catching her eye.

She hustled his way. "Would you like something else?" she asked, flaunting her assets. Clark knew she meant more than booze.

He eyed her one more time. "Not right now."

CHAPTER TEN

"Several of you have asked why I waited so long before calling our first official meeting," Clark started. "Simply put, I wanted you to have freedom to examine leads unimpeded and follow up tips you might have uncovered. Each of you attacked the challenge differently, but collectively your reports demonstrate the strategy worked. You've done one helleva of a job."

The individuals around the table nodded and saluted him, one-by-one. "Your strategy worked," said one, with the others agreeing in unison. "Great idea!"

Feeling at ease, Clark gave the group an encouraging grin and plowed forward. "Things will change tomorrow. Everyone in the city will know who you are; your ability to gain information will be compromised. That said … it simply means we'll need to work as a team to continue our momentum."

"Don't worry, sir," a member piped in. "We're up to it."

"I know you are." Clark nodded. "I have the utmost confidence in you."

"We respect you too, sir," another said.

Clark gave them a sheepish grin. "I hope you'll have the same feeling when our task is completed." He laughed, trying to lighten the atmosphere.

"We're for that," a member said.

"We'll get the bastards," someone shouted.

Clark gave them a thumbs up and moved into his agenda. "Each of you has chatted with the other members, but I want to formally introduce you. It's important for you to know why your colleagues were picked."

Task force members looked side to side, each giving their new cohorts a welcoming grin. Feeling on a roll, Clark continued. "You are an elite group — the finest among the city's best — each of you have an impeccable record of honesty, integrity, and truthfulness."

He turned to his right. "That said, I'd like to introduce our senior statesman, patrolman Leonard Ralston. My father once called him the best policeman in Detroit. He can sniff out a gambling operation before stepping out of his cruiser." Recalling his memories, Clark smiled to himself. *How many times did I go to bed while Leonard and Dad talked into the night? The two of them were like brothers; they lived police blue night and day. Too bad we don't have more cops like them today.*

The elderly man nodded. "I know a little about gambling operations, yes. But I'll tell you … the best Detroit cop ever was Clark's father, Lewis Phillips."

"Thanks, I appreciate that." Clark glanced at the well-endowed woman next to Leonard. "Sergeant Kimberly Weston heads up our squad on child abuse and prostitution and, as you may know, she's worked as an undercover agent." Clark paused. "That's something the two of us have not talked about."

Chuckles circulated around the table.

"And you won't have an opportunity," she zinged back.

Clark's face reddened. Snickers filled the room.

"Next to her is patrolman Will Robinson, thirty-five years on the Northside beat. He knows every informant in town and they know him."

"And they better tell me the truth," Will interjected.

Clark grinned at the baldheaded black man. "And that's the truth. He can see through a lie or made up story like no one you've ever known."

At the other end of the table is Lieutenant Nancy Sterling from narcotics. She's our newest colleague with six years of service in the department. She has a master's from Michigan State University and can recite the details of every drug bust in the city's history."

The chunky petite blonde nodded, said nothing.

"Coming back on the other side is Captain Max Cumberland from precinct eight. He's our logistics expert, *and* can tell you about the city's finest restaurants." With two hundred and forty pounds packed on his five-foot-eight frame, his love for food was apparent. "He knows the new location of a blind pig in his district before the Mafia opens it."

His colleagues applauded, knowing Clark was right on target.

"And next to last, but not least, is Detective Eddie Grissini. He's our resident expert on the Mafia. I've heard he sometimes knows more about the Mafia than the boss-man Jake Nicoletti."

The short, curly-headed Italian-American abruptly jumped up. "If you want somebody rubbed out let me know. For a bottle of wine I can get most anything done."

Puzzling looks shot from those around the table; others were not sure if he was telling the truth. "I'm just joking." He laughed. "Sometimes it might take two bottles."

"Don't laugh," Clark added. "He's telling the truth."

Max chuckled. "I don't know about that … but it sounds good."

"And finally, the guy who's been a part of my life since grade school." He paused for effect, then rolled his name out like a sports announcer … Earl … 'The Pearl' … *Walker*."

Spontaneous applause erupted. Clark waited until he could capture their attention.

"Besides his prowess on the basketball court, Earl distinguished himself by being named the 'up and coming officer' for each of the last three years."

"Here … here," the group responded.

"Thanks all of you and welcome aboard." Clark paused, letting everything soak in, before he moved on.

"As you know, I'm being hounded by the press. Yesterday's report from Max and Kimberly tipped the scales. I'm ready to respond." He turned toward Max. "Would you summarize the information the two of you shared with me?"

"Yes. I'll start and let Kimberly fill in the blanks," Max said, confidently. "Bottom line — we've narrowed the list of suspects in the Nash murder case to four."

"Four? That's terrific," Eddie attested.

"Thanks. We've double-checked and cross-checked every possible suspect. After a few weeks we thought we had our guy — the nanny made a positive identification of Vinny Castintino's mug shot. 'Hallelujah,' I said to myself, I thought it was over."

"So did I when he told me," Clark interjected.

"A week later I showed her pictures of 'Bobby' Boriello, 'Tony' Loria, and Ben Ruggiero, our other three suspects. I couldn't believe it … she waffled, said she wasn't positive … maybe it could have been any one of the four."

"How could she do that?" Will asked.

"I wondered that too," Kimberly added.

"Maybe she was nervous, got scared or someone got to her."

"Someone got to her," Eddie Grissini said, rubbing his early stubble. "Doesn't matter ... now she's no longer a credible witness."

"My gut still says it was Vinny," Kimberly said.

"We're analyzing everything, hoping we'll find a print," Clark explained patiently. He gave the group an odd little smile. "Without her ID we don't have much."

"How many child molester names did you start out with?" Detective Grissini asked.

"Two hundred and seven."

Team members shook their heads in disbelief. "How did you cull that number down so quickly?" a colleague asked.

"Checking their whereabouts was a biggie — some were dead, many had moved out of state and several were in prison. That left about ninety, wouldn't you say, Kimberly?"

"Ninety-three to be exact."

"Next we cross-checked their names with our list of individuals associated with the underworld. And with a little more digging we were down to four. Bingo!"

Clark interjected, "It was more than a little digging; it was hard work — researching, inspecting, and probing — two weeks of intensive investigation."

Another round of applause erupted.

Kimberly and Max gave the group a thumbs-up.

"Great work," Clark said. "Anyone else have another point that might be added to the news release?" He took his time circling the room and making eye contact with each member. "Okay, I'll have PR work up a draft release. Let's take a break."

He stood and hustled down the hallway to the elevator. Two headed for the restroom, another hit the water fountain. The rest stood and stretched, getting to know each other.

When Clark returned, twenty minutes later, the team had reassembled and chatted amicably. He plopped down in his chair. "That's over. Tomorrow you'll be the talk of the town." He laughed and reopened his notebook. "Lieutenant Sterling, would you bring the group up to date?"

"Yes, thank you. A few weeks ago Clark asked me to do some preliminary work on the Nash family, and suggested I start with the father of the murdered boy — Dallas Nash." She paused, catching her breath. "Little did I know where his calculated hunch would take me."

"Why do you say that?" Eddie Grissini asked.

"From my cursory review of his financials it looked like a cakewalk — he wasn't involved. Clark wasn't convinced, told me 'to scrutinize every piece of paper I could find.' I ordered up a complete listing of every check he'd written in the past six months.

"Turns out he had written over twenty-five checks made out to cash for nine thousand and five-hundred dollars in the three months before his son was murdered. That was an unusual number I thought, until Clark described the new federal law. After that I realized it was common practice if you were trying to go unnoticed."

"Why's that?" Will asked.

"Anytime there's a bank transaction, withdrawal or deposit of over $9,999.99, an automatic alert goes to the feds. Anyone not wanting to bring attention to their activity stays under that figure."

Will nodded. "Interesting."

"Has anyone else picked up anything on Dallas Nash?" Clark glanced down the table.

No one offered a word.

"Hmm," Clark murmured to himself. "The guy has been spending like crazy, but not a cent after his son was murdered. That doesn't sound right." He ran his hand through his thick crop of hair. "Lieutenant, let's do a comprehensive workup on his expenditures since January 1st."

"Okay ..." She hesitated, looking across the table. "Want to join me, Max?"

"Sure."

Clark made a note in his pad and glanced up. "I want Earl and three of you, Sterling, Will, and Leonard, to focus on Dallas. See if your street contacts know anything. Snoop around. If he's spending that kind of money someone must have seen him dropping cash." He glanced at his notes — advice from his dad flashed through his mind — keep on digging, probing, don't skip a beat. "What else have we learned in the past few weeks?"

Eddie raised his hand. "The feds are all over the mob. Their connections with the Aladdin Casino in Las Vegas are heating up. They might be able to nail them on this one."

"That reminds me, would you share the first draft of the Mafia organizational chart?"

"I'd be glad to." He distributed the one-pager. "As soon as I've filled in a few more blanks at the bottom, I'll walk everyone through the entire chain of command."

DETROIT MAFIA HIERARCHY

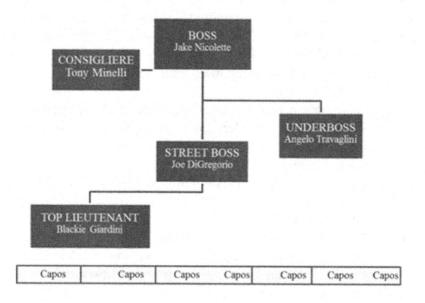

"Sounds good." Clark looked around the table. "Any other unsolved mysteries?"

Will Robinson raised his hand. "There's *the game*."

Clark's eyes bugged. Team members stared, waiting for the next word.

The gray-haired African-American took his time. "It's been out there for a long time. No one knows much about it. Supposedly, high-rollers from Chicago, New York and Jersey are flown in every month."

"Are the feds on it?" Clark asked.

"From what I hear Aladdin Casino has them consumed."

"Looks like an opportunity for us." Clark rubbed his chin. "I'll take the lead on this one. Where do we get started Will?"

"I'll check with my 'T-3s' to see who knows what."

"'T-3s,' what are they?" Kimberly asked.

Will smiled to himself, knowing someone would ask. "It's part of the code we use to categorize our informants. A 'T-3' is the highest rating; it stands for top echelon. It means the informant is very good and highly reliable. Usually they've been providing accurate information for several years."

"How many do you have?"

"Five or six out of a total group of slightly over a hundred."

"Wow, that's amazing." Sounding surprised, Kimberly's interest grew. "How much do you pay them?"

"Depends on the value of the information. Could be a couple hundred, five hundred, or a thousand dollars, if information was just what I needed and proved rock solid."

Clark thanked him for sharing his insights and wrapped up the point. "Let me know when you identify your top source. I'd like to meet with him or her."

"It'll be a couple of weeks."

"Fine," Clark said in an upbeat manner. "Last point for today and," he paused for effect, "the most important one. I can't say enough times how important confidentiality is. Everyone is going to be asking questions, probing, and digging. Much of it will be well intended — a question from a spouse or a friend who's simply interested — but most of the time you really won't know the person's intent. I don't want to lecture you all the time; still, I want to keep the thought fresh and in front of you continuously. We can't afford one slip of the tongue."

"Clark is right," the senior team member said. "I talked to Clark's dad many times about this very point. You can never tell who's connected."

"Thanks, Leonard." Clark said, with confidence. "I'd like us to come up with something catchy — a slogan or quote — that we can put at the bottom of the agenda each week. That way it'll always be there."

"Good idea," Eddie said. "How about 'mum is the word'?"

"That'd be fine. It doesn't have to be perfect. Besides, we can change it whenever someone comes up with a new one."

"I got it," Max said. "Don't be dumb, the word is mum."

"Anyone else?" Clark glanced around the table. "Fine, we'll start with that."

***

THE DETROIT NEWS
September 24, 1978

<small>Today's Feature</small>

FOUR MOBSTERS IDENTIFIED IN NASH KILLING

Today the Detroit Police Department issued the first statement from the Special Crimes Task Force headed by Detective Clark Phillips. The report from the Task Force indicated its search has been narrowed to four individuals, all suspected to have underworld ties.

During its exhaustive two-month investigation, the Task Force culled names from a list of over two hundred known child molesters. The police ask if you have seen or have any information on the men listed below that you immediately contact the chief at your local precinct or call our hotline number at the top of this page:

- Bartholomew "Bobby" Boriello
- Vinny Castintino
- Anthony "Tony" Loria
- Benjamin Ruggiero

A nationwide all-points bulletin has been issued for all four men. For pictures and background information, see related story, Page 3—Suspects.

See related story, Page 5 — Profile of Special Crimes Task Force Members.

***

Clark sat at a table in the far corner of the Sax Club, reflecting on Alsye's problems. *He's a great guy ... deserves better. I hope things are on the upswing for him.*

Ready to order another beer, he looked up. Alsye's trademark smile startled him out of his reverie. Clark stammered, "H-How are you doing?"

"I'm fine, making progress," his friend said unenthusiastically. "Want a beer?"

Alsye nodded. "Make it two. I have to catch up with you."

Clark grinned. "You got it."

The two reminisced over their beer before Clark got to the point. "How's William working out on his new job with Renzo?"

"Terrific. He enjoys working on renovation projects. It gives him more opportunities to use his problem solving abilities. Renzo put him in charge of one of his crews."

"Wow, he must really be good."

"I told you he's very capable … the guys really like him."

"Good for him." Clark took a frothy sip. "How's the rest of his life going?"

A crease appeared on Alsye's forehead. "Ah … not so good."

Clark glanced up with a concerned look. "Why? What's wrong?"

Alsye stared at his bottle of beer. "He's going out with Olivia."

"Olivia … who is she?"

"She's a young woman from Mexico."

"Alsye, she can't be trusted."

"I've tried everything. Whatever I say, William gets pissed off, says I'm interfering with his life."

Clark raised his hands in frustration. "Jesus, Alsye, she's a direct pipeline to the Mafia."

"I told him that. He said 'don't worry, she's not connected in any way.'"

"I doubt that. She'll suck every piece of information out of him she can. Have you talked to Nicole?"

"Yes, she's at her wits' end; she doesn't know what to do."

"Is there any way I can help?"

"I can't think of anything right now."

CHAPTER ELEVEN

Arriving early for October poker, Alsye tossed a box of El Verso 'It's a Boy' cigars on the table and welcomed everyone with his trademark smile.

"Hey, congratulations," Renzo shouted. He pulled one out and bit off the tip. Lighting up, he took a couple of drags. "Mild ... man, this is good."

Ted followed suit. "Nothing better than an El Verso."

The others grabbed a couple and slipped them in their shirt pockets.

"How are things going at home?" Father Dom asked.

Alsye beamed with pride. "Thanks for asking. Baby J. D. is doing fine. Mama is great. I'm so proud of her. Little J. J. doesn't understand what a little brother is all about yet. I'm positive it won't take long for him to figure out what's going on. We're one happy family."

"Good for you, my son."

"Anything else happening?" Renzo asked the guys.

Carlos raised his hand. "I've got one."

The group looked his way with anticipation.

"What is it?" an impatient Renzo pleaded.

Carlos turned toward Clark with a friendly smile. "It's about Clark."

Startled, Clark's eyebrows shot up; he pointed to himself. "Me?"

Slowly and deliberately Carlos said, "Don't sound so innocent."

"What are you talking about?"

"I saw how that hot little waitress looked at you. I thought she was going to wet her pants when you gave her that come-on smile."

"You're out of your mind, Carlos." Clark raised his hands in mock surprise. "She's barely twenty-one."

"Ha, since when did you measure a pussy by how old it was?"

"Shit Carlos, you think I'm going to screw something like that and mess up what I have going with Caroline ... you're out of your mind."

Carlos leaned back and shook his head. "How many times have I heard about someone's pecker making the decision?"

"Yeah Clark," Renzo shouted. "How many times have we talked about that?"

"Enough!" Father Dom exclaimed.

Renzo bit his tongue. "We have some serious business to take care of." He picked up the deck and flipped the cards around the table. "Dealer's choice."

Father Dom won the first hand and after that barely a word was spoken, other than poker lingo, for the next three hours. On schedule, Father Dom made his ritual call, "Break Time."

The guys took care of their business and one-by-one filled their plates and gathered around the table, their focus on Alsye. "What was it like in the delivery room? How did you feel when you first saw J. D.? What was it like being a new father again?"

He responded in ways you'd expect — "It was overwhelming, spectacular. More than I could have ever imagined." The guys continued to jab. Alsye laughed and joked. "It was one of the highlights of my life."

Gathering around the table, it didn't take long before everyone's attention turned back to poker. Several hands were played before Father Dom asked, "Can you tell us anything new about the Nash murder, Clark?"

Clark paused, part of him wanting to tell his friends something — anything significant — yet, knowing he couldn't go beyond limits. "Officially, not much …"

"Here we go again." Renzo tossed his losing cards on the table, his facial expression revealing disappointment. "And, you can't say anything."

Clark covered his mouth with his hand. "My lips are sealed."

***

Following the pattern Clark had established a few weeks ago, he moved the small bedside table to the edge of the bed, covered it with a white towel and placed the only chair in the room on the other side. He lit two candles, turned off the lights, placed a slice of pizza on each paper plate and positioned the bottles of beer to the right side — perfect!

Caroline paraded out of the shower with a bath towel wrapped around her and tucked above her firm breasts. Looking as fetching as ever, Clark pulled out the chair. "Please, my love."

She gave him a peck on the cheek and sat down. "Do you treat all your women like this?"

Clark's mind whirled with excitement; he said gleefully, "Only the special one."

Her forehead wrinkled with her smile. "I bet."

"It's true, sweetheart. I've never done this for anyone but you." She observed the obvious sincerity in his eyes; the loving tone of his voice. "You're the only one," he added.

Picking up a slice of pizza, she smiled knowing she'd never felt this way about a man before. *He's my everything. He treats me like I've never been treated before. I love him so much.* Munching on a slice, she gazed at him. *God, I love him.*

In no time, the two lovebirds had downed the pizza and fallen into a deep conversation, as they often did. Laughing and giggling freely, the two seemed like a picture of the perfect pair.

For Caroline it was extraordinary; most men wanted her body. Clark was different; he was engaging, interesting, and thought provoking. They talked about politics, the city's blight, and the needs of underprivileged kids. *For the first time in my life I'm more than a piece of meat. I'm a real person. He wants me for who I am. I love him so much.* She sipped the last of her beer, and asked, "Had any luck on the Nash case?"

"Same ol' … I can't seem to catch a break."

"Sounds like the kind of project I'd like to work on after I receive my law degree."

"How long before that happens?"

"At my current rate it'll be the end of next year."

"Terrific." He finished off his beer and lifted his head to revel in her eyes. "Hope I have this case solved by then."

"You will." She leaned back, stretched out her legs and twisted her ankles. "My feet are killing me. Could you manage a special treatment tonight?"

"It'd be my pleasure," Clark said, knowing there was nothing he'd rather do than work his way up her backside.

"Which way do you want me?"

"On your stomach, naked."

She flipped the towel in the corner and crawled in bed. "I'm feeling better already."

He tossed his clothes on the chair, grabbed a bottle of lotion from the nightstand and slid onto the foot of the bed. Pouring a small portion of lotion onto his palm, he rubbed his hands together, warming the cream.

Lifting her right foot, he moved his fingers slowly over her toes, and then dug gently into her arch and massaged each pressure point. Her foot went limp. Moving back to her toes, he counted them off, "This little piggy went to market, this one stayed home ..." It didn't take long for his fingers to work their magic. *He's so gentle and caring. It's like I'm the most important one. God, I love his hands ... they're so soft.*

Taking his time, Clark massaged the other foot. Caroline melted into the bed, feeling more relaxed than ever, wanting him more than ever. Unable to wait, she doubled a pillow and slid it under her stomach, elevating her cheeks in the perfect position.

Clark didn't miss the invitation. Sliding onto the bed, he tenderly caressed her calves and worked his way up the back of her thighs. With each touch he could feel the tension unwind — her body was like cookie dough in his hands — moving at a slow, rhythmic pace.

***

Three black '78 Buick Electra's cruised down Monroe in the heart of Greektown. Passing the Grecian Gardens, the cars turned onto the next side street, pulled down the alley and parked behind the restaurant.

A large thug jumped from the front seat of each car, eyeballed the surrounding area and strolled inside the restaurant. Returning to the alleyway a few minutes later, the lead guy gave the all clear sign. The driver of the last car jumped out, opened the back door and stepped aside. Blackie Giardini eased out of the backseat and extended his hand to his mistress. She slipped her right foot on the ground and leaned; showing off her deep cleavage for all to see, then rose and straightened her shoulders.

The men formed a receiving line and stared straight ahead not daring to sneak a peek as she strutted forward. Blackie greeted each with a manly embrace then followed Joey Naples through the back door to the waiting table. Blackie took the center chair, with a clear view of the front door — Vicky on the left, Joey to his right. Three associates sat across from them and the other two henchmen eased in at the ends of the table.

While not the fanciest place, the Grecian Gardens was the city's most popular site for individuals with underworld connections. Murals of the Greek countryside extending the entire length of the side walls gave the place an authentic, old-world feeling. Even better, Blackie loved the hot appetizers and lamb shank simmered in special tomato sauce.

Without glancing at the menu, Joey waved to the middle-aged Greek waitress. "We'll have Agiorgitiko wine, four bottles, an order of Lukániko, your spiced Greek sausage, a plate of Yemistes hot peppers, and the Kalamarakia fried squid. And when we're finished, please bring an order of Saganaki flaming Kasseri cheese for Blackie." He nodded to his left.

Seeing her own reflection in Blackie's sunglasses, the waitress jotted down the orders and hustled through a curtain in the rear. She returned quickly and spaced four bottles of wine between the men. And the feast was on. The men drank and ate hardily, first on the appetizers and then downing their entrees.

Blackie toasted the group, commended them for their dedication and commitment, and ordered a bottle of Ouzo, his favorite anise-flavored aperitif. Taking a sip, he set the glass down and clinked it with his spoon.

All eyes shifted to him; their conversations ended.

"We have some important business to discuss," he started. "Two weeks ago I shared the names of the task force members who were listed in the paper this week. I asked you to collect every shred of information you could find on them — a history of overdrawn bank accounts, loan defaults or high levels of debt. And anything negative you could find on their personal activities, who they're sleeping with, affairs they've had, and any strange stuff they may be doing. So ... who wants to start?"

The guys stared around the table; no one said a word.

"C'mon." Blackie glimpsed at his chickie. "Vicky and I have things to do. We're not going to sit around with you guys all night."

Joey rescued the flunkies. "The boys told me over dinner they were unable to come up with anything substantial. In fact, nothing."

Blackie removed his sunglasses. "How can that be?"

"The committee is clean as a whistle — no financial problems, no personal issues, nothing," Joey repeated.

Blackie rubbed the crease on his forehead. "That's impossible."

"Maybe they're all clean-cut, solid citizens," the mistress interjected.

Blackie shot her a withering gaze. "Quiet, you wouldn't know one if you saw one." She zipped her lips. "Phillips too?" he ventured.

Joey smiled smugly; his mood more optimistic. "He's the chink in their armor."

"Well, let's hear about him," he said in an anxious, elevated tone.

"He likes the women."

"Who the hell doesn't?" Blackie patted his companion on the thigh.

"When he's not at work he's on the make."

"Give me some specifics ... who, when, where?"

"He's banging a black stripper at the Sax Club ..."

Blackie cut him off. "The place up on Six Mile? I thought it closed."

"It did. Some college guys bought it and restored it. It's one of the hottest places in town."

"Who else is he seeing?"

"A medical doctor at Wayne State."

"A stripper and a doctor." Blackie angled his head to the side then back again. "That's a strange combination."

"Those are the most recent ones. From the talk we've picked up it sounds like he has a few notches on his belt."

Blackie smiled. "Sounds like what we're looking for. I want a detailed workup on him, from the first girl he screwed to the ones he's sleeping with now."

"Got it," Joey said.

Blackie glanced at his watch. "I have one more point before we adjourn."

The men straightened back to attention, each one ready to respond.

"The news story made it clear the task force was on us from the get-go. Anyone pick up on how they made that decision so quickly?"

The heavy-set man on the far left side of the table raised his hand.

Blackie nodded. "Go ahead."

"I have it from two different police officers ... Clark Phillips was the lead man from the beginning."

"You're positive?" he asked, double-checking what had been said.

"Absolutely ... everything came from him."

"Damn, he might be smarter than we thought." Blackie tossed his napkin on the table, stood and took his sweetie by the arm. "C'mon honey, we have some business to take care of."

***

Alsye wiped the perspiration from his brow. *I can't believe how close I came to crashing. Ten more feet and the U-Haul would have flipped on its side. I'd have been a goner ... the whole load would've gone up in flames.* Trying to settle his nerves, he pulled off I-75 on the east side of the road outside of Knoxville, Tennessee, and took a breather. *I can't believe that guy cut me off. A half mile later and he'd have had plenty of room to pass.* Alsye walked around his car and checked the trailer hitch and safety chains. *Thank God, they held.*

The rest of the night he drove slower than before, taking his time going through Lexington and Cincinnati, and the remainder of the way home. Arriving in Detroit three hours later than planned, he headed for the main store, not wanting to wake Nicole so early in the morning.

Lights shined brightly over the nearly empty parking lot.

Pulling around behind the building, he backed the trailer up, stopped and rushed around to the rear. He unlocked the secluded storage room in the back of the store and started unloading his private loot. He nearly finished stacking the fruit jars inside when a silhouette in the doorway broke the beam of light. Looking up, he saw the smiling face of Olivia, the Mafia designee.

"What are you doing?" she asked.

"It's nothing, go back and help the customers." She turned and disappeared out of sight.

Alsye finished unloading the brew and locked up.

***

Alsye had already downed a beer when Clark spotted him at a small table along the sidewall. The lunch crowd filled the Cyprus Taverna, one of his favorite neighborhood restaurants in Greektown, not far from his office at 1300 Beaubien. The white-stoned facade made it stand out from the other Victorian-era red brick buildings along Monroe Street.

Working his way down the side aisle behind the black wire-backed chairs, he squeezed into the booth across from Alsye and grabbed a beer off the table. Taking a slug from the bottle, he glanced at Alsye — he looked dreadful — tired and drawn, pronounced dark circles ringed his eyes. "You look like crap. You okay?"

Alsye's eyes rolled up. "Not really."

"What's wrong?"

"It's William; he's gone off the deep end and moved in with Olivia. He hasn't responded to my calls for the past week. I'm sure he's on drugs."

"Are you positive?"

"No question. When something goes wrong in his life, he struggles … he can't handle conflict." Alsye's shoulders sagged, his voice droned. "Nicole and I don't know what to do."

"For good reason."

"I talked to Renzo. He said William missed a couple days of work last month but hasn't been acting differently. He asked one of his most trusted employees to keep an eye on him."

"That's great. People with drug problems are good at hiding their problem — it's like the brain will do anything to avoid cutting off the supply."

"So we've learned. Nicole picked up some literature from the local AA chapter. Apparently addicts, regardless of the type, demonstrate the same kind of behavior."

"You're right. It doesn't matter … drugs, gambling, drinking, eating disorders, or a sex problem. Addicts do whatever it takes — lie, cheat, deny — to cover up the problem. Sometimes spouses, friends and colleagues never find out."

"That's hard to believe."

"Keep trying to reach him. Just because you haven't been successful doesn't mean you shouldn't keep trying. You never know when you might hit the right button."

"Thanks. I'll remind Nicole of that too."

Clark grimaced, trying to come up with a constructive suggestion. "What are you doing about Olivia?"

"Doing?" Alsye looked perplexed. "I can't fire her. William would go off the deep end. I don't know … have any suggestions?"

Clark shrugged his shoulders. "That's a tough one. Let me think about that."

"Want another beer?"

"Nah," Clark said. "I've had enough. But … you can have one if you want."

Alsye inhaled a deep, calming breath. "I'm good."

With that the two men mellowed out, they talked for the next half hour about nothing of importance. Clark felt better, seeing Alsye relax. He talked about growing up in South Carolina, his football career, and his momma.

Gazing across the bar, Alsye leaned back. His mind returned to reality; his face looked troubled once more. "Had anymore thoughts about Olivia?"

Clark chuckled. "I'm not very good at figuring women out." He paused, clearly weighing his options. "My dad always said, 'Never try to figure out a woman's logic — be truthful and open — let the cards fall however they may.' Maybe you ought to have a candid conversation with Olivia. If she has real feelings for him she might be willing to help."

Alsye gave Clark a long stare. "Maybe so. I'll talk to Nicole."

CHAPTER TWELVE

Alsye arrived at his main store early Monday morning feeling refreshed and upbeat. He felt relieved after a talk with Nicole. They agreed he should have a heart-to-heart talk with Olivia. *Half of the stress came from indecision; once we decided upon a course of action I felt a 100 percent better.* By the time the early birds arrived, Alsye had the shelves filled and straightened.

Finishing his chores, he stepped out of the back room. A short Italian-American man walked in and looked around.

"Can I help you, sir," Alsye asked.

The man didn't respond. Two large-sized thugs scurried up and down the aisles; one poked his head in the back room. The bushy-mustached one nodded. "There's no one here, boss."

The head guy walked back to the front door, pulled the blinds and locked the deadbolt.

"Hey, what's going on?" Alsye asked, his voice nearly at shouting pitch.

"That's what we were wondering, Mr. Weatherspoon," the short leader said, on his way to the counter. "Stand where you are and don't try anything foolish."

Glancing nervously at the man's bulging black leather jacket, Alsye watched him slide his hand inside. Alsye placed his hands on the counter. "I'm not moving."

Out of the corner of his eye, Alsye saw one of the henchmen pull a fire ax from the wall panel and almost simultaneously heard the sound of crushing wood. "What are you doing?"

"Relax ... and you won't get hurt," the little guy restated.

One of the big guys slammed the ax into the storeroom door again and again, splintering it into pieces, leaving it dangle by the hinges. "I found it boss. It's here just like she said."

"How many jars are there?"

"Wait a minute, I'll check."

Moments later the voice called back. "About sixty full ones. And enough empty boxes for maybe another hundred and fifty."

The head guy motioned to a lackey. "Open the back door and toss the jars in the alley — bust 'em up."

"Wait ..." Alsye started.

The boss's hand moved upward inside his jacket. "You've been holding out on us."

"That's private stuff. I don't sell it here. I take it to friends' homes."

"Doesn't matter, it's part of your business." He slammed his free hand on the counter. "How long you been delivering this stuff ... to your *friends* ... as you put it?"

"Um, maybe a month or two."

"Let's say it's closer to four. That'd be close to a thousand jars of booze. A tidy sum I'd say. Seems like you owe us a grand."

"You can't do that."

"Who says? You're getting off easy. I'll be back on Friday to pick it up."

"I don't have that kind of money lying around," Alsye said, his voice distressed.

"A grand on Friday." He turned toward the back door. "Okay boys, light it up."

A big guy ran past the counter and staggered as a huge roar ripped through the store. Flames lapped the back-door frame.

"Looks like you better call the fire department before it's too late," the head man shouted. He unlocked the door and stepped outside; his two cronies pushed close behind.

Alsye threw a towel over his head, covered his face with his arm and raced toward the back room. He kicked the steel door shut and turned. Taking a step, he tripped over the ax and fell head-first into a display rack, slicing open his forehead — blood spewed down his face and onto his shirt. Pulling himself up, he stumbled to the phone and dialed 9-1-1.

Within minutes sirens blasted nearby.

Two hours later the chief stepped inside from the charred back of the building. "Is this your first firebombing?"

Alsye nodded, still shaken by the event.

"Good thing they tossed the jars in the center of the alley rather than against your building. Had they broken them against the back of the building the whole place would have gone up."

"Thank God for that."

The chief headed for the door then turned toward Alsye. "An inspector will be by in the next day or two and give you a report you can file with your insurance company. If you have any questions, he'll be glad to help you."

"Thanks for responding so quickly."

The chief smiled. "That's what we do."

***

Clark opened the door to the New Hellas Café, just down the block from the Cyprus Taverna, and pulled a chair up across from Alsye. Rotating for lunch between the two Greek restaurants had become part of Clark's weekly experience — both were homey with friendly staff — best of all was the great food. "How you doing?" he asked, as he slid onto a chair across from Alsye.

Alsye looked up with a blank stare — three empty Old Fashioned glasses perched on the table in front of him — a fourth glass was half full. "I've done only what I've had to do."

"How's Nicole doing?"

"Better than me." A grin parted his lips. "She's one strong lady."

"Have you had time to think about the future?"

"Not really. Nicole and I have talked a little. I've been so frightened … I was scared shitless when the guy put his hand on a gun inside his coat. I couldn't move."

"For good reason. You never know what a guy like that might do."

"When the flames shot inside, my life flashed before me. I thought I was a goner."

Clark wondered how he might help his friend. "Do you need financial help?"

"No. I took the money out of J. J.'s college fund."

"That's not good."

"It's okay. I have a plan to repay it over the next few months."

Clark gave him a doubtful look, not sure his friend was telling the whole truth. "Are you still hauling the white lightening?"

"I … I have one more load planned to help us get back on our feet."

"It's not worth it, Alsye. The poker guys would be glad to help out."

"I can't do that. We're okay."

"Did you get rid of that Mafia girl?"

"No … I didn't want to piss-off William."

"Big deal. Look what just happened. You could have lost your store."

"I know." Alsye shook his head. "But when William gets upset he doesn't think clearly. It'll be a real problem for him." Alsye rubbed his bloodshot eyes, lined with obvious fatigue. "Have any advice on dealing with the Mafia?"

"That's tough to say." Clark rubbed his jaw. "For now just stay on the straight and narrow. We need to buy time."

"Okay." Alsye stood and flashed his mega-smile for the first time in ages. "Thanks for listening. I feel a lot better."

Clark rose and hugged his old friend. "Sometimes the darkest days shed the most light."

Alsye took a couple of steps and turned back. "You're all right."

Feeling good about their conversation, Clark sat down and leaned back. *I hope Alsye can get it worked out with William. I'll give him a call the first of next week.*

* * *

Task force members were already assembled in the McNamara conference room when Clark hustled in, out of breath. "My secretary just called. Tony Loria turned himself in. I have to go to headquarters. We'll reconvene as soon as possible."

"Is he pleading guilty?" Max asked.

"Don't know. The secretary said he walked in and asked for me. I'll be back as soon as I can." Clark turned and walked briskly toward the elevator. *Why is he there? Is he going to confess? Maybe he's going to incriminate someone … who knows.*

Rushing out the back door, he hopped into his car and raced to the Beaubien Street headquarters. Stepping inside, Clark strolled into the interrogation room with a calm and collected air. Officer Smiley, a lanky veteran of thirty-years, had already read Loria his rights; they were waiting for him.

Seeing Clark, Tony shouted, "You're not pinning this on me. One more conviction and I'm in for life."

Clark slid onto the chair across the table from him and took his time collecting his thoughts. "Pinning what on you?"

"I know how you guys operate. Feed the media a crumb or two and beat the drum. Next thing I know I'm guilty before I've been indicted."

"That's an interesting scenario."

"It's not a scenario. I've seen it happen before."

Clark shrugged his shoulders. "So why are you here?"

"I want to set the record straight." The thug pulled a handkerchief out and wiped his brow. "I didn't kill the Nash kid. I was with my girlfriend that afternoon and all night."

"Sure you were." Clark laughed. "And I was cruising on the Detroit River."

"It's not funny. Honest to God I was with her."

Clark gave him a look of disbelief. "Of course, you were humping her and she'll agree."

"C'mon Detective Phillips ... give me a break."

"Give you a break? You're the one who walked in."

"Okay." Tony raised his hands in the air. "What do you want?"

"I want to know who killed the kid," he said coolly.

Tony let out a deep sigh. "Geez, that's huge. I don't know ..."

Clark interrupted. "If you don't know there's no need for us to talk."

"You know I can't say."

Clark's eyes opened wide, picking up on his slip of the tongue. "So you *do* know?"

"I didn't mean it that way."

Clark folded his hands on the table. "Just how did you mean it?"

Tony waffled, "I-I ..."

"Look, you tell me the truth and you'll be off Scot-free, no prison time."

Tony paused to wipe the perspiration from his brow. "It was Vinny."

"Vinny?" Clark asked in a perfectly calm voice.

"Vinny Castintino."

Clark stared him in the eye. "How do I know you're not trying to save your own skin?"

"It's the truth ... so help me God." Tony crossed himself. "I heard it from a capo. You know ... I can't say any more."

"Will you sign a statement confirming all of this?"

Tony rubbed his jaw. "No jail time, right?"

"No jail time." Clark slid a pad of paper and pen across the table.

* * *

An hour later, Clark stepped back into the conference room and plopped down at the table. Questions flew from all directions. He raised his hand. "One at a time."

Going around the table for questions, Clark filled the group in on the details of his session with Loria.

"How are we going to deal with this in the media," Lieutenant Sterling asked.

Grissini, the Mafia expert, raised his hand and spoke deliberately. "I think we should keep it under wraps as long as we can."

"Why do you say that?" Sterling from narcotics asked.

"The longer we can keep the other guys in the dark the better off we'll be. Other than tooting our horn there's no reason to announce it right now. Who knows … maybe someone will speak out of school."

"Makes sense." Clark paused, trying to collect his thoughts. "Where were we now?"

Patrolman Ralston spoke softly. "We're ready to update the group on Dallas's activities from January to July."

"Fine … the floor is yours." Clark nodded and leaned back in his chair.

Opening his notes, the long-time flatfoot took a deep breath then stated, firmly, "Dallas is in serious trouble."

Clark scooted up to the table. Eyes around the table zeroed in on Leonard, pens in hand.

"He went to Vegas for a week each in January, March and May, and stayed in a penthouse suite at the Stardust."

"Did his wife go?" Max asked.

"No. The hotel tab was over fifteen grand for each trip."

"What the hell was he doing?" someone asked.

"Who knows, but he was sure as hell doing a lot of it." The old cop laughed. "And that's only the tip of the iceberg … word on the street is that he's into the Mafia for big bucks."

"Any idea how much?" Clark asked.

"Rumor has it he may owe them as much as half a million dollars."

"Half a million in gambling losses?" Weston questioned.

"There's more to it than that. He's into drugs big-time and loves the women. The kind of prostitutes he demands don't come cheap."

"Has he been seen around town?" Clark asked.

"He frequents a couple of blind pigs on a regular basis."

"Guess he likes one-stop shopping," Earl interjected. Laughter filled the room.

"We need to put a wiretap on his phone," someone suggested.

Clark wrinkled his nose. "I'm not excited about that. It would require a court order. I don't think we have enough evidence to convince a judge." He looked around the room. "Anyone else have an idea?"

"I can keep digging through my informants," Will Robinson offered.

"Yeah, keep on it. You never know what else you'll uncover."

"Will do," the bald-headed insider said.

Earl raised his hand. "I have several contacts on the street. I'll chase down the blind pigs."

"Good, I like that." Clark hesitated, hoping someone would come up with a workable idea.

After some time, Eddie spoke up. "We could run his number through the telephone company."

"We'd have to get a subpoena," Sergeant Weston reminded the group. "Otherwise it wouldn't hold up in court."

"The New York Mob does it all the time," Eddie pointed out. "They pay off an AT&T employee and he runs the phone numbers they want."

A crease crossed Clark's forehead. "What kind of information could we uncover?"

"A listing of all calls, coming and going, from his home phone."

"Could we do the same for his office?"

"Probably; that could produce thousands of entries," Eddie said.

Clark rubbed his forehead. "Do you know of such a person?"

"Ahhh." Eddie gave him a shrewd smile. "Sure ... two or three."

"Hmm." Clark rubbed his jaw, deep in thought — a light flipped on. "Think one of your friends might show you how it works? Nothing formal, you know ... like a demonstration."

"A demonstration ... so we can understand the process." Eddie grinned, picking up on Clarke's indirect request. "I'll see what I can do."

Soaking a piece of pita bread in the broth of his sautéed mussels at the New Hellas Café, Clark jotted a note with his right hand. Concentrating deeply on an upcoming meeting with an informant, he felt a nudge on the shoulder. Glancing up, Miss Hotsey Totsey kissed him lightly on the forehead.

"Haley, what are you doing here?" he said, totally taken aback by her appearance on her day off at the Sax Club.

"Anything you want." She winked and gave him a sexy smile, making sure he knew what she had in mind.

"How did you know I was here?" he asked, still unable to fathom her presence.

She turned to the side, flaunting her modest cleavage in her half-open blouse, unmistakably braless. "What can I do for you, Clark?" she purred.

"Stop, right there." *What is wrong with her? Doesn't she know I'm involved with Caroline?*

She gave him a coy look. "Aren't you going to buy me a drink?"

"Ah ... sure, I guess," he stammered. "What would you like?"

Eyeing him as she sat in the chair across the table, she pointed to his glass of white wine. "I'll have what you're having."

An overweight waitress with heavy rouge applied to each cheek looked at Haley — a smile crossed her plump face. "I see you caught up with him."

"Sure did." Haley straightened her shoulders to make the most of what assets she had.

Clark caught a glimpse and looked away, as if he hadn't noticed. "A Santorini for her and another one for me." He shook his head and leaned back in his chair. *Why is she here? Sure, maybe I gave her a come-on look once or twice, but that was nothing ... yeah, maybe I was a little flirtatious too, but it was all in fun.*

"How did you find me here?" he asked again.

She sensuously ran her tongue around her lips. "You're easy to read. I know about you. Everyone at the Club knows you have lunch at a Greek restaurant every week. Hellas is the best one in town. I figured sooner or later you'd end up here. So I checked around. When I stopped in last week the waitress said you'd probably be here this Wednesday or Thursday. So here I am."

"Ingenious, aren't you?"

She slipped her fingers inside her blouse and eased the edges apart, exposing more of her breasts.

Clark glanced and quickly looked away.

"See anything you're interested in?"

His eyebrows rose slightly, but he didn't look up. *Damn, I can't believe her. She can't want it that bad.*

She didn't miss a beat. "My place is just ten minutes away."

Taking a long sip of wine, he stared at her. *What is wrong with you? Why are you even thinking about it? Caroline is the best person you've ever met. Tell Haley to go home alone and take a cold shower.*

She reached across the table, placed her hand under his chin and gently lifted it up — her eyes made contact with his — she spoke softly, "I'll give you the best blow job ever and more afternoon delight than you've ever dreamed about."

"I can't, Haley." *It might be fun, but I'm committed.* "I ..."

"Shh." She placed her index finger over his lips. "I know you can and I know you *want* to. I've seen the way you look at me."

"That isn't the point." He turned and stared across the room. *One time ... nothing will come of it. If she really wants to, why not?*

"C'mon Clark, I know you want me."

He glanced at her cleavage, pulled out his wallet and flipped a twenty on the table.

She stood with a grin and grabbed his hand. "C'mon, you can follow me in your car."

***

Clark cracked an eye toward the sliver of light coming from the small gap between the heavy drapes. Lying naked on a sweat-soaked sheet, he squinted at his watch — 3:55. *Crap! I can't believe I did it with her. A twenty-one-year-old nothing. What if Caroline finds out? How will I ever explain this to her?*

Coming to his senses, his thoughts centered on Caroline. *How in the hell could I be so dumb? Haley doesn't hold a candle to Caroline. She's everything I could wish for and more. She's the love of my life ... she's my everything. Oh God, forgive me.*

Clark slid to the edge of the bed, planted his feet on the floor and looked around the stark efficiency apartment. Not seeing Haley, he walked into the bathroom, washed his hands and face, dressed, and headed for the office.

The trip was long and slow, even though it was only three miles. Arriving at 1300 Beaubien, he walked up the five flights to release some nervous energy, but couldn't get Caroline off his mind. *How could I have ever betrayed her? Will she ever forgive me?* He trudged onto the next landing. *Please God, don't let her know ... I will do anything. I'll never do her wrong. Oh, please ...* His mind recycled the same thoughts landing after landing.

By the time he reached his office, he was exhausted — mentally and physically — his mind fried, his arms and legs lifeless. He had done the worst thing of his life. He'd been out with lots of women, but had never cheated on one. *Why now? I can't believe I did it. Oh God, what am I going to do?*

Clark slammed the door, trudged to his chair and collapsed onto it. Sobbing into his hands he moaned, "How can I ever make amends?"

CHAPTER THIRTEEN

Staring out the second floor window of the Sax Club, Caroline didn't move when the door opened and Clark strolled in. "How're you doing sweetie?" he asked in his customary way.

She turned slowly away from the pitch-black night and sent him a piercing stare — her cold, glassy eyes sliced his soul.

An uneasy feeling crept over Clark; he locked in place.

"Take off your shoes and socks, put your clothes on the chair, and sit down on the end of the bed," she directed curtly.

Unsure where she was going, he stripped naked and eased onto the foot of the bed. She stepped in front of him with a disdainful look. Clark looked up, not sure where she was heading, hoping to please her as he had so many times before.

She shoved him back, his head landing on the bed with his feet still on the floor. Leaning over him, she ran her hands seductively down his sides, caressing his hips and fondling him — his urges fired.

Still eyeing him with contempt, she slapped his face.

"Ouch ... goddamn," he shouted, rubbing his jaw. "What's wrong with you?"

"Me? You have the gall to ask what is wrong with *me*?" She threw her arms in the air. "You asshole. She gave you a blow job and screwed you, and you ask what is wrong with *me*?"

Clark rose up on his elbows. "Caroline, I can explain. I ..."

Her eyes shot daggers. "You can't explain ... screwing her ... after all of these months, the things you've said ... the things we've done. You're a disgusting bastard."

"It isn't what you think."

"Hah." Wiping a tear from her cheek, she turned and stomped to the window.

Clark stood, slipped on his shorts and stepped behind her; gently, timidly, eased a hand onto her shoulder.

She jerked away. "Don't touch me."

"Please Caroline ..."

She bristled. "Caroline ... don't you ever call me that again."

"Please, let me explain."

"Explain … that's bullshit. She told everyone in the club. How could you embarrass me? All of my friends know. You let a twenty-one-year-old cocksucker …" She bit her lip. "I can't say it. Have you no values … no respect for others?"

"I'm sorry, Caroline." Clark reached for her. "I …"

She pushed his hand away. "Don't come close to me," she sobbed. "Put your clothes on and get out of here."

"But …"

Her look cut him off.

He backed away, slipped on his slacks, zipped them up, and put on his shirt. He took a tentative step toward her. "Please," he begged. "Give me a chance."

"Stop right there." She shot him a long, contemptuous look. "You're no different than the rest of the men I've known."

"Please, Caroline."

"I said, don't call me Caroline!" She shook her head. "Ha … 'give me one more chance.' And the next time, 'give me one more chance.' No way." Stepping closer to him, she shoved her index finger in his face "I've had enough. I'd quit this place if I could just so I wouldn't have to look at you. But I can't afford to do that. I'd ask management to bar you from this place but I know they wouldn't."

Clark stood motionless; his world stood still around him. He hoped against all hope that she might … somehow find a way … a way to forgive him and give him one more chance.

She dabbed her eyes with a tissue, blew her nose, squared her shoulders, and spoke with powerful resolve, "When I'm on the platform I don't want to see you sitting on that damn stool. Sit as far away as possible. Find a place where I don't have to look at your goddamn face. Do you understand?"

Clark didn't say a word; he felt there was nothing he could say. He could only hope for a glimmer of a second chance, any opening, anything.

She turned away then glanced back at him. "Don't answer … just get your ass out of here," she shouted on her way to the door. Opening it, she pointed. "GET. OUT. OF. HERE!"

He followed her directive, walking slowly with his head down, he paused at the door.

"Keep on going. Don't say a word," she demanded. She shoved him out the door and slammed it behind him.

Clark plodded sluggishly down the hallway. He stumbled and tripped on the bottom step, slamming his shoulder against the door below. Stepping back, he opened the door, meandered toward his car, and plopped inside. He stared blankly into the darkness. *What is wrong with me? I had it all. Caroline and I did everything together. We went to plays, went dancing, saw the Tigers, ate at fancy restaurants and best of all, talked about our many common interests. Why did I betray her — one time — how could I be so dumb?*

He jammed the key into the ignition then eased it out. *Maybe I should go back ... maybe she'll reconsider.* "I ought to at least try," he said to the rearview mirror, as he placed his hand on the door handle. He paused and pulled it back. *Shit, after what she said there's no way she'll give me the time of day.*

Wrestling the issue in his mind, he turned the key in the ignition, and gassed it out of the parking lot, squealing onto McNichols. Hitting every stoplight, he pounded on the steering wheel, wondering if he'd ever be the same.

Reaching his apartment building, Clark pulled into a parking slot, cut the engine, and walked inside. His mouth turned down, he stepped into the elevator. *How many times have I stood right here with Caroline in my arms — the two of us as one — it was wonderful!*

***

A wintery November breeze rustled the oaks and swayed the pines that guarded the Grosse Pointe Park mansion. Darkness had set in long ago — German Shepherd police dogs roamed the surroundings — surveillance cameras combed the grounds from above.

A red light blinked, the front gate curled back, making way for the black '78 Buick; it came to a stop in front of a massive wooden front door. The driver stepped out and walked slowly around the back of the car, his eyes scanning the route he'd just traversed. The ten-foot high door opened and a large man stepped into the light of the overarching portico. He said something to the chauffeur and slid back into the doorway.

The driver opened the rear door and stepped back, using his body to shield the passenger from the street side. A silver-haired man with large sunglasses made a comment to the driver as he turned toward the front door.

Greeting him with formality, a doorman pointed down the spacious hallway behind him. The man dressed in black stepped inside and followed the high-polished terrazzo floor past several Romanesque paintings. A life-size marble sculpture of Marc Antony kept company with a statue of the emperor Augustine, and a regal bust of Julius Caesar.

Before reaching the hallway off to the left at the end, the front door opened again. Another man strolled in, his yellow turtleneck shirt extending over the top of a navy blue blazer. The routine repeated several times over the next half hour until nine men had made their way down the marble gauntlet to the meeting room in the back.

Blackie Giardini had already moved a black, high-back swivel rocker close to the Consigliere, Tony Minelli, the Boss's top advisor, and the two were in deep conversation. At eighty-four, Tony looked as dapper as anyone, his perfectly folded white pocket square accenting a smart blue, pinstriped suit.

Members of the leadership council filed in and paid their respects to Jake Nicoletti. The Boss embraced each man and kissed him on the cheek. When the last one had passed, he slid onto the swivel rocker at the head of the table. Jake glanced at the handsome Underboss, Angelo Travaglini, on his right and over at Joe "The Bookkeeper" Norwood, the overweight accountant sitting next to him. Turning back to the left, he nodded to the stoic Consigliere, and grinned at Blackie, the up-and-coming mob star.

Joe DiGregorio, the Street Boss, sat beside Blackie and tapped him on the arm. His top assistant turned and Joe bent his ear in what appeared to be a high-level discussion.

Jake Nicoletti looked at the four caporegimes, commonly called capos for short, seated at the other end of the walnut table. Each man functioned like a corporate division head; each having responsibility for one of the organization's primary activities — racketeering, gambling, prostitution, and drug and human trafficking.

The Boss cleared his throat and turned to Blackie. "I'd like to start tonight's meeting with a status report on Huston Nash."

Blackie gave him a slight courtesy nod. "There are a couple of points worth mentioning. First, the police have at least one sworn statement that Vinny Castintino killed the kid."

"I haven't seen anything in the paper," a capo mentioned.

"I don't like the sound of that," the Consigliere said.

"Neither do I," Jake agreed. "Is the task force still meeting?"

"Every two weeks."

The crease in Jake's brow deepened. "That means they're pursuing something else."

Angelo tossed in his two cents worth. "Knowing Vinny was the killer, they can only draw one conclusion — the kid was under surveillance — that means we're on their radar."

"You're right ..." Blackie rubbed his forehead. "What do we know about Dallas, the kid's father?"

Ray "King" Kingston, the short balding capo for gambling, straightened at the far end of the table. "His name has popped up several times on my rolls."

"The same for me," the capo for drugs agreed.

The heavy-set head of prostitution nodded. "I've seen his name several times too."

"I want a complete profile on him," the Boss said; his voice conveyed a sense of urgency.

"You got it," Blackie said.

Jake turned to his advisor. "Where to now?"

The Consigliere, twenty years the senior to anyone in the room, ran his fingers around the fuzzy patch of hair clustered above his ears. "It won't take long for the authorities to figure out everything we've just talked about. We'll need to move quickly to keep a step ahead of them."

Blackie pursed his lips. "Ten to one, Dallas will cave and want to plea bargain."

"You're right," the Consigliere agreed. "It's time to pick up some insurance."

"Have any ideas?" Jake asked.

His shrewd mentor paused. "Dallas has two sisters. An older one at a university somewhere in California and a younger one at a boarding school out east. I'd say we check out the young one."

"Any particular reason?" Angelo asked.

"A family with their kind of money doesn't usually send the perfect little daughter off to boarding school. I'd wager they're protecting her."

"Anyone disagree with Tony?" The Boss looked around the table. No one raised a hand.

Jake turned to Blackie. "Do it."

"I'll get you something before the end of next week."

"Sounds good." Jake took in a deep breath and sighed. "Let's move on to Clark Phillips. Who wants to go first?"

Hands shot up around the table. "Hold on … one at time. I need to take notes." The Boss opened his pad then listened to Clark's personal escapades. After filling two pages in his pad, he flipped his pencil aside. "Anyone else?"

His glance caught each member's eye, nothing. Checking his notes, he sneered. "This guy must have a perennial penis."

Chuckles filled the room. "A what?" the Street Boss asked, jokingly.

Jake smiled. "I came up with it over the weekend after I talked to you."

"Me?" Questions filled Joe's mind; a frown-line crossed his forehead. "What did I say?"

"It isn't what you said. It was the timing. After I hung up from your phone call my wife poked her head in the doorway and said she was having the landscapers plant some perennial peanuts along the fence." Jake's face glowed. "With my mind still on Clark I cracked up. I said, 'I thought you said perennial penis.' Obviously not amused, she gave me the eye."

Joe guffawed. "That's funny."

"That's only half of it," Jake said, holding back a laugh.

Joe still frowned. "What do you mean?"

"I came up with a definition too," Jake said, trying to contain himself. "A perennial penis pops up every time a pussy *springs* forward."

Laughter bounded off the walls filling the room.

The Consigliere doubled over.

"We need …" Jake hesitated, regaining his composure. "We need to find a hot pussy to get in his pants."

Blackie's grin grew into a smile. "I have calls into L.A. and Philly. I'll get back with you as soon as I hear back."

***

Sharon knocked on Laverne's apartment door, waited longer than usual, then tried the doorknob — locked. Turning toward the elevator, she heard a creaking sound.

Laverne stepped into the hallway. "Sorry, I was on the phone. Wanna come in?"

Sharon held up a bottle of Sauvignon Blanc. "Do you have time for a drink?"

"Of course." She waved her in. "What's happening with you?"

Sharon nodded, excitedly. "I have to talk."

"Oh-okay, I'll get out a couple of glasses." She walked into the kitchen, pulled two small wine glasses from the cabinet and handed them to Sharon. "Here, put these on the table while I'm opening the bottle."

Sharon picked up the glasses, carried them to the small dinette table and sat one on each side. Laverne pulled the cork, carried the bottle to the table and filled their glasses. "Okay, what's going on?"

Seeming out of touch, Sharon stared across the room.

Her friend flopped down across from her and waited patiently for the longest moment. "Are we going to talk?"

Sharon took a long sip. "It's Clark."

Laverne's eyebrows scrunched. "Something wrong?"

Staring at her wine glass, Sharon shook her head. "That's the problem. Everything is exactly right."

"What's wrong with that?"

Sharon bit her lip. "It's not right. We're too different ..."

Laverne cut her off. "Hold on ... first you said he's exactly right then he's not right. You need to slow down and start over."

Sharon slid back in her chair and twiddled her thumbs.

"Do you think you are ...?"

Sharon jumped up and shouted, "Don't say that ... I can't be."

"Okay ... fine." Laverne leaned back and relaxed. "What are we talking about?"

Sharon trudged around the apartment and plopped down on the chair. Looking confused, Laverne shook her head. "Am I supposed to wave a magic wand and make it okay?"

"No ... we're so different. He's had lots of women. Maybe I'll be another notch."

"Could be ... I suppose."

Sharon frowned; her lower lip turned down. "Why did you say that?"

"Christ, I don't know. You've only been around him twice."

"I thought he was really something when he told me Caroline and him were a thing. Now that Ted says he's available I feel like I…"

"Go for it."

"No … I mean yes. I don't know what I mean."

"Christ Sharon, you're going in circles. We're back to square one — he's exactly right then he's not. You're in love then you're not."

"I'm not in love … he's a city slicker on the make."

"Fine, it's over. Forget about him."

Sharon stiffened. "Why are you talking like that? I thought you were my friend."

"Shit, I don't know … have a drink. What am I supposed to say?" Laverne picked up the bottle and filled their glasses, leaned back and stared at Sharon.

Sharon took a sip. "So what do you think?"

"Do you really want to know?"

"Yes, of course. Why do you think I asked?"

Laverne gave her a disgusted look. "I think you should go home, open a bottle of wine and get snockered. When you sober up, look in the mirror and ask yourself the same question. If you feel the same — go for it. If not, tell him to buzz off."

"And that's it?"

"Shit, you asked." Laverne threw her arms up in dismay. "If you don't like that, lay one of the doctors at school. There are plenty of them with the hots for you."

"I'm not spreading my legs for any of them. They're all jerks or pompous asses."

"Fine. Do what you want."

"I don't know what I want." Sharon pouted. "That's why I'm here."

"Crap, here we go again." Laverne pointed her index finger toward her lips. "Read my lips. This is the last time I'm going to say it." She held her breath, trying not to show her frustration. "Look, you have the hots for the guy and you're scared. You're not sure what might happen. Big deal, who in the hell knows anything for sure. There are no guarantees in life."

Sharon raised her eyebrows and gave her a "that makes sense look." "I suppose. I just want to be sure."

"You've got nothing to lose. It's better to take a shot than to shy away and fuss about it. Maybe he's Mr. Right. How would you feel a year from now if you realized he was the one and you found out he was hooked up with someone else?"

Sharon's nod revealed a new sense of confidence. "You're right. I'm going to invite him to my place for dinner this Saturday."

"Now you're cooking." Laverne covered her mouth. "I made a funny."

"Double entendre."

***

Clark took a three-minute walk from the McNamara Building up Washington Boulevard to the Cadillac Hotel. Opening the coffee-shop door exactly at nine o'clock, as instructed by Will Robinson, he looked for the booth tucked away in the back alcove. Barely visible from the door he spied the top of a baldheaded man. Heading that way, the man came into vision — a round face, white fringe around his tan head and a potbelly stomach hanging on the tabletop — just as Will had described.

He extended his hand. "'Morning, I'm Clark Phillips."

"Luis," the old man said with a slight Spanish accent. He grabbed Clark's paw. "It's nice to meet the top dog."

Clark gave him a slight grin and slid in across from him.

The waitress delivered two steaming mugs of coffee and set two sweet rolls on a plate in front of Luis before he looked up again. "Want a couple of sweet rolls too?" she asked Clark.

"One will do it," he said, eying the Puerto Rican man. "Will tells me you're the best at collecting information."

He cracked a smile and nodded. "That's what I do." He stuffed the last part of a sweet roll in his mouth, speaking around it, "Whataya need?"

"You don't waste any time, do you?" Clark asked, and then thanked the waitress for the sweet roll.

Luis grunted. "I'm not here to socialize."

My kind of guy, Clark thought. "I want to know the location of *the game*."

The man's dark brown eyes glazed; he leaned back and grinned. "You rolling dice?"

Clark cut into his sweet roll, knowing he had the right guy. "I need the address."

The overweight man stuffed another chunk of sweet roll in his mouth. "Top dog … *the game*." Luis wiped his mouth on his shirtsleeve. "That won't be easy." He looked Clark in the eye. "Twenty-five hundred."

Clark shook his head, knowing that was double the usual amount.

"It won't be easy … and very dangerous. It'll take some time."

"I have plenty of time," Clark jested. "Two thousand."

Luis didn't blink. "Two thousand, five hundred dollars."

Taking his time, Clark rubbed his jaw. The old man started to slide out of the booth.

Clark raised his hand. "Deal."

"Good." Luis jammed the last of the sweet roll into his mouth. "I'll let Will know when I'm ready to meet."

CHAPTER FOURTEEN

December poker was like Christmas came early. Carlos and Rosa Maria had spent most of the afternoon decorating the room for a Mexican Christmas. Evergreens, moss, and colorful paper lanterns traditionally placed outside the home, filled the room. Large cardboard cutouts of Mary riding a donkey and Joseph standing close beside her stood in the right corner — depicting one of nine "Las Posadas" processions used to celebrate Christmas. In the far corner stood figures of Pestorelas, another celebration of plays that tell the story of the shepherds finding baby Jesus.

Being his typical jovial self, Carlos greeted his friends with a traditional "Feliz Navidad" and handed each of them a shot of tequila. Quickly downing their drinks, they followed Carlos to the appetizer table — there they found three large tins of fresh baked Christmas cookies, two plates of fudge, and four different types of hors d'oeuvres that filled the space between festive poinsettias.

"Enjoy, compliments of Rosa Maria."

"My God, she must have worked all week," Clark said. "It looks wonderful."

Stepping in behind Clark, Renzo popped two more shots. His eyes took in the displays and then searched the table of goodies. "How did you ever come up with all of this?"

"It's unbelievable," Ted said, pushing in behind Renzo.

"It's Rosa Maria. She really gets into things like this."

Father Dom popped a second shot. "I've never seen such distinctive decorations."

Ted nudged in beside Carlos. "C'mon, who came up with all of this?"

"Rosa Maria." Carlos said, looking proud as a peacock. "It was her idea from the start. She's been bugging me for years about having the nine Posadas line our street. I procrastinated. A project like that was the furthest thing from my mind. So when she mentioned doing something special for poker I jumped on it."

"That's only natural, my son," Father Dom said. "Women seem to have more personal insights about things like this. And … I must admit they are usually right on target."

"I suppose so."

"Rosa Maria certainly outdid herself on this," Alsye said, walking in late and overhearing part of the earlier conversation. "We need to do something special for her."

"Right on," Ted agreed. "We ought to send her a dozen roses."

"Perfect," Clark said. "I'll take care of it."

Father Dom raised his hands and spoke a few words about the meaning of Christmas. The guys looked solemnly at each other. One-by-one each hugged Carlos. The glow of his face showed his appreciation.

Renzo eased onto a chair and took charge, flipping the cards. "Dealer's choice."

Father Dom received the first ace and the marathon was on. Playing non-stop, the group raised fifty cents, then a dollar. Acting like high-rollers, they raised again and again. Three of a kind beats two pair. A straight beats three of a kind and a flush beats that. Nothing new, a boat beats them all, unless someone has four of a kind.

Break time extended beyond the normal nine o'clock limit. Ted groused about the sloppy play of the Lions. Renzo commiserated with him.

Turning to Clark, Alsye changed the subject. "Have any news on the Nash murder?"

"Nothing much different than the stories you've been reading in the paper."

"They have several conspiracy theories …"

Carlos butted in. "I don't understand the paper's scenario about the Mafia's insurance. What's that all about?"

Seeing his interest, Clark's eyes twinkled. "It's like any other kind of insurance; it protects against something you don't want to happen. In this case the Mafia uses a person as collateral. They hold someone hostage for protection to make sure no one talks or until they get what they want in return. When a deal is worked out they release the person and both parties are happy."

"Oh …" Carlos wrinkled his nose. "And if it doesn't work out?"

"That's the worse-case scenario."

"Enough of that," Renzo said. "Let's get on with the game."

Sharon opened her apartment door and looked up into Clark's eyes. He pulled his hand from behind his back and presented her a red rose with baby's breath, in a crystal bud vase.

"Aren't you sweet," she said, lifting herself onto her tiptoes and pecking him on the cheek.

"Thank you." Taking a whiff of the aromas coming from her apartment, he glanced toward the kitchen. "What smells so good?"

"Lasagna."

"You can cook too?" he joked.

"C'mon, I grew up on a farm with four brothers." She turned for the kitchen. "There's a bottle of Chianti by the fridge, would you open it?"

"Sure," he said, following behind, enjoying the sway of her ass. "Can I say something first?"

Turning around, she gave him a quizzical look.

"Thanks for inviting me to dinner." The sincerity in his eyes added an exclamation point.

A mystified crease formed on her forehead. "Why did you say that?"

"The other times were arranged; I just thought it was nice of you to ask."

She smiled; their eyes connected for a moment. *I could jump his bones right now.* She glanced away. "Dinner is almost ready. Want to take the salad bowls out of the fridge and pour the wine?"

"That's within my pay grade," he jested.

She placed a plate of lasagna on each side of the table, centered a basket of hot bread and hurried back to the kitchen for the salt and pepper grinder. Clark lit the candles in the center of the table. On the way back from the kitchen, she dimmed the lights. Clark pulled out her chair and stood waiting.

"Well, what do we have here, a gentleman?"

"Only here to serve." He winked.

She giggled. "Sounds interesting."

Clark picked up his glass and toasted. "Here's to a beautiful lady and a wonderful dinner."

"And a handsome man." The two clinked their glasses. "Bon appetite."

Clark dug in. "Wow, this is really good."

"Thanks."

He cleaned his plate and had a second helping. She emptied the wine bottle and he opened another. Light conversation extended throughout the meal as the two laughed and told stories about their different backgrounds. And chatted some more.

"This is the best lasagna I've ever had."

"I'm glad you like it." Her eyes admired his trim body; she tingled with desire. Continuing to measure him, she wondered what he'd be like in bed. *He's been with so many. I bet he's really good. I can't wait 'til I get him in bed tonight.*

Clark didn't look up until he'd cleaned his plate for a second time. "I can't eat one more bite." Rubbing his stomach, he grinned. "Could I take a small piece home for my mother?"

"Yes, of course. There's plenty left." She lifted her plate.

He stood. "Here, let me do that. I'll clean up. You can relax and enjoy the wine."

"Are you sure?"

"Of course. You prepared everything. It's the least I can do."

"Thanks." She eased down and took a long sip of her wine; her eyes followed his every move. *How many guys would do that?* She watched him bend over to put the plates in the dishwasher. *Nice ass. I bet you can do a lot more. I need to get him in the mood.* She cleared her throat. "Would you like an after dinner drink?"

"Ah … just one. I'm taking my mother to the early service in the morning."

Her heart sunk with disappointment.

***

Clark walked into the conference room and stopped cold. Seeing stacks of computer printouts piled in the center of the table, he turned to the smiling face of Detective Grissini. "It looks like one of the contacts came through."

"Your idea worked like a charm," Eddie said. "I told him you wanted a demonstration run of a home number and the corporation, so we'd know what kind of information was available, should we pursue a court order."

"He did it just like that?"

Eddie grinned. "Well … after a couple of beers at a local pub."

"How'd you make it happen?"

"We went back to his office. He hit a bunch of switches and buttons and gave me a wink as I looked the other way. He said, 'Okay. Give me a couple of random numbers off the top of your head.' I read the numbers from the piece of paper you gave me. He turned around and said, 'Fine. I'll have something by the end of the week.'"

"All of these stacks are a result of that?"

"You got it. They're computer printouts of the telephone numbers and addresses for the persons or businesses who called one or two of the numbers. The small pile is all of the incoming and outgoing calls from Dallas's home number. The three huge stacks in the middle of the table are for Nash's corporate office where Dallas works."

"Any ideas how many calls are listed in the three stacks?"

"My friend estimates there are twelve to fifteen thousand entries. It'll take several months to work our way through them."

"That's fine … they're a lower priority anyway. How about the home numbers?"

"Kimberly and I divided them up last Friday. We had everyone in for the weekend, had pizza and sorted."

"How did you sort them?" Clark asked.

"We used our list of individuals and businesses with known underworld connections."

"All of you were here all weekend?" Eddie nodded. "You should have invited me," Clark said. "I would have been glad to help."

"We were so fired up we just dug in." Eddie glanced around the room at his partners. "Whataya say guys?"

The group looked like a promotion for bobble heads. Kimberly piped up, "I was stuck in this room so long even Leonard started to look good."

"Hey, wait 'til my wife hears about that," the old man sparred with a grin. "Actually it was her levity that kept us sane. Otherwise the names would have run together. We had a lot of fun."

"Good for you," Clark said. "So what's the bottom line?"

"I thought you'd never ask … hot off the press." Eddie stood and shared a multipage handout. "Thirty-four names of people and businesses associated with the Mafia on his home phone."

"Wow, that's impressive."

"And, one more thing." He handed out a city map. "I numbered the names and marked the map showing where each phone is located."

"Terrific." Clark's eyes shot around the table. "Where to from here?"

Max spoke up, "We figured if each of us took five or six names we'd be able to work our way through them, interrogate viable connections, and wrap it up by the end of the month."

"That'd be great. Do you really think you can pull it together that quickly?"

"We think it's doable," Lieutenant Sterling from narcotics confirmed. "If not, we'll be off to a great running start."

***

"It's going to be another twenty minutes before the baked potatoes are done," Sharon said. "Want to fix a couple of drinks?"

"I'd be glad to." Clark pushed his stool away from the bar that divided the kitchen and small dinette table, and moseyed toward the kitchen.

"The glasses are on the counter. Tanqueray is in the lower cabinet by the fridge and the tequila is in the freezer."

Clark slid behind her in the narrow galley-like kitchen, sat the booze on the counter and opened the fridge. "I see the olives; do you want a lime in yours?"

"Double lime ... and mix them up with crushed ice in a shaker. I'll get it out for you."

"Anything else?" he jested.

"Don't be smart." She turned with a butcher knife in her hand. "This cuts more than lettuce."

"Okay, okay." Clark backed away, finished his task and turned back. "Are you finished with that knife?"

"Yes." She turned with a smiling face. Clark handed her an Old Fashioned glass and held his high. "Here's to the most beautiful and smartest doctor I know."

She blushed and clinked his glass. "And here's to the city's most handsome detective."

The two smiled. Each took a sip. She leaned closer. "Anything new on the Nash case?"

"Nothing official."

"I understand," Sharon said, continuing to flit around the kitchen; she placed a saucepan on the range and turned up the heat.

"What are you making?"

"A special merlot reduction glaze for the pork chops."

"Sounds wonderful," he said, his eyes glued on her tight, knit slacks. *There's something about her ass. Not the best one I've ever seen but the way she moves; it's hard to explain — a cute little wiggle and wham. I wonder how she'd look parading around in panties.*

Stepping behind her, there was more than a fantasy coming alive. He adjusted himself, placed his hands on her hips, and kissed the side of her neck.

"Oh my God." She backed away. "Look at my arms. Goosebumps down to my wrists."

"Sorry, I didn't mean to scare you."

"It's not that, Clark. Your kiss made me shiver."

"Wow. I didn't know I had that kind of effect."

"Don't get your hopes up." She laughed, leaned over the stove, and tasted the sauce. "Perfect. You're going to like this. Want to pour the wine?"

"Sure, what kind of wine are we having?"

"Sangiovese. There's a chilled bottle over by the fridge."

"Terrific. That's a perfect pairing with pork." He opened the bottle and poured their glasses half full, lit the candles, and dimmed the lights.

She eyed him. "Looks like someone trained you properly."

"My mom." His grin broadened. "Whenever we had a nice dinner she always dimmed the lights and lit the candles."

Sharon sat the plates on the table and joined him. "Did you learn anything else from her?"

"Lots." Clark rambled about his mother, talking about the values she'd instilled in him — the importance of treating others with dignity — being inquisitive by probing to learn more.

Sharon responded in the same manner. "My dad was super. He was kind of quiet but when he had something to say it was worth hearing. And Mom was a dynamo, a real driving force."

"I was very fortunate too." Clark hesitated; casting a gaze around the room while he gathered his thoughts, and broke into a prideful smile. "I owe my entire professional career to my dad — my drive and work ethic come from him. Without that I would have ended up on the production line at Ford."

The two continued to talk late into the night. Sharon reminisced about growing up on the farm; he countered with his experiences growing up in the city. While some of it was a rehash, tonight seemed more meaningful.

Candles on the dinette table flickered. Sharon reached across the table and ran her index finger between his fingers. Her soft smile glowed in anticipation. Their eyes connected. She rose slowly, kissed him lightly on the cheek and eased him into the living room.

Unable to restrain herself, she kissed him passionately and pulled him onto the sofa. The two pawed each other — Sharon loosening his shirt buttons — Clark grappling to remove her blouse. They ripped off their clothes, stripped naked and made love in a hurry. Panting and gasping, they lay perspiring, barely able to move. Sharon eased next to him and snuggled close before the two fell asleep.

Waking up in the middle of the night, the two lovers made their way into her bedroom and enjoyed each other again, this time taking their time to tease and play.

***

Across town in Blackie's favorite hangout, Joey Naples downed a draft and ordered a second. His mistress was not present. Blackie had given her two hundred dollars to go on a shopping spree, as had become a tradition for him the last week of each month.

Munching on a large pretzel, Joey asked. "So how do you want to pursue our boy, Clark?"

Blackie shrugged. "I'm not sure how, but one thing is obvious, the way to his brain is through his dick."

"You got that right."

"Anything you want me to do?"

"I don't think there is much of a chance with the doctor and stripper."

"Heard anything from L.A. and Philly?"

"Not much happening on the California end. Philly is sending a bio and pictures of a couple of broads. After I pick one it'll take a month or two to get her settled in."

"Now, about the young waitress at the Sax Club?" Joey asked.

"Sounds like she's in it for a good time," Blackie said, his tone lacking enthusiasm.

Joey mused. "How about I give her five hundred and see what happens?"

"That'll be fine." Blackie hesitated. "But, I think Philly is our best bet; we need a broad with moxie and big boobs."

***

Opening the door to Laverne's apartment, Ted gave Sharon a friendly hug and winked at Clark. "Right on time. Hors d'oeuvres on the coffee table. Grab yourself a plate and have a chair. I'm pouring the drinks. Everyone want the usual?"

"Sounds good," Clark said. "Want me to help?"

"No, I've already made ours. Yours will only take a minute. Help yourself with the appetizers in the living room."

The lovey-dovey couple smiled at each other and nodded at Ted. Clark filled a plate and slipped onto the sofa. Downing two bacon-wrapped chestnuts before Sharon selected an item; she glanced at Clark's heaping plate. Getting the message, he waited for the others to join the group. Ted delivered drinks.

Looking as lovely as ever, Laverne popped out of the bedroom and strolled toward the group. She picked up her Crown Royal and toasted, "Here's to the best of friends."

Clark raised his glass and took a sip. "And here's to the two best looking women in town."

"I'll drink to that," Ted said, taking a gulp of his scotch.

"The appetizers look wonderful," Sharon said. "It must have taken all day."

Laverne gave her an embarrassing glance. "I cheated. I made the caramelized chestnuts and ordered the rest at the deli down the street." She rose and headed for the kitchen.

Clark licked his chops. "The chestnuts are terrific."

Sharon counted the four toothpicks from the bacon wraps on his plate. He slowed down on the nuts and took a sip of gin.

Ted looked at Sharon. "Did Clark tell you about Carlos' performance at our poker party back in November?"

"Geez no. It slipped my mind." Clark laughed so hard he nearly spilled his drink.

"Carlos came out of the bathroom wearing a long dress and red-haired wig with knockers that wouldn't quit," Ted continued. "I thought Father Dom would go berserk when Carlos plopped on his lap and kissed him."

"Yeah," Clark agreed. "The funniest part was the red lipstick prints Carlos left on his face. Alsye laughed so hard he almost fell off his chair. All of us kept pointing at him; Father Dom kept saying, 'What … what?' No one said a thing about the lipstick that was plastered on his face."

Ted talked over Clark, "When Father Dom came out of the bathroom at break time, he was fit to be tied. He chased Carlos around the table and ripped off one of his boobs. Carlos went nuts, like his dignity had been compromised."

"Too bad you didn't take a video," Sharon said.

"I know … it was one of those spontaneous things we'd never be able to recreate."

Laverne popped her head out of the kitchen doorway. "Okay boys, you can fill the water glasses and pour the wine. The Cornish hens are done."

"Cornish hens," Clark exclaimed. "I can hardly wait."

Sharon gave him a questioning look. "Is there anything you don't like to eat?"

Clark frowned. "Hmm … not much."

Sharon sat warm plates in front of the two men. Laverne followed with the other two plates and dimmed the lights.

Ted emptied a bottle of Sauvignon Blanc and gave a toast. The four took their time enjoying the cuisine and conversation. The women talked about med school. Ted touted his new maintenance staff and how well they were doing. Clark said little.

Laverne turned toward Clark. "Anything new at the office?"

He rolled his shoulders. "There's not much I can say … it's a case in progress."

"I've only glanced at the paper. Could you put the pieces together?"

"Sure." Finishing his wine, he walked her through the sequence of events as they had been reported in the media.

"I bet the Mafia is behind all of this," she surmised.

"Why do you say that?"

"It sounds like a TV plot on one of those criminal shows. They probably had the kid under surveillance and something went wrong."

"I think you're right," Sharon nodded and changed the subject. "How would you guys like to come to my place for the Super Bowl? I'll fix a turkey and you fellas can watch the game."

CHAPTER FIFTEEN

Poker on the third of January celebrated the beginning of 1979 for a second time. Renzo had hats, horns, whistles, and treats, courtesy of Wendy. He'd hung crepe paper streamers from the old fan above and loaded the table with goodies — the room was ready for a festival.

He welcomed each guy with a couple of toots on his horn and a big hug, and directed them to the table to pick out their hats, beaded necklace and noisemaker.

Following protocol, Carlos announced, "These are the best New Year's decorations I've ever seen; everything's here but the dropping of the ball at Times Square."

Ted tried to make up for that, picking up a horn and blasting it like a New York fire truck. The blaring noise filled the room until Father Dom good-naturedly waved his arms in the air, cutting him off. "It's time to move on."

While the atmosphere was as festive as could be, the mood was somewhat dampened — Alsye was home with the flu.

"I feel sorry for him," Carlos said. "He has so much going on."

"I don't know how he's able to deal with it — his momma's death, the Mafia raising his fees and the burning of his store — he's had more than his share," Ted bemoaned.

"I'm proud of you, son," Father Dom said to Clark. "It's wonderful that you've taken the time to talk with him."

Clark puffed up. "We've had some good talks, but sometimes I wonder how much I've really done."

"You'd be surprised, Clark." Father Dom bear-hugged him. "I can tell you from my own experience there's nothing better than having a friend who's willing to listen."

"Yeah, he's right," Carlos jumped in. "Nothing better."

Father Dom nodded once more. "Sometimes it's not what you say; it's more about listening and letting him share his feelings and challenges."

"I suppose." Clark paused. "Anything else I can do?"

Father Dom pressed his lips. "Right now I'd say you're doing exactly what he needs — being a friend who he feels comfortable talking with."

Shuffling the cards, Renzo shifted his eyes to Clark. "Anything else you want to say?"

Clark twiddled his fingers then rubbed his hands together. "I-I … I'll pass."

"I thought you and Caroline were a thing," Renzo said.

"Ah … that ended several weeks ago." He stared at his chips, not wanting to say any more.

"Want to talk about it?"

"I think things are best left unsaid."

"Did you screw that young chick who was hitting on you?" Renzo asked.

"That's none of your business," Clark snapped, stood, and walked toward the bathroom.

"Okay, okay." Renzo called after him. "Dealer's choice."

* * *

After a month of extensive work, the task force gathered around the conference table to present their findings. Earl led off. "I found the two blind pigs Dallas visits. He hits them at least once a week. Everyone knows him by his first name; he drops twenties like they're going out of style. I've talked to his favorite prostitutes; each one is ready to sign on the dotted line."

Eddie Grissini shook his head. "We have Dallas dead to rights." He paused for a moment. "Usually I'd say there's a fifty-fifty chance but … this guy has violated every common sense rule there is. He used his credit card to pay for prostitutes, called on his office phone to illegally transfer funds and, of all things, sent checks to drug dealers."

"I can't believe he did all of that."

Eddie shifted in his chair and shook his head. "He must either be the most arrogant SOB in the world or he doesn't know his ass from a hole in the ground. Either way he's a dead duck."

"Sounds like it." Clark deliberated on what he'd heard. "Anything else?"

"The list is a mile long." Eddie breathed in a deep sigh and grinned to his colleagues. "We have at least twenty-five slam-dunk witnesses who'll testify against him — prostitutes and drug dealers —

even his own secretary will come forward. There are over a hundred credit card receipts for illegal activity with his signature on them. We have photos of him in casinos and blind pigs with prominent women, distinguished leaders, and Mafia strong-men. There are bank withdrawals exactly at the time other bills are paid. Do you want to hear more?"

"I have it, loud and clear." Clark nodded and tossed him a curious look. "What's next?"

"With your approval we'll double-check everything with the State Attorney's office. After that, it's up to you."

"You have it," Clark said.

"Assuming the state's attorney is onboard, you need to decide how and when you're going to confront Dallas and the kind of plea bargain you want to propose, or other deal you want to make."

Sitting patiently, Clark glanced at the team members around the table. "I'd like to hear from the rest of you. What do you think?"

Sergeant Weston wasted no time in raising her hand. "We ought to go for the whole enchilada — life, no parole — there's no use letting him off just because he's a rich brat."

"It isn't that he's rich," the wise-old Robinson interjected. "It's because of the legal team the Nash family can bring to the table. We have to be realistic."

Weston threw her hands up in disgust. "There we go again; it's all about the money."

"What's the typical sentence for cases like this?" Clark asked.

Max raised his hand. "Based on the court cases I've seen he's looking at twenty years. If he successfully plea bargains, probably five years of prison time and five years of parole."

"That's all … sounds like a good reason to bargain," Clark said. "What's in it for us?"

"Hmm … not much." Max took his time to reveal the reality of the situation. "Maybe we can pluck off forty or fifty nobodies, but nothing significant will change."

Clark bristled; his mouth turned down. "So we do all of this work and he gets off with five plus five and in six months things are back to normal, like nothing ever happened."

"You got it," Max agreed.

Clark buried his face in his hands; jerking them away, he slammed his fist on the table. "Damn it, no. I want more."

Eyes widened around the table. None of them had seen an outburst like that from Clark. The team members looked at each other — no one spoke a word — it was like they were frozen in place.

Eddie broke the stillness. "We all feel that way Clark, but trying to nail someone higher is almost impossible. It's never happened in Detroit."

Straightening in his chair, Clark raised his voice. "Just because it's never happened is not good enough. There's always a first time!"

"Agreed," Max's face revealed his dismay. "It'd be a huge challenge. The mob would bring in the best lawyers in the country. The federal prosecutor would be overwhelmed."

"I understand all of that," Clark said, and took a long pause. "Max, have you ever seen more compelling evidence?"

The old pro backed off. "Never; we have Dallas cold, dead to rights ... but it's a leap to a Mafia kingpin. We'd have to have direct testimony or a confession."

"What if we catch one off guard?"

Clark's comment caught the group by surprise. Eddie took his time before asking, "Someone in the higher up leadership?"

"Yes, in the leadership council."

Eddie ran his fingers over his forehead and through his thinning hair. "That'd be highly improbable. The higher ups never talk to anyone. Someone lower in the chain talks to guys like Dallas. They just don't screw up."

Clark perked up. "What if we play on Dallas's arrogance?"

Eddie and the rest of them sat quietly, waiting to see where Clark was headed.

He took his time easing into the point. "You can say whatever you want but Dallas Nash is no dummy. He knows the difference between five and twenty years."

"So what's the trade-off?"

"I want someone in the leadership council."

"Christ, Clark," Eddie said out of frustration. "I've said it before ... that's a leap. For the most part we're dealing with lackeys on the street."

Clark hung on like a bulldog. "Fine, I'll settle for a capo who sits on the council."

"A capo?" Eddie's eyes rolled up and down, left and right. "That's not much easier. We'd need documentation, direct testimony. How do you propose we do that?"

Clark ran his fingers over his mouth and jaw. "We go after King Kingston. He's the capo for gambling."

"Kingston?" Eddie howled.

Clark's mind raced through the reports. "How many times did he talk to Dallas?"

Eddie raised his eyebrows then flipped open his file. Leafing through the report, he counted the entries one-by-one and looked up. "Twenty-five."

Getting the answer he wanted, Clark pressed forward. "How many in the last month or so?"

Eddie made another quick scan. "Most of them were in the past two weeks."

"Right! We have a capo doing lackey work. Something is not right."

"You're right." Eddie backed off. "I hadn't picked up on that."

"Here's what I figure is going on." Clark paused; making sure everyone was on board. "Kingston is turning up the heat on Dallas. He's calling — he's *not* following normal protocol. Someone above is pressuring him. A half-million dollar tab is big money even for the Mafia."

"Seems reasonable," Eddie agreed. "But, how do we get Kingston to incriminate himself?"

Clark's grin broadened into a smile, knowing Eddie had fallen into his trap. "We'll have Dallas wear a wire."

"Christ, the whole thing could blow up," Max said.

Weston shook her head. "It's dangerous as hell, they could ..."

"Wait a minute," Lieutenant Sterling interjected. "Dallas is just arrogant enough to try it."

"I agree," patrolman Ralston said. "We ought to consider it."

Ready to make a proposal, Clark slowed, remembering his dad's advice — let the team come up with the solution. "What should we do, Sterling?"

She scooted up to the table. "We'd have to construct five or six questions. Dallas would have to practice them until he had them down cold. If he doesn't come off totally natural or makes one false statement, they'd pick up on it right away."

Eddie reemphasized the point. "If he messes up, he might not make it out alive."

"And the case would go poof," Will Robinson moaned.

Clark stiffened, sensing it was time to take a shot. "That's a chance we need to take. We'll play on his arrogance. He has to be thinking about five years ... in twenty he'll be in his fifties."

"That's not very old to me," Will Robinson joked. "But for someone in their thirties ... it's an eternity. I think we ought to try it."

"I'm with Will on this one," Earl added.

"I agree," Ralston said. "We'll never be this close again."

"Is everyone in?" Clark asked; his eyes moved slowly around the table, extracting a nod from each one. "Sounds like we have lots of work to do."

***

A relentless and unforgiving pounding hammered Clark's head. He turned over and glanced at the blurry numbers on his clock radio. "Who in the hell is calling me at four o'clock in the morning," he mumbled to himself, picked up the receiver and grunted, "Hello."

"Clark, its Nicole."

His brain shifted into high gear. "Yes, what is it?"

"William is dead. Alsye is so distraught I don't know what to do. Can you come over?"

"I'm on my way." Clark hung up, dressed in a flash and raced across town.

Slamming on the brakes in front of Alsye's place, he jumped out of his car and sprinted up the sidewalk. "Alsye, I'm here."

Rocking on the porch swing, Alsye didn't move. He looked as pale as a black man could be. Clark eased onto the swing, placed his arm around Alsye and hugged him tight.

Staring forward as if in a trance, Alsye rocked.

"It'll be okay, Alsye. We'll work this out."

Nicole flew out the door. "Oh thank God you're here. He hasn't moved since Olivia called."

"What happened?"

"I'm not sure. She tried to wake William but he didn't respond. She called an hour ago."

"Do you know anything else?"

"No. I called the police and gave them our address. They took my name and phone number and said they'd get back to me."

"Do you have any kind of a sedative or sleeping pill?"

"Alsye doesn't believe in that kind of stuff. He's very strong willed about things like that."

Clark nodded, recalling his conversation when Alsye had refused any kind of help from his poker buddies. "I know."

Nicole's eyes opened wide. "What should I do?"

Clark smiled softly, trying to provide a soothing effect. "We need to wait until we get the report from the police." He glimpsed at her stressed face and changed the subject. "Want to make some coffee?"

"Sure, of course. I'll be right back."

Clark placed his hands on Alsye's face and turned his head. "Alsye, look at me." His glassy eyes remained unfocused. "You have to be strong — carry the ball." Alsye nodded. "It's like when you were hurt playing football. The team needs you. Nicole needs you. We need you. Do you understand?"

Closing his eyes, Alsye rocked, unresponsive.

"Alsye, open your eyes and look at me."

His eyelids cracked open.

"William is dead. You have to carry the ball. Do you understand?"

Alsye rocked.

Nicole set a tray with two cups and a carafe of coffee on the wicker end table next to Clark. He poured a half cup and held it in front of Alsye. "Nicole made some coffee for you."

Alsye didn't move.

Nicole pushed Clark's hand closer. "Please sweetie, drink this. It's good for you."

Instinctively, he took the cup in his hand, raised it to his lips, took a short sip and handed it back to her. She glanced at Clark, as if asking for his approval. He nodded and rocked on the swing. Nicole sat in the chair across from them, hoping for the best.

A squad car with flashing lights pulled up in front.

Nicole glanced at Clark; her eyes fearful.

A solemn-faced policeman got out and walked up the sidewalk. Nicole stood and ran out to meet him. The officer said something to her. She covered her face and choked up. He gave her a consoling hug and whispered something in her ear.

Nicole took a deep breath, composed herself, and walked slowly up to the porch. She wiped a tear and eased back onto the wicker chair. "Alsye, look at me."

He moved his eyes up and stared blankly at her.

"They're positive William overdosed. They found him with a needle stuck in his arm."

Alsye rocked.

Clark mouthed to Nicole. "Call a doctor. He needs a sedative."

She nodded and went inside.

Alsye rocked.

A short time later — what seemed like an eternity — an old white Ford stopped in front. A short, stocky black man stepped out, bag in hand, and headed for the porch. Nicole ran down the sidewalk to greet him.

The doctor took one look at him and motioned for Clark to help Alsye into the bedroom. Nicole ran ahead, opening the doors, and pulling back the sheets and blankets. Handling him with care, she helped the doctor strip him down to his shorts.

With Clark's support, she eased Alsye into bed and slid a blanket over him.

The doctor pulled her aside and chatted briefly, nodded and gave Alsye a shot.

Within minutes he was asleep.

A second car arrived. Father Dom stepped out and joined the three around the kitchen table. The doctor outlined his instructions and left.

The priest and Nicole talked for the longest time. Clark chimed in occasionally but mostly listened. Nicole's bloodshot eyes looked up at Clark. "Alsye was William's lifelong guardian. This is going to be extremely difficult for him. I know he thinks he failed William."

***

Two weeks later, Clark slid into a booth across from Alsye, noticing his black friend's tired and worn face. Alsye glanced up, barely cracking a grin; he pointed to the saxophone player on the stage. "That guy is really good. Do you know who he is?"

"Wayne Shorter. He's one of the premier saxophonists in the nation. His name is on the marquee."

"Guess I missed that," Alsye mumbled.

Clark gave him a compassionate smile. "Did you get everything worked out in South Carolina?"

Alsye shrugged his shoulders. "As well as could be expected. The funeral home was packed. There was a long line at visitation. Everyone loved William. He was the kindest person in the world."

"Everything else go okay?"

Alsye shook his head. "I wasn't worth diddly squat. It was like my right arm had been cut off. The paper ran a front page story on William. He'd set all kinds of state football records before he blew his knee out in the state championship game. After that everything was different. He started depending on me for everything ... I let him down," Alsye sobbed.

"You can't say that, Alsye." Clark stiffened his shoulders to make the point. "You did everything you possibly could."

"I made a big mistake. I shouldn't have brought him to Detroit. He couldn't handle the pace of things here."

"You're not being fair to yourself, Alsye. As much as you might want to you can't live another person's life. He made his own decisions. Down deep you know that. Blaming yourself for something beyond your control is not fair to you or Nicole."

"Nicole?" Alsye raised an eyebrow. "Why did you mention her?"

"Because Alsye, think about it ... you're placing an enormous burden on her. She's doing double-duty, carrying her grief and yours too. You need to think about her."

Alsye sobered. "I never thought about that. You're right," he said, with renewed vigor.

He stood, as did Clark, and the two men bear hugged. "You're the best friend I've ever had."

They sat down. Clark asked, "How is Nicole doing?"

Alsye's face beamed. "If it hadn't been for her I wouldn't have made it. She did it all. I don't know what I would have done without her."

"You ought to take a few days off so you can spend more time with her."

Alsye stiffened. "Geez Clark, I can't. I have eight stores to run, employee schedules to complete and a payroll to meet. I just can't not appear."

"You could work from home. I'm sure Nicole would be glad to see you around a bit more."

Taken aback, Alsye seemed surprise. "Yeah I guess … I could do that." Alsye's white teeth sparkled for the first time. "You're right about that, man."

"Is everything back to normal at the store? How are the repairs coming along?"

"They're done. We're up and running, like nothing ever happened. Renzo pulled one of his crews from another job and was ripping off the charred siding before the day was over. By the time the painters finished it looked better than before."

"Guess that's what friends are for."

"He was a lifesaver." Staring up at the ceiling, Alsye hesitated and turned to Clark. "I can't say enough about Nicole. She's like the Rock of Gibraltar. I call her Miss CC — calm and cool."

Clark's mind swirled with wishful thinking. "I hope someday I'll meet a woman like her."

"I'm sure you will." Alsye hesitated. "I mentioned to her I was thinking about moving back to South Carolina. Do you know what she said?"

Clark shrugged. "I have no idea."

"'No way,' she announced. 'We're not running away and hiding. Our business is here, our home is here, and our friends are here. We're not leaving.' There's no waffling with her. When she makes a decision, at most, there's a little quiver in her mouth before she takes off, full bore."

"I don't think I'd want to be around then."

"Can't blame you." Alsye paused. "I just lean back and let her go. The other night she was hammering the bigots in South Carolina, said, 'I'd rather have my boys have to fight their way home on the streets in Detroit than to see them be treated as second-class citizens.' She stomped around the kitchen, plopped down in a chair and slammed her hand on the table. 'We're not moving back. I don't want to hear any more of that kind of talk.'"

Clark mused. "Anything we can do to help her?"

Alsye gave him a puzzled look. "I don't know. She doesn't talk much."

"Does she have many friends?"

"Not really. She talks with her sister on the phone once a week but that's about it."

Clark pursed his lips. "How about I ask Carlos and Renzo to ask their wives to give her a call? Maybe the three of them could have lunch."

Alsye raised his head, looking like an anvil had been lifted from his shoulders. "That's a terrific idea. I know she'd be glad to go."

"Good. I'll do it," Clark said, moving on to his last thought. "There's one more thing." Alsye looked receptive. "I'd like to bring the guys up to speed."

A frown crossed Alsye's face. "Hmm … I've never been much for hanging out my laundry so everyone can see it."

Clark came on firmly. "Alsye, I'm not talking about hanging out your laundry. I'm talking about being open with your best friends. Give it a try. If you don't feel comfortable, I'll end it."

CHAPTER SIXTEEN

Frank McHenry, the city's top criminal interrogator, closed the door to his office and motioned for Clark to have a chair. "I'm pleased you could stop by. I was outlining my thoughts for our meeting with Dallas and his lawyer when it dawned on me you might not be up to date on some of our legal strategies."

"I'm glad you did." Clark's face revealed his relief. "I've been wondering how you planned to proceed."

"How much experience have you had in the interrogation room?"

Clark shrugged. "It's been a while … a review of your plans would be good."

Frank smiled. "I thought that might be the case so I'd like to review a few pointers with you."

"Thanks, I feel better already." Clark relaxed and looked more at ease.

Frank slid his chair closer to his desk. "It's important for the two of us to be on the same page — a blink, hesitation, or a questioning look can give away our strategy. His lawyer will be watching our body language, hoping to pick up a sign or a comment that will bolster their case."

"Guess I hadn't thought much about all of that."

"There's no reason you should have." Frank grinned. "Second, with this guy's ego I'm going to take every opportunity I can to pump him up."

"A little of the Army's 'pride-and-ego down' approach, huh?"

"Right, at least you remembered that from the academy. I'll try to put him at ease … maybe we can catch him off guard and he'll say something he shouldn't."

"Do you think that is likely?"

"You never know what he might say. His lawyer will be on guard too." The old pro paused. "Don't forget we can play good cop/bad cop. That said, if you sense I'm going too far, feel free to move in a different direction."

"Hmm, I don't know about that. I might screw up an angle you're pursuing." Clark tilted his head and gave him a questioning look.

"Well, think about it." Frank hesitated, and then said forcefully, "There's no law or regulation forcing us to tell him the truth — deception is on our side. He'll be trying to hide the truth … we can lie about the facts or exaggerate the strength of our case. We can make misleading statements, so don't be surprised if I say something we haven't talked about. And remember Clark, this is heavy-duty stuff — a no holds-barred contest."

***

Clark followed Frank into the stark interrogation room that looked like most of the rest — four plain walls, an observation glass behind one, and a table with four straight-back unpadded chairs in the middle.

The two acknowledged their adversaries and sat down across from them, Frank facing Dallas while Clark sat across from the lawyer.

Frank opened up as planned, speaking in general terms about the young boy's death and the sympathy he had for Dallas and his family. He mentioned the contributions his family had made to the community and expressed his hope the matter could be concluded in an amicable way.

Dallas leaned back in his chair, looking like Mr. Cool.

His lawyer interceded. "Enough of the bullshit, let's get on to the reason why we're here."

Strike one.

Frank laid out the issues, specifically referencing the twenty-five witnesses who had agreed to testify against Dallas. The lawyer burst into laughter. "That's all you have … a bunch of prostitutes and operators who'll receive a deal from you if they take the witness stand, and a disgruntled secretary. Let's go Dallas." He stood. "These guys are wasting our time."

Strike two.

"Hold on," Frank said in a level tone. "We've yet to begin."

The lawyer slithered back into his chair.

Frank tossed a dozen pictures of Dallas onto the table, showing him embracing distinguished men and kissing prominent women, most of them married to someone else. "How about these photos?"

"Is this a divorce proceeding?" the pro smirked. "You've got a good-looking rich man who enjoys having a good time. It may be a problem for the others. For us, who cares?"

Strike three, one out.

Reaching down in his briefcase, Frank pulled out a handful of papers.

"If that's all you have we're out of here." The defense attorney pushed his chair back. "I still have time for an afternoon martini."

The interrogator raised his hand. "Let's try these on for size." Frank tossed two bundles of paper in front of Dallas.

The lawyer reached over and picked up a stack. "Credit card receipts, so what?"

"Credit card statements signed by Dallas, payable to prostitutes, drug dealers, and who knows who else."

The lawyer read two or three more and slapped them down on the table. He turned and whispered something in his client's ear.

Dallas jerked away and shook his head.

"Got anything else?" the silver-haired lawyer asked.

A hit!

"While you're thinking about it, what about the bank printout showing all of the withdrawals and checks for $9,500 made out to lots of people, including yourself and … many others who'd not like to see their names listed in an ongoing racketeering investigation?"

The lawyer's fist hit the table. "Five minutes with my client."

Another hit, two on, one out.

"Of course." The good guys stood and sauntered out of the room.

Clark couldn't restrain himself. "You nailed him on that one."

"Don't get too excited. The old guy is a wizard; you never know what he may have up his sleeve."

Frank and Clark stepped around the corner and gazed through the one-way glass. "What do you think is going on?" Clark asked.

"Dallas is shaking his head violently. I'd say the lawyer is suggesting a plea bargain."

Looking in, Clark paused. "Dallas just shoved him in the chest and shouted something."

"I can't read lips … it looked like screw you, you're fired," Frank said.

Clark's eyes bulged out with surprise. "Look, the lawyer shoved him back."

"You're right," Frank said. "It looks like he just said, 'You can't fire me. I work for your father.'"

Dallas slumped down in the chair.

"His body language says it all just like you said."

"Right," Frank said. "He's forcing him to agree to a plea bargain."

"Great, we win."

Frank looked over at his trainee. "Not really."

"Why? He's going to prison."

"Right, and tomorrow it'll be business as usual. Prostitutes will be turning tricks. Bookies will be parlaying daily doubles. Blind pigs will open at two and the Mafia will be raking it in."

A sober expression clouded Clark's face. "That's it?"

Frank shook his head, pessimism crossed his face. "We squeezed a pimple and drained the pus; life goes on."

"Frank, I told you before I wanted more." Clark's voice cracked, his face reddened.

"More?" Frank laughed. "We'll be able to round up fifty or so lackeys and put them away."

"Yeah, I know, and in six months everything will be back to normal. That's not good enough," Clark said with renewed resolve. "I want to nab someone in the Partnership."

"No one has ever done that."

"Shit Frank, we have a shot."

"A shot … a shot in the dark."

"No … hear me out."

Frank stepped back and stared with a jaundiced eye. "Okay … let's hear what's on your mind."

Clark spoke with his father's confidence. "Dallas and King Kingston have been talking on the phone two or three times a week since the death of Nash's son. King is on the leadership council. I want him."

"How do you know all of that?"

"Trust me, I know. Our team thinks the Mafia is turning up the heat. Dallas owes them at least half a million dollars, maybe more. I think we should agree to their plea if Dallas will wear a wire to a meeting with Kingston."

"That'll never happen, Clark." Frank gave him a courtesy smile. "It's all uphill."

"Frank," Clark pleaded. "We have nothing to lose; we have to keep playing on his arrogance. If he wants to play ball, I'll agree to five years in prison plus five years' parole. That has to look a helleva lot better to him than twenty years in prison. So, what do you say?"

Frank rubbed his jaw for the longest time. "Okay, here's the plan — we'll play good cop/bad cop. When they propose the deal, I'll play it cool, hem-and-haw, say 'well maybe' and then I'll turn to you. You can go berserk, throw a tantrum, toss your arms in the air — do whatever you want."

With a plan in mind, Clark's demeanor bounded back. "Fair enough."

The two men turned their attention to the one-way mirror and watched Dallas and his lawyer continue to argue.

Without warning Dallas' shoulders drooped; his head slumped.

"Dallas agreed." Frank jabbed Clark in the side.

The lawyer waved them in.

The two lawmen walked unabashedly into the room and took their chairs.

The lawyer fiddled with his pen before looking up at them. "Five plus five."

Frank rubbed his jaw. "Hmm, I don't know."

"You don't know what I mean?" The lawyer shouted. "That's standard procedure. What's the problem?"

Frank turned to Clark. "What do you think?"

Not looking up, Clark shook his head slowly and gazed into the eyes of the lawyer. "You're crazy as hell. We have Dallas dead to rights — twenty years — no deal!"

"You'll never get twenty."

"Fine." Clark threw his palms in the air. "We'll let the judge decide that."

The old lawyer leaned back as his eyes zeroed in on Clark; he didn't say a word.

Sitting motionless, Clark stared without a blink.

Trying to read him, the crafty lawyer rubbed his jaw and glanced away. Nodding to himself, he said, "Okay, let's hear your proposal."

"We want King Kingston," Clark responded without hesitation.

"Kingston? You're the one who's nuts."

Trying to whisper something in the lawyer's ear, Dallas leaned closer. The pro negotiator pushed him away. Dallas nudged him again. The lawyer glanced at him with disdain. "Five minutes."

Frank and Clark stood, walked out the door and closed it behind them.

Rushing to the window, Clark peered in. "What do you think?"

"I think maybe, just maybe, you might have pulled it off."

The two watched a silent shouting match through the window. Both men standing nose to nose, waving their arms wildly, their faces red as beets. Dallas shoved the lawyer and the two broke into a pushing match. The lawyer backed off and tried to calm his client. Dallas didn't stop; he continued to bellow at the attorney. The donnybrook went on for five or six minutes; suddenly the lawyer stopped and turned toward the mirror.

Flailing his arms over his head, he motioned the cops in.

Frank and Clark hurried into the room and slipped onto their chairs as if they'd seen nothing.

The old lawyer took a deep breath and sighed. "What do you want him to do?"

Holding back his enthusiasm, Clark spoke slowly and deliberately. "We want Dallas to wear a wire to a meeting with King Kingston."

"A wire!" The lawyer slammed his hand on the table. "No way…"

"I'll do it," Dallas spouted.

Shaking his head, the attorney clasped his hands over his face.

"What do you want me to do?" Dallas asked, with a level of confidence unseen before.

"We want you to ask Kingston a few incriminating questions."

"That's it?"

"Yes," Frank said. "We'll walk you through several practice sessions and when you're ready … you can set up the meeting."

"Piece of cake," the arrogant playboy said. "I'm ready right now."

***

Super Bowl Sunday started out like a traditional Thanksgiving feast. Sharon had gone all out — turkey, sweet potatoes, cranberries, green beans, wilted lettuce salad, and all of the fixings. By mid-afternoon, the guys had stuffed themselves and were dead to the world.

The women talked over a bottle of Sauvignon Blanc at the dinette table.

Staring at Sharon, Laverne took a long sip. "Don't you think it's crazy?" The eyes of the two MDs connected in wonderment. "The two of us take a cruise with two local guys and *bingo*."

"Huh." Sharon grinned. "I think about that a lot ... how scared I was at first, and now I can't wait to get him in bed."

"Is he good?"

"Good? You wouldn't believe it. Sometimes I wet my pants just thinking about him." Sharon cracked a smile. "How's Midnight doing?"

Laverne shook her head. "At first I had to gulp when ..." She took a sip. "Now he's like silk."

Sharon emptied the bottle in Laverne's glass and opened another. Filling hers to the brim, she set the bottle in front of Laverne and paused. "Sorry, I got carried away thinking about banging Clark."

"You better hope the game doesn't go into overtime."

"I'm fixing turkey sandwiches for pre-game, and warming up the pecan pie at halftime. When the game is over you've got five minutes to get out of here. Deal?"

"If you're that horny we can leave at halftime."

"It won't matter; he'll watch Roger Staubach and the Dallas Cowboys until the very end."

***

The plea bargaining session had been a lifetime high; yet, Clark knew that was a conversation for another day. His strategy for February's poker party was to play it cool, say nothing about work. That worked well until the bewitching hour when Father Dom turned to him. "Clark, you've been unusually quiet, anything new with you?"

He knew that question was coming sooner or later. Still he stammered, "Ah, not much."

"Not much?" Father probed. "You're in an investigation on a big-time case and you can't say a word?"

Knowing he had to respond to Father Dom, a finger nervously parted his crop of hair. "We may have a break in the case. I'd like to tell you more, but I can't."

The priest patted him on the shoulder. "That's fine my boy. There are times when all of us have a heavy burden to carry." Looking around the table, he noticed Ted's curious expression. "Do you have something you'd like to add?"

Ted hesitated and tossed the group a Cheshire cat smile. "Ah, I've hired two handymen to handle the maintenance in four of my buildings. I'm only doing one."

"Are you providing other services?" Father Dom inquired.

"I'm only doing one," he jested. "I knocked a wall out in Laverne's apartment and combined it with the one next door." He stopped cold.

"Is there more?" Father Dom questioned.

Ted looked around the table as if uncomfortable to say more.

Renzo's eyes popped. "Well?"

Ted tried to conceal his embarrassment. "I moved in with her two weeks ago."

"Good for you," someone called out.

"Here, here," the group agreed in unison.

Ted sat patiently, waiting to change the subject. "Maybe there's something you'd like to tell the group," he said, looking pointedly at Clark.

Clark frowned. "Ted, you said you wouldn't say anything until I got back."

"Who me?" Ted pointed to himself. "Did I say anything?"

All eyes switched to Clark.

He finger-tapped the table. "What am I supposed to say?"

"Maybe you ought to share your travel plans."

Carlos' brown eyes doubled in size. "You going somewhere?"

"Yeah, is something happening?" Father Dom asked.

Clark hemmed and hawed. "Sharon and I are going to Aruba."

"Aruba?" Father questioned. "What's this all about?"

"It's not about anything," Clark said defensively. "We're going there the first week in April. Both of us have a little time off coming."

Father Dom zipped his lips. "Sorry, I asked."

Feeling guilty, Clark plea bargained. "Okay, things between us seem to be working out. Neither of us has been there so we thought it'd be a new experience."

"A new experience?" Renzo chuckled. "I can't imagine that."

CHAPTER SEVENTEEN

The guys gathered around a circular booth in a far corner of the Sax Club. Two pitchers of beer sat on the table by the time Ted Moomau, the last one of the group, arrived. Clark got right to the point. "Thanks for coming early tonight. As I mentioned on the phone Alsye has been under tremendous stress. The death of his brother, on top of his momma's passing and the Mafia hitting his store was more than he can handle."

"I understand that," Carlos interjected. "If a guy was ready to pull a gun on me I'd be like Jell-O."

"William's death was extremely traumatic for him," Father Dom pointed out. "Nicole told me the two of them had been like two peas in a pod their whole lives. For some reason, everything changed and William took a backseat."

"I never understood that," Clark confessed. "William was a state football record holder when he blew out his knee. With his stature you would have thought he'd be on his way."

"You never know how a person will react to adversity." Father Dom eased closer to the table. "Football was his life; it gave him identity. When that was gone he felt empty, like there was nothing left for him."

"He had so much to be proud of; it's puzzling that he didn't pick up the pieces and move on."

"Maybe so, but everyone is different. He went into a shell and Alsye became his protector."

"Wow … that in itself is a heavy burden to carry," Ted lamented.

"And worse yet, when William died Alsye assumed a huge sense of guilt," Father Dom said. "For whatever reason he felt like he had let William down."

Clark's face showed his concern. "When I first talked with Alsye, he didn't even want anyone else to know; he wanted to keep everything inside."

"That's not unusual," the priest reminded them.

"Why?" Renzo asked. "We've all been good buddies for years."

"Why is always the toughest question," the wise old man said. "Part of it can be explained by his early life. Alsye is old school; he bootstrapped himself through life and when all of this happened he felt he had failed."

"Failed, shit!" Ted exclaimed. "Eight stores. He's doing better than any of us."

"You're right, Carlos, but for Alsye that's not good enough. He expects more of himself; he is always striving to be the best."

"You're right. He never settles for second place," Renzo agreed and turned to Clark. "So how can we help him out?"

"I'm not sure." Clark admitted. "That's why I asked you all to come early. I hoped the five of us might come up with an idea or two."

"I'm glad you did," Father Dom said. "We can all learn from others. The worst thing for any of us is to close down and keep our problems locked inside."

"Maybe we should set aside some time at the beginning of each poker session to talk," Ted thought out loud. "We could start at six thirty. That'd give us some time to become closer."

"I like that," Father Dom agreed. "If one of us opens up it'll be easier for the next one."

"We ought to give it a try," Renzo said. "This month it may be Alsye who talks most of the time. Next time, it could be Ted and even Father Dom might have something to confess some time."

The group let out a hoot.

Father Dom looked up sheepishly as a sly smile emerged. "We all have times when someone else's voice should be heard."

***

Clark and Sharon walked hand-in-hand through security at Aeropuerto International Reina Beatrix in Oranjestad, Aruba, and headed for baggage claim. After going through immigration, they picked up their luggage, grabbed a taxi and headed for the Marriott. Clark squeezed her hand as they zoomed past the luxurious hotels; they sat quietly in awe, taking in the tropical sites.

Arriving at their destination, Clark handed the bellman a ten and continued to registration. He signed in and within minutes the two were on the elevator to their room.

Stopping in front of the door, Clark kissed her on the cheek. She pulled him tight and gazed up at him; her eyes revealed more than words could say. "I'm so excited … a whole week with you. I can't imagine anything better."

He smiled and raised an eyebrow. "Mmm … this is sounding better all the time."

He unlocked the door and motioned her ahead. Stepping past him, her eyes opened wide in amazement. "Oh Clark, it's wonderful," she exclaimed, running for the sliders and shoving one open — a warm, gentle sea breeze floated in — she took a deep breath and stepped outside. "My God, I've never felt so free." Mesmerized by the tropical breeze, she turned toward him and for the first time said, "I love you."

***

"Want a drink?" Clark asked, after frolicking all morning.

"Sounds wonderful."

The two slipped on their casual wear and headed for the elevator. Reaching the main floor, Clark led the way toward the lobby bar. "Want to sit at the bar or a table?"

"Let's do the bar; I haven't done that in ages."

Clark pointed at several empty stools near the end of the contemporary, half-circle shaped bar. He pecked her on the cheek. "What kind of drink do you want?"

"A Miami Vice; it's half strawberry daiquiri and half piña colada."

The barmaid placed a bowl of mixed nuts in front of them. "Whataya have?"

"Two Miami Vices," he said.

"It's happy hour — two for one."

"We'll go for it," Sharon popped out.

The two lingered at the bar over their second drink then took a long walk on the beach. By the time they returned to the hotel, both were hot and sweaty. She pushed the elevator button and once inside, nailed him with a wet kiss.

Clark raised his eyebrows and as soon as the door opened, hustled down the hallway. Sharon caught up and wrapped her arms around him. He laughed. "Give me a chance to unlock the door."

She stepped back until he cracked open the door then shoved him aside, pulling off her blouse, and purred, "Want to take a shower?"

Clark's eyes widened. "Sounds like another first," he said gleefully.

"I was thinking the same thing," she said. Stripping naked, she eased into the luxurious oversized shower. Clark slid in behind her and closed the glass door.

"God, this hot water feels good," she said. "Would you wash my back?"

He couldn't think of anything he'd rather do. "Of course."

Grabbing a bar of soap, Clark lathered the sponge and gently soaped her shoulders and back. She seemed to melt into his hands — her body moved ever so slightly with his touch. His desires shot up — his pony ready to ride.

Continuing to lather her back, he slid his fingers slowly around her shoulder blades then down her vertebra. "That's so relaxing. I don't know when I've felt better."

Just wait ... I've just begun. He placed his hands on her waist and headed south, caressing her hips and pelvic area. She took a deep, calming breath as if anticipating what he had in mind.

"Step closer to the showerhead and put your hands on the wall."

She did so as hot water streamed down her back — his hands caressing her — her body moving in concert with his touch.

***

The two lovebirds munched on a room service breakfast, then headed for the beach. Pristine sand extended in both directions as far as they could see; crystal turquoise water lapped the shoreline. A cooling trade wind breeze gently ruffled Sharon's hair.

"This is like a dream come true," he said, admiring her beach look.

"I can't believe I'm here with you." She looked up into his eyes. "I love you, Clark."

He held her tight. "You're the best."

The rest of the week followed a similar pattern — late breakfast on the patio, sunbathing, lunch, afternoon delight; then snorkeling, kite surfing, parasailing or enjoying one of the other island activities.

A relaxing, extended dinner at a fancy restaurant set the mood, and the two were back in the bedroom again. Later in the evenings, Clark watched Sharon shoot craps at the Stellaris Casino. *How lucky can a guy be? She's the most gorgeous woman here. She has everything — brains, body, good looks ... God, I love her. Lucky me.* He laughed to himself, while she raked in chips.

That was only the half of it. Back in the room, each night was a different experience — she tied him to the bedpost, seduced him on a chair — and when he thought she'd do it again, she was coy and shy, letting him take her. Not once, but again and again.

Lying under her their last night in the island paradise, Clark gasped for one last time, his exhausted body unable to respond again. She slid off him with a grin. "You said you wanted this to be a memorable experience."

"Memorable?" He laughed. "My mind is a blur."

"I love you, Clark Phillips," she said softly, snuggling close and dozing off.

***

Nicole sat down at a table for four with Rosa Maria and Wendy. "I want to thank the two of you for inviting me to lunch. I don't know the last time I met with one of my girlfriends."

"Me too," Rosa Maria, the shyer one in the group said. "I can't wait to meet Laverne."

"Looks like that won't be long." Wendy pointed to the tall blonde headed their way.

The three stood, introduced themselves, and settled into the comfy chairs.

"I don't know when I was last in a Saks Fifth Avenue," Laverne said.

"It's my first time," Nicole said, her eyes surveying the glitzy surroundings.

"My first time too," Rosa Maria admitted.

"I'm having a glass of wine," Wendy said.

Nicole seemed taken back. "Wine for lunch ... I've never done that."

"Well, this is our first time together; it's a good time to start."

The waitress appeared. "May I get you ladies something to drink?"

"Yes," Nicole ventured. "I'll have a glass of Sauvignon Blanc."

The others rolled their eyes toward her, heads nodding. "Make it four," Laverne said.

The waitress returned in no time, splitting the bottle evenly among the glasses. After a couple of sips the women were engaged in conversation, giggling and chatting enthusiastically. Rosa Maria talked about her two children, the oldest in kindergarten. Wendy shared what was to come, based on her experiences with three kids: seven, nine and ten. Laverne chimed in with some new research on raising children. Nicole listened intently and shared the latest happenings with J. J. and J. D. Each bite of their lunches seemed to melt into conversation, and before long, you'd have thought they were old friends at a class reunion. Their talk soon turned to their men.

Nicole kicked it off. "We're all so lucky to have our guys. Each one is hardworking and goal-oriented. Who could ask for anything more?"

"And they're working all day. I'm so proud Carlos is selling cars, and not sleeping around."

The others nodded.

"I bet we couldn't find many women having lunch today who could say as much," Laverne said.

***

Sharon tossed a pizza in the oven, unfolded two TV trays and placed them in front of the sofa. Clark surfed the movie channels, giving her the choices as she bustled around, and clicked on her selection. By the time she'd cut the pizza, he'd opened a couple of beers and slipped off his shoes.

Sharon laughed and giggled through the love story and snuggled closer to him. Clark opened two more Stroh's and the two chatted into the night, as had become a common practice over the past few months.

"Do you know how many times you've stayed overnight this month?"

Clark shrugged his shoulders like an embarrassed teenager.

"Don't give me that puppy-dog look," she said. "You've been here twelve nights and there are still three days to go."

"Maybe we should shoot for fifteen." He laughed.

"I figured, you'd say that." She hesitated and looked him in the eye. "All of my family goes home to the farm for Easter. It's a big deal for us. Would you like to come with me this year?"

Clark paused, not knowing how to respond. *Seeing her on a regular basis and sleeping with her for a week is one thing, but meeting her parents ... hmm, that's a bigger step than I'm ready to take.* "Ah, I can't. My folks don't have anyone else. If I'm not there they'll be alone."

"Sure, I understand. You have to be with them."

Clark snuggled his head on her shoulder, wondering if she really meant that. *She's the nicest woman I've ever known but meeting her parents ... that's more than a big step; it's a leap.*

***

Clark picked up a bowl of peach cobbler sitting on the kitchen counter. "Hey mom, is it okay if I heat up the cobbler?"

"Sure, go ahead," she called from the living room.

He warmed the bowl in her new microwave oven, added a scoop of vanilla ice cream and headed for the other room. Seeing his mother reading a book in her favorite French Provincial chair, he eased onto the couch next to her and asked, "What are you reading?"

Sitting upright with her nose in the book, she responded slowly, "*The Thorn Birds.* It's a wonderful story ... I can hardly put it down."

Clark tossed her a bewildered look. "What's it about?"

She sighed, put her marker in the book and placed the novel on her lap. "It's about a family in Australia; a young woman and her love for a priest, and his conflict between love for her and responsibilities to the Church." She took a deep breath and turned toward him. "It's very thought provoking; it could have many meanings — deep love for someone, passionate commitment for something, dedication and drive — I just love it."

"Sounds interesting." He looked toward the back. "Is dad out back?"

"Out back?" she repeated. "He's been waiting for you since six. I think he's on his second cigar."

"Guess I better get going." Clark rose and kissed her on the cheek. "Talk to you later." She grinned, picked up the book and buried her head.

Clark set his dirty plate in the sink, turned toward the screened-in porch and slid open the door. "How's the Corona tonight?" he asked, knowing the response that would be forthcoming.

"Perfect … nothing better." Lewis stuffed his stogie in the ashtray and nodded to *the* chair – where his son had sat for their talks since both of them could remember.

Getting the message, Clark took his time settling in, knowing his father was anxious to hear the latest. He kicked off his shoes and leaned back. "How have you been, dad?" he asked, letting his dad stew.

"C'mon, let's hear it. What's happening?" Lewis said impatiently.

Clark smiled to himself; for once he had the upper hand. "The FBI is snowed under so we're taking the lead on sniffing out 'the game.'"

Lewis wrinkled his eyebrows. "I've heard rumblings about that for several years."

"I'm really excited about the opportunity. I met with Will Robinson's top informant … he's digging into it already."

"It'd be something if you could pull that off." His dad's eyes sparkled with pride. "Anything you can report?"

"Not on that, but I heard a great story an FBI agent told me over lunch. It happened about the time Jimmy Hoffa came up missing." Clark ran his fingers through his hair.

"C'mon, get on with the story."

"The FBI had a bug in a coffee shop on Saint Antoine Street in Greektown. Everyone up to the White House was interested in what they might hear."

"I think I heard something about that … tell me more."

"Dominic 'Fats' Corrado is the guy who holds court there with his cronies. Everyone figured they'd all be talking about Hoffa. The techies had placed the bug in the electrical receptacle behind the fridge."

"That's kind of an odd place. Would it pick up the conversations from there?"

"The new equipment can pick up most any sound. Besides, the battery operated ones wouldn't last long enough, and there wasn't another power source in the meeting area." Clark grinned, knowing what was coming. "Here's the best part. The room fills up and the guys start opening the refrigerator door — it kicked on and guess what … the agents couldn't hear a thing!"

"Ah, ha, ha … that's pretty funny." Lewis about choked. "We have the most sophisticated equipment in the world and the damn refrigerator drowns out the conversations."

"Wait, there's more." Clark wiped off a smile and continued to explain. "The next night the tech agents went back in and disabled the compressor, figuring that'd buy a day or two so they could collect good information."

"So what happened?"

"Someone must have noticed the fridge wasn't working in the early morning, so by the time the guys started pouring in they had installed a new refrigerator."

"Isn't that something?" Lewis mused. "It's one more example of how they react."

"You're right, but let me tell you about our guys … the FBI is far more sophisticated than I realized. They have specialists for everything. Whatever is needed they fly in a guy with special skills from Washington; they do everything from unlocking doors to planting bugs and conducting surveillances."

"That must cost them a bundle."

"Not really. The field agents here only need those skills once in a while so it makes sense to bring them in. That way they focus full time on their investigations and the tech agents are brought in to do their thing."

"Makes sense when you put it that way."

"You should see the kind of information their surveillance teams collect. They know everything — when the postman will deliver the mail, when Fat's Corrado comes and goes, when the cleaning people come in — it's amazing how many more details they collect than we do."

"I guess that's why they are the best," dad said, his frustration showing.

"One more point." Lewis rolled his eyes up. "They even have a couple of plainclothesmen in a car parked down the street, so if some cops come snooping by, they take off squealing down the street … and lead them away."

"Why'd they do that?" Dad's lips pursed. "I thought we were all on the same team."

"We are, but sting operations are very secretive and lots of cops talk too much; they'd spill the beans and blow the entire operation."

His old man smiled. "Guess that's something we've talked about."

CHAPTER EIGHTEEN

Clark sat in a small office in the McNamara building, just down the hallway from their conference room. Nervously waiting in anticipation, he doodled on a yellow pad, counting the seconds and minutes. At eight forty-five, he couldn't delay any longer. He pulled open the center desk drawer and grabbed the white envelope.

Flipping through the Ben Franklins aligned in a perfect row, he closed the flap, jumped up, and tucked it into the inside pocket of his black leather winter jacket. He flew down the corridor, stepped into the elevator and hit number one.

In the lobby, Clark took in a deep breath and stepped onto Michigan Avenue — a penetrating chill sliced into him — he pulled his zipper to his neck and marched east.

Turning onto Washington Boulevard, a blustery twenty-five mile an hour north wind blasted his face, shoving him against the building to his left. He lowered his head and trudged up the Boulevard to the Cadillac Hotel. Stepping inside, he paused for a moment, trying to thaw his bones. He unzipped his jacket and rubbed his hands over his tingling cold ears.

Opening the door of the hotel's coffee shop, he saw the top of a familiar tan bald head in the booth tucked away in back. Powering himself that way, he glanced at the steaming mug of coffee that waited across from Luis, and extended his hand. "How are you doing?"

Luis grabbed his hand and, looking up at Clark's rosy cheeks and red ears, the old man smiled. "Much better than you."

Clark grinned and cupped his hands over his ears. "Damn, it's cold out there."

"Got down to nineteen last night. We're supposed to have three or four inches of the white stuff tonight. Once we're done, I'm out of here, going home to curl up with a bottle of Jack Daniels."

"Sounds good to me."

The waitress placed a plate with two sweet rolls in front of each of the men.

"Have to keep up my strength," the pork-bellied gentleman said, grabbing one and shoving a chunk in his mouth.

Clark sliced off a piece and looked Luis in the eye. "What do you have for me?"

Luis took a long sip and straightened his shoulders. "What do *you* have for *me*?"

Clark grinned and pulled the envelope from his pocket, sliding it halfway across the table.

Luis reached for it.

Clark slapped his hand on top of it.

The Puerto Rican looked up and grinned. He pulled a piece of paper from his pocket and put it next to the envelope.

Their eyes connected; both understood the game. Clark raised his hand and pushed the payoff toward Luis' stomach. He grabbed the envelope, folded it and slipped it in his pocket.

"Aren't you going to count it?"

Luis gave him a subtle smile. "Just like poker you never count your chips until the game is over." He grabbed another bite. "Besides, you're the most trustworthy person I've dealt with in the last three months."

Clark nodded, picked up the scrap of paper and folded back the crease. Staring at the info, a deep furrow dug into his forehead. "Two addresses ... what's the deal?"

Luis' face glowed. "I figured you'd need both of them." He paused, acting like he knew he'd piqued Clark's interest, and stared off into space.

Clark shrugged his shoulders, still contemplating, and said, "Okay, I give up. Why do I need two addresses?"

The old man jammed the rest of the sweet roll into his mouth and chewed. Clark knew he had to play the waiting game — the ball was in Luis' court — he finished the sweet roll, wiped his lips, downed the dregs, and called for the waitress. She hustled over and filled both mugs before disappearing again. "The top address on Elmira Street is the place."

"*The game*, I assume," Clark confirmed with a gentle smile.

"Yep." Luis gave Clark a sly grin. "There's a dice game in the basement run by Freddie Salem. It's big time ... connected high up in the Mafia. They finance it and bring high rollers in from the Midwest and East Coast — Chicago, Pittsburgh, Philly, New York, Atlantic

City and Boston — they're all here." He paused, knowing he had Clark's attention. "That's only half of it ... most of the local guys stop there too ... from Jake Nicolette on down."

"Wow." Clark scratched his head. "What's the other address for?"

Luis' routine started again — shoved in half a sweet roll, munched on it, and washed it down with another slug. "It's the house across the street. I figured you'd need a place to set up your surveillance team and equipment. I've talked to the old lady there; she's on board."

On board tossed in Clark's mind. He took a long sip, putting the pieces together. The cash register rang loud and clear. "How much will that cost?"

"Thought you'd never ask." Luis seized a deep breath and sighed. "A grand a month. You pay me up front and I take care of them ... no hassle for you."

"And you take your cut off the top?"

"Absolutely." Luis stared as if saying *what did you expect?* "A guy has to make a living."

Clark let out a long breath. "When do we start?"

"Whenever you want ... let Will know when you have the court order to plant the bugs. We'll meet. You hand me a grand and the place is yours for a month. If you need more time, let me know and I'll arrange for another month."

Clark nodded and moved on to the next stage. "How are we going to get our people and equipment in?"

"That's easy." Luis gloated. "There's an alley behind. You can unload your stuff in the garage and bring things in through the back door — simple as eating apple pie."

"Sounds like a plan."

"Tell Will when you're ready."

Clark nodded, slipped out of the booth, zipped up his jacket, and headed for the door. A gale pushed him down Washington Boulevard and within minutes he was staring at the city map plastered on the wall of the conference room. His fingers pointed to the legend and followed the quadrants to Elmira Street. *Up on the north side.* Making a mental note of its location, he turned and headed for the parking garage.

Within minutes he was in his Mustang headed north on Washington Boulevard. He took a couple of side streets, turned onto

Elmira, three blocks from the address, and pulled over to the curb. Waiting for some traffic to serve as cover, he saw a slow moving van approaching from the rear, the driver obviously looking for a location to unload his furniture.

Clark waited for the van to pass then pulled in behind — perfect — one block to go. Watching the house numbers, he spotted the place on the left just ahead — nothing special — it looked like all of the other homes on the street. A small porch covered the front, three white half-post supports with a brick base below — 1940s vintage.

Getting closer, Clark glanced to the right, where Luis had arranged for surveillance. Another cookie-cutter house.

**

A black car slowed and came to a stop. "We're here," the thug sitting next to Dallas said as he pulled the tightly bound mask from Dallas's face.

Another henchman opened the back door and jerked him out of the car.

Dallas rubbed his eyes trying to adjust to the dimly lit alley. *We must be in some kind of a warehouse district. Everything smells grubby ... filthy.*

The lackey shoved Dallas toward a door with a small light bulb over it. "Straighten up. You're going to meet the boss."

Dallas pulled his shoulders back; his senses went into full operation as he marched arm and arm with the guy. The door opened and two others grabbed Dallas, muscling him down a long dimly lit corridor. Coming to the end, one of the guys opened the door and pointed toward the chair in the middle of the room. He pushed Dallas that way; stumbling, Dallas plopped down on a rickety old chair.

Another guy grabbed his arms, handcuffed his hands behind the chair, and checked them twice before he turned away and walked out.

Dallas looked around the stark dingy room — in front of him was a table with a pad of paper on one side, and three chairs on the other side. He noticed what he thought was a peephole on the far wall. Sitting quietly like Frank McHenry had advised him, he took a deep breath. *They'll wait five or ten minutes, trying to raise your anxiety. Relax as much as you can.* Dallas smiled to himself. *The game is about to begin. My resolve is on — I'm ready to play.*

The door opened, casting a beam of light against exposed cracks on the walls. Three men walked in. Dallas knew by their dress the medium-framed man at the end was King Kingston. The two thugs with him pulled out the chairs on the side, leaving the one across the table from Dallas vacant.

King walked around behind Dallas as if inspecting every hair on his head, and eased down on the middle chair. He smirked, staring at him for the longest time. "So, you're Dallas Nash," he said with disdain and obvious contempt.

Dallas nodded. "A pleasure to meet you, Mr. Kingston."

The brown haired man broke a partial grin. "At least you learned decent manners."

Dallas gawped, not wanting to say a wrong word that might set off an alarm or offend him.

The man ogled Dallas, his right hand on his jaw, rubbing his lips; his piercing eyes penetrating his skull. "So why is it so important for us to talk?"

Dallas took his time to respond. "You've been calling me on a regular basis asking me when I was going to pay up. The last two or three calls didn't seem very nice; in fact, I took them as outright threats."

"Threats … that's an interesting word. Just because you owe us over half a million dollars and have not paid us one red cent in months, you think my calls sound like threats. What kind of a businessman are you? You buy new sports cars, fly around the world, and purchase your wife a mink coat; yet you can't pay us. Hell yes, I'm tired of playing second fiddle."

"That's the reason I wanted to talk."

"You want to talk. Is that supposed to make me feel good?"

Dallas stared without a blink, didn't say a word.

"Cat got your tongue? Maybe Tony should loosen you up."

Dallas glanced to the right, the big guy tapping a blackjack on his palm. "I want to set up a plan to pay off my debt."

"Huh … and when will I see the cash?"

"There's fifty grand in my rear pocket. Take the handcuffs off and I'll hand it to you."

Looking with a curious eye, King cocked his head to the right and to the left, and nodded to Tony. "Take off the cuffs."

The thug got up, took his time pulling a key from his pocket and walked slowly behind Dallas. He grudgingly unlocked the cuffs.

Dallas rubbed his wrists, reached in his pocket, and threw a clip of Cleveland's on the table. "Want to count it?"

"I'm sure there's fifty." King fingered his five o'clock shadow. "So what's the plan?"

"I'll pay you in installments and have the debt paid in full by November."

"What's with November?"

"Over the next six months I'll be receiving a portion of my inheritance. If I know the total amount I owe, I can set up a regular payment plan."

"What's that mean?"

"Regular … cash on the barrelhead every two months."

"How much?"

"I can't tell you until you lay it out. How much is my gambling debt? What do I owe for drugs? For the women?"

King pursed his lips. "It's five hundred and ten thousand in gambling losses, a hundred and eighty grand for drugs and seventy thousand for the women. By my calculation that's $760,000, less the fifty thousand on the table. I'll round it off to $700,000."

"Fine, I'll make payments in the months of May, July, September, and November." Dallas paused, calculating the amount. "That'll be $175,000 each time."

"Too bad some of your other skills aren't as good as your math." King slid his chair closer to the table and shoved the pad in front of Dallas. "Write it up."

Pausing for a moment, Dallas looked up at King. "Why are we doing that?"

"I want it in writing, signed and dated."

"Why?"

"For protection … so I can share it upstairs."

Dallas hesitated wondering why he said upstairs; his mind whirled and then he hit the nail on the head. *He's under pressure from his boss to collect. He wants proof positive that I've agreed to pay up.* Understanding the game, Dallas straightened in his chair. "Fine, you get a copy and I get a copy."

"I don't think so," the capo for gambling grumbled, "why do you want one anyway?"

"Protection. What if something happens to you, Mr. Kingston? Your guys certainly aren't credible witnesses."

A cold stare shot from each of the lackeys' eyes. Tony smacked the blackjack into his hand.

"That's not part of the deal. Write it up."

Dallas's eyes sharpened; he said in a firm tone, "No copy for me, no deal."

King rustled in his chair, ran his fingers around his jaw and over his lips. "Okay. Two copies."

"Deal." Dallas pulled out a pen, prepared two sheets, signed both, and slid them across the table. "Sign and date them."

King picked up a copy and read the promissory note:

I, Dallas Nash, agree to pay the Partnership a grand total of $700,000 in four installments of $175,000, starting on the first day of May and continuing in July, September, and November, 1979.

Dallas Nash	Date	King Kingston	Date

"It looks official."

"That's what you wanted, isn't it?"

King paused for the longest time, his fingers playing a tune on his lips. "I don't think so."

"Fine with me." Dallas slid his chair back. "I guess that finishes our business for today."

"Wait." King hesitated again, took out his pen, signed and dated both copies. Pushing a copy toward Dallas, he said, "I hope that makes you happy."

Dallas folded his copy, slipped it in his shirt pocket and stood. "Nice doing business with you Mr. Kingston." He extended his hand.

King hesitated then grabbed his hand and shook it.

***

Clark met Dallas handcuffed and shackled in the lobby of the McNamara building, guarded by two policemen. One of the officers unlocked the shackles and guided Dallas toward the elevator. The two chatted briefly. Dallas was in high spirits. Arriving in the conference room, Clark introduced him to the task force and asked him to walk them through the scam.

His ego exploded; he spoke gleefully, on and on, how he'd conned Kingston.

Clark interrupted his expository and thanked him for a thorough review. "Would anyone like to ask Dallas a question?"

"Yes, I would," Kimberly stated, obviously chomping at the bit. "How did you ever roll up seventy thousand for prostitutes?"

His eyes slowly rolling up, stopping at her large breasts.

She blushed and looked away.

He gave her a slow, sexy smile; his eyes seducing her — enough for a woman to moisten her pants. "Equipment like yours doesn't come cheap," he said, glancing at Earl. "Have we met before?"

Earl gave him a sheepish, sly smile.

"Yeah, I remember. You're the guy who was hitting on my woman at the blind pig on the east side."

Eyebrows shot up around the room. Earl raised his hand to deflect the looks. "All in the line of business," he told his colleagues. "She's a witness who agreed to testify against him."

Patrolman Ralston shifted his line of interest. "You have over a half million dollars in gambling debt. How did you accomplish that much in such a short period of time?"

"Huh." Dallas looked him in the eye. "That's a question I've asked myself many times. It started small — a couple thousand, maybe three, at a blind pig. They flew me to Vegas. Before I knew it I was losing twenty-five, thirty grand a night."

"And that was it?"

Dallas stared at Ralston for the longest time, then shot him a grin. That was the beginning. Before I knew it I was losing fifty, seventy-five a night at *the game*."

Clark's ears perked up. "*The game*? Were you throwing dice?"

"Yeah, up on Elmira."

"Would you put that in writing?"

"Sure, why not?"

***

The District Attorney greeted Clark with a broad smile. "Job well done. We have just about everything we need on tape to put Kingston away for a long time."

Clark unfolded the promissory note and tossed it on his desk. "Maybe this will top it off."

The DA picked it up and read. His mouth opened wide. "He's a dead duck. How did you get this?"

"King insisted that Dallas put the agreement in writing. At first Dallas wasn't sure why, then it came to him — King was getting heat from above — so he played tit for tat."

"Pretty smart."

"I thought it was superb. I would have never thought of it under those conditions."

"The whole session was flawless," the DA reiterated. "I couldn't have scripted it better."

Detroit Free Press
March 19, 1979

DALLAS NASH INDICTED FOR RACKETEERING

FIVE YEARS IN PRISON AND FIVE YEARS PAROLE LIKELY

Federal Judge James Limbaugh today signed a decree order calling for the indictment of Dallas Nash, of Nash International. His hearing was waived and a court date set for June 3, 1979.

CHAPTER NINETEEN

Exactly at two o'clock in the afternoon, Jake Nicolette called the special meeting to order. His dark brown eyes pierced the souls of each member of the leadership council. Showing his normal restraint, he asked quietly, his raspy voice barely audible at the other end of the table, "How did I *not* know about the impending indictment of Dallas Nash?"

His unwavering stare sliced even deeper — no one said a word — his face reddened, though his demeanor remained calm. In a soft, yet distinctively controlled voice he asked, "Who knew it was going to happen?"

"I heard some rumbling but had no idea they were that far along," the capo for prostitution said quietly.

"What kind of rumblings?"

"The cops were snooping around. A couple of my boys were called in for questioning. It didn't seem like a big deal."

Jake's tone elevated, "Not a big deal." Moderating his voice again he said evenly, "They could have given Dallas twenty. He bargained for five early in the game. Something is going on."

"I've talked to him on the phone several times in the last month or so, nothing seemed to be unusual," King Kingston volunteered.

"Why in the …" Jake backed off, trying to remain calm. "Why would you talk to him? We have lots of guys to do that kind of work."

King gave him an unknowing expression. "I was settling a debt. He owes us big time."

"Big time … how much?"

"Uh, over seven hundred grand," Underboss Travaglini said.

"Who authorized that level of debt?"

"No one," King said. "It was spread out so the individual totals didn't look bad. I just added up all the pieces — five hundred and ten thousand in gambling losses, a hundred and eighty grand in drugs and seventy thousand for broads."

"Seventy grand for broads!" Jake took in a deep breath. "What does he do eat pussy for every meal?"

"We brought in some expensive prostitutes each time he went to Vegas," the tall, slender capo for prostitution said. "When he's in Vegas he goes through hookers like gangbusters. And they're not cheap. He demands the best — first class hookers from New York and L.A. I haven't seen anything like him since Jack Kennedy."

"He sounds like an addict — gambling, drugs, women, and likely booze — he could be a loose cannon," Underboss Angelo said.

"I agree." Blackie nodded. "Guys like him think about themselves first."

King hesitated, "It's no longer a problem. I took care of it last week."

"Well, that's nice to know." Jake said mockingly. "Seven hundred thousand and you didn't take the time to tell me."

"Sorry Boss, he paid fifty thousand and promised to pay the rest." King stood, walked to the end of the table and handed Jake the promissory note. "Here it is."

The Boss's eyes scorched the paper. Jake laid it on the table and buried his reddened face in his hands. Slowly he leaned forward, sat motionless, trying not to blow a fuse. "Okay, let's back up ... how did all of this transpire?"

"King called two weeks ago," Underboss Angelo Travaglini explained. "He said the kid had some money coming in and wanted to settle his debt. Seemed reasonable so I authorized the meeting."

"Who was there?"

"Dallas Nash, two of my guys and me," King said. "We worked out the details and he wrote it up and signed it."

"Why did you have him write it and sign it?"

"Angelo had been on my case. I wanted to have something I could show him."

"Well ... that was very thoughtful of you," Jake bit his tongue. He picked up the sheet and read the note again. "And, I suppose you stuck the name Partnership on it just to make him happy."

"Dallas wrote it up. I-I guess ... I didn't think about that."

"You guess. You didn't *think*." Jake held the note over his head. "It's right here — Partnership — there's no guessing about that."

"I meant to say ..."

"What did you mean?" he asked, cutting off King.

"I-I ... didn't give it a thought."

Jake stared at King; his eyes seething. "Is that all you have to say?"

King pulled a handkerchief from his pocket and wiped the moisture from his forehead. "Ah ... there is one more thing."

Jake glanced up, contempt in his eyes.

"I gave Dallas a copy."

"You did what?" Jake's face turned beet red.

"He said if I get a copy he gets a copy. Otherwise there was no deal."

Jake let out a deep sigh and asked with deceptive mildness, "Who was doing the bargaining?"

King looked up sheepishly. "I was ..."

Jake interrupted, finally letting loose, his voice boomed, "And you let a punk kid take you to the cleaners. How could you be so dumb? You just signed up for a free bus ticket to federal prison. I can see it now. Your ass is grass and the feds will be a lawnmower."

"What do you want me to do?"

Trying to compose himself, Jake rubbed his jaw. "Get your ass into damage control." He glanced around the table. "Angelo, have your guys downtown analyze the plea agreement. See what they can glean from it." He turned the other way. "Blackie, call your contact in the DA's office. See if you can pick up anything."

"Will do; right away."

Jake put on a calm face and pointed his index finger individually at each member. "Get your asses out of here — hit the streets, call in your chits, find out what's going on — someone has to know what's behind the deal."

Jake sat down and stared blankly — no one around the table looked up — he let out a deep sigh. Turning back to the table, he asked, "Enough of that, what else is going on?"

Raising a hand, the Consigliere received a nod from the Boss. "We have to look toward the future. Dallas is a liability. He could spill his guts at any time. We need to revisit our earlier discussions about insurance."

"Finally, someone around here with a brain," the Boss concurred. "You still think his sister in the boarding school is our best option?"

"Absolutely, no question."

"Blackie, take care of her personally; drug her up and put her in a whore house."

***

Clark staggered out of bed after another long week, splashed his face, and made a pot of coffee. Walking down the stairs to his apartment building lobby, he picked up the newspaper, and trudged back to his kitchen. Filling a mug with steaming coffee, he settled into a chair at his small table. The morning sun beamed across the *Detroit Free Press.*

His eyes balked at the glare and he shielded them from the sun until settling into the other chair, and opened up the sports section. "Shit, Tigers lost again," he mumbled and tossed the paper aside.

His mind wandered back over the past six months. *I sure messed things up with Caroline. Sharon asked me to go to her parents' place and I didn't go. How could I be so dumb?* Gazing out the window, his loneliness continued to grow. *One lonely tree, half dead, just like me. I gotta do something today — clean up the place, go grocery shopping — then what? Maybe there's a good movie on.* He picked up the entertainment section and read the movie listings. *Nothing sounds exciting.* Folding the paper, he saw a promo for the Sax Club's afternoon performance of Kenny G. *Can't do better. I'll see if I can get in.*

He took a quick shower and shaved. Feeling refreshed and invigorated, he opened his closet and surveyed his options. The spiffy blue and white plaid shirt his mother had given him for Christmas caught his eye. He put on a pair of newly pressed dark blue slacks, slipped the shirt on and double-rolled his sleeves. Glancing in the mirror for a sign of approval, Clark winked at himself. "Not bad."

He took the elevator downstairs, jumped in the Mustang and drove east for a half mile, north on the Southfield Freeway, until he exited onto McNichols. Approaching the Club, he saw traffic backing up over a block away. He turned right and parked on a side street. Slipping out of the car, he straightened his shirt and headed back to McNichols. Rounding the corner, he walked briskly toward the Club.

A group walked toward him. "They're sold out," one of the guys said wincingly.

Clark ignored them and continued on his way, stopping at the entrance. He leaned close to the doorman. "Can you get me in?" he asked softly.

His buddy grinned. "We're over the fire code; guess one more won't hurt."

"Thanks," Clark said, slipping a five spot into his buddy's hand.

Squeezing in the narrow entryway, he worked his way through the standing room only crowd; a buzz of anticipation filled the place. His eyes searched to the left and the right. Thinking he saw a hand in the air, he turned toward it for a double take. Yep, he saw a waving hand on the far side — a woman pointing to a chair and mouthing, "Over here."

He flipped his hand in the air in acknowledgment and wedged his way through the crowd. Reaching the table, she leaned close to him. "You looked like you were searching for a seat. My friend was unable to come. You can sit here if you want."

"Thanks, I appreciate that." He extended his hand. "I'm Clark Phillips."

Her soft hand clasped his. "Nice to meet you. I'm Abby Thompson."

"Can I buy you a drink to say thanks?"

She gave him a measured look as she nodded. "Sure, I'll have a Manhattan, Canadian Club on the rocks, no cherry." She hesitated a moment and said, "You better order now they just announced last call before the show."

"Thanks." Clark spotted a waitress with a smiling face and waved to her.

She hustled to his side. "What'll you have, Clark?"

"The lady will have a Canadian Club Manhattan on the rocks with no cherry, and I'll have the usual."

"Buy two, get the second two at half price if you order now."

Clark looked at Abby. She didn't blink. "Sure, why not?"

The waitress nodded and headed for the bar.

Abby leaned over to him. "You come here often?"

"Most every week, usually on Friday nights."

She cocked her head. "For the strippers?"

"Nah, our poker group meets upstairs on the first Friday of every month."

The drinks arrived and Clark raised his in a modified toast. "Here's to a most enjoyable performance."

"Thanks." Clinking his glass, she looked toward the flashing stage lights.

Clark eyed her. *I love her short-cropped red hair — and her sharply defined features — her perfect nose, and her slightly raised cheekbones. She's flat out beautiful.*

The crowd gave Kenny G. a standing ovation and like everyone else in the building the two were caught up in the performance for the rest of the afternoon. Clark glanced at her whenever he could sneak a peek. *She's gorgeous. What a body!*

The two oohed and aahed appropriately during the performance; stood spontaneously and cheered along with the crowd.

"Isn't he wonderful? I could listen to him all day," she cooed.

"He's the best. I'm like you. I could sit here all day."

By the time they'd stopped cheering after the final curtain call, the two were exhausted. Flopping down on their chairs, four empty glasses in front of them, Clark leaned across the table, and asked, "You from around here?"

"No, I just moved here from Philadelphia."

"I haven't been there in years," he said, trying to think of something profound then gave up. "I remember going to several great restaurants there."

"Some of the best in the world. The people there are friendly too."

Clark's mouth curled with distaste. "They didn't seem friendly went I went to the Eagles game."

Abby offered her thought. "People love them when they win."

"Sounds like the Lions."

Sharing an understanding look with him, Abby glanced at her watch. "I have to leave now. Maybe I'll see you here again another Saturday. Thanks for the drinks." She rose and left.

Clark looked befuddled. *Did I say something wrong? Maybe I offended her. I can't recall saying anything out of line. Christ, she's hot.*

***

Clark picked up the phone and called.

"Sharon Wilson," bubbled from the other end.

"Sounds like you're in good spirits."

"I was about to call you," she said. "How was your Easter?"

"Terrific. It was great to see mom and dad. He talked shop all day. She's starting to fail," he fibbed, "which reminded me I need to stop by more often. She prepared her usual ham dinner, enough for ten more, I might add. Aunt Helen brought two raisin pies — one for dinner and one for me to take home — she knows they're my favorite. I'm rationing it one piece a day." He rambled energetically then changed the subject. "How'd your trip home go?"

"Spectacular. I'll tell you more next time we're together."

Sounding more like an invitation than something off in the future, Clark measured his thoughts. "I was hoping we might get together some time soon."

"How about an hour? I'll have a pizza ready."

Wasting no time, Clark said, "I'm on the way."

It wasn't long before Clark knocked on the door. She flipped it open, turned, and headed back to the kitchen. "Everything is ready. Grab a couple of Stroh's and meet me on the sofa. I'm dishing out the pizza."

"I'm starved," Clark said, on the way to the fridge.

He placed a beer on each TV tray and eased onto the sofa. Sharon placed two pieces on his plate. "Bon appetite."

Clark devoured the first piece, slowing on the second. "Tell me about Easter on the farm."

She swallowed and sipped her drink. "It was like nothing had changed in twenty years. Dad was his same jovial self, prodding one of my brothers about something he knew would set him off. Mom as always, a bundle of energy, she talked about the meetings she'd had with some aspiring political candidates. I don't want to brag, but sometimes I think she's Mrs. Republican for the county. Without her approval the candidate might as well drop out."

"Sounds like your family is really engaged."

"Engaged … that's not the half of it. You should have seen the antics of my brothers. Dave, he's a year older than me, spun fact after fact about the nation's budget and the crazy big-time spenders in Washington. Steve, the third oldest in the family, didn't listen at all. He's a right winger and preaches the gospel of those nuts."

"Sounds like you had a real donnybrook on your hands."

"My brother, Dan, couldn't squeeze a word in edgewise. He's going to take over the farm when Dad retires." She took a breath. "The shit hit the fan. Gary, my youngest brother, said something positive about the Democrats. You'd have thought there was a nuclear explosion."

"At least each one got to speak his piece."

"Maybe so, but no one really listened." Sharon shook her head. "I went to bed."

Clark leaned over and kissed her firmly on the lips. "You're the best."

"I missed you so much." She gazed affectionately into his eyes, stood and tugged on his hand. "I can't wait any longer."

***

When Clark called Sharon the next night it was more of the same; this time he brought hot and spicy Chinese. Opening her apartment door, Clark stopped cold. His eyes bugged. Sharon stood just inside, sultry in a short black negligee. "Forget Chinese, I'm going American," he choked out.

"Later … did you get something spicy?" she asked, finally hungry for food.

"Szechwan pork, extra hot, and fried rice."

"Perfect. Let's eat at the kitchen table."

"Fine with me."

Clark unloaded the goodies and pulled a couple of beers from the fridge. Popping the tops, he handed one to her. "Here's to the most wonderful woman in the world."

She blushed. "I'll drink to that."

By the time they'd finished, Sharon was ready for more than food. She slinked around him, caressed his ears and kissed him on the neck. Wasting no time, she loosened the buttons on his shirt, unbuckled his belt and headed south. Slipping her hand inside his shorts, she fondled and purred, "Want to do something special tonight?"

***

Sitting at the end of the Ghostbar in The Whitney, one of Detroit's iconic Gilded Age mansions, Clark took in the opulence of the past. Built in 1894 by David Whitney, Jr., a lumber baron and one of the wealthiest men in the city, the mansion now housed Clark's favorite getaway bar. The dark paneling and high-gloss mahogany bar made it a cozy place to talk with a friend over a cold one.

Catching Ted's eye, Clark waved. "Over here."

Ted sent him a high-sign, sauntered past the polished bar and pulled out a heavy wooden stool with a cushion seat. Glancing around at the artwork and the Tiffany windows, he raised his eyebrows. "Pretty fancy place for an after work beer."

Clark's grin turned into a smile. "Happy hour; prices go up at six."

The bartender pulled out a white towel and wiped the bar top. "Whataya have?"

"Do you have a dark beer on tap?" Ted asked.

"Sam Adams."

Ted nodded. "Make it two," Clark added.

Ted turned his stool toward Clark. "So what's so urgent that we had to meet today?'

"It isn't urgent." Clark fidgeted with his napkin. "I-I ... want to talk about Sharon."

Ted perked up. "You getting engaged?"

"No, it's nothing like that."

"Well ..., what is it?" Ted pressed.

Clark tossed a hand up. "It's that she ... she's too comfortable; she's starting to sound more and more like we're married."

Ted contorted his face. "Too comfortable ... married ... what's wrong with that?"

"Comfortable ... maybe that's not the right word. I just feel like I've fallen into a pattern whenever I'm at her place. Like we're in a routine."

"You're not making sense." Ted leaned back with a confused look on his face. "Am I missing something here? Maybe you ought to start over."

"It began earlier this year when she asked me to go to her parents' farm to meet the family over Easter. That seemed like a big step, making a commitment."

"So, what's wrong with that? You've been talking about how much you like her."

"I do ... but the idea of meeting the family is a step beyond that. I don't want to give her the wrong impression."

"Wrong impression. Christ, you banged her for a week in Aruba."

"That was different."

"Different? Not according to Laverne. Sharon thought it was special."

"It was," Clark acknowledged, trying to keep things in proper perspective. "Things are just moving too fast. I'm not at that stage yet."

Ted stared at him. "Are you seeing someone else?"

Clark shifted uncomfortably and looked away. "No."

"I don't think you're telling the truth. C'mon, 'fess up."

Clark tapped his fingers on the table then ran them through his hair. "Well …I … I met this woman at the Sax Club."

"Now, we're getting somewhere."

"No. It wasn't like that." Clark defended himself. "We just talked."

"Big deal, so you talked to another woman."

"It was more than that," Clark admitted, an excited tone in his voice. "I had a good feeling about her. I'd like to see her again."

"Are you telling me everything?" Ted asked, his inclinations suggesting something more. "You sure you're not involved with her?"

"No, I'm not … yet … if Sharon was the right one, I don't think I'd be having these feelings. I've been with a lot of women but I'm not a cheater. Doesn't that make sense?"

Ted paused. "You cheated on Caroline, didn't you?"

Clark glanced quickly away then looked back at him. "Yes, one time, and I've hated myself ever since. I don't want to hurt Sharon."

"Now you're making sense." Ted chugged his beer. "Why don't you tell her you're not ready to make a commitment? And that you think the two of you should slow down."

"Hmm, I don't think I can convey it in a way she'd understand."

"Christ Clark, you can't have it both ways."

Clark gazed at the bar's elegant wall décor for a moment and turned back to Ted. "Sometimes another woman can say things better. You think Laverne would talk with her? Maybe say that I confided in you?"

Ted pursed his lips. "That's a lot to ask of Laverne."

"C'mon Ted, you're always saying, 'what are friends for?'"

Ted took in a deep breath. "Okay, but you'll owe me big time."

CHAPTER TWENTY

The lights dimmed — two minutes to show time — Clark's hopes of seeing her dwindled. He took a long sip of Tanqueray and glanced at the front door one last time. The lights flickered and the up-and-coming saxophonist was introduced.

Abby appeared out of nowhere.

His heart twitterpated.

He pulled the empty chair closer to him and motioned for her to join him. "It's great to see you. How have you been?" he said without thinking.

"I've been snowed," she said, ignoring his flustered greeting. "This is the first time I've been out since the last time I was here." She stroked her short hair. "I decided this morning that I needed a break."

Clark grinned, needing to hear more than that. "Same for me."

The lights dimmed for the final time — the performance was ready to begin — unable to keep his eyes off Abby. *She's unbelievable. I've never seen anyone so distinctive — short red hair, pencil-fine features, perfect complexion — she's gorgeous.*

The two sat in awe, marveling at the performer's skill, hitting notes most wouldn't try. Abby leaned closer to Clark. "He's fabulous. How old do you think he is?"

I had the same thought about you. Clark nodded. "Twenty-four or twenty-five."

The performance ended with a rousing roar that echoed through the club. Shouts filled the room, cheering and applause continued for minutes. Raphael Ravenscroft stepped from behind the curtain and sat down on a stool. "Thank you, thank you," he said calming the crowd; he wet his lips and picked up the saxophone. "Here's my latest — 'Baker Street.'"

A hush fell across the bar. Abby and Clark sat motionless, captivated by his performance. After another standing ovation, the two eased back onto their chairs.

"He's as good as anyone I've ever heard," Abby gushed.

"You can say that again." Clark paused. "Wanta grab a burger?"

Abby stared at him for the longest time before she spoke. "I ... don't know ... I have plans ..."

He cut her off. "There's a little place not far from here. It won't take long." Seeing her glance at her watch, he figured she'd say no.

She looked up and gave him the sexiest smile ever. "Sounds perfect. My car is parked by the front door. I'll drive."

"Fine with me."

Abby led the way outside and stopped in front of a new red Corvette.

"Wow, this is something."

She gave him an embarrassed look and unlocked the doors. "I bought it last week ... got a special deal with my GM employee discount."

Sliding inside, Clark's eyes opened wide. He rubbed his hand across the leather dashboard, smiled and quickly fastened his seatbelt. "Turn right when you leave the parking lot."

"Will do." She pulled onto McNichols and sped east for a mile or two.

Clark slid his right hand down and firmly gripped the seat. "You can slow down. We're almost there." He pointed. "There it is on the right — Marcus Hamburgers."

"It's not very big, is it?"

"No, but wait 'til you sink your teeth into one of their burgers ... they're to die for."

She whipped into the driveway and slammed on the brakes, the 'Vette rocking in the parking space.

"I'm glad your brakes work," he jested.

She jumped out of the car and was standing in front of the restaurant before Clark closed the door. Waiting for him to open the front door, she stepped in — stopped and stared in amazement — her mouth dropped open. "I've never seen seating like this. There are no booths or tables ... only swivel stools in a horseshoe-arrangement."

"Pretty cool, huh?"

"It's darling. I love it."

"I knew you'd like it." Clark took her by the arm and guided her to the two vacant stools at the end.

Abby eased down and looked around — a throng of regulars filled the place — the guy next to her chomped into a bun. She leaned close to Clark and whispered, "What is he eating?"

186

Clark glowed. "I wondered how long it would take you. The hamburgers are cut in a rectangular shape to fit hotdog buns."

She shook her head. "This is truly unique. I have to tell the women at the office."

"Wait until you taste the burgers. They're great."

"I'm ready to give them a try." Opening the menu, she marveled at the wide selection.

Clark pointed to his two favorites.

"Let's order both and share," she proposed.

"Great idea." *We ought to share more than burgers.*

Their burgers and fries arrived in no time. Slicing her burger in half, she waited for Clark to cut his and the two traded.

"What do you think?" Clark asked, after she'd taken a couple of bites.

"I can't talk while the flavor lasts," she joked, and took another bite.

Clark finished the first half. "You mentioned you work at GM. What do you do?"

"I'm a section manager in the technology division. I work in the headquarters on Renaissance Center on the riverfront."

"Wow, that's impressive."

She giggled. "I'm not sure about that … but I can hardly wait each day to get into the office." She paused, running her fingers through her short crop of stylish red hair. "Where do you work?"

"I'm a detective in the Detroit police department," he volunteered.

"Really … I have such high regard for the kind of work people like you do."

Clark lowered his brow; gave her a distressful look. "Some days it seems like we're fighting an endless battle."

"I read about that huge news case, and read an article on the Nash indictment … guess that was a big-time, white collar crime."

"Ah … sort of. Most of his troubles are centered on how he used his personal assets."

"Guess I didn't understand all of that technical stuff. Is it wrapped up?"

"We're on the downhill side, still looking at the spinoff issues."

She looked at him sincerely; her eyes bewitching. "I'm always amazed how you guys can figure things out the way you do."

"If I had some of your computer magic maybe I'd be able to crack the Detroit Mafia. They're such a close-knit family it's almost impossible to penetrate their network."

"They can't be as tight as the Philadelphia Mob."

"Hmm, I don't know. The Philly Mob is probably more violent. The Detroit Mafia is more low-key; everyone is either married to someone or connected in another way."

"Well good luck," she said, glancing at her watch. "I really must be going."

"Sure, my treat." He picked up the check and paid the bill, hustled outside, and slid into her purring Corvette. "What did you think of the burger?"

She smacked her lips. "Never had better."

Squealing out of the parking lot, she raced toward the Sax Club. Clark glanced at her out of the corner of his eye. *Her nipples stretching the limits of her sweater. Her face is perfect, even sexy when she's not trying to be.*

Following his directions past the Club, she turned on the side street and jammed the brakes. "Thanks for the drinks and burger."

"My privilege." He stepped out of the car and started to close the door then stuck his head back inside. "You going to the Sax Club next Saturday?"

She paused, looked him squarely in the eye. "Probably … maybe around five o'clock."

"Maybe me too, I'll see you then."

She grinned. "I'd like that."

He closed the door and watched her peel away. Climbing into his car, Clark adjusted himself, his mind fantasizing. *Goddamn, she's the sexiest woman I've ever seen. Great body and one of the brightest women I've ever met. She has her head screwed on right and knows what's happening in town.*

***

Clark strolled nonchalantly into the Sax Club, looking as if he didn't have a care in the world. Her hand shot up from a two-person table on the right. He waved and sauntered her way; seeing her gave him an instant feeling of anticipation.

Before he arrived at the table, she called out, "Clark, it's great to see you again."

"How have you been?"

She gave him a whimsical look. "Busy, like always."

Her face seemed lovelier than before; even his fantasies were nothing like this.

"Got the Mafia figured out yet?" she jested.

His mind was not on the Mafia. "I don't think I'll ever figure them out."

Abby gave him a slow grin. "Hey, you have one of the most unenviable tasks in the city. There is no way you can turn everything around overnight."

He gave her an unconscious shrug. "Guess so ... how's your life going?"

She smiled softly. "I'm exploring the city and enjoying it."

"Found anything special?" Clark's eyes said more. *I'm ready to explore too.*

She gripped her glass stem and stared across the table. "As a matter of fact I have," she said, her eyes returning to him. "A colleague introduced me to her favorite restaurant — The Whitney — it's on Woodward near Wayne State."

"I've gone to their Ghostbar, but I've never eaten there. I've heard it's pretty fancy.".

"It has a wonderful old-time atmosphere."

✳✳✳

Clark was surprised by how often he'd thought about her during the week. Saturday morning he was up early, made a pot of coffee, had a bowl of Wheaties and quickly skimmed the *Free Press*. His mind kept drifting back to her cute red hair; her vibrant personality and how she seemed to know so much about everything. *She's unreal!*

He finished his household chores quickly and headed out to J. L. Hudson's in Northland to pick up a new shirt. He found the perfect blue pinstripe to go with his dark blue sports coat — three hours to go.

He shined three pairs of shoes, pressed his pants, ran a load of laundry and emptied the dishwasher — two hours to go.

Flipping on the Tigers, Clark settled in with a beer and watched the Tigers score six times. Looking at his watch, he jumped up. "Holy shit, I should have left ten minutes ago."

He brushed his teeth and hit the road.

Strolling casually toward the best table in the Club he took his time. Once seated he ordered his usual and asked the waitress to bring a Manhattan with no cherry, in case she arrived. Waiting anxiously, his heart sank as the stage lights flashed.

The door opened; framed in the doorway, she stood like a Goddess as she scoured the crowd for him. Clark sighed happily, stood and waved. She gave him *that smile* and headed his way.

As she neared the table, he rose and extended his hand. "I thought you might not come."

"I've been looking forward to it all week ... got caught up in traffic."

The waitress delivered her drink.

Abby smiled. "Wow, you're on top of everything."

I'd rather be on top of you.

"Here's to a wonderful performance." She raised her glass, clinked his and taking a sip, slid closer to him, positioning herself on an angle for full view of the stage. "Have you been here long?"

Clark forced himself not to stare at the profile of her tits. "Since ten o'clock this morning," he joked.

"I love your sense of humor," she cooed, placing her hand on his thigh. She caressed him briefly then put her hand back on the table.

Clark redirected his urges, shifting his thoughts to the stage. The lights flickered. Wanting to jump her, he settled for adjusting himself.

The performer ended the first set. Again the two stood and cheered, clapping and shouting. Easing back in his chair, Abby's hand returned to his thigh, slightly higher than before. Clark took a deep breath, hoping his tool got the message. She gave him a sly sexy smile.

He swallowed hard and leaned back in his chair. "Excuse me," he said, trying to mollify his urges. Half rising, he said, "I have to make a pit stop."

She smirked, knowing the real reason. *Blackie was right. This guy has one thing on his mind. I need to take my time, lead him along, and bang the hell out of him.*

Watching the end of the last performance, his anticipation grew.

"I have to go now." She made a move to get up.

Clark's hopes dropped. *Shit, I can't believe it. How could I have misread her?*

"Just joking." She laughed. "How would you like to go out for dinner next Saturday?"

His hopes were revived. "Yes, I'd like that," he said, trying to sound calm and collected.

She stared at him; her mind whirling. "Let's go to The Whitney. It's about half way to my place and it'll be an easy drive home for you."

Clark hesitated, knowing it was a very upscale restaurant. "I'll buy."

"No. It's my treat."

Clark started to speak. Her fingers crossed his lips before he could utter a sound. "I'll make reservations for seven thirty, is that okay?"

Clark's glow said it all.

***

Clark opened the door to The Whitney and turned toward the dining room. An arm slid around his waist. "You're right on time," she said.

"Hey, I wouldn't miss this for anything."

Abby took his hand and nodded to the maître d' who led the way. Following behind, Clark appreciated the dark wood paneling, leather-backed chairs with brass studs, and the sparkling crystal glassware on white tablecloths. *I'm glad I'm not picking up the tab.*

The maître d' pulled the chair out for Abby. Clark eased in across from her. She ordered a bottle of Beaujolais and looked up from the menu. "Anything look particularly good?"

Clark looked at the prices. "Ah … I'm not sure."

She pointed to the menu. "I'm thinking about the tenderloin, lobster oscar."

He looked at the price and gulped to himself.

The wine arrived; the sommelier offered her a taste and poured their glasses half full.

Abby gave him *that smile* and raised her glass. "Here's to a wonderful evening."

"I'll drink to that." Clark clinked her glass, and asked, "Have you settled on the tenderloin oscar?"

"Yes. I haven't had lobster since I left Philly."

"It sounds good … hmm, I'm having the roasted salmon."

"My friend had it the last time I was here; she said it was very good." Abby refilled his glass.

Caesar salads were served and the two entered into casual conversation sharing experiences about youth and growing up in the city. They talked about everything from A to Z, never disagreeing on a single thing. *How refreshing; someone who understands what's going on in the city.*

He couldn't take his eyes off her — her dark green sequined cocktail dress that carved around her breasts left little to his imagination. He adjusted himself once and again.

Their eyes connected. Clark became lost in time. She gave him a slow sexy smile and asked, "How would you like to have dinner at my place next Saturday night?"

Clark's heart leapt; he acted calm and cool. "I'd love to."

***

Strolling into the lobby of the Millender Center, one of Detroit's most upscale residences, he checked in with the man on duty then took the elevator to the penthouse. He'd barely touched the buzzer when the door opened wide, and there, standing before him was the most gorgeous woman in the world. Her thigh-high, formfitting white dress accentuated her shapely body. Turning to welcome him, she showed off the exquisite contour of her breasts.

Clark gazed at her and pinched himself. "You look beautiful … your dress is spectacular." *That's putting it mildly; it looked like she was wearing nothing at all.*

"Thank you," she purred. "It's a little something I picked up this week." She ran her fingers around his collar. "I love your Nero shirt."

"It's a little something I picked up this week," he jested.

She giggled. "Okay smarty you can fix us a drink. The olives and booze are on the counter. I'm taking the Brie out of the oven."

"I can handle that."

By the time he'd fixed her Manhattan and his gin, she had placed crackers and a round of cheese on the small table overlooking the twinkling lights along the riverbanks.

"Don't you just love the view?" she said, parading toward him.

He eyed her then gazed out the full length picture window. "It's unreal."

The two chatted while finishing the Brie. "We're having strip steaks rare and twice-baked potatoes; I hope that is okay."

"Rare, that's the way I like it."

"You can fill the goblets with ice and water and pour the wine while I'm taking the salad out of the refrigerator."

He placed the glasses of wine next to the goblets and joined her at the small table overlooking the river. They talked about nothing special and emptied their wine glasses. "There's a bottle breathing on the counter above the wine cooler," she suggested.

"I'll get it," he said, and refilled their glasses.

Like magic the steak and potato appeared before him. "Bon appétit."

He raised his glass and clinked hers. "Here's to a very special woman."

She took a sip and sent *that sexy smile* his way. "Thanks, and here's to a handsome man."

Clark cut into his steak and looked up. "This is the most tender strip I've ever had."

"Thank you," she said.

She's so sexy, more than candy apple. She knows more about baseball than any woman I've ever met. She loves to travel, has been everywhere. I can't believe how interesting she is. She asks questions, understands the inner city. Loves my stories. Has a subtle and dry sense of humor. And is so easy to talk to. Noticing her smirk, he wondered if she had something else in mind. I hope so, he fantasized.

She emptied the second bottle. Clark felt a tingling in his cheeks; he knew they must be glowing. She changed the music to a soft jazz station. "Would you like to dance?" Feeling tipsy, he gathered himself and reached for her hand. The two slow danced for the longest time, her hands caressing his back and lowering to press lightly on his cheeks. The room began to spin. His eyes blurred.

Next thing he remembered, she was humping him like a bronco-rider, screaming and flaying her arms over her head. *God, she's unreal.* He was on top, gasping and pushing with all his might. And again, she was on top, sliding slow and easy, driving him home one more time.

He lay still, totally spent. *I don't recall how many times we did it. Doesn't matter, she's the most wonderful ... exciting woman I ever met.*

His nostrils twitched ... *do I smell bacon?* He paused and took in a deep breath. *It's bacon ...*

"You going to sleep all day?" Abby called. "It's ten o'clock. Your omelet is almost ready."

CHAPTER TWENTY-ONE

MORNING STAR
New Chatham, Massachusetts
April 16, 1979

COED MISSING AT CHATHAM HILL

The Rector at Chatham Hill, an all-girl's boarding school, today confirmed that Samantha Nash, daughter of Mr. and Mrs. Huston Nash of Grosse Pointe, Michigan, was missing from her room. Miss Nash was present at the school's group dinner and sing along Friday night. She did not attend classes on Monday, the FBI agent confirmed.

"Clark, this is Oscar. Thanks, for returning my call. I read the bulletin on Samantha Nash. Anything more you can you tell me?"

"I sent one of our task force officers there as soon as I read the AP report. She should be meeting with the FBI agents about now. I talked to the chief there; he's sure it was done by pros."

"Why's that?"

"Her roommate went home for the weekend. When she returned Sunday night she noticed one of the drawers ajar in Samantha's chest-of-drawers. She thought that a bit unusual since Samantha is such a tidy freak. When she wasn't back by eleven that night, her roommate called the front desk. The police arrived shortly after that."

"Did they find anything?"

"No, the place was clean as a whistle. The only prints were those of Samantha and her roommate. A medium-size suitcase from under her bed was missing. The chief figures the intruders filled it with clothes and personal items."

"Do you have any information on her?"

"Not much. According to the roommate Samantha was a loner. She'd been seeing a counselor on a regular basis to help improve her self-esteem and confidence. My lieutenant will be meeting with her roommate and counselor this afternoon."

"Sounds like you're on top of everything."

"The chief there seems overwhelmed. There's never been a major crime in Chatham. They only have a couple of deputies so we'll carry a lot of the load."

"Do you have any pictures of her?"

"The roommate gave the chief two. I'll drop them off when they come in. She's a blonde with a chopped-off Dutch-boy hair style, five-foot-five and maybe twenty pounds overweight."

***

Rosa Maria stood at the front door of her Mexican restaurant to welcome the group. Laverne arrived first and marveled at the archways, the tall potted palm trees hanging over the booths, and the continuous mural wrapping all four walls.

"Where did you ever come up with the idea for this motif?"

Rosa Maria beamed with pride. "It's a copy of my parents' restaurant in Puerto Vallarta."

"Oh my … Ted and I will have to come here."

Nicole stepped in and paused. "This is not your local Taco Bell," she jested.

Wendy nudged in behind her. Having eaten there many times, she handed Rosa Maria a bouquet of yellow roses. "Here's a special thanks for our hostess."

"How sweet. There's a table for us over there." She pointed. "Please seat yourselves. I'll get a vase so we can use the flowers as our centerpiece."

Rosa Maria returned in no time with the vase in one hand and a pitcher of margaritas in the other. She placed the vase in the center of the table and filled their large goblets.

"I can't drink all of that," Nicole said.

"We'll see." Rosa Maria held her glass high. "Here's to an afternoon of good times."

"Yes, and here's to Rosa Maria," Wendy toasted.

"Here, here," the group chimed.

"We're having five courses, tapas style, so take your time."

"Sounds terrific!" Nicole added.

The group nibbled chips and salsa, and chatted. Rosa Maria refilled their glasses. It wasn't long before Nicole raised the topic of the day. "Let's go around the table and share the ideas we've come up with for doing something with the guys."

Ideas flowed like the river in the mural behind them — we could go to a play, see a performance at the Fisher Theatre, enjoy a nice dinner out, or maybe eat here.

"Better yet," Laverne added. "We could have dinner at the rooftop restaurant downtown."

"Woo, I'd like that," Nicole said.

"How about going to a ballgame? They're always talking about the Tigers," Wendy suggested.

Rosa Maria's confidence grew. "We could buy box seats. They'd love that."

"Hmm, I don't know." Laverne finger-rolled her long blonde hair. "Maybe we should do something more private … like fixing them a romantic dinner. Ted could move the furniture around at our place and make it look like an elegant restaurant."

"Ooh … that would be fun," Rosa Maria added.

Laverne threw her arms in the air. "I have it," she blurted, then covered her mouth as if afraid to share her thoughts.

"Well, what is it?" Nicole asked excitedly.

"We could do … an upscale fashion show."

The three other women looked at her in wonderment.

"I saw one on TV once. It was really something," Wendy said.

"I've never seen one. What would we do?" Rosa Maria asked.

Laverne loosened the top buttons of her blouse and leaned forward, showing off her décolletage. "Wear something sexy and dance around your guy like you're seducing him."

"I don't know," Nicole said, her voice revealing her qualms. "I've never done anything like that."

"Each of us could wear something new and strut around my apartment. We could ask Father Dom to be the MC. He could flip the lights off and on and introduce us."

"Wouldn't that be neat," Wendy agreed. "We could each dance to our own special song."

"I could wear my special Mexican sundress and do the cha-cha," Rosa Maria said.

"It sounds like fun. I could wear a traditional countryside party dress and dance to one of Renzo's old time favorite Italian love songs. How about you, Laverne?"

"That's easy. Ted loves Nancy Sinatra's 'These Boots are Made for Walkin.' There's a pair of red short shorts and matching halter top I saw at Dillard's last week that would be perfect."

Rosa Maria's eyes bulged. "That'd be something else."

Laverne looked at Nicole; her head turned away, staring at the mural. "What about you?"

She didn't respond, turned slowly and cast a firm eye toward group. A smile burst free, brightening her face. "Yes, I'm going to do it!" She nodded to herself.

Wendy frowned. "Do what?"

"Alsye has always wanted me to wear a black negligee and perform for him. I just couldn't bring myself to do it."

Rosa Maria looked surprised. "You're going to do it in front of everyone?"

"Sure, why not. We're all friends. Besides I won't have these much longer." She gestured as if lifting her breasts. "They're at least two sizes larger since I've been nursing J. D."

"Are you positive?" Rosa Maria asked.

"Yep, I'm going to buy an outfit on the way home so I can start practicing."

"I'm excited." Rosa Maria bubbled. "I can't wait 'til I see you."

Wendy jumped up. "Wait 'til the guys hear about this. They'll go bananas."

"Let's not say anything other than we're all getting together at my place," Laverne said.

"Yes, I agree," Nicole said. "Let's keep the details secret. That way it'll be a big surprise."

"How about June at my place," Laverne said. That'll give us a month to prepare."

**

Later that week a line of thunderstorms pounded Detroit. Walking in late for the May poker party, Ted brushed the water from his jacket. "Where is everyone?"

198

"Don't know," Father Dom said, munching on a handful of chips. "I got here before the storm hit. Looks like the early bird gets the worm."

Renzo walked in practically on Ted's heels, placed a large umbrella in the corner and grabbed a Stroh's. Carlos followed close behind and headed for the table of food.

Slipping in behind them, Alsye glanced at Father Dom then took a longer look. "What's with you?"

Strutting like a peacock, the priest smiled. "Nothing," he fibbed. "I was thinking about a project I'm working on. I'll tell you more when the details are finalized."

With a frustrated look, Carlos said, "Now you sound like Clark … can't say a word."

"You talking about me?" The rarely late Clark slouched in with a sheepish grin.

"You look like a drowned rat. What happened to you?" Alsye asked.

"I got caught by a downpour in the middle of the parking lot."

Father Dom stepped up and looked Clark in the eye. "What's the latest?"

Knowing the word was out, Clark grinned. "Okay, you didn't hear this from me … Dallas waffled on his testimony."

"Why?" Alsye asked. "I thought you had everything you needed."

"We did until his sister got kidnapped from the boarding school in Massachusetts."

"Yeah, I remember reading about that. Guess I didn't put the two together."

"He's in a tough spot. If he goes forward with his testimony his sister dies."

"You have a signed plea bargain; doesn't that count?"

"Hmm, yes and no. If they back him into the wall he could claim he signed it under duress. If the judge agrees, he might not honor the plea bargain, and could sign a court order forbidding the use of any information Dallas has provided."

"That would be a disaster," Renzo spouted.

"Worse yet … the mobsters go free," Alsye projected.

***

Abby opened her apartment door and stepped back. Clark's eyes flashed her body, head to toe, then moved slowly up her high black boots and fitted black leather pants. He paused at her dark tan cotton top clinging to her large breasts. Wanting to stop there, he glanced upward and caught her smile. "I love the purples and greens in your brown scarf." She wrapped it tighter around her neck, letting one end hang to her waist.

You'd think I just landed at de Gaulle airport in Paris. She said we were doing French tonight. I never imagined she'd start out like this. She's the most gorgeous woman I've ever known. He stammered to get the words out. "Y-You look fabulous … like a fashion model."

She pecked him on the cheek. "It's French. Do you like it?"

"Like it? You look terrific." He thought about asking if they were doing everything in French, but thought better of it. Instead he took his hand from behind him and handed her a bottle. "Here's the wine you asked me to bring."

She grabbed the bottle and held it up. "Domaine Huet Chenin Blanc. Perfect, you're going to love this Vouvray. Wait 'til you taste the hints of honey and apricots; it's to die for."

So are you. "Are we having it now?"

"No silly, I'm putting it in the freezer. It goes wonderfully with the sear-roasted wild salmon with leeks and artichoke ragu we're having for dinner."

"Sounds fancy."

She rolled her shoulders. "Hmm … maybe. Wait until you cut into the crisp exterior of the salmon and taste the juicy inside — it's the best."

"I can hardly wait."

"You won't be disappointed." She headed for the kitchen. "You can fix drinks while I'm finishing the salads. Everything is on the wine bar." She pointed across the room.

Clark headed that way and made her a Manhattan and his usual. Walking back toward the kitchen, he couldn't take his eyes off her profile — her formfitting tight top. *Her breasts look like grapefruits.* His thoughts went wild. *To hell with dinner, let's do it now and after dinner too.*

"How are things going at work?" she initiated her probe.

Taking a seat on a barstool, Clark tried to come up with something that made sense then changed the subject. "Should I open the wine?"

"Yes, and fill our glasses. Dinner is ready."

Clark poured the Chenin Blanc and carried the half full glasses to the small round table in front of the picture window. Abby placed their warm plates on the table, flipped her insulated gloves to the side, and joined him. "Bon appétit."

Clark lifted his wine glass. "Here's to the most spectacular French woman I've ever met."

She gave him a sweet sexy smile. "I hope I can live up to that the rest of the night."

"There's no question in my mind," he said, without looking up, then took a bite of the salmon. "This is wonderful. Terrific. I've never had better."

Oh shit! Clark's fantasies shot wildly. *I'd like to see her lose it. Nothing better than watching a woman shooting out of control.*

The two talked about baseball — the Tigers and the Phillies — then went on to the magic of the city. Waiting for the opportunity, Abby went back to her agenda.

"I noticed the hearing for Dallas Nash was postponed. What's that all about?"

"Hmm, it's complicated. He's worried about his sister and a lot of stuff related to the Mafia. I can't say much," Clark said, placing his silverware across the plate and changing the subject. "That was an outstanding dinner. I don't think I could eat one bite more."

"I'm glad you liked it." Abby stood, knowing she'd pushed far enough, and topped off his glass. "There's a tray of aperitifs on the wine bar. You can put it on the coffee table and help yourself. I'm slipping into something more comfortable."

I can hardly wait. "No problem." Clark downed the last of his wine, placed the dishes in the sink and set the tray on the coffee table as requested.

Slipping off his shoes, he fixed an amaretto on the rocks and leaned back on the huge white U-shaped sectional. *How lucky can a guy be? Growing up in the inner city with not much at all. And now look at me ... sitting here in a plush downtown apartment with the most attractive woman I've ever seen. She's smart; has a great body. What more could a guy ask for?*

Her bedroom door opened and she slinked toward him wearing a short, filmy black negligee and holding a white, terry cloth robe in one hand.

Clark zeroed in on her body, his eyes moving slowly up her legs to her skimpy black bottoms and up to her bulging breasts.

Stopping in front of him, she turned from one side to the other. Giving him a perfect angular shot, she held the pose. "What do you think?"

Clark paused, unable to say what he really thought. His smile told her what she wanted to know.

Their eyes connected.

Still holding his gaze she said, "Want to get more comfortable?" and handed him the robe.

"Sure." Clark grabbed the soft, masculine cover-up and slipped into the guest bedroom. Returning moments later, the robe tied loosely around him, he joined her on the sofa. The two chatted about everything imaginable; each responding as if they'd spent their entire lives together. Clark fixed another round and leaned back.

She caressed his bare thigh that had escaped the robe, then took a sip of Brandy straight up. "Here's to the best night ever."

Clark picked up his glass. "I'll drink to that."

The two continued to chat intimately. Clark slid closer. Abby snuggled against his chest and lifted her head slightly. "I don't understand why a handsome guy like Dallas Nash, with all of the money in the world, could get so messed up."

Clark raised his brow trying to clear his head so he wouldn't slur — it didn't help — he mumbled, "I'm not a psychologist but I assume he has some strong addictive personality traits. People don't come in neat little packages. He seems far more susceptible than most to drugs, gambling and sex. The Mafia preys on people like him. He kept digging himself in deeper and deeper in debt; he owes the Mafia big-time. We made a deal with him and he spilled the beans."

"Sounds like you were lucky. It isn't easy to get much on them."

"You're right about that," he said, running his fingers down her side. He slid his hand under her top and inched up. She pecked him on the cheek and planted a wet kiss on his lips. The two French kissed, caressing and fondling wildly. She ripped off her nighty and leaned back on the sofa, giving him full range of her naked chest.

Clark downed the last of his drink and gazed at her firm breasts pointing at him. He squinted trying to make sure he hit the target and sent his mouth into action — teasing and nibbling on her right nipple, then sucking on the left. She moaned and pulled his head into her cleavage. He kissed and sucked — his burning desires firing — his urges ready to deliver. He gasped once and again, ready to lose it.

Trying to catch a breath and slow his libido, he raised his head and laughed, "We wired him."

She pushed him back and stared him in the eye. "Wired ... whom?"

"Dallas Nash. And we got the other bastard dead to rights."

She kissed him tenderly and ran her forefinger over his lips. "I'm sorry, sweetie, I don't understand."

He smirked, slurring his words, barely legible. "We wired Dallas when he met with one of the big guys in the Mafia."

"Geez, this is starting to sound like a movie script."

"I can't wait to see King's face when we play the tape in court."

"Who's King?"

"King Kingston, he's the capo for gambling."

"A capo ... what's that?"

"He's like a director, kind of like your boss, the head of technology." Trying to focus his blurry eyes, Clark placed his index finger over his lips. "Shh ... all of that is top secret."

"My lips are sealed," she said, pushing him down on the sofa and ripping open his robe. Her soft hands caressed his pecs and explored lower, fondling his manhood.

Abby rose, slipped off her bottoms and slid on top of him. Taking her time, she eased down, pushing harder, yet moving slowly up and down.

Clark joined her fluid rhythmic motion; their bodies locked, rocking as one.

***

Standing in the front lobby of the Roman Village Cucina Italian restaurant in Dearborn, Wendy welcomed the group. She gave Laverne a hug before turning to point toward the mural that extended along one wall depicting the Italian countryside.

"How did you ever find this place?" Laverne asked.

Wendy bubbled with pride. "Anthony Rugiero, the owner, is a member of our church. He's very active in the community."

Laverne stepped inside the dining area. "White tablecloths ... and look at those table arrangements, how quaint."

"Wait 'til you hear the entertainment he's providing for lunch."

"Entertainment?" Nicole said, joining the group.

"When I told Anthony about the group he insisted on doing something special. He wouldn't take no for an answer."

Rosa Maria slipped in behind Nicole. "Sounds exciting."

The waitress escorted them to a round table tucked away in the corner of the colorful mural that wrapped three walls. Laverne gazed at the panoramic view of the Italian countryside. "I feel like I'm sitting in an outdoor restaurant in Tuscany."

The waitress filled each of the wine glasses with Chianti. "It's on the house," she said. "Compliments of Mr. Rugiero ... Enjoy."

"That's very nice." Wendy said. "Please give him our regards."

The waitress nodded and disappeared.

Rosa Maria oohed and aahed over the specials. "I can't believe the number of selections."

"Let's all order something different so we can get a taste of everything," Nicole suggested.

"Great idea," Laverne added perkily.

The waitress topped off the wine glasses and took their orders.

Settling into a jovial mood, each woman updated the group on recent activities as they giggled their way through lunch.

Laverne turned to Nicole. "Have you completed your routine for the party?"

Nicole's face glowed; her shy grin broadened into a smile. "Yes," she bubbled. "Do you want to see a preview?"

Rosa Maria's eyes opened wide. "Right here?"

"Sure, we're the only ones in this corner of the room," Nicole said, stood and gyrated through several sexy, provocative moves.

"Wow," Wendy said. "I can't wait to see the whole show."

"You?" Laverne clapped her hands. "I can't wait 'til I see Alsye's face."

Rosa Maria nodded. "It's going to be something else."

"I called Father Repice. He agreed to MC and asked that we work up a brief introductory script for each of our routines," Laverne said.

"He'll be wonderful," Wendy agreed. "I remember when he hosted at the church two years ago. He was a real hoot."

Stepping into the doorway, an old Italian man strummed his guitar, leading a group of three other men into their alcove. Dressed in traditional attire — dark pants and shirts, colorful neck-bandanas and matching caps — each played a few introductory notes on his instrument and flipped his cap with a flourish, to the lead guitarist. He stomped his foot and led the group into a medley of patchanka-style Italian folk lullabies and serenades.

Each man took his turn showing off his skills; first the tall one with the accordion, the baldheaded flutist, followed by the tubby one playing two tambourines. The guitarist sang with each rendition while the others chimed in with backup one-liners.

The women applauded and cheered for more.

The old man nodded and the quartet played two more of their favorites, and asked each one of the band members to step forward.

Each bowed in his own particular way.

Wendy stood, leading their enthusiastic applause, as the rest joined her. She thanked the performers and handed the lead man a twenty.

The guitarist shook his head. "No, no, not necessary. Mr. Rugiero take care of everything."

CHAPTER TWENTY-TWO

A black hand turned the doorknob of a third floor apartment in an old tenement building on Detroit's east side. Pushing the door open, a strong urine stench filled his nostrils. The hallway light broke the darkness. His eyes zeroed in on his bounty — a blonde woman curled into a ball on a small bed, with a sheet tucked under her chin.

Stepping inside, he flicked on the wall switch — a faint light fell from the blackened bulb hanging on a cord in the middle of the room. He mopped the moisture from his face against his shirtsleeve and dabbed the other side. *Christ, it's hot in here. For fifty bucks you'd think they'd at least provide a fan.*

He closed the door, locked the deadbolt and turning his head to the right, glimpsed a grimy sink and stained toilet, dirty towels stuffed on a wall bar, and a wastebasket overflowing with debris. Off to the left, plaster and paint chips covered the floor; a straight-back chair sat in the corner beside an end table with someone's initials carved on the top.

He walked to the woman's side and ran his fingers through her course, matted-hair. Ripping off the sheet, he stepped back and admired her body. "Nice ass. Turn over, let's see your boobs."

Slowly, ever so slowly, she turned onto her back — breasts like melons filled her chest. He stared at a dream come true. *Where the hell did they find you? The stuff for the two last years has been scrawny teenagers. It's been a long time since I've seen a real piece of ass.* "Where are you from?" he asked.

Her glazed eyes cracked open; her mouth quivered and closed without uttering a word. "Doesn't matter." He lifted her right arm, examined it and laid it down; picked up the other one — a checkerboard of needle punches scarred her flesh. "Into the heavy stuff, huh ... guess you won't be saying too much."

Shuffling toward the chair, he kicked a path through the rubble along the way and plopped down. He slipped off his loafers and socks, and hung his shirt and pants on the chair back. Standing, he tugged off his bulging Jockeys, freeing an oversized erection.

He strode toward her and looked down at his prey for a moment and plopped his blubbery frame onto the bed. He leaned over and kissed her lightly on the cheek.

She didn't move. Her lovely face seemed even lovelier.

Wrapping his hand around the back of her neck, the man lifted her head and kissed her firmly on the mouth. His arousal sparked; he French kissed her — his lips smothering her face, his mouth drooling on her neck, while his hands molested her breasts.

Groping her body, he pulled her tight to him and pressed with all his might.

She lay breathless, unresponsive, like a train-car on a siding.

He rose onto his knees and spread her legs. "Hold on, baby, the express is about to arrive."

With the full force of his two hundred and fifty pounds he jammed against her. Her body jerked and withered as if every ounce of life had been squeezed out. With no regard for her, he rose and slammed against her again, unmercifully. Pawing at her breasts, he savagely increased the pace, pounding feverishly.

Gasping for a breath, his urges peaked — ready to fire — perspiration spewed down his sides and onto her face. He shouted, "Put your arms around me, you bitch!"

She slowly raised one arm then the other, flopped them on his back and dug her fingernails in, breaking the skin. "That's more like it … finally … a little spunk."

***

The last capo took his seat. Jake cleared his throat and called the meeting to order. "We have an untenable situation." The men around the table came to attention, no one blinked. "I have it from a very reliable source that Dallas Nash had a wire on when he met with King."

"No, that's not possible." Kingston shouted. "We ran him through the standard security process. He wasn't nervous nor did he break a sweat. He never paused or hesitated. He spoke with total clarity throughout the entire session."

"I don't know anything about that. All I know is that they have the full conversation on tape and you're in big trouble."

King flopped back in his chair and stared off into space.

Jake ran his hand across his face then tapped his fingers on the table. "Damn, I didn't like this from the beginning." He took a deep breath and sighed, as if contemplating. "Okay, here's the deal. King, I want you to pack your bags immediately. You're moving to my place on Biscayne Bay in Miami. The boys there will set you up in your new assignment."

King nodded. "Yes sir."

"Take your wife with you and all of your valuables; we're going to torch your place."

King stood. "You can't do …"

The glare of Jake's eyes shrunk him down into his chair.

"Sorry Boss. I'll tell Virginia right away. We'll be on the road this weekend."

"Don't rent a U-Haul. Destroy your credit cards. Close your bank accounts and don't leave a record of your past around. Use cash from now on. And don't fly or take any form of public transportation where you have to sign in. I don't want to see one piece of paper with your name on it; not a trace that you ever lived. Do you understand?"

"Yes sir. My office will be clean as a whistle tomorrow."

Jake turned to the Consigliere. "Where to next?"

"He needs to destroy every file he has, at home and in the office."

"Makes sense." Jake looked around the room. "That means all of you, too. Don't leave a shred of potential evidence in any of your offices."

"Yes sir!" came firing back from around the table.

Consigliere Minelli continued. "It won't be long before the police will mount a citywide investigation of Kingston. We need to spread the word, tell everyone to clam up — like no one ever heard of him. Going forward, we need to compile lists of the stoolies they meet with, the people they call, and those they interrogate. Our guys must follow up with each one … find out what questions were asked and what was said. Someone will tip us off to their strategy."

Jake stood, his cold eyes focused on each man as he pointed to them. "I want a 110 percent effort; remember, this time we're trying to save King. Next time it may be your ass that's on the line." He stared around the table, and uncharacteristically shouted. "Do you all understand?"

Vigorous nods came from every head.

Taking a deep breath, Jake sat down with a heavy sigh and turned to Blackie. "Tell us about the Nash girl."

"The operation went like clockwork. The boys slipped in her room, gagged and blindfolded her, filled a suitcase and were out in no time. No one saw them coming or going."

"Where is she now?"

"Drugged up in a whorehouse on the east side."

"Good. Let's move on to Dallas."

The Boss recognized King's waving hand. "I've talked to Dallas twice on the phone. He understands the situation — if he talks, it's goodbye to his sister. In my last call he emphatically pleaded, 'don't worry, the plea bargain is off.'"

Tony Minelli turned to their chief legal counsel, William Bufalino, Jr., who'd joined the group for this session. "Can he do that?"

The legal brain spoke without hesitation. "Yes. Even though he signed the agreement he's still in control. He can allege he signed the plea bargain under duress. If the judge goes along with that he could disallow all of Dallas' testimony against King."

"That has to be our single most important goal," Jake emphasized. "Do you think Dallas knows that?"

"Probably not," the legal counsel said. "Only a person with a legal background would know he can change his mind without retribution."

"We need to pound that into his head," Minelli said.

"My exact thoughts," said Jake with emphatic conviction. "Who should do it?"

"Someone not at this table," the Consigliere stressed. "We must keep our distance."

"How about my Joey," Blackie suggested. "He has a good head on his shoulders."

"Joey Naples, perfect, I like him," the Boss said. "Have him meet with Bufalino so he understands the concept and any nuances pertaining to this situation."

***

Clark walked into the team meeting and half-heartedly called it to order. *We've lost our edge. With Samantha in their hands, Dallas is like Jell-O.* He glanced up and spoke slowly. "Anyone have a thought on where we go from here?"

Old pro Ralston was quick to respond, "We don't have a choice."

Clark gave him a perplexing look.

"We have to ignore the kidnapping. We can't let their actions affect our plans. Otherwise, we're locked into their game."

"That's hard to do," Clark confessed. "It has to be weighing on Dallas' mind. He isn't going to cooperate as long as they have his sister."

"There's nothing we can do about that," Ralston emphasized. "It's only natural for him to back off and be ambivalent. He knows one wrong step and his sister is dead. We have to help him through all of this. If nothing else ... buy time ... ask the judge for a postponement. The longer we can delay action the greater the likelihood something will turn up in our favor." The veteran cleared his throat. "We need to be calm and help Dallas stay that way too."

Clark ran his hand across his face, collecting his thoughts. "What do you think they're doing now?"

"They have the upper hand and know it; they're in the catbird seat. They'll likely crank up the pressure on Dallas and fight a postponement. Their goal is to get him to cave, rescind his agreement, and the sooner the better. On the streets they'll be snooping around, trying to glean as much information as they can. I expect they'll play it close to the vest; yet, at the same time try to figure out what we know and where we're headed."

"That means it's time for us to strike," Clark said with renewed vigor. "We need to take the offensive."

"Sounds like the Phillips of old." Patrolman Ralston winked. "We need a plan that doesn't trigger a negative response from them."

"And we have to find out everything on King Kingston we can," Earl said.

"Have any ideas on that?" Clark asked.

"Hit the streets. Contact every stoolie, prostitute, bookie, and penny-ante thief we can — find out what they know about King. We have to be like bulldogs, and sniff out every little detail about him."

"That makes sense." Kimberly Weston smiled, compassionately. "But we have to help Dallas too. If not, everything else is for naught."

"Excellent point," Clark said. "He's going through hell and it's going to get worse as the Mafia turns up the heat. We need to bolster his spirits and confidence. And most importantly, give him hope something good will happen."

"That'll be tough," Eddie said. "They're going to try every sleazy trick in the book to make him scrap the plea bargain. Starting with the threats on his sister's life."

Clark straightened upright in his chair. "We need him to think clearly and not react quickly to their tactics, just like he did when he was with King."

Eddie shared a pessimistic look. "This may sound cruel, but he's our only bargaining chip. They are not nice people. When he recants the plea bargain we have nothing ... his sister's life is not worth a plug nickel."

"Excellent point," Will Robinson agreed.

"I agree too, but this is his sister ... it's going to be tough on him," Kimberly said.

"Right, that's why we have to keep him focused on them and the games they're playing," Clark reemphasized. He stood and asked, "Anything else on him?" Hearing nothing, he turned to Earl and changed the subject. "Would you update the group on our surveillance efforts at the house across the street from Freddy's game?"

"A pleasure." His eyes brightened. "It's really something to see. I've never worked with an FBI surveillance team before. These guys are real pros — that's all they do twenty-four-seven, three hundred and sixty-five days a year."

"How many are there?" Eddie asked.

"There were six the two nights I was there. I'm sure a couple dozen are assigned to the unit. The living room of the house is loaded with listening devices ... three or four guys with headsets on. They don't miss a beat."

"How'd they get the bugs inside Freddy's place?" Max asked.

"That's an interesting piece of the pie. After a week of surveillance, they sent in a team one night when everyone was gone to bug the place, cameras and all. With the bugs in place, two undercover agents — William Randle and Allen Finch — went in posed as local gamblers and cased the operation."

"I'd like to hear more about that. Could we meet them and see the room?" Weston asked.

"Good question." Clark nodded. "I know they wouldn't do that with regular cops, but they might with our special team."

"That'd be good," Earl chimed in. "They're posting a gallery of those who've been there. It's really an impressive display of the biggest mobsters in town."

***

Clark pulled up a chair at his old stomping grounds and sat down across from Alsye. He glanced up and slid a beer in front of Clark.

"Are you getting things sorted out?"

Alsye popped his patented cheek-to-cheek smile. "I'm doing much better. Thanks."

"Good for you. You've gone through a lot of crap."

"Crap ... you don't know the half of it."

"Half of it?" Clark cocked his head and gave him an inquisitive look. "There's more? Like what?"

"It's the Mafia. Everywhere I go I see one of their thugs. Guys are in each of my stores every day. My employees are really nervous; several have called in sick. Two threatened to quit."

"Why? Are they intimidating your staff?"

"No, not openly; it's their presence. They're snooping around, checking things out. They make everyone feel uneasy. On the first of the month, the bagman is there waiting at eight o'clock in the morning." Alsye abruptly stopped talking and took a slug of his beer.

"Your finances okay?" Clark asked his friend.

Alsye didn't look up.

"What is it Alsye? You having problems?"

Alsye blotted a tear with his handkerchief. "J. J.'s new medication is three times more than before. I need extra money to stay afloat."

"You could borrow from the guys. We'd all be glad to help."

"I can't do that." Alsye looked dreadful — disheveled, his eyes bloodshot with fatigue and worry. "I'm having a friend haul a truckload of booze up from South Carolina twice a month."

Clark stared at him.

"You're not driving to South Carolina by yourself are you?"

"I hired a driver."

"A driver?" Clark straightened in his chair. "Christ Alsye, that's one more possible leak."

"No way. He's an old high school buddy. He's solid as a rock."

Clark shook his head. "Alsye, this is not going to work. You have to find another way to make ends meet." Clark's voice elevated. "Jesus Christ Alsye, are you crazy? You're playing with dynamite."

Alsye seemed disengaged.

Clark waved his hands in front of his face. "Hello, is anyone home?"

With a double take, Alsye stared at Clark, who kept talking. "Alsye, I'm concerned for your safety. The Mafia doesn't fool around with things like this."

"Nothing is going to happen. I've rented a storage unit in Taylor Township, south of town. Whenever I run low I bring a carload in. I'm really careful."

"I don't care how diligent you are. Sooner or later they are going to find out. You can't hide something like that from the Mafia forever."

"Don't worry, Clark. I have it all worked out."

"There has to be another way." Clark motioned to the waitress for another round. "I'm telling you, Alsye … bootlegging is not going to work. You have to stop … right now. Do you remember what happened once already?"

A new waitress placed two bottles on the table. "Want anything to munch on?"

"Yeah, give us an order of chicken fingers with extra hot sauce." Alsye said, without looking up. He took a long sip of his beer.

Alsye took another slug; his eyes wandered aimlessly toward one of the dancers then vacantly beyond.

"I assume you haven't said anything to Nicole about this."

Alsye threw his arms in the air. "Christ no, Clark, she'd throw a hissy fit."

"And rightfully so." Clark looked at him thoughtfully. "Have you given any consideration to her? What if something went haywire? How would she deal with everything?"

"I told you, Clark. Nothing is going to go wrong."

Clark rubbed his fingers around his chin. "We need to discuss this some more. Will you talk to me about your finances next time?"

"Well … okay, if you insist." He stood and walked out without waiting for his chicken fingers.

CHAPTER TWENTY-THREE

Ted stood at the front door of Laverne's apartment and greeted Renzo, Carlos, and Alsye. "Your assigned seats are in the living room," he said.

"Assigned seats?" Renzo questioned.

"Where are the tables?" Alsye asked. "I thought we were having a romantic dinner."

"So did I," Carlos said, looking around the apartment at the unusual arrangement.

"I don't know a thing." Ted led the way to the living room and pointed. "Alsye and Carlos, you have the two loungers on the sides. And Renzo, you and I are on the sofa."

"How come there is so much space in the middle of the room?"

"Hey don't ask me." Ted shook his head. "When I got home tonight Laverne told me to push everything back and slide the coffee table to the side. Hell, if I knew what was going on in her mind, I'd be the richest man in the world."

"That's for sure," Renzo agreed.

"The women are in the bedroom. Laverne has loaded the dining room table with heavy hors d'oeuvres. Pick up a plate and help yourself. Oh, I almost forgot, she said your wives made your favorite dessert so save a little room." Ted pointed toward the table. "Go ahead. I'll fix the first round of drinks; after that you're on your own. Everyone want the usual?"

Grunts and groans flowed from the three.

Ted called from his mini-bar. "I'll set your drinks on the side tables and TV trays where you're supposed to sit so don't screw up."

One by one the guys filled their plates and returned to the assigned seats. Ted set their drinks at the location for each of them, loaded his plate and joined the group. Renzo downed a couple of appetizers and turned to Ted. "What are they doing in the bedroom?"

"Shit, I told you I'm not a mind reader … they're women."

Alsye cleaned his plate and went back for seconds. Carlos followed suit and when he returned asked, "We supposed to sit here all night?"

Ted grimaced out of frustration. "Okay, I'll check to see how much longer they'll be." He stood, walked over to the bedroom and knocked on the door. Laverne cracked it open and poked her head out with a stern look on her face.

He paused. "Should I fix another round of drinks?"

She smiled pleasantly. "That would be nice dear; make them doubles."

"Okay." He raised his eyebrows and turned for the portable bar. "Laverne said to fix everyone a double. You might as well have some more to eat."

The doorbell rang.

"Carlos, could you see who that is? I'm fixing the drinks."

"No problem." He set his drink on the TV tray and headed that way. Opening the door, he stopped cold and hesitated. "Father Dom … what are you doing here?"

"Laverne said there was a party and she needed someone to keep an eye on you guys."

"Whatever." He turned toward the living room. "Hey guys, look who's here!"

Renzo stood and shook his hand. "Welcome to the party."

Ted turned. "Great to see you Father Dom, Stroh's or vodka tonight?"

"Vodka. Make it a double on the rocks."

"Grab a plate and help yourself. The hors d'oeuvres are wonderful," someone said.

Father Dom fixed a small portion of treats and joined the guys. Ted brought in a tray of drinks. "I fixed another one for you Father so you could catch up."

"Sounds good to me." He took a long sip and looked toward Ted. "Are you celebrating something special tonight?"

Ted gave him a blank look. "Damn if I know. I'm just the maintenance man."

"So I recall." He turned to Alsye. "How are you doing?"

His smile popped. "Much better, thank you very much. The guys have been great and Nicole has helped a lot. And things at the stores are going fine."

"Good for you, my son. Nothing like good friends to make things better."

The bedroom door opened. Laverne strolled over to Father Dom and whispered something in his ear. He nodded and followed her into the hallway.

The guys looked around at each other, curiosity wrinkling their brows.

"Don't look at me," Ted said. "I've already pleaded the fifth."

Carlos pointed at Ted. "C'mon, you know what's going on."

"No, honestly … I don't."

"There's a ten-by-ten area in front of us. Laverne must have said something when she had you move the furniture."

He threw his arms in the air. "I told you. I'm the maintenance man."

Alsye laughed. "Sure."

Laverne stepped into the hallway. "It's show time."

Father Dom flipped the living room light off and on, and dimmed the lights. Glancing down at his script, he cleared his throat. "Gentleman, tonight you're privileged to witness a one-time only extravaganza. Direct from Las Vegas four beautiful women — here for one reason — to fulfill your personal fantasies."

The guys looked at each other not knowing what to say.

"For Alsye, the dream of his life," Father said, turning on the tape recorder — the theme song of "The Stripper" filled the room. "The one … the only … Miss Nicole," he said with a flourish.

Nicole stepped seductively out of the bedroom, dressed in a short black negligée and spike heels, and strutted to the middle of the room.

Alsye froze in place; his eyes bulged. Slinking to the rhythm, she moved slow and easy. His mouth dropped open. With his eyes glued on her, his trademark smiled exploded. She began her stripper's routine — flaunting her assets — sensually running her hands down and around her trim body.

Alsye cheered for more. And she delivered. Moving closer to him, her pelvis rotated within inches of his face, and she shifted into high gear. Running her hands over her enhanced breasts and down along her side, she placed her hand under his chin, pulled his face in front of her private area and went to town, grinding in slow motion.

Alsye threw his arms in the air. "Okay, okay, you win."

"Later, dear." She ran her hand softly along his chin as she turned and walked slowly toward the bedroom.

Alsye stood and cheered. The others followed suit with their applause.

The music stopped and the lights brightened.

The other three men exchanged glances, questioning who would be next. Father Dom flashed and dimmed the lights. The music started. "And now, a special treat, the hot tamale from Mexico City." He majestically swept an arm toward the bedroom door.

Rosa Maria sashayed to the center of the room, her hips shifting side to side, her long white dress flowing behind. Carlos stared at her breasts bulging from her low-cut neckline. She straightened her shoulders and flaunted even more.

Carlos slid to the edge of the couch.

Going into a cha-cha routine, she tossed her hips and moved her ass suggestively to the music. Carlos stood and called for more. She winked, acknowledging his obvious desire and swaggered even closer to him — her body danced wildly as she tossed her head, flinging her hair from shoulder to shoulder.

Carlos collapsed on his chair and wiped his brow. She leaned over one last time, his eyes never wavering from her breasts. She kissed him on the cheek and strutted to the bedroom as the lights brightened and the music stopped.

Ted and Renzo looked at each other. Ted said something unintelligible.

"And now, from the mountains of southern Italy ..." Renzo's brain went on high alert. "We have a traditional delight. Wendy, dancing to one of Italy's most beloved ballads."

The music began with a flowery intro and the lights dimmed. Wendy strode down the makeshift runway dressed in formfitting, black leather slacks and a tight red sweater.

Renzo jumped up. "Go for it, baby."

She threw him a faint smile and flowed to Frank Sinatra's golden voice. Renzo sang the famous words *All The Way* with her, leaped up and held her tight, slow dancing to the sensuous song. Their bodies intertwined with comfortable lust, swaying to the notes of the tune. The music stopped. He kissed her on the cheek and whispered in her ear. "Thank you, darling."

Father Dom flipped on the lights. Renzo watched his wife's sexy bottom disappear into the bedroom.

The guys rustled and poked fun, knowing Ted was the final one.

"Ted, what do you think is in store for *you*?" Alsye asked.

"Who knows, if it's anything like I've seen for you guys the party is over — I'm sending you home — without dessert!"

Father Dom worked the lights. Ted leaned back on the sofa. An unmistakable intro began to blast through the room — Nancy Sinatra belted out "These Boots are Made for Walkin'!"

Laverne pranced out like a sex queen, wearing short red pants and a halter that wouldn't quit. Flaunting her ass, she gyrated slowly toward Ted turned and danced energetically to the beat. Ted eased excitedly to the edge of the sofa and fell onto the floor. She leaned over and pulled him up, her cleavage pressing into his face and sang, "These boots are gonna walk all over *you*."

Ted pulled her tight and kissed her wildly.

The lights brightened and she danced off into the bedroom.

The guys cheered and hooted for more. The women paraded out, hugged their men, and strolled back down the hallway.

A half hour later, dressed in their regular attire, the ladies strolled into the living room as if nothing had happened. Each man grabbed his special gal and whispered sweet nothings in her ear. The couples hugged and kissed.

"Looks like it's time for me to leave," Father Repice announced.

Laverne extended her hand. "Thanks so much for helping us out, Father. You made tonight a real success." She stepped closer and kissed him on the forehead.

"Thanks, that's reward enough for me."

***

"How are you doing, man?" Clark said, slapping Alsye on the back. He plopped down next to him. "The beer's on me."

Giving him a confused look, Alsye leaned away and stared at him. "You all right?"

"I'm fine, why?"

"Why? … slapping me on the back and offering to buy the beer is not like you."

"I had a good week, but most of all I was thinking about you on the way over."

"Me?" Alsye didn't move; he stared, questioning Clark.

"Yeah, I was thinking about our last conversation and what a big step that must have been for you."

"You lost me." Alsye raised his eyebrows.

"Bootstrapping yourself, having to be in-charge all of your life, it's pretty amazing that you were willing to talk with me and lower the wall you've built up."

Alsye stared at Clark for the longest time and choked up, mumbling, "You're my best friend ever."

Clark threw his arm around him. "You're my best buddy. Let's have another beer."

Clark motioned to the waitress and she wasted no time delivering the Stroh's. The two reminisced about growing up, and chatted about the Tigers.

Taking a long sip, Clark looked Alsye in the eye. "You know what?"

Alsye shrugged his shoulders. "No ... what?"

"I think the two of us ought to tell the guys about your financial issues."

"Hmm." Alsye picked up a beer and glanced at the pole dancers doing their thing. "I don't know. You know I'm ..."

Clark cut him off. "Alsye, it's no different than talking to me. We're all good buddies, friends. So what do you think?"

"You really think I should?"

"Absolutely. Father Dom will be there too."

Alsye twisted his lips into a grimace, and sighed. "Okay, but you'll have to take the lead. I don't want it to sound like I have my hand out."

Clark gave him a fatherly hug. "I'll take care of everything. We can talk before poker."

Alsye took another sip. "Okay, but don't make it sound like a big deal."

"Thanks. I won't." Clark ordered another round.

He glanced around the room then leaned closer to Clark. "The Mafia boys are hanging around more and more. The other day I caught one out back going through the trash container."

"That's not a good sign. They're sniffing around too much. I think they're on to something. You need to stop selling white lightening. Right now ... end it."

"It isn't easy Clark, I need the money."

"How much do you need?"

Alsye seemed uneasy. "Hmm, a couple of grand."

"That's all?" Alsye nodded. "Done," said Clark. "I'll get it from the guys when we meet."

"Thanks, I really appreciate that." Seeming relieved, Alsye found his missing smile and changed the subject. His mouth turned down again. "Something happened this week in my store that you may be interested in."

"What's that?"

"One of my regulars stopped by last Friday, bragging about a chick he'd banged two Saturdays ago."

"So." Clark scowled. "What's that have to do with anything?"

"He said she was a blonde with big boobs. Apparently the Mafia had been providing young stuff from South America for some time. He thought she was a big deal."

"A blonde with big boobs ... did he say anything else?"

"Hmm, not that I recall ... oh yeah, he said she was so drugged up she probably didn't know what was happening."

Clark paused; his mind whirling. "When will he be back?"

"Friday, like always. He comes in to cash his check."

"Would you mind if a couple of our undercover detectives show up and ask him a few questions? She could be the missing Nash girl."

Alsye shrugged his shoulders. "Fine with me."

***

Two undercover cops lingered in the back row of Alsye's main store on the lower east side. Slightly after seven o'clock, a large black man set a twelve-pack of beer and a large bag of chips on the counter. Alsye nodded. The two policemen moseyed out the front door.

Alsye cashed the man's check and made change for the groceries. Opening the door, the man walked outside and headed for his car.

Patrolman Will Robinson stepped in front of him and flashed his badge. "Detroit PD. We have a couple of questions."

The guy's eyes opened wide. "I didn't do anything. I just came in to cash my check."

Eddie Grissini stepped closer. "That isn't what we want to ask about."

"Look, I'm married and work on the line at Ford. I'm on my way home. My wife has dinner on."

"It will only take a few minutes," Eddie said. "Unless you want to talk downtown."

"Downtown? Christ, I didn't do anything."

"Fine, you don't have anything to worry about. Ready to talk?" Eddie pulled him aside. "Where were you last Saturday?"

"At home watching the Tigers," he said trying to avoid the issue.

"Will your wife verify that?"

"Ah … sure."

Eddie stuck his face nose-to-nose with the man. "You can do better than that."

"Honest, you can ask my wife."

"Cuff him," Robinson said. "Sounds like he'd rather talk down at the station."

"Wait," the guy pleaded, talking in a low tone. "This is between the three of us, right? My wife will never know?"

"Right." The man wiped the perspiration from his brow. "Where were you?" Robinson pressured.

"At a place on the east side."

"C'mon, we're not going to pry every word out of you. Give us the facts."

"I was at this whorehouse on East Warren. It's run by the Mafia. I go there a couple times a month. Two weeks ago I met this blonde with big jugs. I went back again last week."

"That's all?"

"Yes, that's it. I screwed her. Is that what you want me to say?"

Will pulled a photo of Samantha out of his pocket. "Is this the woman?"

The guy glanced at the picture. "Yeah, that's her."

Will grabbed the photo and jammed it in his face. "Look carefully, are you sure?"

He studied the shot. "Yes, that's her. I'm positive."

"Where's the house located?" The guy hesitated. "Would you rather invite us over for dinner with your wife?"

He sighed and gave them the address.

***

"Play ball," shouted the home plate umpire at Tiger Stadium.

Clark and Abby settled into their box seats as the first Red Sox batter stepped up to the plate. "C'mon Billingham, strike him out," she bellowed.

Clark's brow curled. "I thought you were a Phillies fan."

"I am ... tonight I'm rooting for the Tigers." She cupped her mouth, "Strike two ... give him an outside curve ball," she yelled loud enough for everyone around them to hear.

"You know your baseball, don't you?"

"Of course, I told you I was a Phillies fan."

"Oh ... so what do you know about the Tigers?"

"I know they're supposed to do better than they've been playing. Ten wins and eighteen losses in June is pretty crappy. They need to ramp it up." She shook her head. "How can they be playing so poorly? They've got Billingham, Slaton and Wilcox in the rotation; Milt May, Jason Thompson and Ron La Flore can hit with anyone. With Lou Whitaker and Alan Trammel around second base they should be near the top of the division."

"My buddies and I have been saying that all year." *Damn, she really knows baseball. I've never known a woman who could rattle off facts like that.*

The couple had three beers each, two hotdogs and a tray of nachos. They hollered and cheered throughout the game, helping the Tigers pull out a win.

On the way home, Abby snuggled close to him. He put his arm around her and pulled her tight. She chattered happily all the way. Clark came dangerously close to saying something he shouldn't have about *the case*; he caught himself and clammed up.

I've never had such a comfortable, wonderful feeling for a woman in my whole life. She's not like all of the others. She's warm and affectionate, a great cook and smart as hell — knows everything about computers, baseball and what's going on in the world. What more could I ask for? I love her.

Heading down Michigan Avenue, his mind wandered back to the last four weekends at her place. They'd been like three-day orgies. *She goes non-stop. What a turn-on. Whenever I tried to seduce her, she ended up on top. God, I love her!*

He pulled into the parking structure, opened the door for her and the two headed for the elevator. Stepping inside she threw her arms over his shoulders and hung on his neck. Rising on her tiptoes, she whispered in his ear, "How can I make you happy tonight?"

He smiled and pecked her on the cheek. "You already have."

"You're so sweet … I could kiss you all over."

His eyes brightened. "That'd be a good start."

CHAPTER TWENTY-FOUR

At precisely three o'clock Saturday afternoon, six heavily armed policemen wearing flak jackets and helmets burst into the front door of the rundown apartment building on East Warren. Three SWAT team members broke down the rear door.

"Hands up, don't anyone move," the lead officer shouted to the bruiser seated at the front desk.

Hysteria reigned — doors opened and slammed female shouts and screams echoed down the hallway — commotion raged through the three floors.

A handcuffed, half-dressed man was led out the back door. Three scantily clad women were herded close behind.

Two cops scurried upstairs. The sergeant and his assistant took the steps two at a time to the third floor and flung open the door of room #312. The older man rushed in and the assistant flicked on the light. "There's no one here," the sergeant shouted, and said to the younger one, "open the window and let some fresh air in here."

The rookie SWAT member followed orders.

Heading down the hallway, the sergeant called over his shoulder. "Stand in the doorway until the crime lab people arrive. "I'm checking the rest of the rooms on the floor."

The greenhorn assumed the position; arms folded across his chest.

Minutes later, his supervisor returned. "The rest of the rooms on this floor are clear."

An officer from the first floor appeared. "The guy at the front desk said the blonde with big boobs was moved two days ago."

"Did he say anything else?"

The sergeant turned to Earl Walker, the lead man on the bust. "No ... other than she had been turning tricks on a regular basis."

Earl ran downstairs, picked up the phone and dialed.

"Clark Phillips," the voice on the other end responded.

"It's Earl. The room was vacant. The guy at the front desk said they took her to another location two days ago. The crime lab folks are dusting for prints."

"Anything else?"

"Not yet. If we uncover anything, I'll give you a call."

"Thanks." Clark turned back to the conference table and slammed the phone down. "They moved her two days ago. The crime lab people are doing their thing now."

"Damn," Detective Grissini, the Mafia expert, blurted. "They were tipped off."

"How do you know that?" Clark questioned.

"I've seen the same thing too many times for it to be a coincidence; they knew."

"That's impossible. Only those of us in the room were aware of the plan. The squad members weren't informed until late this morning."

"I don't care if you were the only one ... I'm telling you the Mafia was tipped off."

"At least we know she's alive," Kimberly from the prostitution squad said, drawing a positive note from the bust.

"That's important," Nancy Sterling of narcotics said, giving a sigh of relief. "That's something we can share with Dallas. Any shred of positive news will be good for his morale."

"You're right about that," Kimberly agreed.

"Damn." Clark scribbled a note on his pad. "Let's go back to Kingston. What are your informants telling you, Will?"

The inside-scoop aficionado looked up, sheepishly. "No one even heard of him. They've been told not to say a word."

"You're pulling my leg."

"No, it's true, Clark," patrolman Ralston interjected. "We came up with zero, too."

"Zero? How can that be?" Clark ran his index finger across his upper lip. "There's no way they could have anticipated us moving so quickly."

"Maybe not, but they did."

"I'm telling you, Clark. The word is out," Eddie restated his point.

Clark looked puzzled; his mind whirled trying to trace everything he'd said — everyone else in the room was doing the same. Coming up blank, he asked, "What else do we know?"

Captain Cumberland raised his hand. "Did anyone read the fire report for last week?"

Clark looked around the table. "It doesn't look like it, why?"

"Listen to this entry for Thursday." He paused, making sure he had everyone's attention. "At four o'clock in the morning, three units were dispatched to the residence of Mr. and Mrs. Raymond Kingston. Upon arrival the home was engulfed in flames. It was declared a complete loss."

Clark scowled. "I don't get it."

"Something is fishy." Patrolman Ralston stroked his jaw. "No one ever heard of Kingston. Now his house is gone. Next thing we know there'll be no evidence he ever existed."

"Hey, I wouldn't be surprised by something like that," Eddie admitted.

"A person can't just disappear off the face of the earth," Clark prognosticated.

"I've heard of crazier things," Max said.

"We have to keep digging. Someone out there knows something," Clark said. A frown settled on his face; his brain searched for an answer. Unable to come up with a clue, he asked, "Anyone else have something for today?"

Will Robinson straightened in his chair. "I do." Eyes around the table shifted in his direction. "We're halfway through our analysis of the questionable calls to and from Nash International. So far we've identified three hundred and eight calls in the past three months."

"That's a lot of calls from mob related numbers," Clark said.

"My back of the envelope calculation says five per work day," Grissini offered.

"That doesn't seem likely," someone said.

"I agree," Clark said. "Can we be assured that all of these calls were to and from Dallas?"

"I don't know," Sergeant Sterling said. "Tracing land-based calls to and from a number is easy. I don't know if we can segregate calls to various extensions in a corporation."

"Eddie, can your contact help?" Clark asked.

"Let me check."

The group sat in silence while he paged through his black pocket-sized notebook. "Here he is." He pulled the phone from the center of the table, picked up the receiver and dialed.

"AT&T," the group heard from the receiver.

Eddie asked for his friend and listened to the beeps. A man's voice answered.

"Paul this is Eddie, I have a question. I have three hundred and eight calls to and from a corporate number. Can you sort the calling numbers by the extension involved?"

A long pause followed.

"You don't think so?"

Eddie's head bobbed and weaved like a boxer. "You're not sure." He pursed his lips. "Will you try?"

He listened to his friend for a long spell. "Let me give you the number." He read the main number for Nash International and hung up. Turning to the group, he said, "He's never tried to do anything like that. He's going to check with one of his technology gurus. It'll take three or four days."

***

Eddie barged into Clark's office. "I have them."

Glancing up in surprise, Clark asked, "You have what?"

"The calls to Dallas' extension … forty-two of the calls were to him."

"Forty-two? Is that all? You're positive?"

"Paul double checked it twice. Two hundred and sixty-six went to the executive suite."

"The executive suite … Huston Nash?"

"I guess so."

"Call the team together. Tell them I'll be over in a half hour."

By the time Clark arrived at the McNamara conference room, Eddie had briefed the group.

Before sitting down, he asked, "What do you think about Eddie's finding?"

Max blurted out, "It's why Samantha was kidnapped and drugged up. It wasn't all about Dallas; they were buying protection against the old man, too."

Kimberly gave him a blank stare. "I understand why they may drug her up but why put her in a whorehouse?"

"That's part of it." Eddie spoke up. "They had no plans of setting her free."

Kimberly looked impassive, curious. "I don't get it."

"It's low maintenance and no need for a guard," Eddie added.

She shook her head in disgust.

Earl grasped the plan. "They were using her for insurance; they had no plan to ever set her free."

"Right." Max spoke from across the table, "One thing for sure we can never apply our logic to the mob's actions."

"Max is right, dealing with them is an entirely different ball game," Ralston said.

Clark deliberated quietly; his fingertips combed his thick crop of hair. "Let's assume it's all about both of them." He paused, his mind whirling. "Put your thinking caps on. Work independently the rest of the week. Pursue your own inclinations, don't talk to anyone else."

Eddie gave him a perplexed look. "You're always telling us to work as a team."

"I know, but this time is different." Clark rolled his shoulders. "We'll get to that. For now, I want each of you to act as if you were the only one on the case. Don't limit yourself — think creatively — hopefully you'll come up with something."

Ralston grinned. "Sounds like something your dad would try."

Clark smiled with the comparison. "Let's see what you can come up with by Monday."

***

Sliding into a chair at the beginning of the next week, Clark looked around the table. "Anyone come up with anything new on Dallas?"

Blank looks stared back at him from around the table.

"Okay, how about Huston?"

Nothing but silence.

Sterling shook her head. "I'm stuck on why. Why would Huston be a target?"

Max nodded in agreement. "Something is going on. It doesn't make sense on the surface."

Kimberly raised her hand. "I spent the entire weekend reviewing his financials. Everything looks normal except for the late Sixties. During an eight-year period his net worth increased six-fold."

Ralston piped in, "There was some inflation then."

Max Cumberland's eyes brightened. "That might account for a doubling but not six times."

"He'd have to have hit a gold mine," Earl jested.

"Sounds like you've found something that needs to be investigated, Kimberly." Clark's face glowed. "Let's everyone team up with her. See what kind of investments he made. Check out his personal life. Find out the kind of activities he was involved in. Who was he associated with? Run down everything that looks remotely questionable — there has to be an answer."

***

Sitting in the corner booth of his favorite neighborhood bar, Blackie made small talk with his mistress. She pecked him on the cheek and snuggled close. He whispered a sweet nothing in her ear, kissed her lightly on the lips, placed his hand on her upper thigh, and caressed gently.

Joey slid in on his right, followed by his two associates, each taking a seat on the side. "I have some troubling news to report."

Blackie removed his hand from her thigh and gave Joey his full attention.

"Saturday the police busted the place on East Warren where we'd been keeping the Nash girl. Fortunately, we moved her two days earlier."

Blackie's dark, thick eyebrows curled down. "Was it a regular bust?"

"Hmm … no. They went through the motions, but it was obviously aimed at the girl."

"Why do you say that?"

"Two cops immediately rushed to the third floor room where she had been held. The crime lab people were there in no time — she was the target."

"Someone tipped off the cops. I want to know who."

Joey looked at his two henchmen. "Go back to the house. Question the manager and the whores. Find out who was banging the blonde."

Blackie's face reddened. "There's a weasel out there. Get me a name."

"Right away, boss." Joey turned to his cronies. "See what you can find out. On the double."

The two slid out of the booth and scurried for the door.

Blackie turned to Joey. "How'd your telephone conversation go with Dallas?"

"Really well. I described the scenario Bufalino had laid out and told Dallas this was his chance to save his sister."

"How'd he react?"

"He got all choked up, said she wasn't a strong person and that he'd take care of business. He sobbed most of the time. Apparently, the two were close; he kept talking about things they did as kids."

"Sounds like we have him by the balls." Blackie pursed his lips. "Keep the pressure on him. We need him to withdraw the plea agreement as soon as possible."

***

Seeing Joey open the door and the lackeys standing behind, Blackie withdrew his hand from inside her blouse and kissed his mistress lightly on the cheek. She closed the middle button on her blouse leaving the others undone, proudly showing off her braless décolletage.

Joey called from the doorway. "We found the guy."

"Good." Blackie patted the cushion next to him. "Let's hear it."

Joey slid in on the right. The two soldiers assumed their positions at the end of the booth. "Wait 'til you hear this," Joey spoke pridefully. "We traced one of the guys who'd been banging her to the convenience store we've been watching."

Blackie's heavy brows came together. "The one owned by Alsye Weatherspoon?"

"Yeah, that's the one. The guy stops there every Friday night to cash his check. Last week an informant saw two guys with him, he assumed they were undercover cops. It looked like they got what they wanted. That was the day before the bust."

Blackie rubbed perspiration from his forehead. "Weatherspoon is connected with the police?"

"More than that … he's a regular at the Sax Club; and guess who his drinking buddy is?"

"Christ." Blackie threw his arm up. "How in the hell would I know?"

"Clark Phillips."

"Clark Phillips!" Blackie paused. "So *that's* the connection."

"And that's only half of it," Joey said, looking proud of himself. "The boys trailed Alsye all week and guess where he led them?"

"Jesus Christ, Joey, how in the hell would I know?" He said again, waving his hand. "Get to the point."

"Alsye has a bin rented at one of the storage facilities in Taylor. And hear this, it's loaded with fruit jars — moonshine. Weatherspoon is transporting fifty to sixty at a time in his trunk, each time he makes a run to his store."

"Son-of-a-bitch. I knew something was going on."

The associates stared at Blackie; his face beet red with anger. "Put a scare into the SOB."

Joey perked up. "The storage unit is located in a remote part of town. It'd be a good place to rough him up."

Blackie nodded. "Give him a lesson he won't forget."

Joey turned to the shorter lackey, rubbing his hands anxiously, waiting for his orders. "Teach him a lesson."

"My pleasure."

CHAPTER TWENTY-FIVE

Alsye pulled his banged-up '71 Cadillac in front of the storage unit, cut the engine and popped the trunk. Looking in all directions, he unlocked the storage bin door, surveyed the empty parking lot again, lifted the trunk lid and started loading fruit jars.

A car pulled into the far end of the lot and parked between two storage units, almost a block away. The driver glanced at the bigger guy. "Ready to go?"

The heavyweight nodded to his superior; the two henchmen slipped out of the car and walked briskly behind the units. Easing between Alsye's unit and the one next to his, the guy in charge spoke softly, "I'll grab him from behind and pin his arms when he leans into the trunk."

The big one grunted, stepped behind him and waited for the signal. Alsye carried a box of jars from the shed and slid them into the trunk. The short, pug-nosed guy sprang forward from behind, wrapped his arms around Alsye's chest and locked his arms against his side.

Alsye jostled trying to free himself. "What are you doing?" he shouted.

"That's what we were going to ask you," the short, stocky guy said. He manhandled Alsye, turning him to face the big thug. "Guess we'll have to teach you a lesson." He nodded to the enforcer. "Have at it."

The bruiser stepped forward and unloaded a powerful left to Alsye's stomach. He hit him with a right and a left under the ribcage. Alsye doubled over, gasping for a breath. The big guy aimed a fist at Alsye's face and threw an uppercut to his jaw, sending him sideways to the left. Alsye's eyes rolled back. Blood gushed from his mouth. He mumbled something and closed his eyes. The heavyweight threw another hard right, opening a deep gash above Alsye's right eye that sent blood flowing freely from his face. Alsye's head fell limp. The bruiser continued to hammer Alsye unmercifully, a left and a right to the body and another right.

"That's enough," the little guy said, loosening his grip and pushing Alsye inside the doorway; his body landed on a stack of fruit jars, splattering moonshine in all directions. "C'mon, let's get out of here," he barked.

"Go ahead. I'll clean up." The bruiser stepped inside and kicked Alsye; his blood-soaked torso barely moved. The guy picked up a fruit jar, popped the lid and poured booze over Alsye's head. "Here, have a drink." He laughed. "It's on the house."

"Hurry up," his buddy called, now less than ten yards from the car.

"I'll be right there." The thug picked up another jar, sloshed out of the shed, closed the door, and slammed the jar onto the concrete driveway. Pulling a cigarette lighter from his pocket, he laughed.

"What are you doing?" his buddy called.

"I'm giving him a house warming."

"Stop, that stuff is all over you!"

The slow-witted heavyweight chuckled and flicked his lighter. Flames leaped from his hand to the pool of alcohol surrounding him. He flayed his arms, trying to put out the fire. "Help me, I'm on fire!"

"I'll get a blanket out of the trunk," the headman called.

"Hurry," he shouted. Kicking at the flames, he slipped on the greased pavement and tumbled to the ground, cracking open the storage unit door.

Flames rushed inside — a horrendous explosion flashed — the ground shook, sending debris into the sky. Hot coals peppered the lot. The little guy scrambled under the car.

A second explosion erupted, igniting Alsye's car. Metal fragments flew like bullets, pieces of the Caddy filled the parking lot, smoldering like stumps in a forest fire.

Pulling himself from under the car by the door handle, the pint-size henchman looked at the gaping opening where the row of sheds once stood. "Frankie, shit!"

He stared at the twisted steel framing where three units once stood. Flames leaped from the piles of rubble next to the blazing car. His eyes shifted to the burning heap lying where the doorway used to be. "Oh Frankie, no." He saw another pile of flaming debris where the shed had stood. "Oh my God, they're both gone."

***

Flicking on the noon-time news, Clark sat in his office chewing on a white-bread, baloney and cheese sandwich. A SPECIAL REPORT flashed across the screen.

He turned up the volume. "About ten thirty this morning, the Taylor Township Fire Department responded to an explosion at the Taylor Self-Storage Center. By the time the trucks arrived, three storage units were nothing but smoldering rubble," the young female reporter announced.

The camera scanned the ruins, filling the screen with the gruesome video.

"The fire chief speculates that two people were in the structure when it exploded." She pointed to the charred car. "The police are checking the vehicle number of the car to determine its owner. This is Rachel Salinger reporting for WXYZ-TV, live in Taylor Township."

Recalling Alsye's comment about a storage shed in Taylor, Clark stared in shock, hoping what he had seen was not what he thought it was. He picked up the phone and called Ted, followed by Carlos, and Renzo to see if any of them were watching. No one answered. He called Father Dom and told him of his speculation.

"What do you think we should do?" Father asked.

"Go to their place and check on Nicole ASAP, just in case my instincts are correct."

"I can't tell her I'm making a house call."

Clark's voice sharpened. "C'mon Father, you've done this before. Tell her the truth. Say it's a long shot but we thought it'd be good for you to be with her, just in case."

"What if it's a false alarm?"

"All will be forgiven and forgotten … imagine how she'd react to a phone call or a knock on the door about Alsye from a stranger."

Father Dom agreed. "I'm on my way."

***

It was three o'clock when Clark received a call from his friend confirming the car vehicle number belonged to Alsye Weatherspoon. "Damn." *I knew it was him. Why Alsye? There was no one better than him — he worked hard, was a wonderful husband and father — a great friend. I'm going to miss him so much.* Clark choked up and sucked in a deep breath, knowing what he had to do.

He ran his hand over his jaw in thought, picked up the phone and called Renzo's home. Wendy picked up. He described the findings. "It's becoming more likely that one of the bodies is Alsye."

"Oh no," she moaned. "Renzo won't be home for another hour or so. I'll leave him a note. I'm on my way to Nicole's."

He repeated the same conversation with Rosa Maria and Laverne. "We're on our way."

Clark jumped in his Mustang and sped across town. Seeing several cars parked in front of Alsye's place, he rang the doorbell and walked in. He came face to face with Nicole; her eyes were red and glazed.

"Do you think it's true?" she ventured, obviously not wanting to hear Clark's response.

"They're not positive yet," he said, not wanting to reveal his true thoughts. He pulled her tight and they hugged for the longest time.

Nicole sighed, pulled away, and squared her shoulders. "I want you to meet my oldest." She sounded as if nothing had happened. She pulled her son close to her.

"This is number one, J. J."

The cute two-year-old with Alsye's smile extended his hand like a diminutive grown-up. "I'm glad to meet you, sir. Where do you work?"

Taken aback by his poise, Clark cleared his throat. "I'm a policeman."

The little tyke's eyes brightened. "My daddy's best friend is a policeman."

Clark's eyes welled. "Your daddy is a wonderful man."

"Yep, I know," the miniature Alsye said and ran off to play in another room.

Clark said something to Father Dom and sat down on the chair next to the sofa. Nicole eased onto the sofa next to the priest. He put his arm around Nicole and held her firmly.

She broke down. "I know it's him," she sobbed.

"There's always hope, my child."

The phone rang. Clark hustled over and picked it up. His mouth turned down and he choked. "Yes ... I will."

Nicole screamed, "I knew it ... I knew it."

"Let it out my child ... let it out." The old priest held her as tight as he could.

"Why Father … why? Alsye never hurt a flea. Why? I don't understand why?"

"Sometimes we can't know why. God has different ways for all of us to serve him."

She sat still for a long moment and then pushed her hands against him. "I have to fix dinner. Alsye will be home any time. I have to get up."

Father Dom firmed his grip on her shoulders. "Nicole, he is not coming home."

"No. You're wrong." Nicole pushed against him, trying to free herself. "I'm cooking dinner — collards, black-eyed peas and barbecued ribs — his favorite."

Father Dom held her face in his hands. "Look at me, Nicole."

She turned her head toward him, her eyes slowly connecting with those of the priest.

Softly, slowly, he said, "Nicole, he is not coming home."

She stared blankly. "He isn't coming home, is he?"

The priest shook his head. "No, my dear, he isn't."

Nicole closed her eyes and leaned her head on his shoulder. Moments later, she stirred and pulled away. "I have to turn on the oven. Alsye will be home any time."

Father Dom held her tight. "Nicole, he's not coming home."

"He's not coming home," she mumbled, and eased her head back onto his shoulder.

Father Dom took his time consoling her, lightly stroking her hair and whispering prayers of consolation. She closed her eyes.

Clark mouthed, "Is she asleep?"

Father Dom mouthed back. "I think so."

Still resting against him, she rustled; her head shot straight up. "I heard the garage door. He's home. I have to set the table."

Father held her in place. "Nicole, he isn't coming home. He died in the fire."

Her eyes widened. "You're lying. Father, why are you lying to me?"

The priest gave her a most compassionate smile and squeezed her hand. "Nicole, Alsye is dead. He isn't coming home."

She rocked in his arms. "He's not coming home. He's not coming home."

Father Dom repeated, "He's not coming home."

She fell back on the sofa, crying, still mumbling, "He's not coming home."

The two rocked on the sofa 'til after dark.

Friends and neighbors came and left. The guys slipped into the dining room. Wendy gave Father Dom a break, sitting by Nicole's side. A neighbor stopped by and took the boys to her house.

Nicole remained on the sofa, dazed and periodically dozing. Once she sat up straight and stiff, her voice clear, "I can hear Alsye. He's coming home."

Wendy ran her fingers through her hair and pulled her close. "Nicole, Alsye is dead. He's not coming home."

"Alsye is not coming home," she reiterated and fell asleep.

***

Waiting at baggage claim, Clark waved to a tall, attractive African-American woman. *It has to be Nicole's sister. She could be her twin.* "Hi, I'm Clark Phillips," he called. "Are you Natalie?"

"Yes." She rushed forward, flung her arms around Clark and hugged him. Stepping back, she eyed him. "You look just like Nicole described."

"I hope that's good." He chuckled.

She smiled with a wink. "It's very good."

Clark picked up her bag and rolled it toward his car. Chatting as he drove along I-94, she asked about his job and thanked him for being there when Alsye and Nicole needed him. Clark shared his feelings about Alsye and filled her in about the details of the disaster.

Arriving at Alsye's place, Clark slowed and parked in front. Natalie sprang from the car, ran onto the porch and shoved open the front door. Racing inside she came face to face with Nicole. The two embraced in the middle of the room, swaying and hugging as if they were the only two people in the world. Neither said a word; nothing needed to be said — Natalie was there.

Nicole mumbled, "Alsye is not coming home."

Tears ran from Natalie's eyes. "I saw him from the plane on his way to his new home."

Nicole backed away. "You saw Alsye?"

"Yes. His smile was as big as always. He said, 'Tell Nicole I love her.'"

238

Nicole squeezed her with all her strength. "Natalie, you're a God-send."

The next few days were filled with friends and well-wishers. Casseroles, hot dishes and soups lined the kitchen counter. Natalie made arrangements for visitation hours and the funeral. Nicole seemed oblivious to the activity surrounding her. The two sisters had long talks about their childhood and the importance of family. Natalie reminded her of the trials they'd experienced when their mother passed and after their father's death. She repeated again and again. "Nicole, now it's your turn to stand tall for your boys; that's what Alsye would want."

***

Nicole sat at the grave site, dressed in black with a black veil hiding her tears. Father Dom looked over the casket. "Dearly beloved we are gathered here to recognize a great man, a wonderful father and husband," he began.

Tears streamed downed Nicole's cheeks; she held J. J.'s hand and rocked J. D. on her lap.

Father Dom continued for a couple of somber moments, blessed the casket, stepped to Nicole's side and whispered in her ear, "Be strong, my child."

Holding back a sob, Nicole nodded. Natalie stood close to her and the two stared at the casket one last time. Clark stepped to their side, took J. J. by the hand and escorted him to the car. Natalie carried J. D, squeezing him tight, Nicole cried all the way. Natalie consoled her as they climbed slowly into the back seat. Clark sat quietly in the front seat with J. J. on his lap.

Pulling into Ricciuti's driveway, Nicole took a deep breath and sighed. "Clark, I want to thank you for all you've done. Alsye always said you were his best friend. Now I can honestly say you're my best friend too. I really appreciate all you've done."

Not being much for words in situations like this, Clark hugged her. "You'll be fine. We're here to help." He took J. J. by the hand and led him inside. Waiting inside, each of her friends took one more turn consoling her.

Nicole veered away from the throng of people and took a chair in the living room. She sat alone, staring blankly at the walls. The others talked quietly in the dining room around the table of hors d'oeuvres and punch.

The hour grew late. Nicole stood and walked into the other room. She faced the group with determination. "I appreciate your friendship so much. I can't tell you how important all of you have been in our lives. You've treated Alsye and me like family. We felt like we were your brother and sister. You're simply the best friends anyone could have. I'm so blessed to be able to call each of you a friend."

The group smiled graciously. "The privilege is ours," Carlos said.

She raised her hand. "I'd like to say something ... Alsye and I talked often about a time when one of us might be gone. We agreed the remaining one would move on as if we were two. I will learn how to run the stores. J. J. and J. D. will have a good life. They will grow up to be fine young men that will make you and Alsye proud." She hesitated and brushed a tear aside. "One last point ... I will not bend or turn the other cheek to the Mafia. Alsye and my great- grandparents were slaves. I will not lower myself to being a slave to them."

"God bless you," Father Dom closed.

***

Two weeks later, Laverne and Rosa Maria slid out of Wendy's car and the three walked slowly up the steps to Nicole's front door. Looking at each other, Wendy took the lead and knocked.

Nicole's look-alike sister opened the door. "Don't say a word. Let me see if I remember ... you're Wendy." She extended her hand to her and looked to Wendy's side. "And you're Laverne."

"Right." The two embraced.

Natalie turned. "And you're Rosa Maria."

She smiled. "That's pretty good for only meeting us one time."

"I cheated." Natalie laughed. "Nicole told me who you were when you were on the way over."

The three followed her to the dining room table where Nicole waited. She rose and gave each one a hug. "It's so good to see all of you. I hope you're all well."

"We're fine," Wendy said. "How are you?"

"Much better ... have a seat."

Natalie headed for the kitchen. "I'll get some tea. We have sweetened and unsweetened."

"Sounds good," Rosa Maria said. "May I help?"

"I have it," Natalie said, returning within moments with two pitchers of tea. She left again and returned with a tray of glasses filled with ice.

"I want to thank you for helping me get over the hurdle ... you guys are the best," Nicole said, raising her glass in a toast. Casting the group a reassuring eye, Nicole spoke firmly. "Natalie and I have had some long talks and we've agreed it's time for me to pick up the pieces and get on with my life."

Wendy gave her a questioning look. "Nicole, these kind of things can take a long ..."

"That's what we talked about." Nicole's voice rose stronger. "I have a new resolve."

Her friends looked at each other not knowing what to say.

Nicole stood, stepped behind her chair, and placed her hands on the chair back. "I want to reiterate what I said the other day." She paused. "Alsye and I had a pact ... whoever went first the other would carry on just like the two of us were still alive."

Laverne smiled. "Yes Nicole, but so soon. Don't you think you should...?"

"Nope, we agreed. Sitting around moping won't accomplish a thing. Natalie helped me understand — I have responsibilities, people depend upon me, I can't be wasting time — there are things that need to be done."

Laverne raised an eyebrow. "Good for you."

Wendy raised a fist. "More power to you."

Nicole looked thoughtfully at her friends for a moment, and spoke with conviction. "I'm following through with our plan."

Overpowered by her display of confidence, her friends sat in silent awe.

"I have a five-point plan and won't stop until each goal has been reached."

"Sounds impressive," Rosa Maria said. The others agreed.

"First, I will raise our boys in a way that would make Alsye proud. Second, I will learn how to manage our stores. Third, I will create a Neighborhood Watch Program in each of the communities where we have a store. Fourth, I will take a stand on every issue that makes a difference in our community. And fifth, I will not pay the Mafia one red cent as long as I live."

"Nicole, I know you have strong feelings, but the Mafia ..."

She cut off Rosa Maria. "Not one cent. My great grandparents did not achieve their freedoms only for me to give in to slavery again. Not one penny!"

Her sister cast a disconcerting eye. "Nicole, those are very laudable goals, but …"

"Natalie, you know me. I intend to accomplish each one."

Natalie shook her head and glanced around the table. "You better be ready … when she sets her mind to something, it's going to get done."

CHAPTER TWENTY-SIX

Clark shuffled through his file and looked up. "Let's bring everyone up to date on Huston Nash. Who wants to start?"

Eddie raised his hand. "This guy is a piece of work." Chuckles raced around the room.

"He has a great image," patrolman Ralston said. "His record of support for civic endeavors and giving to worthy charitable projects is unmatched in the city."

"He has to be one of the top philanthropists in the country," Max emphasized.

Ralston gave Clark a puzzled looked. "I'm intrigued though, by the changes in his wife."

"How so?" Clark asked.

"Ten years ago she was the queen of the ball. Her photo played across the social pages every weekend; and if there was a major event she was front and center standing by Huston. I thought she was the most attractive woman in the world."

"Is this a true confession?" Max asked.

"I'm sure I wished something like that once or twice … and just like *that* she disappeared. I don't recall seeing her in the paper since."

Earl glanced at Ralston. "Maybe she was tired of all of the hoopla."

"Hmm maybe, but … people don't change that dramatically overnight."

Clark gave him a quizzical look. "What triggered your observation?"

"The family picture after her grandson was killed. She looked like a dowdy, old-fashioned housewife. It just jumped out at me, like night and day."

Eddie drew a frown. "So what's this mean for us?"

"I'm not sure." The old-timer shrugged his shoulders. "It just popped into my mind; maybe nothing."

Clark looked toward the other end of the table. "Kimberly, want to tell the group about your findings?"

"Yes." Sergeant Weston glanced at her notes. "In 1961 Huston accepted an appointment to a small savings and loan in Grosse Pointe. In '63 he was named board chairman for another bank in Sterling Heights."

"Where's this going?" Eddie asked, impatiently.

"Hold your horses," she said. "Both were declared insolvent in 1971 and closed before the end of the year. By that time Nash's personal wealth had grown six-fold."

"Maybe he made some great investments."

"Could be, but there's more. I made a list of the other directors, and … guess what?"

"Okay … okay, I give up," Eddie said, again pulling her chain.

She flashed him a disgusted look and continued. "The board of directors for both reads like the membership of the Italian-American Club."

"Do you think they were connected to the Mafia?" Eddie asked, with renewed interest.

She wrinkled her nose. "Next time, wait until I'm done before you spout off, huh?"

"Yes, mama," he said respectfully.

Clark intervened. "Since you're hitting it off so well, I want Earl and the two of you to head up our continuing investigation of Huston. See if we have any information on the board members."

***

August poker was something the guys *had* to do. They left a chair vacant for Alsye and bowed their heads. Father Dom delivered a personal eulogy. The sober conversation turned to Nicole.

"I don't know how she will be able to deal with everything," Carlos said.

"She's very strong," Renzo said. "I think the monthly meetings with the women will be helpful. It'll give her a good outlet and a chance to talk."

Father Dom picked up on the point. "That's a lesson we all learned from Alsye."

"I still can't believe it," Renzo bemoaned, turning toward Clark, "Have you been able to reconstruct what happened?"

A watery-eyed Clark shook his head. "Alsye mentioned to me that he had moonshine stored in Taylor. We figure a couple of Mafia thugs followed him out there. Maybe they wanted to put a little fear into him … who knows. They beat him up pretty bad. The coroner said he had a broken nose, a dislocated jaw and four cracked ribs."

"Sounds like they used him for a punching bag," Ted said.

"We think so."

"The paper said two bodies were in the rubble. Any ideas on the second guy?"

"His body was just outside the door. The fire chief figures there may have been white lightening on the ground. He could have dumped a jar, or maybe it seeped out from inside. Who knows after that? He could have been smoking a cigarette or playing around with a lighter. Anyway the juice ignited. Alsye didn't know what hit him."

"Damn, I hate it," Carlos said.

"I'm sick and tired of the Mafia doing this, doing that and no one does a thing," Ted said.

"Next thing we know they'll be moving in on one of *our* businesses," Renzo grumbled.

"They better not mess with my car business," Carlos said emphatically.

"What would you do?" Clark asked

"I-I … I don't know but …"

"You do the same thing as Alsye, and you'll end up the same way. These guys don't mess around."

Carlos hesitated, catching his breath. "I know but … I'll have to give more thought to that. Hopefully, I won't have to worry about it."

"Clark, are you positive Nicole will work her way through this?" Father Dom asked. "Maybe I should have some meetings with her."

Clark's gaze contemplated the old man. "Right now, I'd suggest you hold off on that thought. She'll have her struggles in the weeks ahead but I believe her resolve will carry the day. She's serious about raising her boys the right way and giving them the privileges she didn't have. I can tell you one thing … if she gets her dander up, I wouldn't want to be in her way."

***

Clark eased into his chair at the conference table. Meeting with the subcommittee of Eddie, Kimberly and Earl, he asked, "Did you get all of the information you needed?"

"I can't believe it. How'd you come up with so much in two weeks?" Kimberly asked.

Clark gave her a sly smile and winked. "Magic I guess."

"Someone had to pull a lot of strings," Earl said smugly, knowing Clark had the inside track with the FBI.

Clark flipped his hands up. "I called an old friend. He made a call to the Federal Home Loan Bank and ... bingo."

"Who are they?" Kimberly asked.

"They're the counterpart of the FDIC who protects your savings. They oversee activity of the savings and loans. The country is divided into twelve regions; the office for our area is in Indianapolis."

"You sound like a banking aficionado."

"Now you know as much as me." He gave her a curious look. "So what kind of information did you get?"

"Everything ... examiner reports, bank reports and CPA reports for the years in question."

"And?"

"The year-end statements for the two savings and loans were amazingly similar. There were tremendous financial gains from one common holdings — Atlantic Off-Shore Drilling."

"Sounds like they hit a big oil strike," Clark surmised.

"That's what we figured, too," Earl said.

"FHLB examiners signed off each year so they had to be on the up and up," Eddie said.

"What's next?" Clark asked

"There's a lot of banker jargon we don't understand. We need someone — a banker or CPA — to walk us though this so we can make sense of it."

"The feds can bring in a team of examiners in a couple of months."

"A couple of months!" Earl exclaimed. "We need to know something, like ... next week."

"Hmm." Thinking to himself, Clark rubbed his lower jaw. "I have a good friend who's a bank vice president. I'll give him a call. Maybe he can help speed up the process."

***

An attractive redhead opened the door to the dimly lit neighborhood bar and headed for the glow in the far left rear corner.

Seeing a woman on the right side of the booth, whose figure wasn't half of hers, she smiled to herself. The curly headed Italian man on the left eyed her. The man in the center nodded for her to take a chair at the end of the table. He removed his sunglasses and gazed at her cleavage as she leaned forward to sit down.

"I'm Abby Thompson from Philly."

"So I figured. I'm Blackie Giardini." He slipped his glasses back on. "Glad to meet you. I appreciate the information you've provided."

"That's the deal." She stared him in the eye. "Why was it so important for us to meet?"

"I like to have an image of the person I'm talking to on the phone."

She gave him a repulsive look, and quipped, "I'm sure you have my photo."

"Maybe, but I … like meeting people so I can look them in the eye."

She smirked. "Enough of the bullshit … get on with it."

Blackie seemed taken aback. "Have you heard of King Kingston?"

She paused for a moment. "What's the deal?"

"He's one of our guys who got himself into big trouble. He had a meeting with Dallas Nash and said some things he shouldn't have."

"So, what's that got to do with me?"

Blackie leaned back, realizing she was one tough broad. "I want to know everything you can learn from your boy, Clark. We have to get King out of this mess."

She sat motionless without comment. "I told you about the wire."

"Yes, but I need more."

"How much more do you want?"

Knowing the game, Blackie grinned. "I'll add another grand."

"Make it two." She grinned, knowing she had the upper hand.

"Fair enough." He removed his sunglasses and looked her in the eye. "How about Clark and you taking a little trip to Mackinaw Island? It's the best place in Michigan this time of year."

"Never heard of it. What's it like?"

"It's elegant … has great food. It'd be a wonderful getaway at the Grand Hotel. "I'll even throw in an extra five hundred for incidentals. You can drive there in five or six hours."

"Make it a grand."

* * *

Abby pulled her Corvette into a far corner of the parking lot at Shepler's Mackinac Island Ferry and turned off the ignition. Grabbing a large green floppy hat from the back, she slid out and took her time adjusting the hat. She modeled her light tan blouse and formfitting dark green slacks in the door's window reflection. Clark pulled his carry-on bag and her small suitcase from the storage area and followed her into the terminal building.

He bought the tickets and a couple of Cokes and led the way onto the ferry and up the stairs to the open-air upper deck. Snuggling into two seats in the rear, they held hands and cuddled. Clark whispered sweet platitudes in her ear.

She cooed and giggled. He pecked her on the cheek. "This was a great idea. How did you ever come up with such a thought?"

Abby's cheeks broadened into a smile. "A friend at the office said the place was spectacular. So I said, why not?"

"Wait 'til you see the hotel. You'll be overwhelmed," Clark said.

"The pictures in the newspaper ad looked magnificent."

"No, no." Clark waved his hand. "Photos don't do the place justice. When we walk inside you'll feel it … the atmosphere … it reeks with character and ambiance."

"Spending a weekend with you," she snuggled closer, "what could be better?"

Clark kissed her lightly on the lips. "You're the best."

The ferry chugged away from the dock. Abby rested her head on Clark's shoulder and snuggled close for the rest of the trip.

Stepping off the ferry, the two walked up the steep incline to the main street. Clark hailed a buggy driver who reigned the horse to a stop. Jumping down, he patted the horse and loaded their luggage in the back of the carriage.

Driving up the hill toward *the* hotel, the driver played tour guide, giving the two a brief history of the island, and stopping in front of the world's longest porch. The driver sprang from the buggy, helped Abby down, and placed the luggage in front of the bellman.

Paying the driver, Clark deposited two extra bucks in his hand and nodded to the bellman standing by their bags. "Phillips, party of two," he said.

The senior African-American nodded with a grin, welcomed them and led the way to the elevators.

Clark frowned and tapped him on the shoulder. "We haven't checked in."

"No need, sir. Everything has been taken care of."

Clark turned to Abby. "You think of everything, don't you?"

She gave him a come-on glance. "I try to when it comes to you."

Wait 'til I get you in bed. I'll do the thinking.

"Your first time here?" the bellman asked.

"Not for me. It is for the lady." Clark acted like he was in charge.

The old man turned to her and said pleasantly, "Welcome to the Grand Hotel."

She smiled at his cute grin and winked at him.

"I'm sure you'll have a lovely stay. If you need anything, just call. My name is Harold."

"Thank you, Harold. That's very kind of you."

He opened the door to their suite and waved them past him, to enter. Placing their bags on the racks, he adjusted the air conditioner, briefed them on the hotel amenities and headed for the door.

Clark pushed a five into his hand. "Thank you, Harold."

He grinned and closed the door. Snuggling against his back, Abby wrapped her arms around him and whispered, "I want you, Clark. I can't wait any longer."

He turned and planted a firm kiss on her lips. She gave him a long French kiss. Clark's urges fired, his hands tugging and pulling at the buttons on her blouse.

"Take your time sweetheart," she said, stepping back and sensually unbuttoning her blouse for him. Clark stripped naked, ripped back the blankets on the king bed, and slid his lower torso under the sheet. Playing coy, she paraded to the bedside and took her time unhooking her bra and slowly sliding off her panties.

She eased under the sheet and climbed on top, straddling him — her large, firm breasts brushed his chest. He ran his fingers around her breasts and took his time teasing one nipple and the other.

The two wrestled playfully, soon falling into passionate lovemaking — Clark led the way and then Abby was on top. Clark tried not to come too soon. She caressed his shoulders and ran her hands down his sides. Taking her time, she watched him squirm — his breath shortened, he gasped and swallowed hard. She knew one more move and he'd explode. Seizing the opportunity, she slammed against him.

"Oh my God," Clark called out.

***

Dinner that night combined the perfect view of a glistening sunset over the Straits of Mackinac with a gastronomical treat. Sitting at a table for two in the elegant dining room filled with crystal and sterling, the two barely took their eyes off each other. Clark ordered Muscovy duck breast as an appetizer and Abby opted for the Mexican white shrimp with horseradish. Both passed on the soup and salad.

Clark tore his attention away from her long enough to order a braised veal shank for his entree; Abby chose the baked Mackinac whitefish.

After ordering another bottle of wine, Clark reached across the table and gently squeezed her hand; he ran his index fingertip up and down the top of her fingers. She smiled softly, biding her time. He picked up his glass of Pinot Noir by the stem and swirled the wine — his fantasies whirling more than the wine — Abby's lovely face seemed even lovelier with each swirl.

Over dinner he adjusted himself twice before enjoying a demitasse served in the parlor. Listening to soft music played by the hotel's own orchestra, the two held hands and discreetly kissed. She whispered something in Clark's ear. He smiled broadly, took her by the hand and strolled to the elevator.

Stepping inside the room, the two took their time loosening each other's buttons one at a time — he tossed his shirt aside; she laid her blouse on the chair. Slowly, sensually, she removed his slacks, and took privileges with his bulging shorts.

Stepping back, they eyed each other and finished stripping. In the moonlight that streamed through the balcony door, the two gently caressed each other. She admired his sculpted body. Clark couldn't take his eyes off the most perfect woman he'd ever seen.

Slowly they inched toward the bed. Clark collapsed on it, his emotions drained. Abby eased down and slid on top, straddling him. She ran her hands across his pecs and inched further down.

Clark's engine roared. The two made passionate love late into the night.

Early in the morning, Abby snuggled close to him, ran her fingertips around his pelvic area, toying and teasing. Clark placed his arms over his head, knowing he could spend the rest of his life with her. She slid on top and wasted no time taking him to his limits once and again, before watching him explode.

***

Clark took a stroll around the grounds the next morning, picked up a newspaper and was back in the room before breakfast arrived.

He could hear Abby in the shower when the doorbell rang. Clark opened the door and held it, while an African-American man placed a carafe of coffee and their breakfast orders covered by sterling-silver lids, on the small table in front of the window. Clark handed him a tip and the man scurried away.

"Breakfast is here, darling."

Abby opened the door and paraded out, her long dark blue, filmy negligee leaving nothing to his imagination. Clark's sex switch flipped on, his eyes taking her in. "How am I supposed to eat when ..."

She cut him off. "We could eat later?"

"Hmm, you're hot ... breakfast is hot ... my omelet won't stay that way long."

"And you think I will ..."

"Have some coffee." He laughed and filled her cup. "I'll see what I can do later."

She gazed into his eyes. "You promise?"

"You'll have to wait and see," he jested and unfolded the paper. The headlines jumped out:

𝔇etroit 𝔉ree ℜress
August 30, 1979

BODY OF MISSING WOMAN FOUND AT DETROIT YACHT CLUB

The body of millionairess Samantha Nash was found early this morning floating face down in the Detroit Yacht Club pool. Missing since April of this year when she was abducted from her room at a boarding school in Massachusetts, she'd been the subject of a prolonged police investigation. Both of Miss Nash's wrists had been slashed. The police found a razor blade near her shoes and have tentatively listed the case as a suicide.

"That changes everything," Clark mumbled.

"What's that, dear?"

"Samantha Nash, the woman I told you about. Her body was found face down in the Detroit Yacht Club pool."

"Oh ... that's terrible. Do they know what happened?"

"It's been tentatively listed as a suicide. There was a razor blade next to her shoes." He sliced into his omelet and read further; his mind racing over *the case.* "She had to use a code on the gate to get into the pool area. Hmm, this changes everything. Dallas had recanted his plea bargain because of his fear for her. That's out the window now. We can move full speed ahead."

"It'd be a real feather in your cap if you could nab one of the higher ups."

"It isn't about me, sweetie. It'd be a real big step for all of us." Clark stretched his arms over his head. "God, I feel great. Want to take a bike ride around the island?"

"That sounds like fun."

"Should I order two bicycles or do you want a bicycle built for two?"

"Hmm, I don't care. Get what you prefer."

"Okay. I'll order a bagged lunch so we can stop halfway."

"Perfect."

CHAPTER TWENTY-SEVEN

Dallas Nash and his lawyer followed Frank McHenry into his office and took their places at the conference table across from Clark. Pulling out a chair next to Clark, Frank glanced at Dallas, nervously fidgeting his hands.

"What can you tell me about my sister's death?" he asked, in a distressed tone.

Knowing he had to give Dallas the straight facts, Frank didn't beat around the bush. "We're positive it was a suicide."

Dallas grimaced, trying to sort out his thoughts. "I wouldn't think she'd have the courage to do something like that."

Clark eased into the topic. "Maybe she figured they were not going to release her."

Dallas gave him a questioning look. "Why do you say that?"

"We're still piecing things together but it isn't a pretty sight."

"What does that mean?" Dallas asked in an elevated tone. "Did they abuse her?"

Clark took a deep breath, wanting to tell the truth in the least hurtful way he could.

"C'mon, don't dance around." Dallas' face reddened. "I want to know the facts."

Clark hesitated, knowing how much the truth would hurt. "From the needle marks on her arms it's obvious she was heavily drugged. She likely drifted in and out of reality. They were keeping her in a whorehouse. …"

Dallas cut him off, "A whorehouse … why was she there?"

"We have some theories but I have to tell you … they forced her to turn tricks."

"Oh my God, no. Those bastards. She was so innocent." Dallas pulled out his handkerchief and wiped his eyes. "She didn't deserve that." He blotted a tear, put his handkerchief away and took a deep sigh. "Okay, tell me the rest. How did she get to the Yacht Club?"

"We're not positive." Clark gave him an unconscious shrug. "She could have conned a guy ... promised to go to bed with him. Maybe she tucked away twenty bucks and used it for cab fare."

"That sounds just like her. She was no dummy. I bet she figured out she was being used as a hostage for them to get something from our family, and planned the whole thing."

"Planned?" Clark looked perplexed. "Why do you say that?"

"We were raised with the thought of kidnapping in the back of our minds. When we played cops and robbers as kids, she always came up with a way out. The Yacht Club was a favorite getaway place — she'd race away in our yacht or be a stowaway."

"So do you think she was capable of suicide?" Clark asked, making sure what he'd heard was correct.

"Normally, I'd say no, but from the abuse she was going through it'd be a natural reaction. She always said she'd rather be dead than be used. I'm sure it was her way out. She never would have been able to live with herself after that."

"And she used the Yacht Club to tell you."

"Right ... being found there says it all." Dallas pursed his lips and cracked a grin. "Now it's my time to give back to her. What else do I need to do to finalize the plea bargain?"

"Nothing," Frank said. "We'll complete the paperwork today and see you in court next week."

"Thank you," Dallas said, relief evident in his voice. "Guess I'll be changing my pinstriped suit for a wide-striped outfit." He stroked his jaw. "Made any progress in locating Kingston?"

"Not yet," Clark said. "We issued an APB and are trying to track down his whereabouts. The Mafia has done an outstanding job of covering his tracks. I expect it'll be some time before we catch up with him."

***

Clark opened the door to The Whitney and headed for the Ghostbar. Seeing Nicole waiting in a black leather barrel chair at the end of the shiny, mahogany bar, he hustled her way. She gave him a faint smile. "I ordered a Tanqueray with three olives for you. I hope that's okay."

"Perfect," he said, looking at her puffy eyes. "How are you feeling?"

"I'm fine … as long as I stay busy." With a double-take look, she admitted, "As a matter of fact I feel like crap."

"I can understand that," he said in a sympathetic tone. "I think about the boys and you often. How are they doing?"

"Better than I would have ever imagined." Her smile grew. "Fact is, I don't know what I'd do without them."

"Let me know if there's ever a time when I can do something for them."

"That's so kind of you." She let out a deep sigh; her eyes softened. "I'm so fortunate to have so many good friends. Wendy, Laverne, and Rosa Maria have been particularly helpful. They've been there to lend a helping hand whenever I've called."

"Guess I would have expected that. They're all special."

She took a deep breath. "I'm glad you could meet me today. I have some questions for you."

Clark's mind spun; his eyebrows shot up. "I'll be glad to help in any way I can."

"I'm creating a Neighborhood Watch Program around our main store," she stated excitedly.

"I've heard lots of good things about them. How can I help?"

"I have material from the local chapter, but it doesn't say much about making connections with the police department. That seems particularly important; can you help?"

"Of course," he said anxiously. "A couple of thoughts come to my mind." He paused while she opened a small notepad and pulled a pen from her purse. "I'd suggest you have a sit-down chat with the chief at your precinct. It'd be good for him to meet you and have a sense of your overall vision."

"Makes sense. Eventually I want to extend the concept to our other stores."

"Wow, that's pretty ambitious."

She stroked her black wavy hair. "I don't have a choice, Clark. I can't stand by and watch the neighborhoods go downhill in fear."

"Too bad we don't have more people like you." His warm smile revealed his respect for her. "Once you get your organization together I'd give the street captains' names, addresses and phone numbers to the chief. That'll give him a person to call if there's an issue in their area. I'd also ask him to send a representative to your meetings. The presence of a police officer will add significantly to your credibility."

"Hold it," she said, flipping the page and continuing to write. "Those are great ideas. That will relieve some of the anxiety of the people who are leery about the process."

"It's especially important to have an officer at the first meeting," Clark pointed out. "It'll go a long way toward demonstrating that it's a two-way partnership."

Nicole underlined the point. "Yes, I'll call the station first thing Monday."

Clark finished his gin. "I'm having another. Want a refill on your Coke?"

"Might as well."

He glanced over at the barmaid and made a circular motion for another round. Nicole glanced at her watch. "I have to leave pretty soon. I have one last question."

The drinks arrived.

Clark took a long sip. "Let's hear it."

She leaned closer. "I have no intent of paying the Mafia goons."

A deep crease sliced his forehead. "Nicole, that's extremely dangerous. You can't do that. First, we'd need to have an extended talk about your decision. You just can't …"

Nicole interrupted. "No need to talk, Clark. I've decided."

Clark saw the resolve Alsye had mentioned in her eyes. A smile filled her face. "I'm serious, you know."

"I understand." Clark's eyes sharpened. "Do you have a plan?"

"I'll just say no when hoodlums ask for money."

"And then?"

Nicole leaned back in her chair. "They won't know how to react … so they'll leave and go back to get their marching orders."

"That's probably accurate." Clark folded his hands. "What happens next?"

"They'll come back with their hands out. I'll say no and tell them I want to talk to their boss. They're know-nothings. I'll hold my ground until they come up with a name."

"That's perfectly logical, Nicole, but these guys aren't logical. They may threaten you or bust the place up. It's too dangerous. I can't let you do that."

"I'll keep you posted."

"That's not good enough. The Mafia is my business. Nicole, you have to give further consideration to all of this."

With a questioning look, she thought about what he said. "What do you think I should do?"

"It has to be a cooperative plan — it's we, not you — at a minimum there has to be plainclothesmen in the store and outside."

Nicole looked away. "Oh-Okay."

Clark paused, feeling that she wasn't fully on board. "Do the goons come at a regular time?"

"It's always the same, between 8:30 and 9:00 a.m. on the first Monday of the month."

"I'll have undercover men there at eight"

"If you say so." Her pout turned into a partial grin. "That's fine."

***

Clark could hardly wait to get off work at five o'clock. Within minutes, he was in his car heading for Abby's place. It had become a regular routine; she was there waiting for him. He smiled to himself. *After all of the women I've been with, I know she's the one. She's the best; her actions prove the feelings are mutual. We've gone everywhere together — gone to plays and the theater, enjoyed dinners at the finest restaurants — done everything. And best of all is the sex — in the shower, on the toilet, on the counter in the kitchen, standing against a column in the hallway, on a lounge chair on the balcony — it doesn't matter — she goes non-stop.*

He unlocked the door and looked down the hallway. She was not in sight; soft jazz music filled the room. Taking a few steps in, he saw her perched provocatively on the dining room table; her bare legs dangling over the edge.

"What's going on?" he asked with high hopes.

She loosened the string holding her top. "What do you think," she said, running her fingertips around her breasts and down along the top of her skimpy red panties. "Welcome home delight."

"You gotta be kidding."

She hooked her fingers inside the top of her panties, slipped them off and let them fall on the floor. "Do I look like I'm kidding?"

Shaking his head, Clark swallowed hard. "Not. At. All."

"You just going to stand there? Take your clothes off."

"I can handle that." He hurriedly stripped to his bulging Jockeys.

Her index finger beckoned him. "Drop your shorts."

He slipped them off and eased closer. Placing her hands on his hips, she moved her fingers down his side and fondled him.

"You don't mess around, do you?" he gasped and closed his eyes, trying to rein in his urges. She slammed a hand on each of his cheeks and pulled him tight. Wanting her more than ever, his heart rate rocketed. "Take it easy."

She leaned back on the table and locked her legs around his torso.

***

Squeezing into the cramped surveillance room, Clark proudly introduced the members of his task force. Oscar Westerfield, the FBI's lead man on the sting operation, made a few comments about each of the operatives and turned to FBI field agent Robert Barenie.

"Could you show the group some of the video clips you've put together of the mobsters coming and going from the house across the street?" Westerfield asked.

"I'd be glad to." Barenie pointed to a monitor. "Slide over here so all of you can see."

Clark's team huddled around him. He flicked on the box-size computer and waited, slowly the screen brightened. "Here's Freddie Salem standing in the front door." The agent paused. "I guess I should properly introduce him; here's 'Freddie the Saint' Salem. He runs the crap game for local gamblers and some big hitters out east. To the right is Edward 'Baldy' Sarkesian. He's another gambling lieutenant for the Mafia. And in the lower right side of the screen is Henry Allen Hilf. He's the most prolific bookmaker in town and often helps Freddie run the game." Barenie glanced over his shoulder. "Any questions?"

The group stood in awe. They collectively shook their heads.

Earl pointed to a different screen. "Show them some of the frequent visitors."

"You're a perfect straight man." Barenie laughed and flipped on the other screen. "Here's Freddie again on the left, and two of his crew members. In the center is William 'Buffalo Bill' Gibera and on the right is Frank 'New York Frankie' Inglese." He flipped to another surveillance photo. "This is Frank Versaci, another underworld bookmaker." He paused. "That's just a small sample of what we have." Barenie said, flicking off the computer and turning around in his swivel chair. "I understand someone wanted to meet the guys who have been inside."

"Yes, I do." Kimberly raised her hand.

"Well then, turn around and I'll introduce them to you." Two men stood inside the doorframe. "These guys have cased the joint a couple of times. They'll go in a half hour prior to the rest of the agents on the night we make the bust." He pointed to the handsome, dark-haired one with a thick black mustache. "This is undercover FBI agent William Randle."

The agent eyed Kimberly and extended his hand. "Nice to meet you."

"To his right is his sidekick, Allen Finch."

"I'm glad to meet all of you," said Finch. "We've heard a lot of good things about your work."

"Thanks," Clark said on behalf of the team. "Earl and I are looking forward to joining the group on the night of the raid."

"We're getting close to wrapping it up." Barenie stood. "Anyone have a question they'd like to ask?"

Max raised his hand. "How do you get in the place?"

Randle grinned. "We've been seen in several local gambling places and blind pigs. The two guards outside know us as local gamblers, so we can come and go with ease. On the night of the sting, we'll go in and case the place one more time to make sure everything is a go, and I'll give the signal for the rest of the guys to come over."

"That sounds kind of risky." Earl shook his head. "I'll be the last one in."

A roar filled the room. Embarrassed, Earl hung his head.

"It's a little risky," agent Finch admitted. "We'll all be wearing bulletproof vests. Don't worry Earl. There'll be a dozen or so agents in front of you."

Earl's smile opened wide; he wiped his brow. "I'll be way behind."

"Anyone else?" Looking around the group, Barenie glanced back at Kimberly. "You look like you'd like to ask something."

Her faced reddened. She bit her lip.

"Well?"

She looked into agent Randle's sexy dark brown eyes. "Is he married?"

Barenie gave her a broad smile and extended his left hand, revealing his wedding band.

Kimberly pouted in mock disappointment. Laughter filled the room.

CHAPTER TWENTY-EIGHT

A tall, slender African-American man followed Clark into the conference room and laid a large stack of papers on the table. Clark placed his arm around his shoulders. "Folks, this is Lawrence Brown, the banker friend I mentioned. He's the senior vice president at American Savings and Loan. Lawrence, along with two of my buddies, went to school together at U of D; he handles all of our banking business."

"If you're a friend of Clark, you can't be too bad," someone joked.

Lawrence raised an eyebrow, studying the group thoughtfully. "I'm not sure if that's a ringing endorsement or not," he jested.

Leonard spoke up. "I've known the Phillips family for over fifty years. You're obviously okay."

"Thank you, sir." He sat down in the chair next to Clark.

"Lawrence, please share the summary of Huston Nash's banking activity that you walked me through over the weekend."

"Gladly," he said, opening his leather-bound notebook. "I've done a quick and dirty review." He laughed. "That's not a banking term. Clark is always on my case for using banker's jargon."

"C'mon Lawrence, that's only when you're talking about my loan application."

He smiled at Clark's wit. Getting down to business, his mouth turned down. "Here's the scheme I figure he used."

"Scheme?" Eddie questioned, raising an eyebrow.

Lawrence grinned. "That too is not a banking term. At least I got your attention."

The group enjoyed a laugh at Eddie's expense.

Lawrence ran his fingers down his notes. "First, you'll be glad to know that Atlantic Off-Shore Drilling does not exist. It's a dummy corporation based in the Bahamas. If you go there, I'll lay odds it's a storefront operation."

"Storefront operation?" Eddie questioned. "For what?"

"Money laundering."

Eddie threw his hands in the air. "Why in the hell didn't that get the bank examiner's attention?"

Lawrence shook his head. "Good question."

"Do you think they were on the take?"

"Hmm, not all of them. More likely two, maybe three."

"I don't understand," Ralston said.

"Let me back up." Lawrence loosened his tie. "The primary focus of the examiners is assessing the viability of loans and protecting depositors. Most of the team members focus on bank loans — remember their primary purpose is to protect the consumer. Out of the nine-person team the FHLB sends, only one person has responsibility for assessing investments."

"So if you grease his or her palms you'd be home free?" Earl suggested.

"Almost ... the team chairman would have to be in on it too."

"Interesting." Max mused. "So you pay off two members, you get the report you want."

Lawrence gave him a regretful nod. "Right."

"Any idea how much Huston could have raked in?"

"Both of the savings and loans were medium-sized ... someone could have skimmed off two or three million dollars a year."

"From each bank?" Kimberly asked.

"You got it, five or six million a year is certainly in the game."

"Wow." Earl's eyes brightened. "No wonder his portfolio skyrocketed."

Kimberly looked confused. "I don't understand. I thought the feds monitored every transaction over ten thousand dollars."

"Great point." He gave her a pleasant smile. "That's right for banking transactions ... deposits and withdrawals. Again, protecting and monitoring consumers is their primary focus. In this case, we're talking about investments. There are no federal reporting requirements for internal operations. No one checks on investments or wire transfers. Whatever a bank records on their books is the official record."

"I can't believe that." Eddie looked shocked. "That leaves the whole area open to devious actions."

"You're smarter than I thought." Lawrence joked.

***

Rosa Maria opened the door to Roman Village and stepped briskly toward Wendy. "I'm glad you scheduled the meeting here. It has a real homey feeling. I think Nicole will feel comfortable in a casual environment like this."

"My thinking too."

Laverne strolled in and joined them in the foyer, followed by Nicole. Each one gave Nicole a firm hug and whispered something in her ear, and headed for their corner table for four.

Wendy, Rosa Maria and Laverne settled into their seats. Nicole remained standing and spoke firmly. "I want to thank the three of you for all the things you've done. I don't know how I would have gotten through all of this without each of you. Thanks again."

"We did the same things you would have done had similar circumstances happened to any one of us."

"That's nice of you to say, Wendy."

"I'm not just saying it, Nicole, I know you."

Nicole blew them a kiss and joined the group. "You women are the greatest."

The waitress filled their glasses, emptying a bottle of wine. Laverne held hers high. "Here's to the good times that are ahead."

"I'll drink to that," Nicole said.

Each woman ordered a small pasta dish with a salad. Halfway through her salad, Wendy laid her fork aside. "How are your plans progressing to establish a Neighborhood Watch Program?"

"Surprisingly well," Nicole perked up at the question. "Lots of people on the blocks surrounding our anchor store are excited. I have brochures on how to get started that I'm going to hand out at our first meeting."

"When is that?"

"Next Tuesday. I've hand-delivered over four hundred fliers in a six-block area. Our church is making their community center available. I've sent special invitations to the two newspapers and all of the television stations."

"That sounds exciting," Rosa Maria said. "I'm looking forward to seeing you on TV."

"I hope you do."

"Wouldn't that be something? Maybe we'll have a celebrity with us next month."

"I'm not interested in being that. I just want to clean up our neighborhood. I know that would make Alsye proud."

"Good for you," Wendy chimed in.

***

THE DETROIT NEWS
September 3, 1979

JUDGE ACCEPTS NASH'S PLEA BARGAIN

As expected, Judge Harold Baines sentenced millionaire Dallas Nash to serve five years in the Milan Federal Penitentiary after which he'll be on parole for another five years. His testimony remains under lock and key in the federal prosecutor's office.

***

A dim light from the kitchen broke the darkness of Abby's exclusive riverfront apartment. Sitting at her small table, as she had with Clark on a regular basis over the past few months, she stared blankly at the city lights lining the Detroit River. Paying little attention to the recently opened, half empty bottle of Canadian Club on her right, she clasped her hands over her face.

How did this happen? She picked up the bottle of Canadian Club, filled a glass and added a dab of vermouth. Stirring slowly, her mind played back the movie of her life. She'd been an all-state track star, setting a Pennsylvania state record in the four hundred meter dash. A success at every endeavor she'd ever attempted — she graduated from college with honors in computer science and landed a high paying technology job. All of that, she chuckled to herself, to become the highest paid call girl in Philadelphia.

Big deal. The Mafia paid me to seduce him, get all the information I could and to share it with them — twenty grand per month plus all expenses — better than three months' pay back in Philly. But it wasn't supposed to work out this way.

She refilled her glass and stirred. *Shit. I've screwed high rollers, big-name execs, celebrities, and sports stars without becoming involved. How can this be? Everything was fine until we went to*

264

Mackinac Island; without warning it happened ... I fell in love with a detective on the Detroit police force. It can't be ... it shouldn't be. Damn, I love him so much.

She took a long sip and stared at the flowing river; the twinkling city lights now barely visible in the morning sun. *I have to tell him. I can't go on hypocritically pumping him for information, spilling my guts to the mob ... and then jump back in bed with him like nothing has happened. Geez, I hate myself. I can't wait any longer.*

***

Abby opened the door and looked at Clark tenderly — smiling like a Cheshire cat — she gave him a light peck on the cheek and tugged on his arm. He drew a long white box from behind his back and gave it to her. "This is for the love of my life."

Her eyes welled. "You're so wonderful, Clark. I love you."

"I'm so glad," he mumbled, trying to say more, but he choked up. "Go ahead ... open it."

She hurried to the kitchen, placed the box on the counter and loosened the gold bow. Opening the box, she stared at the small envelope lying on top of green paper, opened it and read it aloud:

Abby,
To the most extraordinary woman I've ever met. I love you.
Forever, Clark

She stared at the card, unable to move. A tear trickled down her cheek. She brushed it aside and pecked him on the cheek. "You're such a sweetheart."

"Go ahead."

Her hand slowly pulled back the wrapping. "Yellow roses, they're beautiful, and baby's breath ... I can't wait 'til I see them in a vase."

Her tears began to flow freely. Sniffling, she wiped her face with a tissue and thrust her arms around his neck, planting a wet smacker on his lips. "I love you, Clark Phillips."

He eased his mouth from hers. "I'll love you forever."

"You're the best." She looked up with glassy eyes.

Still embracing, Clark glanced past her into the kitchen; the lights were out. "Do you have plans for dinner?"

"I was thinking we might order in something."

"Fine with me." Clark stood and headed for the wine bar. "I'll fix a couple of drinks and we can talk about it. Want the usual?"

"Yes. I'll put the hors d'oeuvres on the coffee table. You can join me on the sofa."

"Sounds good."

Sliding onto the sofa, Abby sat pensively, clearly not her usual self. Clark handed her a Manhattan and clinked her glass. "Here's to you, darling."

She gave him a faint smile and took a slow sip.

"You okay?"

"Ah … there's something on my mind," she said; her voice weepy, shaky. "I need to …"

"Go ahead," he urged, while filling his plate. He turned to give her a questioning look as she remained silent.

She hesitated a moment longer. "Clark, I don't know how to say this."

He scowled and placed a chunk of pickled kipper in his mouth.

"C'mon it can't be that bad," Clark said, in a playful, joking manner.

Her sorrowful eyes, pleaded. "I want you to hear me out before you judge me."

Clark smiled cheerfully. "Of course I will."

She took a deep breath.

Waiting patiently, he waved his hand in front of her blank stare. "I'm still here."

Her lips didn't move for a long time, she spoke softly, "I … I work for the Mafia."

Stunned with her admission, Clark's eyes glazed as he realized the implication. He cocked his head and stared at her for the longest time. Sitting dumbfounded, motionless, he looked like he'd been punched in the gut. "I-I don't understand."

"Clark, you said you would hear me out. Let me explain."

He jumped up and shouted, "You don't work for GM, do you?"

She paused, not sure, afraid how he might respond. "No, I don't. I *was* a computer science major in college."

He kicked at the sofa. "And you didn't get a GM discount on your Corvette?"

"No, they bought it for me to drive." She pleaded again, "Please Clark, please ... you promised to hear me out."

He flopped back on the sofa. "Okay ... get on with it," he said sharply.

"I'm from Philadelphia and was hired by them to get as much information as I could."

"Hired? You were hired to seduce me and ... screw all night."

"No ... no. It wasn't like that." She wiped a tear from her cheek.

Clark straightened on the edge of the sofa. "Well just how was it?"

"Well, at first it was ... and then I fell in love with you."

"And that makes it all right?"

"No, none of it was right."

"None of it ..."

She cut him off. "No. I didn't mean it that way. You're not listening ... you're not hearing what I'm saying."

"I'm hearing exactly what you're saying. You're a whore from Philly hired by the Detroit Mafia to screw me and pump out as much information as possible. Yes or no, is that what you're paid to do?"

She shouted, "No Clark, you don't ..."

He screamed over her. "Yes or no, is that what you were paid to do?"

Her face paled. "Clark, that's not fair."

"Fair!" he yelled. "Look who's talking about being fair." His face beet red, he gasped, barely able to speak. "One. More. Time," he said evenly. "Yes or no, is that what you're paid to do?"

She buried her face in her hands, and said without looking up, "Yes."

"Now ...what part don't I understand?"

"I admit it, Clark. That's the way it started ... but ... it's different now."

"Oh, so they're not paying you now?"

"No." She paused. "I'm still being paid ..."

"So what's different?"

"It's different now because I love you."

"You love me. Ha ... so when did this big change occur? A week ago, two weeks, last month?"

"It just happened. When we were on Mackinac Island it was so magical. I've never felt that way. I've been head over heels in love with you since."

"When the authorities found the body of Samantha Nash, did you tell them what I told you we were going to do?"

Abby lowered her head. "Yes ... and I'm so ashamed of myself."

"You slut. You've lied and cheated for months and now you say you're in love with me. You squealed to them about our plans. I can't believe it."

"Clark, please listen to me. You're only hearing what you want to hear." She held her breath, hoping she had his attention. "Originally it was that way Clark, but now it's different ... I love you."

"That's what you say." He waited, letting the silence lengthen. "Yet, you're still leaking my information to the Mafia. Will it be different tomorrow or the next day?"

"I'll never change," she sobbed. "I'll love you forever."

"Forever ... ha!" He slammed his hand on the coffee table. "Get out of here. Pack your bags and go back to Philadelphia. I don't ever want to see you again."

"Clark, don't say that. I want to be with you forever."

"Sure." He laughed bitterly. "And I want to live with a whore who I can't trust from one minute to the next. I'm out of here." He stood and bolted for the door.

"Wait." She rose to rush after him. "I know where King Kingston is!"

Clark stopped in his tracks and slowly turned to face her. "You know *what*?"

"Please sit down. I'll tell you everything I know." She pointed to the living room. "After that you can do whatever you want to do."

"Fine." He sat in the chair across from the sofa. "Tell me about King Kingston."

"He's living at Blackie Giardini's Florida place on Biscayne Bay in Miami."

"How do you know that?"

"Blackie mentioned it at one of my meetings with him."

Clark's mouth dropped. "You've been meeting with him on a regular basis?"

"Not at first, but yes, I've been meeting with him every two weeks for the past six weeks."

"How could you be meeting with him and at the same time say you're in love with me? You're a goddamn hypocrite, whore, a liar and a cheat."

He stood and stomped out the door.

"Clark, please don't leave," she shouted after him. "I'm so sorry Clark. Please, I love you."

***

Clark fumbled for his apartment key, shoved it in the lock, and opened the door. Slamming it shut, he shouted his frustration, "Goddamn, son-of-a-bitch, asshole …." He stumbled across the living room, kicked the stuffed chair, and banged his fist on the kitchen counter. "Son-of-a-bitch. How can you be so goddamn dumb?"

Pulling a bottle of Tanqueray from the cabinet, he grabbed a water glass and ripped opened the fridge. Seizing a jar of olives, he opened the lid and jammed a toothpick through three of them and tossed them in the glass. He filled it with ice and gin, and took a long sip then shrieked for everyone in the building to hear, "Goddamn, son-of-a-bitch …!"

Walking slowly back to the living room Clark plopped down in his favorite leather chair. *How could I be so dumb? Why didn't I see through her? All the things I told her … I've always been careful in the past … never divulged a key fact. My big mouth could have hurt someone. All the time I was screwing a snitch-whore. Now look at me … one more notch on her belt. And now, of all things she wants me to forgive her. That's bullshit! If my dad knew about this he'd give me a tongue lashing, a swift kick in the ass, and lecture me all night.*

CHAPTER TWENTY-NINE

Clark sat at the conference table with the task force members, waiting for the call. Right on time, eleven o'clock, he picked up the phone. "Clark Phillips."

"This is Captain Gonzales, head of the Miami swat unit," the speaker phone summoned.

"Did you get him?" Clark asked, anxiously.

"Yes, sir. It went just like clockwork. We've had the house under surveillance for the past ten days to establish his daily routine. On schedule the driveway gate opened at nine-thirty and the driver took Kingston and his wife to the IHOP a half mile away. Our team was waiting there. We nabbed him when he stepped out of the limo."

"Did you have any problems?"

"No. He surrendered without incident."

"Great job. Thanks for the update."

"No problem and ... good luck on your prosecution."

"Thanks," Clark said, and hung up the phone.

"I can't believe we nabbed him so quickly," Kimberly Weston said.

"How did you ever figure out where he was?" Will Robinson asked.

"Sometimes you play a hunch and hit it right," Clark fibbed, as the pats on the back continued. Thoughts of Abby swirled through his mind; images of her flashed — in bed, at a fancy restaurant, watching the Tigers, on Mackinac Island, and standing naked in the shower. *Damn, how could I be so dumb?*

"Ready for an update on the bank examiners?" Kimberly asked.

Deep in thought, Clark didn't look up.

"Clark?"

"Yes of course, go ahead."

She kicked off the report. "The findings confirm what Mr. Brown had speculated. Huston raked in millions from both banks. It was laundered through their location in the Bahamas."

"No wonder his net worth shot up," Max said.

"We checked out the names of the other directors. They received an annual hundred grand stipend — most of them are known mobsters or connected with the Mafia."

"How did individuals with their backgrounds ever get approved to serve on the boards?"

"That's another case. The investigator thinks some money exchanged hands. He pointed out that information systems are better nowadays than they were fifteen years ago — not much detail was available on individuals back then."

"Listen to the name of the one person who served on both boards," Kimberly said.

Clark gave her his full attention, and repeated her disclosure, "Angelo Travaglini, the Underboss?"

"Yes. The number two man in the Detroit Partnership."

"Do the examiners think we might be able to nail him too?"

"Hmm, they're not positive from the information they've uncovered thus far. Huston for sure. His signature is on every document."

"Anything else?"

"Mrs. Nash was the secretary to each board. She received an annual stipend of fifty thousand dollars."

Clark's eyes widened. "A tidy amount for a part-time job."

"I guess so." Weston laughed.

"So what does it look like for Huston?"

"He's going to be in the federal pen in Milan for some time. They'll have him on several counts — money laundering, tax evasion, racketeering — and who knows what else. The FBI has taken over the case. We're now back-up for them."

***

Detroit Free Press
September 30, 1979

DETROIT MOBSTER NABBED IN FLORIDA

EXTRADITION TO MICHIGAN IS IN PROGRESS

Ray "King" Kingston was apprehended yesterday at the IHOP restaurant just after leaving a mansion on

Biscayne Bay, one of the most exclusive districts in Miami. He surrendered to federal agents without incident.

Blackie's lieutenants gathered in the booth of his favorite neighborhood bar. His mistress was not invited. Joey ordered a couple pitchers of beer and waited for the waitress to fill their glasses and leave.

After a quick sip of his drink Blackie pounded his fist on the table. "How in the hell did the feds find out about Kingston's location?"

Not a word was spoken. Not one of the soldiers looked up.

"Well ... I'm waiting," he said, impatiently; his face reddened. "I want to know ... Now!" he shouted. "I have to report the details to Jake. There's a leak and I want to know where."

"Who else knew?" Joey asked.

Blackie stared him in the eye. "The guys up the ladder and ..." He stopped, his mind obviously twirling a hundred RPMs per second. "Red, from Philly."

"Maybe she's the source," Joey ventured.

"That cunt ... I don't think so. The Philadelphia Mob Boss personally vouched for her. They've used her countless times. Her record is flawless."

"There's always a first time."

"Hmm, I don't think so. She was a damn good source of information on Clark Phillips."

"Do you want me to call her in?" Joey asked, "Just to make sure?"

Blackie ran his hand across his lips. "She left yesterday, said she had pumped Clark dry."

"Maybe she got tired of giving him blow jobs."

"I don't think so. She's a top-notch professional." Blackie's eyes refocused on those around him. "I want each of you to retrace every conversation you had about Ray. Someone, maybe unknowingly, said the wrong thing to the wrong person. I want to know who it is. That person is a liability. We'll meet in two days right here at the same time. I want a name!"

***

Blackie and Joey were in the same seats as the last time when the guys filed in. A group of long faces surrounded the table.

Blackie's eyes shot fire. "I'm waiting!" No one looked up. "God damn it; I want to know … who's the stoolie?"

His lieutenant spoke for the group. "Each of the guys has scrutinized every conversation they've had recently. I'll vouch for them — the leak did not come from this table."

Blackie's mouth turned down. "So you're saying the Philly Boss let me down."

"Maybe she got the hots for Clark."

"A pro like her … she's been with the most famous, richest guys in the world. She could have had any of them." He sighed. "And you're telling me she picked Clark Phillips, a detective on the Detroit police force, to fall in love with? C'mon, give me a break."

Joey spoke up. "Maybe her pussy is like Clark's pecker."

Blackie snapped his head back. "What does that mean?"

"Clark's pecker makes his decisions; maybe it's the same with her pussy."

"She's a pro … I can't believe that. I want everyone to keep digging. I want an answer."

***

Clark walked into the poker meeting room.

"Our hero has returned," Renzo shouted.

"Hail to the chief," Ted called.

"Shall we kneel before his majesty?" Father Dom asked.

"Get out of here." Clark waved his arms over his head. "You guys are crazy. We captured one guy."

"Yeah … a big fish," Carlos declared. "It's a first ever — one of the big Mafia honchos."

Clark smiled and conceded the point. "You're right about that. It shows they're vulnerable after all."

"Who's next on your list?" Ted asked.

"I wish I could say," Clark admitted. "When you're dealing with these guys it's one step at a time. You never know when a lucky break may occur."

"So capturing King Kingston was a lucky break?"

"Hmm, not lucky … just something we didn't anticipate."

"Sounds lucky to me," Carlos concluded.

Clark fluffed his peacock feathers. "You can call it anything you want. We've got the bastard behind bars."

"Here, here," Renzo shouted. "Dealer's choice!"

The guys gathered around the table and waited for the first ace. Father Dom was the lucky one. He grabbed the deck and shuffled the cards. "Seven card stud, deuces wild."

The cards, conversation and jokes flowed like normal. Father Dom had half of the chips when he called, "Break Time."

"It's about time," Ted admitted, having lost more than anyone else.

The group made their usual pit stops, filled their plates and settled into their regular spots — a chair still vacant for Alsye.

Clark gestured toward the chair. "We'll never replace Alsye, but it's time to fill his chair. Earl Walker has been a great friend ever since we played ball in high school." He paused letting his suggestion sink in. "I recommend that we add Earl 'The Pearl' Walker to our group."

"That's a no brainer as far as I'm concerned," Renzo said.

"Me too." Carlos agreed. "Maybe after all of these years I can get even with him. He'll be great; he has a good head and a dry sense of humor."

"Sounds good to me," Father Dom agreed. "It's about time we heard some new stories."

"I'm all for it. Maybe *he'll* tell us what's going on in the police department." Ted laughed.

***

The women met at the Roman Village in Dearborn for the third consecutive month. Wendy took charge. "I'm so pleased to see how well you're doing," she said to Nicole.

"Me too," Rosa Maria said. "You have so much energy."

Laverne butted in. "It's her resolve; she's a woman on a mission."

"You're all right," Nicole agreed. "When I talked to my sister after Alsye's death, I decided I had to make a choice. I could do like most people, keep on trucking and adjust to a new reality. Or, I said, I could say enough is enough. I'm going to make something of my life."

"I understand that," Rosa Maria said, "I had a sister who became a wall flower and wilted on the vine after her husband passed away."

Nicole squared her shoulders. "I recalled the stories from my great grandparents. They didn't have a choice. They simply did what their master said. There were the times when my grandmother couldn't eat in a restaurant, go in a public bathroom, or stay in a nice hotel. I owe it to them."

"That's a real statement of who you are," Laverne stated.

"It really isn't about me. My boys are not going to grow up as second-class citizens. They're going to walk tall like every other man in the world." Nicole paused and took a deep breath. "Like Alsye. I don't have a choice!"

"That's a tremendous declaration of your resolve," Rosa Maria said. "If most people had half of your commitment our city would be ten times stronger."

Nicole gave her a polite smile. "I don't know about that, but I'm going to make a difference. I'm not going to be trampled on. I'm going to keep pushing."

"Nicole, that'll take an enormous amount of energy and perseverance," said Laverne, with a worried look.

"If I don't, who is going to show the way?" she said confidently, "We're going to reclaim our community. It doesn't belong to the Mafia. It's our property, not theirs. It's our store, not theirs. It's our children's future, not theirs. They have no right to interfere with our lives."

"Nicole, I know you're passionate, but you can't take on the world in one swoop," Wendy warned. "You need to move slowly, one step at a time."

"I'm doing just that. First, we'll secure the neighborhood around the main store — the others fall in line, one at a time. I'm stopping my payments to the Mafia. I'm not giving them my savings for my boys' college educations."

Laverne bristled. "Nicole, that's too dangerous. They don't act like normal people. They only know one course of action — bully, coerce, intimidate and threaten — do whatever it takes to get their way."

"Maybe so…but if I lie down and don't fight, I might as well be their slave. The freedoms that generations of my family have fought for will be lost. I can't allow that to happen."

"Have you talked to Clark? What was his reaction to all of this?"

"Yes, he was leery too, but finally agreed, as long as we work together."

***

Oscar Westerfield and Robert Barenie greeted Clark and Earl, and the four sat down at a small table in the surveillance room. "I appreciate the two of you coming in for a briefing on such short notice," Westerfield said.

"No problem." Clark grinned. "Earl is anxious to lead the team in."

"No way." Earl's eyes bugged out. "The only way I'll be leading is on the way out."

Barenie laughed, gave him a thumbs up. "You have some time to think about it. We're only doing a walk-through tonight to make sure when we hit Freddie Salem's we've got everything right."

"I know," Earl said, "but my palms get sweaty just thinking about it."

"It'll be like shooting a free throw in an overtime game," Oscar pointed out. "It's only normal to be nervous the first time."

"I was nervous every time I shot a free throw."

Clark gave him a pat on the back. "Sure you were; and you never missed one."

"You'll be fine. See that monitor over there," Westerfield pointed to the screen in the corner. "We have mini cameras in the basement ceiling so we can keep track of every move of the gamblers."

Earl raised his eyebrows. "That helps."

"Here's the procedure we'll follow. When we get the all clear signal from undercover agents Randle and Finch, two other agents will walk up to the front door and place the two guards under arrest. With the way cleared we'll storm the place — break down the door and rush for the basement — they won't know what hit them. A couple of agents will take anyone upstairs into custody." Oscar paused and winked at Earl. "By the time you get there everyone will have their hands up and I'll be reading them their rights. All you will have to do is help frisk them."

"Sounds easy enough but I'll feel better when it's over."

"Hey, we've all been there." Barenie winked. "We've all had butterflies the first time or two. After that it's old hat."

Clark looked across the table at Westerfield. "Do you have a timetable for when it's going to happen?"

"Hmm … not a timetable, but there's less than a week left on the court order for the cameras and bugs … and I don't want to go through all of that again."

Earl gave him a puzzling look. "Is that a problem?"

"Yes and no, sometimes it can be and other times it's just a hassle. The procedure is much tougher than most people think. The guidelines for surveillance activities like these are incredibly strict. You have to develop probable cause, present it to a federal judge, and get him or her to buy in. It can be a brutally time-consuming process."

Earl looked surprised. "You'd think they'd be very willing to help law enforcement people capture the bad guys."

"I agree, but it's not quite that simple. You're dealing with freedom of speech, invasion of one's personal rights and a slew of other things. So they give us twenty or thirty days to do the job. Every five days we have to come back with a progress report."

"That takes a lot of manpower," Clark interjected.

"You bet." Oscar continued. "It's all very structured and if not done right the defense attorney can have the whole damn wiretap thrown out and poof, there goes the entire case."

Earl gave him a thoughtful glance. "Does that happen very often?"

"More times than I'd like to admit. I've seen a lot of cases thrown out because a good defense attorney attacked the best evidence we could have — the bad guys saying incriminating things — and the judge ruled it was obtained illegally or was a violation of this or that. Judges are very protective of freedom of speech." Oscar looked up, somewhat embarrassed by the length of his response. "I guess that's more than you ever wanted to know. Any other question about the planned raid?"

The two cops looked at each other and shook their heads.

"Good. One of these nights, you'll get a call late in the evening telling you to be over by one o'clock. We'll have another briefing before we hit the place, probably between three or four in the morning."

CHAPTER THIRTY

Nicole handed the customer his change and looked up.

An overweight Italian-American with long dark sideburns and a receding hairline stepped to the counter. To his right, a thin man with a blue long-sleeved shirt rolled below his elbows stood fidgeting nervously.

"We're here to collect the four hundred dollars for the month," the heavy guy said.

Having practiced her line, Nicole said, "Excuse me?" in a firm tone.

"You know, to collect like always," he said, abrasively.

Nicole gave him a hard look and then spoke in a stern tone. "I'm sorry, I've just taken over after my husband's death; you'll need to be more specific."

He softened his tone. "It's for protection services."

A crease wrinkled her forehead. "Do we have a contract?"

"Sort of ... it's an understanding. We make sure your stores are not vandalized or damaged."

"I don't even know your name."

"It's Thomas Lewis ... I go by Tommy."

"Well Tommy ..." She brushed her hair to the side. "I'll have to think about it. You'll need to come back next week."

"You don't understand ..."

Nicole cut him off. "Me?" she asked, elevating her still firm voice. "What didn't *you* understand?"

The hoodlum backed off and glanced at his cohort. The thin man shrugged. Turning back to her, Tommy Lewis said, "We'll be back next week."

"Better yet," ventured Nicole, "What is your boss's name? I want to meet with him about this so-called service."

"Uh, I'll tell him," Tommy said without giving her a name. The men hurried toward the door.

No sooner had the two bagmen stepped out the door than a plainclothes officer walked in. "You okay?" he asked.

"Yes, I'm checking in with Clark."

He nodded and walked out.

Nicole picked up the phone and called him. "Clark, I just had my first visit from the Mafia. They wanted their money for this month."

"Are you all right?" he asked with concern.

"I'm fine. I told them I would have to think about it."

"Think about it? You can't say that."

"I did. I wanted them to know that this Tommy guy and his scumbag, scrawny buddy were not going to jerk me around."

"Tommy?" Clark paused. "Do you know his last name?"

"Yes. It's Lewis ... Thomas Lewis."

"Oh shit," Clark mumbled. "Does he have a dark mustache, goatee and long sideburns?"

"Yep, that's the guy. Do you know him?"

"Only by reputation. He's Thomas 'Tommy Gun' Lewis. He's one of the most feared mob enforcers in town. He works directly under crime family captain Dominic 'Fats' Corrado. You don't want to mess with either one of them."

"Well, whoever he is I told him I wanted their boss's name."

"Why? What are you going to do?"

"I want to meet with him. Do you know his name?"

"Not really. The ones that came into the store are several layers down in the organization."

"Well ... who do all of *their* bosses report to?"

"Nicole, I can't ..."

"Clark, I called you because I want to know their boss's name."

"They all report to the Street Boss."

"Okay, I'll talk with him."

"Nicole, you can't. The higher ups don't talk to anyone outside the organization."

A long pause followed. "Okay, I'll talk with his assistant."

Clark took in a deep breath and sighed. "Okay, but we'll do it my way, agreed?"

She paused. "Fine, what's his name?"

"Blackie Giardini."

＊＊＊

A week later, to the hour, two henchmen walked in the front door. The big one leaned on the counter. His lackey stood by the door.

"I'm sorry, sir. You and your friend will have to wait over there by the freezer." She pointed. "I have two customers ahead of you."

He smirked and motioned his buddy toward the coolers.

A scruffy guy wearing an old Tiger's ball cap walked in the door, tossed her a subtle grin and went to the back of the store.

Nicole checked the items for the two waiting customers, took a deep breath, and waved to the two. "Guess you're next."

"We're back to pick up the cash," the big guy said.

"Yes, I thought about the four hundred dollars and decided I'm not paying it."

The short thug next to the head guy gasped, "You're not paying …"

She interrupted. "Listen here. I've never seen you in my life. We don't have a signed contract. I'm not going to hand over four hundred dollars to a total stranger."

"You don't have a choice …"

"We all have choices," she bristled, cutting him off. "I want to talk with your boss."

Looking surprised, he stammered. "I-I … I'm sorry that's not possible."

"Fine … I'll talk with *his* boss."

"I'm telling you, that's not possible.

Nicole sighed, showing her frustration. "Well then … I'll talk with Blackie."

The large dark-haired man stepped back and said something to his associate. The little guy gave her a peculiar look and slid up to the counter. "You know Blackie Giardini?"

The guy wearing the ball cap pulled a six-pack from the beer cooler and stepped up behind the two bagmen. The little guy nudged the guy in charge and nodded to the customer behind. "We better leave," the lackey said, looking up to the bruiser.

Nicole sensed she was in control. "I told you I wanted to talk with Blackie. Don't come back until you have arranged a meeting with him."

He nodded and led the way out.

The ball cap guy set the six-pack on the counter and paid the tab. "You all right?"

***

Blackie sat in his regular elevated booth of his favorite neighborhood bar, his mistress on his left and Joey Naples on his right. "Tell me again, who is this woman?"

Joey opened a small black book. "Nicole Weatherspoon, she took over the business when her husband was killed in that storage unit fire in Taylor."

"Oh yeah, such a tragedy."

"She gave the boys a hard time, said she wasn't paying and wanted to talk with you."

"Sounds like a spunky woman. How'd she find out my name?"

Joey shrugged. "Don't know."

"How much does she owe per month?"

Joey glanced in his black book. "Four hundred dollars."

The front door opened, casting a stream of light into the dimly lit bar. An attractive African-American woman walked in and squinted, trying to adjust her eyes.

"This way Mrs. Weatherspoon," a deep voice said.

She followed the sound, making her way through the maze of tables. Reaching the booth she surveyed the seating arrangement and pointed to the vacant chair in front of the booth. "I assume this one is mine?"

"That's right," the man in charge with the sunglasses said.

"Thank you." She sat down and asked, "Are you Mr. Blackie?"

A small grin appeared and then it was gone. "Yes. And I want to share my condolences. Your husband's death was an unfortunate tragedy."

"Thank you for your consideration," she said, holding her emotions in check, looking directly at him. "I'm sorry to ask … do you have an eye problem?"

Blackie shook his head.

"I tell my boys it's only proper to take their ball caps and sunglasses off when they come inside. Would you mind removing yours, sir?"

Joey didn't move a muscle. His mistress bit her lip trying not to grin.

Blackie hesitated for a moment, took off his glasses, folded and slid them inside the pocket of his black sports coat.

Nicole glanced at the floozy and back at him. "Is this your wife, Mr. Blackie?"

"No, she's a friend."

Nicole wrinkled her brow and noticed the woman's deep cleavage. "Does she always dress like that so early in the day?"

Blackie burst out laughing. Joey followed suit. Blackie's girlfriend self-consciously pulled up her halter top.

"Thank you." Nicole looked Blackie in the eye. "I'm here to protest the four hundred dollars your men tried to collect. I asked them for a contract so I can understand exactly the type of services I will be receiving. They said there isn't any contract. Is that correct?"

Joey responded, "Yes, that's the going rate for your stores."

"It's common practice," Blackie added.

"Common practice!" she exclaimed. "My great grandparents were slaves. It was common practice for the white men to rape the women and beat the men. Just because it was common practice didn't make it right."

Joey stammered. "You don't understand. That was different then."

"Oh yes, I understand. At the end of the month they had nothing left. I am not a sharecropper ... I'm not a slave, and I don't see why I should pay anything."

Joey swallowed and glanced toward Blackie — the boss's face contorted and twisted, his cold eyes pierced hers. "If I don't charge you, how do you expect me to collect from the others?"

"I really don't care about the others, Mr. Blackie. That's your problem."

"How old are your boys?"

"One and three," she said confidently, sensing a break in his demeanor.

"How long do you propose not to pay?"

"Until they've finished college."

Blackie laughed, burying his face in his hands. "Look, Mrs. Weatherspoon ..." he looked at her with waning patience.

She cut him off. "You look here, Mr. Blackie. My boys deserve a college education far more than you need the money."

"The money is not the point. It's the fact that I ..."

"Fine. If the money is not the point — we agree. I don't have to pay. Thank you, I knew you'd understand my position." She stood and extended her hand. "I think we should shake on that."

Blackie stared at her, rose slowly, and shook her hand.

"Thank you very much, sir." She turned and walked briskly toward the front door.

Joey glanced at his boss. "What happened?"

Blackie grinned. "We just got snookered."

"What do I say to the boys?"

"Tell them she's paid in full and not to stop there anymore."

***

Several blocks away Nicole stopped in the parking lot of a small, mom and pop restaurant and walked in. Clark pulled his Mustang into the lot, jumped out and double-timed it inside. Sitting down across from her, he asked, "How'd it go?"

Her smile broadened. "Just like Alsye used to say, 'piece of cake.' We agreed I didn't have to pay."

Clark stared in shock. "You don't have to pay … this month?"

"Nope, I don't have to pay until the boys are out of college."

"College? You have to be shittin' me."

"No, I'm not," she said, then described the essence of the meeting with Blackie. She paused at the end. "So there, what do you think about that?"

"I can't believe it. How'd you ever build up the courage to do that?"

"Courage?" She leaned back with a grin. "I never thought about that. I just did it." She laughed. "Wait 'til the girls hear about this."

"The girls? Wait 'til I tell my staff. They'll think you're Wonder Woman."

"That's cute, Clark. And thanks for having your guys hang around. That really made a difference." She glanced out the window. "Do you mind if I change the subject?"

"Not at all; it's your nickel." *I can't believe she did it. She's the most confident woman I know.*

"You won't believe the progress I've made on the Neighborhood Watch Program. We're meeting every other week; last time we had over eighty people. They're putting up signs … things are happening."

"Good for you."

"That's not the half of it. There's a police officer at every meeting, and he's engaged. Thanks for the suggestion, he makes a strong statement. Captain Kelly at the precinct has assigned an extra patrolman to walk the beat. There are squad cars all over."

"Sounds like you've really created a strong partnership."

"It's amazing. Each step seems to generate five more ideas. Sometimes, I feel like I'm the one putting on the brakes so we don't jump too fast."

"Hey, that's a nice problem to have. Effort like this requires a steady hand to keep things on course. Otherwise people lose interest."

"You're right. All of the national material repeatedly says 'move slowly, take one step at a time, and build momentum.'"

Clark's encouraging expression gave her positive vibes. "Sounds like good advice."

"We have another group that's excited about cleaning up the neighborhood. A lot of urban communities have a citizen-based effort to beautify their community. They're calling the five-block area in each direction from our store, "Eastside Streetscape.""

Clark gave her a thumbs up. "I like that."

"People are painting their store fronts, putting baskets of flowers out front and mowing grass on vacant property. Our councilman said he was going to push for a special district designation for our ten blocks. If it passes they'll resurface the streets and spruce up the city's plantings. The power company has agreed to put up attractive 1890's street lamps. Can you imagine? Six months ago the place was the pits."

"It's exciting and thanks to you …the area is becoming a community again."

"A community again." Nicole smiled at him, a friendly smile. "I like the sound of that — that'd be a great slogan."

Clark passed it off. "I'm glad I could contribute something."

A slight frown creased her brow. "You okay? You don't sound as upbeat as usual."

Clark tried to appear as if he was perking up. "I'm okay, it's …"

"What is it?" she interrupted.

"My girlfriend and I split," he said, wearing his broken heart on his sleeve.

"I'm sorry to hear that," Nicole said, her expression showing real compassion. "I had heard good things about the two of you."

"Good? It was great." Clark's mind wandered; he hadn't slept very well since the breakup. All night he kept waking up, thinking about Abby. "I was sure she was the one."

"What happened?" Nicole asked with great concern.

Clark ran his hand through his hair. "Sometimes things aren't what they seem to be."

"You're not the first one to say that." Nicole straightened. "You won't believe how many times one of my friends has said the same thing."

Clark's shoulders drooped. "Right now I'm in shit city."

"You have to pick up the pieces and move on. Why don't you call Sharon?"

"Sharon …I gave her the cold shoulder several months ago. I'm positive she doesn't want anything to do with me."

"Don't be so sure about that. Laverne says she's always talking about you. Why don't you have Ted set something up?"

"Do you really think she would come?"

"Nothing ventured, nothing gained."

"Hmm, maybe I will." He glanced appraisingly at her, unable to believe the amount of enthusiasm she has. *She's a bundle of energy. I wish I felt the same way.*

***

Six soldiers filed into Blackie's sanctuary and slid around the table.

He waited impatiently for the last one to be seated. His mistress snuggled close, her halter top snug, barely showing a hint of cleavage.

"What did you find out?" he asked, sharply.

"Not a thing," his senior guy said.

Blackie curled his thick, dark eyebrows. "Nothing?"

"There's a rumor in police headquarters that Clark Phillips pulled Kingston's location out of his hat. Everyone was shocked. The only thing he said, 'sometimes you have to play a hunch.'"

"A hunch?" Blackie ran his fingers around his lips. "The guy in the fire, Alsye Weatherspoon, was a friend of Clark's, right?"

"Yes," Joey said. "Clark meets regularly at the Sax Club to play poker with a group of guys. Alsye was one of them."

"Who are the other ones?"

"Don't know."

"Hmm." Blackie's lip curled into a snarl. "I want to know who they are and what they do. There's a rat somewhere in all of this."

CHAPTER THIRTY-ONE

Water goblets and wine glasses, a bottle of Castello Svevo — their favorite ruby red wine with a hint of licorice — waited with a basket of fresh Italian bread. They walked in and took their regular seats. Blackie Giardini, who was becoming a regular, eased in at the end. Jake Nicoletti raised his glass. "I'd like to make a special toast today." The eyes of the others zeroed in on him. "This toast is to Angelo Travaglini."

Angelo glanced up, more startled than the others.

Jake gave him a familiar nod. "As you know, Angelo and I have been at odds over some of his personal antics." The boss winked at him. "Angelo has reformed. He's back with the woman he's loved for years. This toast is to Angelo and the love of his life."

"Here, here," the others rejoiced.

"Good." The Boss nodded. "Let's order."

Each of the men ordered a special of the day, broke bread and downed a glass of wine. Lunch was served. They talked about family matters and shared stories about the accomplishments of their children and grandkids.

Jake pulled his napkin from his lap, wiped his lips and moved to the first agenda item. "Do you think King has a chance of beating the rap?"

Consigliere Minelli looked him in the eye. "No way. They have a credible witness, the entire transaction is on tape, and a copy of the agreement. He's dead meat."

"I agree," the Underboss said.

"Where to now?" the Boss asked.

The Consigliere shook his head. "We ought to do a good faith effort but … beyond that he's a dead duck."

"You mean just have our lawyers go through the motions."

The old advisor nodded. "Maybe add a little pizzazz to make it look like we're mounting a strong defense, but there's no use giving away anything important on a case we can't win."

"Makes sense," Angelo agreed.

Jake nodded. "Let's run with that."

Blackie refilled their glasses.

"Let's move on to Detective Phillips' friends. What do we know about them?" Jake asked.

"They're all straight-arrows. Carlos Montes owns some used car showrooms in center city — 'Buy American' is his theme."

"Yeah, I've seen those. He has several locations."

"Right. By all indications he's highly successful."

The Boss pursed his lips. "Who's next?"

"Ted Moomau. He operates five small apartment buildings, mostly on the Northside. They're clean and well maintained. One is in the upper/middle price range."

"Hmm, who's the other one?"

"Renzo Ricciuti. He has a small construction company on the southwest side. He seems to have quite a business to remodel, renovate and restore buildings."

"Can we put indirect pressure on Clark through one of them?" Jake asked.

"Sure," the Consigliere said. "But we'd have to be careful … do things subtly."

"I'd suggest we start with Renzo," the Street Boss said. "We're always in need of someone to retrofit a blind pig."

"I like that," Jake agreed. "Blackie, take care of it."

"Will do. I'll send a couple of the boys out the first of the week."

"Move slowly," Jake cautioned. "You know, tear down a construction fence, and mess up some of the finished work. That'll set things in motion."

"I'll make it look like some street gang activity and we can up the ante." Blackie said.

Jake smiled for the first time. "I like that. Anything else?"

Blackie shook his head.

"Good. Let's move on to Huston."

"It's been ten years since I've had any dealings with him," the Consigliere said. "Has anything changed?"

"Nah." Angelo smirked. "He's the same old spineless guy. He presents a terrific image but down deep he's a wimp."

"That's what I figured … guess a zebra doesn't change its stripes."

"Should we be concerned about him in the trial?" the Consigliere asked.

"He'll do whatever his wife, Barb, says," Angelo volunteered. "She wears the pants in the family."

Jake winked at Angelo and shifted the conversation. "How about the other guys who were on the bank boards with you?"

"Five of them are still alive. None of them are particularly strong."

"How do you think they'll react under pressure from the feds?"

"I have reservations about all of them."

"Reservations? What kind?"

"Each one has raised his family and is well off. They're all upstanding men in their community. I don't think any of them would trade that for jail time."

"I agree." The Consigliere nodded.

Jake rubbed his jaw. "Down the road the feds may reopen the bank cases. It could be a real problem for you, Angelo."

"I was thinking the same," he said. "They're all liabilities."

"You need to take care of the problems," the Boss directed.

"I agree." The Consigliere nodded his head.

Angelo double nodded. "I'll take care of them over the next few months — a slow process, make it look natural or like an accident — I don't want to set off any alarms."

***

Ted sat down across the table from Clark and pushed the three empty Stroh's bottles aside. "Hitting the bottle a little more than usual, aren't you?"

"I guess. I'm not a good one to be home alone at night."

"Interesting you said that."

Clark glanced up with a curious look.

"Nicole told Laverne you broke up with Abby."

"Yeah, sometimes things don't work out."

"Ha ... so I've heard. Laverne says Sharon mentions your name quite often. Have any interest in getting back with her?"

Clark tossed him a look of disappointment. "I left her kind of high and dry."

"That's not the impression I get from Laverne."

Clark's eyes brightened. "Oh, what makes you say that?"

"Sharon thinks she was pushing too hard and scared you away."

"Hmm, maybe it was some of that, but …"

"Hey, whatever else doesn't matter. How about Laverne and I set up a casual dinner next Saturday night and see how it goes?"

***

Ted opened the front door and greeted Clark with a manly hug. "How have you been?" he said, acting like they had not talked in some time, in case the women were listening.

"I'm doing fine." Clark stepped back protecting a bouquet of mixed-colored flowers in his hand behind him. "I have a little something for Laverne."

"She's in the kitchen with Sharon."

"Guess I might as well make my grand entrance." Clark pulled back his shoulders and walked in, exuding confidence. "I heard there are two lovely women in here." He handed the flowers to Laverne. "Something special for the hostess."

"Aren't you sweet?" She gave him a peck on the cheek, opened a cabinet and pulled out a vase. "Would you arrange the flowers in this?" she asked Sharon.

"My pleasure." She glanced at Clark. "Nice to see you."

"Same here." Clark did a double take. "I like your hair. When did you get it cut shorter?"

Turning side to side, she fluffed her hair. "Thank you. I decided to change styles two months ago."

"It looks very nice." Clark smiled too, tilting his head slightly to continue his appraisal.

She looked up with a faint smile. "Thank you."

"I'm fixing the drinks. Everyone having the usual?" Ted asked.

"There are two platters of hors d'oeuvres in the fridge," Laverne said. "Clark, would you get them out and set them on the coffee table?"

"Sure enough."

Ted sat the drinks next to the appetizers. The two men filled their plates and waited. Ted glanced in the kitchen. "Hurry up Laverne, we can't hold off much longer."

"You guys can start. We'll be there in a minute."

Ted grinned. The two men dug in.

The women joined them a short time later and took over the conversation. Sharon had plenty of questions for Clark — Kingston, Dallas, Huston — he took center stage, weaving together the stories published by the press as a collage of mysteries.

Downing a second gin, he leaned back. "Gosh, I guess I've done most of the talking."

"Not a problem," Sharon said. "I'm glad to hear the update."

"How are your mom and dad?" he asked her, trying to shift the attention to Sharon.

She bubbled as usual. "Mom is the same. She has a hundred and one projects going on. I worry about her health but she's happy, so I try not to say too much."

"Probably just as well. That's who she is. How about your dad?"

"He's happy as a lark. He just bought a new grape picker. He picks our grapes and contracts with other farmers in the community to pick theirs."

"Wow, a grape picker," Clark repeated, with no concept of what it might be like. "I'd like to see that. How does it work?"

Sharon gave him a puzzled look. "It's fairly simple ..."

"Another time," Laverne called from the kitchen. "Dinner's ready."

"Sorry." Sharon jumped up and ran to the kitchen. "Guess I was talking too much. I'll fill the water glasses."

"Everything is ready as soon as Ted slices the pot roast."

"I'm on the way." He pulled the cork from a bottle of Sangiovese and handed it to Clark. "Here, you can pour the wine."

"Got it."

The four had a leisurely dinner — lots of conversation for the women and plenty of food for the men. After cleaning up the dishes, Laverne and Ted excused themselves to the game room, challenging each other to a game of pool.

Clark filled two small glasses with ice and poured a Grand Marnier for Sharon and an Amaretto for himself, and joined her on the sofa, occupying the other end.

Both tried to initiate an easy going conversation, but it lagged. Sharon broke the ice. "There's something I'd like to say."

Clark waited, not sure how to respond.

She paused, looking for the right words. "Clark, I've thought a lot about my behavior last spring and want to apologize for my actions."

"Apologize ... for what? There was ..."

"Wait." She raised her hand. "Let me finish."

Clark flashed a forgiving smile. "The floor is yours."

Sharon took her time explaining how she felt, and then looked him in the eye. "I just got a little too emotional. I didn't mean to push you into a corner. I hope you understand."

"You don't have to say another word. That's over and done."

"Maybe, but I want you to know I've never done that before. I don't know what happened, I just wanted to be with you all the time."

Clark gave her an affectionate smile. "It wasn't just you, Sharon. The feeling was mutual."

"When I asked you to come to my parents' home for Easter I thought your jaw was going to hit the floor. You said you had to be with your parents, and I knew I'd stepped over the line."

"It wasn't your fault. At the time, meeting your parents just seemed like a big step. It wasn't that it was wrong, I just didn't ..."

She slid closer and placed her fingers over his lips. "Let's not talk about that anymore."

"Good idea ... that's water over the dam. Why don't we go out a few times and see how things go?"

"I'd like that."

Ted cracked open the door and poked his head out. "You guys want to play some cards?"

***

Detroit Free Press
October 27, 1979

MOBSTER INDICTED FOR RACKETEERING
PLEA BARGAIN UNLIKELY

Ray "King" Kingston was indicted today on several counts of racketeering and extortion. Kingston is one of the few high ranking members of the Detroit Mafia ever indicted. Captured in Florida last month, he has

been held in the Wayne County Jail without bond. A trial date will be scheduled for early next year.

Feeling better after his reunion with Sharon and reading today's headlines, Clark walked into the conference room with renewed vigor.

Patrolman Ralston was the first to shake his hand. "You made your father proud today."

Clark responded with a big hug. "Thanks Leonard, it's a tribute to the hard work of everyone around the table."

Other members of the task force lined up to congratulate Clark. By the time the mini celebration ended, Clark was on a real high. "As soon as we get off today, we're meeting at the Sax Club … drinks on me."

"Hey," Max shouted. "Meeting adjourned."

The group laughed and took their chairs.

Clark paused reflectively, collecting his thoughts. "I want to thank all of you for a job well done. When we came together who would have ever thought we would achieve an 'airtight indictment' against one of the top capos in the Partnership."

"This is just the beginning," one of the team members said.

"Here, here," the group agreed.

"So what's next?" another shouted.

Clark took a deep breath and sighed. "That's hard to say. After this year … I'm still amazed at where we are today," he said, collecting his thoughts. "I assume we'll wrap up the Huston Nash case by the end of the year and start digging again."

***

"Most of you know Earl Walker," Clark said to the poker group. "As I mentioned last time, he's a college buddy of mine. He asked me to pass him the ball and we've been friends since."

Chuckles popped around the table.

"Hell, that's all you did when you guys played us," Renzo said.

"You can say that again." Carlos raised his arms like he was guarding a basketball player.

Shaved head and still trim as ever, Earl's eyes twinkled, setting off a broad smile. "It's indeed an honor to join such a distinguished group. You have spoken of the camaraderie of the group. I've heard

293

you praise one another, never finding a reason to say a sharp word. This is a real privilege and I look forward to being one of you."

"We're glad to have you on board, my son," Father Dom said, on behalf of the others.

Renzo ruffled the cards. "Dealer's choice!"

By break time you'd have thought Earl was a long-standing member of the group. He started out telling college stories about Clark, Carlos and Renzo, and then the tide turned, he became the brunt of the jokes.

Renzo shuffled the cards and paused. "I had a fence ripped down on one of my construction sites last weekend."

"Did the vandals do any damage?" Clark asked.

"They punched holes in most of the drywall. I'll have to replace it all."

"Where was the watchman?"

"Wouldn't you know it was the only site I didn't have one. The security company said they were shorthanded and couldn't send anyone that night; they'll have someone there this week."

"It always seems to work out that way, doesn't it?"

CHAPTER THIRTY-TWO

Underboss Angelo Travaglini passed a second basket of hot Italian bread. Each man took a slice and dabbed it in the traditional dish of olive oil and herbs.

Finishing off a house salad, Jake turned to Blackie. "Give the group a briefing on the work done on Renzo Ricciuti's construction site."

Blackie laid down his fork. "Everything went as planned. We paid off the scheduler at the security agency so the coast was clear. The guys knocked down half of the fencing around the perimeter and busted up two or three rooms of new drywall. This week the night watchman will be trapped in the port-a-potty while our work is being done."

"Are they going to tip it over?" Angelo asked.

"Yep, the door will be on the ground."

"I like that." Street Boss DiGregorio laughed. "That'll give him something to talk about."

"We'll have a couple of the guys meet with Mr. Ricciuti the following week." Blackie added. "This weekend we'll stop by one of Carlos Montes' dealerships and flatten a few tires and do a little keying. The next week we'll have some fireworks. That ought to get his attention."

"Sounds good to me." Jake looked around the table and turned toward Blackie. "Another job well planned." Blackie beamed and dug into his salad.

Jake glanced across the table at Tony Minelli. "Did the lawyer say anything about his meeting with King?"

The Consigliere responded immediately. "I was about to raise that point. Kingston seemed very unsettled. He said he'd never seen King so uptight."

Jake gave him a look of concern. "Do you think the cops are getting to him?"

"He didn't say that. He only mentioned that King seemed extremely nervous."

"You're right," Joe DiGregorio echoed. "That doesn't sound like King at all."

"That's what I thought too … otherwise I wouldn't have said anything about it."

"Maybe the prospects of being in prison are starting to get to him," Angelo said.

"That's what's bothering me. Once you get in that mode, a plea bargain sounds good."

"The paper reported that a plea bargain was unlikely," Blackie reminded the group.

"They don't know anything," the Underboss said. "They probably heard the case against him was air-tight and figured there'd be no need to bargain."

"Don't believe any of that crap in the paper. If cops have a chance to get information on anyone around this table they'll give him the moon," the Consigliere said.

"That's what worries me." Jake's eyebrows drew together. "Any thoughts on what we ought to do?"

Eying the Street Boss, Angelo glanced at Tony.

Taking his time, the Consigliere stroked his gray sideburns. "I hate to say this … King has been a really good man … but I'm afraid he's a liability."

Jake glanced toward Blackie and caught his nod. Angelo gave him one too. The Boss took a long sip of wine, deep in thought. "Next time the lawyer meets with King have him ask him if he needs a belt."

***

Walking in with the other women to their newly adopted Italian restaurant in Dearborn, Nicole could hardly restrain her enthusiasm. Waiting until Laverne had taken the last chair, she jumped up with a glass of Chianti in her hand. Nearly spilling her wine, she paused to wipe the outside of the glass.

"That was close," she giggled. "I'm so happy about the progress our community has made. The Neighborhood Watch Program at our main store is in full operation. We have a team of street captains and signs up all over. The police are there all the time. It's like night and day."

Wendy rose. "I want to propose a toast." Laverne and Rosa Maria stood and held their glasses high. "Here's to Nicole and the wonderful things she's accomplished."

"Here … here," the group chimed.

"It's the people that have made the real difference," Nicole said with a blush.

"No, no." Wendy's smile grew. "You may have worker bees, but none of it would have happened without a queen bee."

"Maybe so. I can't believe how fast the city people moved. The curbs and sidewalks have been repaired or replaced and there's ten blocks of new asphalt. The cable for the new streetlights is in and by spring the 1890's street lamps will be in."

"That's truly amazing," Laverne bemoaned. "I can't even get someone to return a call."

"I have two of my managers at the north side stores starting the same process with neighbors around those stores."

"Wow. You're a regular dynamo. Next thing we'll know, you'll be in the mayor's office."

"Not me," Nicole said emphatically. "I'm a doer. I don't have time for political stuff."

The waitress poured a half glass of Chianti for each of them and took their orders.

Wendy's lips quivered. "Did you hear about the damage on one of Renzo's worksites?"

"No," Nicole jumped in. "What happened?"

She described the damage that had taken place.

"I'm not an expert, but that doesn't sound like a gang of kids … sounds like the work of thugs. You ever had any problem with the Mafia?"

Wendy shook her head.

"Four cars on one of Carlos' sites were damaged the other night, too. He'll have to have the sides repainted from where some kids keyed the doors."

Nicole frowned. "Have you had problems like that before?"

"Not one. Carlos was always saying how he had to 'knock on wood,' because he'd never had problems with the local kids."

Laverne finished her entree and changed the subject. "Did you know that Clark and Sharon are back together?"

"No," the group said in unison.

"He broke up with the other one … I think her name was Abby."

"Did any of the guys ever meet her?" Rosa Maria asked.

"No. She was some type of computer expert at GM headquarters."

"Ted thought it was strange that the guys didn't meet her," Laverne added. "Sharon has been talking about him since they broke up. Clark was in the dumps so Ted and I thought it might be good for both of them. We had them over for dinner a couple of weeks ago. Turns out they've been seeing each other since. They're dining out at some fancy place this Saturday."

"Good for them," Rosa Maria said. "He's such a nice man."

"He was a life saver for me," Nicole added. "I don't know how I would have made it through everything without his support and guidance."

"I hope it works out. I think Sharon and Clark are a good fit."

***

Sitting across the table from King in the police interrogation room, the Mafia's number two lawyer started down a long list of questions regarding his defense. Half way through the briefing, the lawyer stopped and spoke in a low tone. "I have a question for you."

King gave him a confused look. "What's that?"

"Do you want a belt?" he whispered.

King's face flushed; he stared blankly.

"I-I wore two belts today."

King didn't move; his eyes glazed, he mumbled, "Yes, I do."

The lawyer loosened a belt and slipped it under the table. King took a deep breath. "I don't think we need to talk anymore," he mumbled.

The lawyer nodded. He stood, knocked on the door, and waited for the officer to unlock it from the outside.

***

The maître d' guided Sharon and Clark to a small table for two at Cliff Bells. She glanced around at the dark paneling and 1930's motif. "This is wonderful. How did you find it?"

"One of the guys on my task force recommended it," he fibbed. "He brings his wife here on special occasions. He said you can't go wrong with anything you order. Red or white wine?"

"I think red … something light."

"That's what I was thinking too. I'll order a bottle of Beaujolais. It's nice and light."

"Perfect."

The sommelier took Clark's order, returned in no time, and offered him a taste.

"Excellent." Clark licked his lips. The sommelier filled their glasses and disappeared.

Sharon glanced through the menu. "Everything sounds so good. I don't know where to start. Why don't we order different starters and share."

"Great idea," Clark said, trying to narrow his choices. "The plate of smoked salmon and country pâté sounds wonderful."

"I'll order the seared sea scallops with corn puree."

Clark eyed her. She had that look; vulnerable as hell. "Yes, that was my other choice."

The waiter returned, took their appetizer order, and jotted down the mix of roasted veal and beef tenderloin and Caesar salads they had agreed on.

Catching the waiter's eye, Clark winked. "We'd like to take our time."

"Yes sir, by all means," the slender man with a narrow mustache grinned.

Sharon chattered about her family most of the way through the hors d'oeuvres and finally turned to Clark. "I'm sorry I've been babbling so much."

"Not a problem. I enjoy hearing about your parents and brothers. It sounds like you all were really close when you grew up."

"There wasn't much difference in our ages."

"I can tell when you're talking about them, you were tight with them. It sounds like one of those big happy families … you know, the kind we used to see on television."

"I never thought about it that way, but I think you're right."

Clark's lip curled into a wry smile. "My brother was ten years older so it was like being an only child."

Sharon stopped and stared at him. "Wow, everything I've been talking about must really seem weird to you."

"Hmm, not weird … different; different in a good way."

"I've been reading lots about you in the news. Sounds like you have a great PR agent," she jested.

His grin broadened into a smile. "I have a truly great team."

"I think you're being overly modest. Finding out all of the stuff about the Nash family, locating that mobster in Florida and putting him behind bars. That was a real accomplishment."

Clark puffed up. "Nabbing him really did make me feel better. To get one of the head guys in the Mafia was exciting."

"And a feather in your cap."

"Hmm ..."

"Come on Clark, from what I've read you deserve lots of credit on that one."

"Well, thanks," he admitted humbly.

***

Sipping a Diet Coke through a straw, Sharon gazed out a window in the Wayne State University Hospital cafeteria; her mind floating into fantasy land. She envisioned Clark naked, lying on his stomach in her bed. *I love his ass.*

"Where are you?" Laverne asked.

Glancing up, Sharon shook her head. "What ... I'm right here."

Laverne cocked her head to the side. "I don't think so. I've been standing here for a minute. You never noticed."

"Oh." She tried to dismiss her reverie. "I was off in a dream world."

"I guess. Was Clark with you?"

"Yes. I can't stop thinking about him."

Laverne placed her tray on the table, sat down, and removed the Glad Wrap from her salad. "Did you invite him up after dinner Saturday night?"

"No. I ..."

"You didn't bang him? After six months ... you must be crazy."

"I wanted to but I didn't want to push things."

"I bet he was ready to push his thing."

"Ha, ha."

"So how was dinner?"

Sharon's face glowed. "Unbelievable ... spectacular ... I've never been in a more elegant place. And Clark ... you should have seen him. He looked so sexy in a black Nero shirt and brown leather-like sport coat. I've never seen him looking so spiffy."

"C'mon, you've been with him lots of times."

"No, I'm telling you. He was special. Twice I had to hold my breath so I wouldn't moisten my pants."

Laverne's long eyelashes flipped up. "You've got to be kidding me."

"No, I'm not. If he would have touched my hand I would have lost it right there."

"Are you going out this weekend?"

"Yes. I'm taking him to see the Pistons."

"The Pistons ... how romantic." Laverne said mockingly. "Aren't we going first class?"

"He loves to watch them. I figure one for him ... one for me."

"Now we're talking." Laverne opened up again with a knowing smile. "You banging him after the game?"

"You bet. He's driving my car so we have to come back to my place. I'm inviting him up and having my way with him all night." She winked at Laverne.

***

Renzo waited anxiously at a rear table for Clark to arrive. Ten minutes late, his friend burst in the front door of the Sax Club, glanced left and right, then walked briskly to the table. "Sorry, I'm late. I got caught up in an issue at the office."

"No problem. I'm pleased you could make it."

Clark gave him an inquisitive look. "Why was it so urgent that we meet this afternoon?"

"The Mafia hit my jobsite again," Renzo said, nervously.

"How do you know it was them?"

"I just finished with the detectives at the precinct. They said it was clearly not gang activity. It was done by professionals."

"How much damage did they do?"

Renzo shook his head despairingly. "Two weeks of work."

"I thought you had a night watchman."

"They turned over the port-a-potty and trapped him inside."

"I'm sorry, Renzo." Clark laughed. "Your situation is bad but I can see him now, inside the crapper, yelling for help."

"It is kind of funny when you think of it that way," Renzo admitted. His smile didn't reach his eyes.

Clark regained his composure. "It sounds fishy to me too."

"Yeah, the chief said the same thing. He's going to check out the security agency."

Clark nodded. "Won't be the first time an agency has been in cahoots with the mob."

"What do you think I ought to do?"

Clark let out a long sigh. "You've never had one of their people contact you?"

"Hell no, the first thing I would have done was call you."

"These guys are not spontaneous like gangs. The mob takes action in a more calculated, planned way, thought out to the nth degree."

"So, what does that mean?"

"For some reason they want your attention. Maybe they have a job for you."

Renzo's mouth curled up with distaste. "A job, like what?"

"Geez, I don't know ... maybe it's some kind of a construction project."

"They don't build things; they tear them down."

"Hey, you're in the business, you know better than I."

Renzo's frustration grew; he drained his glass empty. "That doesn't help any. What do you think they're going to do?"

Clark's face contorted into a grimace. "I'll give you odds; ten to one ... you'll have a visitor within the week."

"A visit ... from whom?"

Clark shrugged his shoulders "Some lackey from the Mafia."

"What do I do?"

"Play it cool. Act dumb. Be nice as you can and ask as many questions as you can. The guy will be a nobody; he'll likely tell you more than he should."

"Then what?"

"Give me a call right away."

CHAPTER THIRTY-THREE

Detroit Free Press
November 28, 1979

MOBSTER FOUND DEAD IN JAIL CELL

Early this morning, Ray "King" Kingston was found dead in his cell at the Wayne County Jail. It's reported that he hung himself. Details of his death have not been released. "King" Kingston was one of the highest ranking members of the Detroit Mafia ever arrested. His trial was scheduled to start early next year.

Clark arrived early for the specially called eight o'clock meeting. Waiting for the last task force member to arrive, the team chatted quietly, filling in time —anxious until they could talk about King's death.

Kimberly popped her head in two minutes late and seeing one vacant chair, sauntered over to it and glanced at the clock. "Guess this morning's event captured everyone's attention."

"It seems that way," Clark mused, and got to the point everyone wanted to hear. "I have the same question — how could something like this happen?"

"You're right about that," patrolman Ralston spouted on behalf of the rest.

Clark rolled his shoulders. "Unfortunately, I can't add much."

Max Cumberland expressed his frustration. "Clark, we have policies, procedures and protocols. There's no way a prisoner could have a belt in a cell. It isn't possible!"

"You're right, Max, but ... it happened."

Eddie rubbed his jaw. "You can tell internal affairs to call off the dogs."

"Why?" Clark asked. His colleagues turned to give Eddie their full attention.

"I don't want to sound condescending, but they're not going to find out anything. I checked his visitor's list. King met with nineteen people — his wife, colleagues, friends and legal counsel — none of them will know anything. Internal affairs will conduct intensive interviews with every staff member that could have come into contact with him — none of them will know anything."

"That's not possible," Lieutenant Sterling stated. "Someone has to know."

Eddie smiled. "One of the things you'll learn when dealing with the Mafia is never to say 'that isn't possible.' They know how to get things done."

"Why would King commit suicide?"

Eddie looked her in the eye. "He didn't have a choice."

"Why? What do you mean?"

"I'm sure the top guys decided he was a liability, figured he'd spill the beans when push came to shove."

***

Clark drove Sharon's new Camaro to the Pistons' game at the Silverdome in Auburn Hills. She asked Clark a hundred questions about King's death on the way there.

"Sharon, I keep telling you. We don't have a clue to what happened. Like it was reported, he hung himself."

"How? Why? I don't understand."

"We're not sure. He had almost twenty visitors. Any one of them could have slipped him a belt. It could have been smuggled in to any inmate or by someone on the staff."

"Why do you think he did it?" she asked.

Clark tried to weasel out, without answering her. "That's a question to be answered by someone above my pay grade."

Sharon kept digging. "Can you say what you *think* happened?"

"Hmm … it's likely the Mafia had a sense he'd testify against them rather than face the prospect of spending the rest of his life in prison."

"So how did he get the belt?"

Clark shrugged. "There are countless sources, ranging from another inmate to his wife."

Sharon looked uncomfortable and grimaced. "That'd be a tough thing to do — give someone I love a tool to commit suicide. I don't think I could do something like that."

Clark flipped his right hand in the air. "Who knows? Every relationship is different."

Sharon paused, feeling she might be pressing him too much. "Let's change the subject," she suggested. "What are the chances of the Pistons winning tonight?"

"It looks good to me. They're ten and five and the Bucks have a losing record."

"I hope it's exciting," she said, pointing toward the end of the parking lot. "Take one of those places so it'll be less likely that someone will ding my car."

"You got it." Clark parked next to an island of planted trees. "There, at least one side is protected."

She smiled, grabbed his hand and held it until they reached the gate. Clark bought a couple of sodas and two bags of peanuts, and led the way to their seats. Sharon jabbered, spouting one sports fact after another. "No one thought the Pistons would start out like this, everyone playing so well together."

"I didn't know you were into basketball."

"After being a cheerleader and watching four brothers play, I guess it's in my blood. While I was an undergraduate at Michigan State, I officiated girls' basketball."

"Wow." Clark leaned back in his chair with a look of surprise. "I would have never thought that about you ... that's amazing."

She curled her lip sarcastically. "Because I was an official?"

"No, because you can do so many things. My life seems routine compared to yours."

She gazed intently into his eyes. "That's only because our backgrounds are so different."

"Hmm, maybe so. Still, I can't believe you know all of the stats for the Pistons."

She laughed. "No different than you knowing the life history of every Tiger player."

"Touché."

Short conversations continued at every pause during the game. Clark's feelings grew with his admiration. *She's so easy going ... like an old friend. It's fun to be with her.*

The Pistons beat the Cavaliers 121 to 105 and, once again, M. L. Car and Kevin Porter led the way. Walking back to the car, Clark replayed the game highlights in conversation. "Cleveland doesn't have a big man. We should have fed Bob Lanier inside. He could have scored a bundle."

Sharon's eyes settled on Clark. "You're absolutely right. I've been saying that all year. Cleveland was easy tonight, but when the Celtics come to town they have to get it in to Lanier."

In the car, she slid close and snuggled her head on his shoulder — her tone more relaxed and comfortable. Clark didn't say much; most of the time he responded amicably to her comments and kept his eyes on the road. It was almost eleven when he pulled into her parking spot and cut the engine.

Not sure what she was thinking, he slipped out of the car and opened the passenger door. Sharon grabbed his arm, pulled herself out, and fell against him.

"Sorry." She took a step and tugged his arm.

Clark looked down at her.

"Would you like to come up for a drink?"

Clark's desires jumped; a caution sign flashed, knowing he didn't want to move too quickly and offend her. "Ah … maybe a short one. I have some heavy duty work in the morning."

She leaned back seductively on the car. "If you don't want too, that's okay."

"No, it isn't that …"

"I wouldn't have asked if I didn't want you to come in." She gave him a sly, sexy smile for the first time in months.

He pecked her on the cheek. "Seems reasonable to me."

She grabbed his hand and the two strolled inside. Pulling him into the elevator, she rose up on her tiptoes, threw her arms over his shoulders and planted a wet kiss on his lips. Pulling her to him, Clark responded with one of his own.

Sliding down on her feet as the door opened, she led the way to her apartment, unlocked the door, and headed for the kitchen. "Amaretto on the rocks or Grand Marnier?" she called out to him.

"Hmm, I think I'll change … Grand Marnier on the rocks."

"Two Grand Marnier's coming up. Make yourself comfortable on the couch. I'll have them ready in a minute."

Clark sat near the end of the sofa and stretched out his legs. "Thanks for suggesting we see the Pistons tonight. That was a great game."

"I go four or five times a year. Laverne and I have gone the last couple of times. She enjoys the event — she's a big people watcher."

Sharon handed him his glass and clinked hers against it. "Here's to starting over."

"I'll drink to that." He took a sip. "Do Laverne and you see each other much in med school?"

"Not really. She's into pediatrics and I'm in the research lab all day. We usually meet in the cafeteria two or three times a week. That's the only safe place."

"Safe?"

"The doctors are always on the make. There is safety in numbers." She laughed.

Clark raised a brow. "I thought that only happened on TV."

Sharon shook her head. "The stuff you see on television is mild compared to what actually happens."

"Really," Clark said, wondering if that was an opening line — his mind overruled his desires.

Looking like she had expected something else, she leaned back and took a sip. "I still can't believe what happened to King. His wife must feel awful. And what if she helped him ... that'd be terrible."

Sensing an opportunity, Clark downed his Grand Marnier. "I really need to go."

***

Father Dom was ill for the December poker gathering but Renzo's jokes and antics filled the void. By break time Clark had laughed so hard he nearly cried. The others around the table were in the same condition. Renzo continued his craziness while sprinkling in questions about Kingston's death: "How could something like that happen? How'd he get the belt? Do you think it was really a personal decision or didn't he have a choice?"

Clark followed with the same responses he'd shared with Sharon. Ted turned to Earl. "How about you ... can you say anything?"

He winked at Clark. "Sure, I have heard from an inside source that ..." He grinned. "... I shouldn't say a word."

"Damn, now we have two know-nothings."

Laughter flowed around the table.

Renzo's face sobered when someone asked about the destruction he'd had on his job site. "Yeah, I'm still pissed off. The chief at the station said he was sure it was the Mafia."

"It sounds like it," Clark agreed.

"Any thoughts on why they did it?" Earl asked.

"I don't have a clue … maybe it's because I know Clark." He laughed.

A crease crossed Ted's forehead. "Don't laugh; maybe there is something to that."

Heads around the table turned toward him. "Why do you say that?"

Without a pause Ted said, "Carlos mentioned he'd had some cars keyed and tires flattened. In the last ten days I've had three robberies in one of my buildings."

Clark straightened in his chair. "Wait a minute, Ted may be on to something. Hold on," Clark said, jumping up and picking up a scrap of paper from the table on the other side of the room. Sliding back in his chair, he said, "Okay, give me the details of the incidents."

His three buddies shared the specifics of the situations they had experienced. "Interesting," Clark said, running his fingers down the dates. "All of this started after Kingston was indicted. Ted's right. They could be targeting you guys as a way to get to me."

"I want each of you to keep copious notes of anything that seems out of the ordinary."

***

Kimberly stood at the end of the conference table waiting for Clark to arrive.

Stepping in, he eyed her. "What's with you?"

Her smile stretched across her face. "I'm ready to give everyone the low down from the investigation of the feds on the bank examiners."

"Well, what are you waiting for?" Clark flipped his notebook aside. "Sit down and get on with it."

She sighed. "It's a little overwhelming, but once you understand the process you'll see how they pulled it off." She paused for effect. "Normally, the FHLB office in Indianapolis sends an eight- to ten-member team to review a savings and loan every twelve months. Their focus is to protect consumers — ensure deposits and evaluate loans."

"Yeah," Ralston said. "It's like Clark's friend hypothesized."

"Right. Pay off two and you're a winner."

"So what did they do?" Max asked.

"The feds tracked the transfers from Atlantic Off-Shore Drilling. Just like Lawrence speculated, a five-thousand-dollar wire transfer has been sent to the team chairman every month since the first review. And a twenty-five-hundred-dollar transfer went to the investment evaluator on the same schedule."

"Wow." Clark was exasperated. "Sixty grand to the chair ..."

"I understand that," Will Robinson interrupted. "But the scam went on for five years. How did they pull that off?"

"Good point," Kimberly said with a smirk. "Since the bottom line of the two banks was so good, the FHLB wasn't concerned about them failing. The office was short of staff so they extended their review from twelve to eighteen months."

"Did they pay off another team?"

"No. Again, they did not follow the norm of sending a different team."

"Why not?"

"Who knows, maybe someone's palm was greased. Anyway the same team returned." Kimberly rubbed her hands together. "Bottom line, the two top dogs were reappointed. And, they got another set of transfers — five thousand and twenty-five hundred dollars — for who knows how long. And the bank got another eighteen months."

"Let me see if I have this right." Will Robinson calculated in his head. "Now they're headed for a review in fifty-four months — three eighteens — right?"

"So what happened?" Max asked.

"They learned that a new team would be coming, and as an astute businessman, Huston looked for a merger." Kimberly flipped her hands up. "That was an easy call. His banks had several pursuers. And in no time each of his banks was gobbled up by a bigger competitor. It was a win-win situation for everyone."

"How so?" Leonard asked.

"When the mergers took place the FHLB closed the doors on the two banks. The Mafia was home Scot-free; they'd laundered millions of dollars. Huston Nash was a rich man, received a seat on each of the new banks, along with a lucrative stipend."

"Why does a guy of his stature do something like this?" Eddie asked. "He had it all!"

Ralston shook his head. "Greed, it's a familiar theme in our society."

CHAPTER THIRTY-FOUR

Nicole followed Rosa Maria in the front door of the Roman Village and headed for their spot. An open bottle of Chianti was on the table. Laverne and Wendy were deep in conversation.

"Have you solved the world's problems, yet?" Nicole kidded.

"No, we're talking about the trouble our men are having with the Mafia."

Nicole quickly sat down and asked, "What kind of trouble?"

She listened intently as the women updated her on the latest happenings. "I don't like that. It sounds very much like what they did to Alsye. It's a slow process, one step at a time until they get what they want; or snuff you out in trying."

"That's what I told Renzo," Wendy blurted. "I said you need to be careful so this doesn't get out of hand."

"I know," Rosa Maria said. "But you know how stubborn our macho men can be."

"I'm learning that more every day," Laverne admitted.

"Tell them to play it cool." Nicole's face flushed. "Stress to them … you don't want to end up like me."

"Yes, I'm going to remind Carlos tonight."

"Me too," Laverne agreed.

"Have they talked to Clark?" Nicole asked. "They have to follow his lead."

"Will do," Wendy said. The other two confirmed it with a nod. "He said to keep track of every event and emphasized to play it cool." Wendy turned to Nicole. "Enough of that. How are your many projects coming along?"

"They're going much faster than I ever anticipated. People are fired up. It's like they've wanted to do something for a long time, but no one took the first step."

"It's like that most of the time," Wendy agreed. "A lot of people need someone like you to take the lead."

Nicole paused, reflecting on her comments. "I never thought about it that way."

Laverne gave her a curious look, "You mentioned you were introducing neighborhood watches at your other locations. How's that going?"

"Hmm, slower than I had hoped. People are excited but I have to train my own staff and help others organize things."

"Better to move slowly than too fast," Wendy added.

Nicole nodded her acknowledgement. "It didn't take me long to learn that. In the beginning it was one step forward, two back."

"You're a real dynamo, Nicole." Rosa Maria said, shaking her hand. "I don't know how you are able to do all of that."

"It comes naturally for me." Nicole's smile broadened. "Did I tell you that I received a plaque from our chamber chapter last week?"

"No, what's that all about?" Rosa Maria asked.

Nicole looked embarrassed. "Woman of the Year, Eastside Chamber of Commerce."

"Woman of the Year! Why didn't you tell us sooner?" Laverne asked.

"I didn't want to sound like I was bragging."

"Bragging?" Wendy shook her heard. "You ought to be tooting your horn."

"I want to see." Laverne's eyes lit up. "Bring it next time so I can take a picture?"

"Let's have a Christmas party. That way we won't have to wait until next year."

"Great idea," Rosa Maria agreed. "Will you bring it?"

Nicole paused, and reluctantly said, "Yes."

***

Clark walked slowly down the magnificent corridor of the Detroit courthouse; its classic marble floors flanked by bronze statues, led the way to the maze of chambers. He glanced up at the intricate hand-painted domed ceiling, and opened the door to the "Million Dollar Courtroom." Pausing in the doorway, he marveled at the numerous species of marble and the bench carved from East Indian mahogany. *Every time I come here, I wonder at the beauty of this place. It's remarkable. It has to be one of the most elaborate courtrooms in the world.*

He took a seat in the gallery and continued to gawk.

The prosecutor's team, followed by the defendant's lawyers, entered the courtroom and spread their materials out on the two massive tables below the judge's perch.

The bailiff entered the room and announced, "All rise for the Honorable Judge James Limbaugh, presiding over the U.S. District Court for the Eastern District of Michigan."

The black-robed bald-headed judge took his seat and, looking stern, gaveled the session to order and motioned for everyone to be seated. "The federal court of the Eastern District of Michigan is now in session to hear the case of the U. S. Government vs. Huston Nash."

The judge shuffled a stack of papers and looked down at the defendant. "Mr. Nash, will you please rise?"

Looking feebler than his years, the old man rose slowly and stared at the judge.

Judge Limbaugh glared at him for a moment and then read the charges. "Mr. Nash, you are charged with one hundred and forty-two counts of money laundering, tax evasion, grand larceny, and racketeering. How do you plead?"

"Guilty," Huston replied softly.

An undercurrent of whispers filled the room.

The judge gaveled. "Order, we'll have order." He nodded to the defense attorney. "Will the defense counsel approach?"

The silver-haired attorney rose and approached. The judge leaned closer. "Does the defendant understand the consequences of his plea?"

"Yes, Your Honor." He looked the judge in the eye. "He'd like to make a statement."

Judge Limbaugh nodded and looked at the defendant. "Mr. Nash, I understand you'd like to make a statement, is that accurate?"

"Yes sir."

"Please rise and do so."

Huston Nash pulled himself up and placed his hands on the table in front of him for support. Clearing his throat, he spoke quietly and deliberately, "I am respectful of the normal legal procedures, but I'd like to waive my rights to a trial by jury. I am guilty of all charges and do not want to put my family through the agony of long days of testimony that will be of no value other than to fill the record with facts to which I've already pleaded guilty."

A rumble rippled across the courtroom.

"Order, I'll have order," Judge Limbaugh gaveled, and stared at Mr. Nash. "Defense counsel, approach."

Huston's counsel stepped forward and leaned toward the bench.

The judge whispered, "This is a highly unusual request. Are you positive Mr. Nash understands the consequences of his statement?"

"Yes, he'd like you to honor his request and proceed directly to sentencing."

"Thank you." The judge rubbed his shiny head, pondered for a moment and banged on his bench. "The court will take a fifteen-minute recess. Will defense counsel and Mr. Nash please join me in my chamber?"

The two stood and followed the judge through the huge doorway.

Fifteen minutes later, the three came out and took their positions.

The judge gaveled. "Court is now back in session. Will the prosecutor approach the bench?" The judge turned his head to the other attorney's desk. "Will the defense counsel come forward too?"

The two attorneys paraded forward.

The judge spoke softly to each one. Catching a nod from each he motioned for them to return to their seats. His eyes surveyed the packed gallery as he cleared his throat. "The court has accepted the request of Mr. Nash. Sentencing will commence on January 4th 1980, at 10:00 a.m. This court is adjourned." He gaveled.

Befuddled by the events, Clark sat watching the courtroom empty. *What's going on? Why would he do that? Does he think the judge will be more lenient on him?*

*****

Clark glanced around the Perkins restaurant, not far from his apartment. He spotted his three buddies sitting in a corner booth. Catching Ted's eye, he headed that way and plopped down. "It must be important for us to meet so early on a Monday morning."

"We all had problems over the weekend," Renzo said, diving right into the reason for the meeting.

"Okay. Let's hear about them."

The three looked at each other.

"I'll start," Carlos said. "The Mafia burned one of my cars last night and at seven-thirty this morning two cronies were in my office. The one in charge asked if I knew you. When I nodded he said,

'Here's the deal. We want three cars a month at four hundred dollars below wholesale.' I said, 'Are you crazy? That'll cost me twelve hundred a month. I can't do that.'"

Carlos continued with the thug's response, "'Figured that would be easier than us having to collect a grand a month,' the guy said. I gave him a bewildered look, and asked, 'Where am I supposed to dig up that kind of money?'"

"'I really don't care,' he said. 'You're selling plenty of cars. I'm positive you'll find a way.'"

"'I won't have any profit left,'" I told him.

"'Figure it out,' he snarled at me. 'We'll be back after the first of the year.'"

"Is this the first time you've heard from any of the Mafia?" Clark asked.

"Yes, you said to let you know right away."

Clark turned to Ted and started to ask, "What ..."

Ted cut him off. "One of my renters was robbed at gun point and had her eye blackened."

"Was she hurt badly?"

"No, but she was scared shitless; said she'd have to move to a safer location. I can't handle many situations like that."

"Did anyone stop by to see you?"

Ted nodded. "A tall, handsome Italian-American guy and a short little runt stopped by. I got the same question — 'Do you know Clark Phillips?' Sure, I said, and then he said they wanted to rent ten apartments each, with a two hundred dollar discount per month. They were going to put twenty women in them."

"Prostitutes?"

"He didn't say that, but I assume so. With women like that in my buildings I might as well close up. All of my residents will move out."

"Did he threaten you in any way?"

"No. Like Carlos, he said he'll be back after the first."

Clark glimpsed at Renzo. "I assume it's pretty much the same for you?"

"Yep. They ripped apart one of my construction sites Friday night. Two of the guys came by Saturday morning."

"What'd they have to say?"

"The guy in charge asked if I knew you. When I said yes, he said, 'we want you to remodel some blind pigs for us.'"

"Did he say exactly what they want?"

"Yeah, they want the work done dirt cheap. I'm supposed to take a loss on every job. Clark, my prices are the lowest in town. The goon said, 'it'd be better than paying us every month.'"

"So what kind of remodeling are they talking about?"

"The whole shebang — new electrical, plumbing, drywall, and carpet on the walls. They want to have a first class whorehouse/casino." Renzo wiped the perspiration from his brow. "Even if I could afford it, the word would be out on the street. I wouldn't be able to get a decent job anywhere in the city."

"Are they going to show up after the first of the year?"

"You got it."

"At least we have a few weeks to map out a strategy."

"A strategy? Clark, I want to kick some ass."

Clark smiled at Ted and shook his head. "That was Alsye's first thought. You can't do that. You'll be playing into their hands."

"I know that but it pisses me off."

"Hey, you're not the lone ranger. We have to maintain our cool."

"Do you have any immediate thoughts?" Ted asked.

"Obviously I'm their target. The first question from each one sounded like they were reading a script. That was intentional."

"Why?"

Clark sucked in a deep breath. "They want to make sure I get the message, loud and clear. Back off or your friends will pay the price."

"Back off? On what?"

"Huston … the Mafia … everything."

"I understand that," Ted said, with a swipe across his forehead. "What do you want us to do?"

Clark stroked his chin. "Take your time. Have them come back another day. We need time to come up with something."

"What if they get pissed off?"

"Back off … don't aggravate them. Remember, you're dealing with thugs. They only know one way to solve a problem — don't give them a chance to react — if that route isn't available they'll go back and get their marching orders."

CHAPTER THIRTY-FIVE

Clark took his time dressing for the Christmas party, knowing tonight was the night he'd been waiting for. He knew by the way Sharon had come on after the Pistons' game there was no doubt in her mind. *It must be seven or eight months since we did it. I wonder if she slept with anyone else ... hmm, I bet not. I need to move easy tonight.*

He slipped on his slacks, his favorite shirt, and primped one more time in front of the mirror. Grabbing a sweater, he turned and sauntered toward the front door. Out of the corner of his eye he noticed a blinking light on his telephone. *Someone must have called while I was in the shower. Maybe Sharon wants me to pick her up.*

He walked back to his desk, hit the blinking button and waited.

"You have one new message," the computer voice droned, "First message: 'Clark, it's Abby ... I know you hate me but I miss you terribly. I've started over. I'm a computer analyst with a fortune five hundred company here in Philly — honest to God I am. Can we talk?"

Clark raised his hand to delete the message then pulled it back. "I think about you every day and wish you'd call. I'd do anything to see you again. I'll fly to Detroit; meet you halfway. I'll do whatever you want; just say it and I'll be there. Please call me; I want to hear your voice."

Clark plopped down on his desk chair and stared across his dark apartment. *What the hell! Does she think I'm some kind of a robot? Calling me ... why would she do that? She lied and cheated; worse yet, sucked critical information out of me and gave it to the Mafia.*

His mind drifted through the times they'd done it, the places they'd gone, the things they'd experienced together. And that special time when she'd seduced him on the dining room table. *Shit, I can't believe she called — that bitch — she has a lot of gall. She got paid for screwing me ... and now she wants to make amends. What kind of a woman is she?*

Reaching for the delete button, he paused and played the message again. *Damn ... a whore!* He slammed the phone down and bolted for the door.

Driving to the restaurant took longer than he'd planned — a light mist began to fog his windshield — traffic was a bear and worse, he hit every red light. Abby was there at every stop — waving from the corner by the light pole, sitting in the car next to him, sliding closer and caressing his thigh — *Shit! I can't believe this. Here I am thinking about a goddamn whore and in five minutes I'll be with the nicest woman I've known.*

Arriving at the banquet room in the Roman Village Cucina a few minutes late, he examined the Christmas decorations Carlos and Rosa Maria had put up. *Twice as many as they had done for poker last year and much more elaborate.*

"The decorations look great," he called to the two of them.

"Thanks." Carlos pointed to Rosa Maria. "She gets all the credit."

Rosa Maria hurried over, stretched up and pecked him on the cheek. "Thanks Clark," she whispered in his ear. "Thanks, for helping Carlos deal with the Mafia."

He smiled at her. "Hey, we're all in this together," he said softly, and then shouted over the music, "Merry Christmas everyone."

Sharon darted over and grabbed his arm. "I thought you had a problem."

"Nah, it's drizzling … the traffic was horrible."

She rose up on her tiptoes and lightly kissed his cheek. "I can't believe this. After all that's happened we're together again."

Clark smiled wide. "It was meant to be."

She gazed up; her yearning eyes connected with his blue eyes. The two spontaneously embraced. She planted a wet kiss on his lips. "Merry Christmas, darling."

"Merry Christmas to you," he whispered, and pulled her tight.

She made a hand gesture as if her heart was fluttering, and laid another smacker on him.

"C'mon Sharon, you need to share him with the rest of us," one of her friends called.

Clark backed off realizing the two of them were the center of attention.

Laverne came to their rescue. "I want to introduce our newest love birds."

Everyone stood and cheered.

Ted winked at her. "C'mon Sharon go for it, plant one more on him."

Sharon gave him a faint smile, rose up and nailed Clark.

Everyone applauded.

Following a second round of drinks, the group settled down. Father Dom gave the blessing and the guys dug in.

Earl sat next to Nicole. Although not really a date, he was obviously uncomfortable. He hadn't dated for several years. His first wife had died of leukemia seven years ago. Nicole rambled constantly. He listened and shared an occasional thought.

The group went through appetizers and several bottles of wine. The four-man musical group appeared. Jovial times were back again.

Nicole and Rosa Maria danced to the pleasure of all. The rest of the group soon joined in.

Earl walked over to the bar and grabbed a can of Stroh's. Renzo stepped off the dance floor and headed for the table of booze. The rest of the guys followed. The women gathered in the corner with Wendy.

Laverne stood and tapped her empty wine glass with a knife. "During this festive season, I want you to know that we have a celebrity among us."

The group turned, giving her their full attention. She asked Nicole to stand beside her. Holding something in her hand, Wendy eased to Nicole's other side.

Laverne took a half step forward, and said, "Here's to our own woman of the year," then took her time reading the inscription from a note card.

Wendy held the leadership plaque over her head and handed it to Nicole, giving her a giant-sized hug. The group roared their approval.

Clark grabbed the microphone from Laverne and stepped next to Nicole. "Can I have your attention," he boomed then moved the mike further away. "Please, just for a minute."

The group settled down and focused on him.

"I know many of you have read 'The Thorn Birds.' It seems to me that we have our own thorn bird. Nicole has demonstrated the ultimate in leadership skills and dedication. She's worked tirelessly — on a mission — to rally forces to improve our community. Nicole Weatherspoon, you're the first "Thorn Bird of Detroit."

Cheers and applause filled the room.

Nicole took the microphone and raised her hand.

A hush fell over the room.

"I want to thank all of you. You're the best friends a person could have." She paused brushing her hair aside. "I want you to know this award is not for me; it is for Alsye and what he stood for." She hesitated and wiped a tear from her cheek. "This award is for both of us, the thorn birds of Detroit."

The group showered her with hugs and kisses. One by one the women had their picture taken with her. Ted snapped a group picture. The band of the same old four men struck up an Italian country love song and the partners filled the dance floor.

Seeing Earl standing alone, Nicole extended her hand. "Looks like I'm your only choice."

His eyes opened wide. "You're the best one." He took her hand and the two joined the group, dancing at a modest distance apart to the slow melody.

When the music ended Laverne grabbed the hand mike. "I have another announcement."

The group stopped and stared.

Ted took the microphone from her. "I guess that's my cue," he said quietly.

"Speak up," Renzo shouted.

He moved the mike closer. "During the dance this young lady accepted my proposal." Laverne held up her left hand, flashing a shiny rock.

Shouts and cheers reverberated off the walls. Laverne made her way around the room showing off her multi-carat engagement ring. Returning to Ted, she kissed him on the cheek.

The band began an Italian wedding song and the newly engaged couple floated across the floor.

As the tune ended, Renzo picked up the mike and said, "I have an announcement too."

The smiling faces turned with a sense of wonderment. What's next?

He laughed. "Dinner is served in the main dining room."

***

Clark followed Sharon to her parking garage, jumped out of his car, and rushed over to open her door. Taking her hand, the two strolled into her apartment. She stepped in and pulled him tight. "I had a wonderful time tonight. Thanks for inviting me."

"You made it perfect."

"You have some of the greatest friends ever."

"Hey, they're your friends too." He kissed her softly on the lips. She followed with a long, firm kiss. The two embraced, holding each other affectionately for the longest time. She rose on her tiptoes and kissed him gently on the lips. "Would you like an after dinner drink?"

"Sure. I'll fix them."

Sharon headed for the sofa and slipped off her shoes. "God, that feels good."

Clark returned with her Grand Marnier and his Amaretto and joined her, sitting close.

"Wasn't that nice what Nicole said about Alsye?" she said.

"Yes. I really miss him." Clark seemed happier as he began to recall the good times. "Did you know about Ted and Laverne?"

Sharon mused, "I had an inkling. She's talked about him a lot in the last week or so but didn't say a thing."

"They'll make a great team."

"So what's on your agenda now that you have the Nash case all wrapped up?"

"It'll be on to the next challenge. You know a detective's work is never done."

"You stole my line." She giggled.

Clark's face brightened. "On the first Monday of the new year the judge will sentence Huston Nash. But before that, I'm taking off the week between Christmas and New Year's." He gave her a sly smile. "Are you doing anything special?"

"No, not really." She took a sip, set her glass down, and snuggled closer. "What's it like to be at a sentencing?"

"Hmm … it's kind of strange. You know what's going to happen, but you kind of feel sorry for the person. There are really no winners." He hesitated. "Do you want to go with me?"

"Oh … I don't want to interfere."

"You won't. I'll just be watching. Besides, you'll love the courthouse. They call it the 'Million Dollar Courtroom' … it's spectacular."

She pursed her lips. "You're positive it'll be okay?"

"Of course."

"Sure … why not."

"Great, I'll pick you up. We can talk details after Christmas." He shuffled as if getting ready to leave.

"Are you going somewhere?"

"Well …" Clark started to respond then realized what she had said. "Ah … no."

She gave him her sexiest smile and started to unbutton her blouse. "I wondered how long it'd take you to catch on."

"I'm a slow learner."

"Sure you are," she said, tongue-in-cheek then flipped loose a button on his shirt and slid her hand inside.

He kissed her on the neck while his fingers nestled inside her blouse, inching down to the top of her bra. "I'm not that slow."

She smiled softly. "The slower the better."

***

Sharon sat on the edge of the courtroom bench, admiring the stately oak furnishings and the ornately carved cabinetry. "This is like a movie scene."

Clark leaned over. "You never know. Maybe it will be someday."

"Wouldn't that be something? I could tell my friends we were there."

"It's nice but don't expect too much." Clark winked; his mind whirled with excitement, recalling the week the two of them had just spent together. Glancing at her sweater, he was reminded again how she had smothered him with her breasts. *God, she was good.*

"How long will it take?" she asked softly.

He leaned to her side. "It'll be over in a flash."

"All rise for the Honorable Judge James Limbaugh," the bailiff called.

A stout man with a commanding presence, dressed in a black robe, strode forward and took his seat behind the bench. He gaveled the session to order. Completing a few opening remarks, he nodded toward the defendant. "Mr. Nash, please rise."

Showing wear from his ordeal, the tired, silver-haired man rose slowly, his head bowed. "I have taken into account your guilty plea and your remorse, but I cannot ignore the list of counts — tax evasion, money laundering, bank fraud, and racketeering. You've violated the code of ethics entrusted to men with your level of responsibility. Your behavior has been despicable; you have disgraced your family, your corporate partners and the community as a whole. With the severity of your betrayal of the public trust, I sentence you to twenty years in the Milan Federal Correctional Institute in Milan, Michigan. This court is adjourned."

Huston Nash collapsed into his chair. An attractive blonde female in her early thirties rushed his way and threw her arms around him. He stood and the two embraced. They kissed as if they were long-lost friends then talked until an officer tapped him on the shoulder.

She stepped away from him, wiping her tears, and watched the officer cuff him.

"Do you think that's his daughter?" Sharon asked.

"It looks like it," Clark agreed, his right arm holding Sharon tight.

A tall, stately woman in her early sixties, very attractive, waited for his lawyer to finish.

Sharon slid closer to Clark and eased up on the hard wooden bench, trying to get a better view. "Who's that?"

Clark shrugged his shoulders. "I don't have a clue."

"She looks kind of familiar, don't you think?"

Clark shook his head. "I never saw her in my life."

"There's something about her." Sharon continued to stare.

Mr. Nash finished with his lawyer and turned, coming face to face with the woman; his somber face and loathing eyes turned away.

Sharon whispered in Clark's ear. "That's his wife. I know it is."

"The Betty Crocker-type in the picture?" He grimaced; his forehead wrinkled. "I don't think so."

"No, I'm telling you, Clark, that's her. I can tell by her eyes."

"Are you positive?"

"Yes. I remember that look." Sharon cocked her head. "Why did the two of them act that way?"

Clark's brow curled into a light frown. "What way?"

"Like they hate each other."

"I didn't notice."

"Hmm, maybe it's a woman thing ... there's something between them that isn't right."

Clark frowned, wondering what Sharon meant by that. *A woman's thing. What the hell is she talking about?*

The gallery emptied. Clark and Sharon lingered, taking in one last look at the spectacular décor. Gawking up at the ceiling, Sharon walked slowly out of the courtroom into the long marbled-floor hallway and grabbed Clark's arm. Pulling him close, she rose on her tiptoes and whispered in his ear. "Don't turn around right now, but Mrs. Nash is talking to a handsome Italian man in the far corner. She's cozied up real close."

Clark took his time, turning slowly so he could see the other end of the hall. Taking a quick glance, he turned back to Sharon — his eyes wide open, shining brightly. He gestured for her to come closer. She slid next to him.

He whispered. "The guy facing this way is Angelo Travaglini. He's the Underboss for the Detroit Mafia; their number two man."

"Underboss?"

"I'll explain it later."

"What do you think they're talking about?" Clark shrugged. Sharon glanced again. "He just kissed her on the cheek and … it wasn't like he was kissing his sister.

"Jesus Christ." Clark's mind scrambled; he covered his mouth.

"What is it?" she asked.

"He was on the two bank boards with Huston. She was the secretary."

"So?"

"It all fits."

"What fits?"

"She used to be the queen of the ball and now she's Miss Nothing whenever she's around Huston."

Sharon gave him a blank look. "I don't understand, Clark."

"Ten years ago Mrs. Nash was the celebrity of every ball in town; one day, she was gone from public life." Rubbing his jaw, Clark paused and his eyes brightened. "She's faked it all these years."

"Faked what?"

"She stayed with Huston to keep up the image, but she was his wife in name only. She backed out of everything because she was having an affair with Angelo." Clark cocked his head to the side. "Oh my God … it was the two of them."

Sharon eased closer.

"The two of them set up Huston. He took the rap for her." Clark shook his head. "We just convicted the wrong person!"

324

Hi Readers,

I hope you enjoyed *Sax Club*; additional novels in the "Thorn Birds of Detroit" series will be available soon.

If you didn't get an opportunity to read *Gloom and Doom,* please do. It is a Free eBook that sets the stage for the "Thorn Birds of Detroit" series. Other Free eBooks related to the series are also available to readers everywhere.

Detroit was a fast-growing boom city in the 1960s. But unknown to most, under the surface corruptive forces including the Italian, Greek and Black mafias and many gangs were at work. The *Gloom and Doom* novella is a synopsis of the tough life in the inner city of Detroit in the years after the 1967 riots. It was a violent time. The new historical fiction series, *Thorn Birds of Detroit* begins in the late 1970s. Les Cochran weaves a tale of the underworld and the effort of citizens to fight back from a state of anguish and despair.

Go here to get your free copy:

http://lescochranblog.com/gloom-and-doom-2/

Share with others who are interested in historical fiction about Detroit and the mafias that controlled the city.

Cheers to Readers Everywhere,

Les Cochran, Author

IN THE WORKS

BLIND PIG is the second in the "Thorn Birds of Detroit" series. Continuing his **SAX CLUB** ventures, Detective Clark Phillips takes on the Detroit Mafia. This time he isn't the only one; his best friends have rallied with him. Tired of paying monthly taxes to the mob, the guys unite around the wife of a fallen friend. She will not be bullied or succumb to the ways of the mob. Clark and his friends devise a tricky plan to close down an illicit revenue stream.

In **LAST CALL** the third novel in the "Thorn Birds of Detroit" series, Clark Phillips carries on his crusade to root out evil in Detroit. This time his focus is on the Mafia's top guys and gangland connections with some of Detroit's biggest names. Despite his feelings about the Catholic Church, he pursues Mafia money-laundering schemes, under the guise of the Church

DO YOU KNOW A THORN BIRD?

Write about his or her efforts

Your tale about a thorn bird may be included in an upcoming book in the "Thorn Birds of Detroit" series.

I'm looking for real stories about regular people who made a difference in turning around Detroit. Share your insight about a thorn bird that didn't give up, and brought about change under extraordinary circumstances.

My goal is to base some of my episodes on real people. The thorn bird tales I accept will be fictionalized in my "Thorn Birds of Detroit" series. It's your opportunity to tell a story that needs to be told.

There are no gimmicks; simply follow these guidelines:

- Submissions should be no longer than ten pages, use Times New Roman font, double-spaced with one inch margins.

- Submit your manuscript to: thornbirds@LesCochran.com.

If your story about a thorn bird in Detroit is selected you'll be recognized in the acknowledgements. Or, if you prefer you may remain anonymous.

Additional Information: www.LesCochran.com

***

Episodes may be changed or modified to fit the particular story. Submitters must agree to waive all literary rights. The author does not accept material that may be considered depraved or illegal, pedophilia, rape, incest, necrophilia, bestiality, racially intolerant or sexually explicit. All individuals must be eighteen or older.

Other Books by Author Les Cochran

Steve Schilling, a highly successful (and very sexy) university president weaves his ways through the politics, sex and backroom machinations of academic life. Later, the first female president of the United States recruits him to lead the reform of public education. His leadership abilities are equaled only by his lovemaking skills, resulting in "Steve-a-mania" obsession from his lovers, as he treats each as if she is the only one—OMG!

Go To: **http://amzn.to/2baf4La**

CPSIA information can be obtained
at www.ICGtesting.com
Printed in the USA
FSOW04n2026240916
25332FS